HELP DARLI̶N̶G̶
ONCE I NEED YOU TODAY REPEAT TODAY
1.15 VICTORIA ARRIVES DENE 2.20 BLESSINGS
JULIE PS BRING PINS

'Did you bring a dress?'

Startled, Janna tore her eyes away from the butler's
dark-suited back to face Julie. 'No, I thought . . .'
She heard herself begin to stammer, bit her lip.
Had she misunderstood completely? Had Julie
meant her to make up a dress in advance, without
fittings, consultations, patterns? 'I've got the pins,'
she finished, lamely. A faint rustle from behind
her, where the butler was standing motionless.
Could you hear a smile?

'I meant for you.' Julie put her hand to her mouth.
'Didn't I say? I meant to, really I did. I want you to
stay for the ball.'

Also by Catherine Nicolson in Sphere Books:

CHASE THE MOON

SILK

Catherine Nicolson

SPHERE BOOKS LIMITED

Sphere Books Limited, 27 Wrights Lane, London W8 5TZ

First published by Michael Joseph Ltd 1987
Published by Sphere Books Ltd 1987
Copyright © 1987 by Catherine Nicolson

TRADE
MARK

Set in Plantin

Printed and bound in Great Britain by
Cox & Wyman Ltd, Reading

CHAPTER ONE

London Bridge. Janna halted, suddenly dizzy. People swept by her on every side, buffeting her like the cold air off the river. Traffic roared, making it hard to think. Her hand shook as she searched the inside pocket of her winter coat. Was it still there? If she'd lost it –

Fingers met paper and she let out a small breath of relief. Yes, it was still there. But now another fear hovered at the edges of her mind, eating away at the moment's relaxation. Was it enough?

Janna looked round, just once. Quickly, before she could change her mind, she set down her case, wedging it precariously against the parapet, and took out the small brown envelope. The notes fluttered in her hand. She counted once, lost track, tried again. Her head swam. It was no good, she couldn't be sure. And yet – it would be all right, it had to be. They'd said it would be all right.

But everything was so strange. Her coat, heavy and stiff, as if it were made of cardboard. Her feet, in their unaccustomed shoes, seeming somehow far away, as if they didn't belong to her. The light, so bright it made her eyes water. Long-forgotten scents of tar, dust, petrol. And the noise. It was that most of all that unnerved her, the rattle and clang of the great city, with herself trapped inside it like a mouse in a bell, dreading the stroke of twelve.

'You'll be met. It's all arranged.'

Someone jostled Janna's elbow and she almost dropped the money. Panic stirred inside her, cold and slow as the snail-grey water below. She squeezed her eyes tight shut, willing the deep inward tremor to go away. If she could just rest for a moment . . .

But there was no room, no time, only people, an endless, faceless stream. Quickly Janna stuffed the notes back into her pocket and picked up her case. She'd barely turned before the flood enveloped her, carrying her almost bodily, breathless, stumbling, over the bridge and beyond.

'Liverpool Street. It's not far.' Every step brought Janna a little nearer. She'd know when she got there. She remembered from the last time. Dim light filtering down from grimed glass set in a vault so high she'd thought she was in a church. It seemed a place for tombs, and endings, and farewells. Pigeons trotted and strutted on the overhead walkways. There must be a hole in the roof, she remembered thinking. Pigeons aren't allowed in church. And then, terrifying, the scream of a train departing. That was the last thing she remembered.

But she was better now. She drew herself up a little, straightening her shoulders under the safe dark wool. Not cured yet but better, much better. Everyone said so. And now it was up to her to go home and stay better, always.

'You must be very glad, to be going home.'

Yes. Janna's fingers tightened on the handle of her suitcase. She'd looked forward to this moment for so long. She'd go home, and everything would be the same as it was before, only better, like her.

I'd rather die.

Janna flinched. Who could have spoken? A cool, clear voice, ordinary, almost matter-of-fact. She glanced quickly to either side. It's not true, she wanted to say to whoever it was. You have no right to say such a thing. Home is where I'm going. It's where I belong.

No. The voice was a whisper now, so close that she knew it could only come from inside her mind. You belong nowhere. The best that you can hope for is that one day you will look in the mirror and there will be no-one there at all.

Janna dropped her head. The panic inside her that had been slow and cold was now hot and hard, a snake coiling up from the pit of her stomach to wind itself round her body, so tight she couldn't breathe. The truth. How could she have

2

forgotten, even for a moment? The truth never went away or changed. It was simply – there. It would be there, waiting to greet her on the station platform, when she got home.

Clumsily, her case banging against her legs, Janna began to run. She ran head down, blindly, without a thought in her mind. All she knew was that she must get away, right away, from the hubbub of Bishopsgate and its greedy, prosperous roar, from the station and its busy, well-ordered, inexorable trains, from the startled faces and curious eyes that saw through her winter coat to the ugliness inside, but most of all from that small, sure voice that told her simply, over and over again, no, no, you belong nowhere, there is no home for you, anywhere in the world.

And then, suddenly, it was another city. She turned into an alley, felt rough cobbles under her feet. Now she was running back through time, over stone sets. Fleur-de-Lis Street. Blossom Street. Elder Street. Trampled flowers in the gutter. A sooty maze of little houses with broken windows and peeling doors. Rubbish smoking at the end of a cul-de-sac, and not a soul in sight.

Janna leaned against a small crooked wall. It seemed harder to breathe now that she'd stopped running. Her lungs burned with the effort of taking in enough air. She waited, patiently, for the voice.

But it didn't come. There was only silence, a silence so ancient, so complete that even the voice could not break it. Silence, and the smell of ashes.

And yet . . . she felt better here. Almost at home, amongst the grime and clutter. Nothing to live up to, nothing to lose. A small street, barely a street at all, eaten up with decay and neglect, and yet it was alive. Set like a jewel in a patched-up shop-front was a window full of saris, scarlet and gold. At the alley's end a Rolls Royce prowled past, a city beast, lordly and strange. Janna melted against the wall.

Then, it was all right again. She was alone. Just her and the blackened walls and the uneven puzzle of stones beneath her feet.

Now the fading light was stippled with rain. Janna hardly

noticed it. She didn't know where she was going, didn't care. It was enough to be alone. She slipped down another alley, turned the corner and found herself in a wilderness. A truncated row of abandoned houses overlooking what seemed like an endless waste, misty and surreal in the dying light. Much had been broken, nothing built.

It was a miracle that one house, one sound tooth in a row of rotting stumps, was still intact. A shell, reduced to its essentials, everything of value long ago stripped or stolen, every pane of glass on the ground floor and upper storeys a dark star, but a house still, no more, no less. It pleased her, that simplicity. The house let her see at a glance exactly how it had been built, brick on brick. Windows, doors, walls. An anatomy lesson. Nothing to hide, every bone bare.

Janna shivered. It was getting cold. The rain was falling harder now. Her body felt empty, strangely light. She touched the railings, gently, as if the house might disappear. But it stayed there, facing her, with what seemed a small, gap-toothed smile. She looked down. The windows of the basement, protected behind thin iron bars, were still whole. Rubbish had silted up against the basement door. Slowly, in the depths of her mind, a thought stirred. It was hard to look at a door without wondering if it might open, this time. Without meaning to, hardly aware of what she was doing, she crept down the narrow mossy steps, each worn curve leading her on. It was only when she pushed the door and it opened silently under her hand that she realised how sure she'd been that someone would call her back.

The lintel was low, so low that Janna had to duck her head as she went in. Something brushed against her hair and she felt a moment's fear. Nothing moved in the hall at home except the hands of the big brass clock. Mother wound it at the same time each evening. I learned to live from that clock, Janna thought. A cold metal face over the taut spring. Time. So much of it, a frozen fountain of days.

She closed her eyes. When she opened them she could see a little better. She was in some sort of narrow hall, all bends and angles. Ahead the corridor lost itself in shadow. Close by in

4

the left-hand wall was a small panelled door, barely wide enough for a cupboard. It was slightly ajar.

But there was no-one in the small, low-ceilinged room, no-one at all. Apart from a lop-sided deal table propped against the window-ledge it was completely empty.

Empty. A well of emptiness, deep and cool. A treasure house.

Two steps took Janna to the table. She leaned against it, felt it rock back against her, felt herself breathe for the first time. With that breath she took in the smell of the house, tasted it. Old. Empty. Safe. She stayed by the window, motionless, and watched the last light leave the sky, invisible as an animal in its underground lair.

With the night came cold. Janna became aware of it slowly. It was polite, the cold. It didn't intrude. It touched her gently, first her hands, then her face, so gently that she didn't even shiver. It was her friend, the cold. It made the boundaries of her body disappear, her mind go still. No need to think or feel or remember. There was just her, and the house, and the cold.

So simple, after all. Janna felt her eyelids growing heavy. Why had she been running, that girl? She seemed like a stranger now. There was a much easier way. All she had to do was stop. Cease. Fade away into the walls like twilight. Become part of the silence. Invisible, untouchable. Just herself and the house and after – just the house.

Stiffly, Janna turned. The movement seemed to last for ever. In the darkness the walls of the room seemed insubstantial, as if she could drift through them if she tried. But there was nowhere else she wanted to be.

Yes, it would be easy. She could curl up there at the hearth, like a cat before an unlaid fire, and sleep. The stone flags would feel no colder than her own body. It was a small hearth, just right for the room. Surrounding it, a diminutive chimney-piece, cast-iron. Beneath the rust, flowers curled.

Pretty. The thought came to Janna from a long way away. She wondered how long it was since anyone had seen those flowers bloom. Blackleaded, they would shine like silk.

But who would do it? Janna found herself listening for a

reply, but the house was silent. Or perhaps not entirely. There were small creaks and rustles, as if it breathed.

As if someone were waiting, there in the darkness, patiently, to see what she would do.

CHAPTER TWO

'Anything else?' The shopkeeper's eyes rested curiously on Janna's hand, curled tightly round the handle of the wire basket. Looking down, Janna saw that the lace-edged cuff of her nightdress protruded from her coat sleeve. It had been so cold last night that she'd put on every piece of clothing she had. Heat rose to her cheeks. She tugged at the sleeve, uselessly.

'Blacklead.' Janna's voice came out high and small. She moistened her lips. Her tongue felt dry and huge. 'Please.' She looked back at the woman, begging her to understand. She wouldn't be able to ask again.

At last the woman turned away to rummage in a shallow cardboard box behind the till. Dusty tins of shoe polish, an amber block of beeswax, an embroidered leather pincushion covered in rusting pins, a packet of coloured chalks ... Janna's heart sank. Then the woman surfaced, triumphantly, in her hand a small striped tube. 'Zebra,' it read. 'For all grates, stoves and ironwork. Take a shine!'

'That what you wanted?'

Janna nodded, unable to speak. She could feel the woman's eyes on her, feel the pressure of her curiosity like a physical weight.

'Not much call for that nowadays, you know. From round her, are you?'

Panic rushed over Janna in a choking, salty wave.

'It's all right, ducks.' The woman winked. 'I'll mind my business, you mind yours.'

Janna paid, hurriedly, a mindless scatter of coins, gathered up her purchases, fought her way through the pounding in her head to the door. She could feel eyes on her spine like

7

needles, had to stiffen every muscle against the need to drop everything and run, through the glass and splintering wood, away from the lights and the multi-coloured shelves that shouted and that terrible, friendly smile.

Out of sight at last, Janna leaned against a wall until her vision cleared and her pulse subsided. Despair remained. She didn't know how it worked, the human machine, with its nods and smiles, its automatic words. But she would try to learn – she had to. If only she knew where to begin.

'Children are better seen than heard, but best not seen at all.' She shivered suddenly, remembering. How often she'd lain in the bath at home, the water cloudy with carbonated lime, and stared at her own body. If she kept quite still it almost seemed to disappear. But in the end, as the water chilled around her, she had to move, and her body was back with her, just the same.

Something cold and wet trickled across her wrist. She looked down and saw that the lid of the cottage cheese carton had come loose and discharged a thin yellowish-white fluid. Revulsion spiralled up from her stomach. Oh, to be thin . . . glass thin, smoke thin, thin and fine as a needle, transparent as ring silk, light enough to float on a breath of air.

Suet crust, short crust. She could taste it now. Pastry. That was Mother's gift. You needed cold hands for pastry. Yet it came out of the oven so hot, so flaky – Janna could see herself still, stuffing the burning crust inside her mouth behind the kitchen door. But no matter how much she ate, she was always hungry. She got out of the bath colder than when she got in. She rose from the table emptier than before. There was something in her that nothing could fill.

But no more. Please, no more. Janna pressed the hard shape of the brown loaf to her chest, feeling the crust give. 'I am all right,' she said to herself, aloud, testing the words. 'I am alone.'

At last, Rose Alley. The smell of soot, and old brick, and dandelion leaves. A stage set, dusty, paper shutters hanging. All the players long ago moved on. Not a face, not a sound. Just herself, in the wings.

Next time, she thought, I'll wait till ↯
time –

Suddenly afraid of what she might find,↯
down the basement steps. The door had n↯
could push it open, as she had done.

But the door was as she'd left it, the lit↯
unchanged. And yet something was different. It felt right to
her now, the brush of the lintel against her hair, as if the house
was reaching out to touch her, as if it, too, had to make sure.

This time she made herself tap on the small inner door, to
remind herself that she had no right to be there, that at any
minute, any hour of the day or night, she might be discovered.
And yet, as she entered, letting the room enclose her, its
papery smell, its silence, she was shaken by a joy so sharp it
was almost pain.

Carefully, she laid out her purchases on the three-legged
table. First, the food. She knew the exact calorific content of
each item. Vitamins, minerals, fibre, protein, carbohydrate,
fat. A precarious balance, a high-wire act. An orange, because
it took so long to peel. Bread, a small loaf, to be eaten down to
the last crust, dry. A bottle of mineral water. Last, the cottage
cheese. She would have liked it colder but she had no choice.
She would have to protect herself as best she could against its
full taste, slightly salt, like tears.

She turned away. This was her test. She had to know the
food was there and yet not eat it before time, to prove something to herself. To live with it. Discipline. She must build
herself now, brick by brick, or fall.

The orange glowed, hypnotic, imprinted on her retina.
Quickly, she picked up candles and matches. She'd never
realised how bleak a night could be without light or fire. Her
next night would be easier. But she mustn't think of the next
night, not even the next hour, it was too dangerous. The
house was under sentence of death. This was just a temporary
arrangement, a sort of reprieve. She mustn't settle, even in
her mind.

All the same, just in case, she lit a match, softened the base
of one candle and set it ready on the tiles before the hearth.

le didn't count. One candle was simply – sensible.

glanced back, just once, at the table. Sunlight fell on
provisions, a single clear, implacable beam. She turned
away again. No, it wasn't time yet. She wasn't ready. She
needed to take strength from the house again, from her small
cold kingdom, her underground domain.

Down the corridor, where last night there had been only
shadows, she now saw a stair, narrow, irregular, with a slender carved balustrade. Looking up, she realised with a stab of
dismay that it had been blocked off at the top. Lumps of fallen
plaster littered the treads. No-one had bothered to come down
to the basement to clear them away.

Janna touched the banisters. They stood upright and
defiant, as if outraged at the insult to their dignity. She could
see marks of the chisel where some long ago craftsman had
shaped each one into a long barley sugar twist. The corner
knob fitted exactly into the palm of her hand. Smooth, even a
little warm.

Quickly, Janna drew back her hand. She didn't want to
think about the stair leading nowhere. It came too close, said
too much. She turned away to another door, not ajar this time
but rusted tight into its hinges. She tugged it open and found
another room, even smaller than the first. But here the quiet
was broken by a small, regular ticking sound. In one corner
was a stone sink. Above it, a single tap, from which water
dripped onto the discoloured surface. Cautiously, Janna
caught a drop on her finger, tasted it. It was pure and cold.
Eagerly she turned the tap full on, but no more water came.
She stared at it, frowning. It felt as if her mind was flexing
muscles long unused. She wished she'd learned more about
such things. That water had to come from somewhere.

At last, high on the wall, bound about with ancient rags,
she discovered a pipe with a stopcock. She turned it, hopefully. There was a groan, deep and protesting, followed by a
disconcerting rattle. Then, startling her, water gushed wide
and full into the sink, spattering the dusty floor like a blessing. Janna plunged her hands under the tap, not minding the
cold. The water sang and shone. She cupped her hands,

10

drank. She hadn't realised how thirsty she was. She splashed her face. The cold brought tears to her eyes.

She turned off the tap, patted her face dry on the corner of her sleeve. With the same sleeve she polished a small hole in the grime that covered the back window. Pressing her face to the glass, she gasped with surprise. From the front all she had seen was a wasteland, but here was a secret place, a jungle in the heart of the city. Brick walls overgrown by roses, turned vicious in their old age, with thorns the size of darning needles. A scattering of self-seeded vegetables from some long ago planting, green and tall, light-starved, a forest of strange things sprouting and sprawling behind the bars. Outside in the street it might be winter, but here, where no-one could see, spring had come, unchecked, uninvited, to make the earth its own.

Squatter's rights. Janna smiled. She liked those plants, coiling so fiercely up towards the light. She liked the bars too. They were a cage, not to keep her in, but to keep her safe. Behind them, in the top few inches of sky, she'd be able to see the sunrise.

The top sash didn't open more than a crack. Rain had got in and swelled the frame. But there was enough of an opening to let in a drift of green air, the smell of damp earth and the small faraway sound of a dog barking.

Yes. It was time. Slowly, Janna retraced her steps down the corridor, pretending. That this was just an ordinary day, that she was someone like other people, going about her life calmly, doing the things that everyone did. The sort of person who could look in a mirror and smile.

She lifted her head, deliberately relaxed the muscles in her neck and shoulders. Time to eat. Time to confront the old enemy, the one inside. The caged beast.

Slowly, counting the seconds, she made herself look. Carefully, so that not a drop fell, she prised the lid from the tub of cottage cheese, laid it neatly aside. It shone. She closed her eyes for a moment, willing herself to think of how she would feel when this was over and she was safe again, all the demons laid to rest until another day.

It will be all right, she told herself. I won't sit down. I will take them, the bread and the cheese and the orange, to the hearth, and stand. It will be safer there. The chimney-piece will help me. I will think of how it will look when I've polished it. I will see my own hand going up and down, round and round. I won't think of the taste, or the feel of the food going down. I won't think of it as food at all. It will be simply fuel, fuel for my fire.

After it was done she swept every crumb from the hearth and tipped it into the grate. She rinsed the cottage cheese container under the tap till the last swirl of white disappeared down the drain. It would be a cup, a good one. She put it on the window-ledge to dry.

Then, and only then, with a sigh of relief so deep she hardly dared acknowledge it, she settled down to blacklead the grate. When it was finished she sat back on her heels and smiled a small, weary smile. It had been worth it. Now the secret flowers curled and twined, glossy and sleek, as if they were alive.

She leaned closer. If only beauty could keep you warm. So fine a grate deserved a real fire. But what could she burn? She hadn't thought further than blackleading the grate. The hearth seemed to beg, a baby blackbird's open beak. Feed me. Make me live.

Anxiously Janna considered. There were so many things she needed. Her gaze fell on her blackened hands. Soap, for one thing. And a broom. She looked round the dusty room. Oh, she'd dearly love a broom. A blanket, maybe. A paraffin stove.

But of course she could afford none of those things. The money for her fare home would barely cover food, let alone fuel. No matter how she added up sums in her head they all came to the same answer.

And darkness wasn't so very far away. Already the pale sunlight had shifted from the window. It now fell long and oblique on the demolition site opposite, highlighting the desolation, the scattered stones, the fallen beams.

The demolition site. Janna's mind moved slowly, considering. There might be wood there. Old planks, rafters – perhaps something small enough to carry?

12

The twilight received her, friendly, anonymous, the same shade of grey as the coat she wore. Janna felt herself blend invisibly into the wasteland. She picked her way carefully amongst the rubble. Tall plants whose names she didn't know, purple in the fading light, grew between the blackened stones.

The bigger pieces of wood were heavier than they looked. She abandoned several, regretfully. They were old and well seasoned. They would have burned the whole night long. But there were plenty of smaller pieces, broken jambs and lintels, fragments of lath, sticking up out of rotting plaster a little sadly, like so many ribs. Janna worked quickly. Suddenly she was filled with energy, a deep warm glow inside that was almost happiness. Every scrap of kindling she found seemed like a piece of the future rescued, made real. The knowledge that it would soon be dark only made her work faster. It wasn't that she was afraid of the dark, she'd always liked it, but she was afraid of losing track of her carefully gathered hoard. She turned stones eagerly, skinning her knuckles, had her coat snagged and ripped by big protruding nails, but she didn't care. Slowly but surely her small stack grew. Soon she could begin to ferry it back home.

And then, as she stood upright for a moment to ease her aching back, Janna saw something strange. Gliding silent and ghost-like along the line of yellow lamps that marked the edge of the road was a long silver shape. Janna stared, almost forgetting her pile of kindling. It was so sudden, the apparition, it seemed to come from another world. She watched as it came nearer, apprehension stirring at the base of her spine. Now she could see it was some kind of vehicle, huge, with shining featureless sides. What was it doing here? Why had it come?

Suddenly at the end of the lane it turned and with the same strange silent motion came bumping and swaying across the demolition site. Janna could hear the long grass brushing against its gleaming sides, hear the spurt and crackle of small stones under its tyres. She watched, frozen into immobility as it swayed to a noiseless halt in the middle of the site, effectively blocking her own exit to the road. Twin headlights opened up wide, fixing her in their gaze.

Terrified, Janna dropped instantly to her knees. Through half-closed eyes she saw the wild plants around her, all life bleached out of them by that hard white stare. Automatically she threw her arms round her pile of wood, buried her face against the dark wool of her sleeve. When she looked up again, peering cautiously round the wood, she saw a frenzy of activity. Men in overalls were everywhere, shouting, gesticulating, swarming in and out of the pantechnicon, carrying with them bales of cable, aluminium rods, strange machines fenced around with baffles and grids. They worked swiftly, expertly, as if they did this every day of their lives. The clang of metal on metal was interspersed with shouts, whistles, crisp one-word commands. A dynamo thumped once then settled to a contented whirr. Somewhere a switch was thrown and the demolition site erupted into brilliant light, as sudden and bright as if it was the Blitz all over again.

The light hit Janna like a blow, taking all the breath from her body. And yet she couldn't look away.

Shutters clanged, and the light changed, striped fans reaching out across the wasteland, transforming it into something magical and strange. Janna's throat constricted. It's a festival, she thought, a festival to welcome the spring. Or a wedding, or a party. Excitement filled the air, so real she could almost touch it. Something wonderful is going to happen, she thought. And I'm going to be allowed to see it. She felt privileged. She dug her nails into the palms of her hands. If this is a dream, she thought, I don't want to wake up, not until I've seen all there is to see.

And there was more, more than she could have imagined. Out of the pantechnicon and into the blaze of light came a woman, the most beautiful being Janna had ever seen. Tall as an angel, graceful as a tree, a fantasy creature enclosed from head to toe in metallised silk. Janna drew in her breath, silently. What a dress – but the woman transcended it. Her smooth, boneless arms were the colour and texture of doeskin. She seemed almost transparent, like a pillar of light. And yet,

14

somehow, Janna knew that if she touched her she would be warm.

And slim. Janna looked, wistfully. A lovely, comfortable slimness, with no hint of struggle or strain, every curve sculpted and smooth. Perfection.

Pain lanced through Janna's heart so suddenly that she felt faint. She'd thought she'd forgotten. She'd tried so hard, to forget.

'While you have been away I have had your room re-done. I have put the dolls into the local sale of work. You are too old for dolls.'

Janna trembled, pinned by memory. The lace, the scraps of silk she'd collected so painstakingly, a bird feathering her secret nest. Gone, all gone. And the dolls. So slender, so egg-shell smooth, every curl as crisp as the first day. Her heroines, never soiled, never defeated. The lovely ones. All gone.

Fiercely, she scrubbed at her eyes with her sleeve. She'd thought it had gone with the dolls, this hunger, this passion for happy endings. But now, looking into the magic circle of light, she could feel it burn inside her all over again.

Julie smiled. Somewhere behind the lights there was a clatter as some vital piece of equipment dropped from a technician's nerveless hand. Julie's smile didn't waver. She was used to it by now. It had followed her around for the best part of her life. The Julie Effect. Sometimes she felt as if the core of a tornado must be located somewhere just above her left shoulder. She barely moved yet daily around her portfolios shed like confetti, lights shattered, men tripped down invisible stairs, spectacles splintered underfoot.

So, because she was used to it, and because she had exactly an hour to finish this crucial set-up and wing her way Westwards to an interesting, maybe even a significant date, she smiled on, patiently, and hoped that no-one, this time, would break a leg.

'OK, Julie.' The director. Crew-cut hair, red-rimmed eyes, rumours of impending divorce. 'It'll be coming down right there.' Julie glanced across the lunar waste of rubble to a slightly smoother plot outlined with red marker lights. An assistant director was peering hopefully up into the spring twilight.

'You're sure this is going to work?'

The director cast a haunted look over the wasteland that surrounded them. They could have been anywhere, post-holocaust. Only the line of yellow lamps along the road they'd come linked them to civilisation.

'It's going to be great.' The director spoke with determination. 'Let's face it, it's got to be. No way can we shoot this one twice.'

He was right. Julie's confection of a dress had barely been completed in time as it was. She could tell from the anxious expression in Wardrobe's eyes that the problems found with the prototype hadn't been resolved quite to her satisfaction. But there was nothing Julie need do about that. She was sewn-up, literally. All she had to do was be – Julie. The Most Beautiful Woman in the World.

'Hair!' The two boys, insistent as parakeets, descended on her, brandishing spray.

'Ouch!' An acrid mist caught Julie in the eye. One boy gave her a mock-malevolent look. 'Fortunes of war, darling. This has got to stay, and I mean *stay*!'

Far in the distance Julie heard a solid thwack, thwack, thwack, like creamery butter hitting a wooden board. She felt her spirits rise. This was crazy – crazy and fun, like some sort of circus, the bit she liked best. Now it hung above them, amber lights winking, deafening them all with its noise.

'OK, Julie. This time give it everything.'

She felt nylon thread snap onto the concealed fastenings at her back. She felt eyes, out there beyond the lights, fasten onto her as invisibly. Client, director, storyboard deviser, agency man – all glued to Julie in her extraordinary dress.

'Lights. Action. Julie.'

Slowly, because the dress was extremely tight as well as irreplaceable, and because slowly was always best, Julie walked. As she walked she felt the hush lengthen and expand, like the moment over a candle-lit table when a man's eyes turn to velvet. She let that pulse slide into her walk, that breathlessness, that languor. Where had she come from, this girl in her extraordinary dress, where she was going to, picking her way so delicately over the stones? Out of the future into now . . .

Julie felt the wind machine start up on cue, amplifying the rush of air from the helicopter as it rocked like a ballerina towards the ground. It touched, light as a feather. She advanced towards the machine in her silken armour, outfacing it, outclassing it.

'For nights when anything can happen – Allways, the new hairspray from Futures . . .'

The rotors spun, the rush of wind intensified, lifting the panels of Julie's dress. A speck of dust entered her eye. She ignored it. As she hit her mark she felt the tug on the nylon wire at her back. Nothing happened. She smiled on. There was a sound of rending silk.

A horrified, wordless whisper, an agonised intake of breath from the darkness behind the lens. Julie stopped. Around her dangled pathetic shreds of a good idea. The boys hovered, checking her hair like well-oiled machines, but she knew there was very little point. There weren't two dresses like this one in the world.

'Wardrobe!' The director went from whisper to bellow in the blink of an eye. 'What happened?'

Anxious hands fumbled at Julie's waist. 'Well . . .'

'No, don't tell me.' Julie could see the dollar signs ringing up in his eyes. 'Is it repairable?'

'I don't know.' Wardrobe was near to tears. It had been a long day.

The director spun on his heel. 'Cut that engine, for God's sake, I can't hear myself think!' Silence, thick enough for murder. He glanced at his watch. 'We've got exactly forty-five minutes before our police permit runs out. It may not look it, but this is a residential area.' He ran a hand through his half-inch of hair. Julie saw panic flare in his eyes as he spotted something over her shoulder. She turned to see the client, complete with minions, advancing steadily over the stones. It should have been comical. It wasn't.

The director gripped her arm like a vice, spun her round. 'Don't let him see the back of that dress, whatever you do. And you!' His eyes fastened on Wardrobe. 'I want you back here in twenty minutes flat with Julie and a dress that works. I don't care how you do it. Go!'

Smiling till their faces ached, Julie and Wardrobe backed away.

'Just a run-through, Mr Benson.' Hysteria bubbled in the director's voice and was abruptly checked. 'Wonderful product you have there, though. Not a hair moved, did you see?'

Julie and Wardrobe turned tail and fled, bumping and stumbling over the stones.

'What on earth are we going to do?'

'Beats me.' Julie began to laugh. It was as much as she could do to walk at all, clutching her dress together at the back with both hands. 'For nights when anything can happen, remember?'

'No!' The word was torn from Janna, halfway between a gasp and a moan. She'd seen it happen with her own eyes, but she couldn't believe it, couldn't bear it. The dress, that beautiful dress, so clearly the result of many weeks of love and labour, reduced between one second and the next, to nothing, glittering shards.

The lights went out, all at once, plunging the wasteland into a darkness blacker and bleaker than before. It felt suddenly cold. It's the end, Janna thought. There won't be any more, because of the dress. They won't be able to mend it. No-one will know how.

She squeezed her hands into two tight balls. They seemed to burn and itch with the longing to touch that silk, make it whole again. Because she knew. It was the only thing she knew, but it was hers, that small nugget of knowledge, so painfully acquired. She knew, because of the dolls.

But there was no point in her knowledge. It weighed on her, heavy and useless. She could never tell anyone, never explain.

And yet Janna couldn't seem to tear her eyes away from the long silver shape of the pantechnicon. What were they doing in there, the two women – what sacrilege were they contemplating? That fabric – it must have cost forty pounds a yard at least. She'd never seen anything like it. Perhaps it had been specially milled, for this one night. Irreplaceable, like the dolls.

It was then that she knew she couldn't let it happen, not again. She'd let the dolls go without a word, without a murmur. They'd meant too much. But now . . . As she picked her way carefully over the rubble in the darkness Janna whispered a small silent prayer to whichever god took care of magpies and children, gypsies and other lovers of things that shone. Please, one more doll. The last one, I promise. The very, very last.

She reached up to tap on the ribbed aluminium door and her courage almost failed her. It was so tall and wide. Streamlined, modern, ice-cold under her hand.

'Yes?' A small face peered down irritably. 'Who are you?'

'I –' Janna swallowed hard. It was the girl in the short skirt. She wished it had been the other one, the one who looked as if the world was her friend. But she couldn't go back now. 'I've come about the dress.'

'Really?' The voice took on a hopeful note. 'Come on in!' A flight of aluminium steps unfolded like a conjuring trick. Janna hesitated. The metal looked thin and insubstantial, as if it might disappear as suddenly as it had come. She held tight to the handrail, felt the big vehicle dip as she entered, the way a web flexed when a fly landed on it. As soon as she was in she wished she was back there in the friendly darkness. It was so bright, with a flat, alien brightness that hurt her eyes. The air tasted of plastic and freshener. Somewhere in the background, a complacent, somehow sinister sound, a generator thrummed. Janna felt suddenly trapped. There was nowhere to go. The long narrow space was neatly sectioned off into separate areas, each with its own clearly-defined function, like the interior of a submarine. One end, half blocked off with fibreboard partitioning, held a sort of lounge, bare and

19

impersonal with its padded PVC seats and imitation wood-veneered table. The other held a mass of shelves and boxes spilling over with hardware – film cans, upright in their racks like soldiers, tripods, metal legs sprawling, an octopus-like tangle of cable, the single, malevolent violet eye of a huge lens.

'Hi.'

Janna swung round. In the middle section, standing by a full-length mirror studded round with bulbs, was the girl in the silver dress. 'I'm Julie.' She smiled and spoke at the same time, making it look easy.

Janna blinked. She knew she was staring but she couldn't stop. Close to, Julie wasn't just beautiful. She had something else, a sort of inner light. She looked as if every part of her was brand, shining new. The way a horse-chestnut kernel looked for the first second it was out of its prickly green shell. Moist, glossy, perfect. Only Julie, somehow, kept that look. She shone, like a racehorse or a sunset or a butterfly, as if she'd been polished and burnished and wrapped under cellophane so that nothing could ever dull her shine. Not a pore, nor a crease, nor a blemish showed on her skin, with its velvety texture, its even colour, from honey through to cream. Hair yellow as the dandelions in Janna's alley, eyes blue and white as Wedgewood china, and as if that wasn't enough, with all the light came warmth, effortless, unthinking, reaching out to Janna where she stood and drawing her inside its circle, irresistibly. Before she knew it she could feel the muscles of her face loosening under its spell, as if her face were being remade in its own reflection. A strange feeling. Janna felt the treacherous warmth reach deep to touch her bones. I will try, she thought. A smile, a little one. Next time.

Julie laughed, a deep, throaty, golden chuckle. Suddenly she swivelled round, exposing a flawless expanse of naked back.

'What do you think?'

Janna winced. It was just as she'd thought.

'I know.'

'You know?' The small girl swung round to stare at Janna in surprise.

'I mean . . .' Janna felt her cheeks grow hot, fumbled for words. 'I saw.' She gestured stiffly towards the door. 'Out there.'

The small girl gave her a curious look. Behind the owl glasses and panda make-up her eyes were disturbingly acute. 'How come? Do you live near here?'

'Yes.' Janna heard herself begin to stammer, felt a cold sweat break out over her skin. 'Just – just across the road.' The words would barely come. She tensed in an agony of anticipation. She'd said too much already. But she could hardly explain that she'd been out there all along, watching.

Mercifully, the small girl shrugged. 'Oh well, now you're here, you'd better let me take your coat.'

'No!' Janna shrank away, clutching her coat together at the neck. The small girl eyed her in astonishment.

'But it's boiling in here!'

'I don't mind.' Janna's words jostled and spilled in her haste, unnerving her. 'Really!' She hated the note of desperation in her voice.

'Leave her be, Lucy.' That golden, lazy voice again. 'If she wants to keep her coat on, why not?'

Janna nodded wordlessly. How simple Julie made it sound, how natural.

'Oh, please yourself.' The small girl shrugged again. 'I've got more important things on my mind.' She picked up a pair of large dress-maker's scissors from the table, and advanced on the dress. 'I don't know.' She shook her head doubtfully. 'I just can't work out what went wrong. The thread was supposed to give way.' She gave a tentative tug, snipped, tugged again. There was an ominous rending sound.

'Wait!' It took Janna a moment to realise that it was her own voice, a little hoarse, protesting. The small girl glanced at her sharply over her spectacles. Janna felt her face begin to burn. What had possessed her? She had no right.

'Here.' She felt cold metal in her hand. The scissors. 'You try.' Janna looked up to see Julie smiling down at her. Her eyes were so direct, so purely friendly with their wide black pupils, their look of sheer unfocussed gaiety, that Janna found

21

herself smiling back. It's a crazy world, Julie's eyes said. Welcome.

'But, Julie!' The small girl had her hands on her hips, her lips compressed into a tight line of disapproval.

'It's OK.' A liquid shrug, a laugh like honey. 'What have we got to lose?'

'Speak for yourself.' The small girl's voice was tart. Without looking at either of them she whisked up her jacket and stamped to the door. 'But if he asks, I'm going to tell him it's got nothing to do with me.' The aluminium door slid to behind her and she was gone.

Janna looked at Julie anxiously.

'Don't worry.' Julie gestured airily. 'If you can help she'll be pleased. If you can't – well, we'll have done our best, won't we? Nobody can ask any more than that.' She pirouetted neatly to present her tattered back.

'But what about my hands?' Janna held them out, black from the grate, dusty from the old wood.

'No problem.' With sudden, almost childlike glee Julie swept an array of bottles and phials and multi-coloured powders into an open drawer, lifted up the tray they'd rested on and revealed a miniature recessed basin, complete with doll-sized taps and tiny paper-wrapped tablets of soap. 'How's that?'

'Wonderful.' Janna spoke with feeling. She turned a tap and real hot water gushed. When she'd finished she found Julie waiting with a bright pink paper towel.

'Now, to work!' Julie's eyes were sparkling. For a moment Janna wondered which Julie would enjoy more, success or disaster.

Tentatively Janna touched the metallised fabric. It was warm. She thought hard. She understood silk, the strongest and the weakest of fabrics, the kindest and the most forgiving. It was a creature of moods and whims, demanding a firm but loving hand. A few strategic snips and the sculptured panels fell back off Julie's shoulders, revealing a simple white slip. Good-to-average lace, machine stitching.

'Well?' Julie turned round inquiringly. 'What went wrong?'

22

She touched the fabric gently with one long pearlised nail. 'It was supposed to come off when these strings were pulled, like a butterfly's wings.'

Silently Janna picked up the garment, brought it closer to the light. She took a length of dangling thread, bit it, tugged it. Yes. Just as she'd suspected.

'Polyester.'

'Oh.' Clearly Julie didn't understand what that meant. 'Not strong enough?'

Janna shook her head. Words came easily now. These were facts, her friends, they wouldn't let her down.

'Too strong. Look, it's cut right through the fabric. It should have been silk, pure silk.'

There, she'd said it. A whole sentence – two – without a stammer or a strutter. A lecture even! Janna felt her cheeks go hot with relief. Julie listened, she understood. A real conversation!

'I see.' Julie nodded sagely. 'So what do we do now?'

'Well . . .' Janna hesitated. Faced with Julie's smile, she wanted to promise miracles. She didn't want to see her face fall, but some incurable honesty made her speak the truth. 'Start again.' She looked down at the material in her hands, reluctantly. 'It's the best way.'

'I was afraid you might say that.' Julie's expression was philosophical. 'The trouble is, we've only got five minutes to spare.'

'Five minutes?' Janna felt her eyes go round. She shook her head. 'Impossible.'

Julie said nothing, she simply waited. When Janna looked at her again she saw something in her eyes. Trusting, confident, willing to take a chance. Putting herself in Janna's hands. No-one had done that, not since the dolls.

'Listen.' Janna's voice was gruff. She didn't know whether it would work, she didn't even know whether she dared. But she would try. Because it had never occurred to Julie that she wouldn't. 'Stand over there, absolutely still. I'll see what I can do.'

*   *   *

'This has got to be it, Julie.' The director's voice was stern. 'The machine's got barely five minutes flying time left and we've got ten before we're thrown into jail.'

'Don't worry, it's going to work.' Julie soothed him automatically, though she doubted if he heard her. By now he was beyond anything, simply pacing up and down, muttering gently to himself. 'It will, I promise. There's nothing to go wrong this time, nothing. Just pins.'

'Pins!' He cast his eyes upwards in despair. 'All this high technology and we're down to pins? I can't bear it.' He stared at her. A sudden bellow. 'Cut the pink! And that necklace. It may be Cartier but it's got to go.' Obediently Julie unclasped it, let it drop unheeded amongst the other stones. A production assistant scrabbled.

'Cue lights. Sound. Action. OK, Julie, go for broke.'

As Julie began her mute, brightly-lit walk across the rubble for the last time she felt a twinge of anxiety. Not for herself, or the client, or the seconds and pounds that were ticking away by the clock, but for that funny little girl with the white face and shuttered eyes, whose great idea this was. Such a strange girl, so shy, so stiff, like a wind-up toy with a broken spring. How did any girl get to be like that, in a world full of pretty clothes and fast food and telephones? She reminded Julie of a creature she'd seen on a TV documentary about endangered species. An ai-ai. She'd always remembered it, scuttling across some remote forest clearing with a haunted backward glance. Only ten of them left in the whole world, and she could see why. It wasn't the witch's claw on its front paws that made it an outcast, it was the expression in its eyes.

Those eyes. The eyes of a night-time creature, huge and pale.

'Are you sure it won't tear again?' The girl had given her a look, half timid, half proud, so exact a scaled-down copy of the professional's look that Julie had been getting all her working life that she almost laughed.

Keep your beautiful nose out of this, the look said. This is my province. I *know*.

And now, despite all the odds, Julie had faith in those

small, sure hands. No witch's claw maybe, but something of witch's skill.

The big moment. No tug of nylon wire this time, no heroics. Just the merest, infinitesimal caress as the silk parted behind her back. Now held only on her shoulders like a moth's outspread wings it flared out, rippled briefly in the onrush of air, and was gone.

'That's it! Cut. Thank you, everybody.' Wardrobe hurried up with a coat. Julie felt a moment's anti-climax. Being beautiful was lonely work, in the end.

'Just pins, eh?' The director was at her shoulder. Relief seemed to have taken ten years off his age. 'Wonders will never cease.'

'It's the way they're put in, apparently. Like origami, you know? Very, very difficult – except when you know how.'

'Don't tell me. Come and look at the monitor.'

Glued to the tiny flickering black-and-white screen they watched. Yes, it was all there, diminished but intact. The rush of wind, the fluttering fabric, the single, magical moment when Julie took wing.

'See what I mean?' Exhaustion and satisfaction was in the director's voice. 'It'll win an award, just you wait.'

As she watched the replay, fascinated, Julie realised he was right. It was just the kind of ad the industry liked, a Chinese puzzle, a piece of sleight-of-hand. Executives and clients alike would watch those two minutes over and over again, trying to see the ropes, the mirrors, the wires, talking knowledgeably of back projection and colour separation overlay, trying to work out how it was done, trying to pin it down . . .

'Difficult, you say.' The director gave her a mournful look. 'I suppose that means it's going to cost us a fortune?'

'No.' Julie shook her head, obscurely pleased at the surprise on his face. 'I tried to persuade her to put in a bill but she wouldn't.'

'Maybe she's expecting us to send her something.' The director grimaced a little sourly. 'Probably hopes she'll do better that way.'

'I'm afraid not.' Julie played her trump card. 'She wouldn't tell me where she lived or anything. Not even her last name.'

'Really?' The director's eyes were round, half-relieved, half-outraged. Clearly he didn't know whether to accept the news as a compliment or an insult to his craft. 'You mean she did it for nothing, nothing at all?'

'Well, there was something.' The director's face fell.

'What?'

'Oh, nothing much.' Julie gestured airily. 'I gave it to her. I thought you'd want me to. You can take it out of my fee, if you like.'

'Oh, yeah?' The director eyed her suspiciously. 'What was it, exactly?'

Julie smiled.

'Soap.' She said the word with deep satisfaction, remembering the girl's face as she'd pressed the three bars into her hands, knowing she'd guessed right, knowing that that was what she'd like, beyond anything. Three small bars of rose-coloured, gardenia-scented company soap.

And that was only one of the evening's mysteries. As Julie mounted the trailer steps she couldn't help wondering what would happen to that girl. There was something about her that made her hard to forget. Not just the way she looked, with her fine brown hair savagely cropped, like a child of ten, a small, delinquent boy, though that was striking enough. No, it was something else. The expression in her eyes, an intensity, a sincerity that burned. For a moment, there in the brightly-lit trailer, with the generator humming and the quiet intermittent click of the air-conditioning cutting in and out, Julie had the strange sensation that she herself was looking out through those eyes, at a world grown suddenly fearful, full of shadows and dangers. She'd never had that feeling before, and yet, somehow, she recognised it. As if she'd mislaid something or someone, missed by chance some never-to-be-repeated opportunity, failed to make the right move at the right time.

You're being silly, Julie, she told herself firmly. Just because she didn't respond to your famous charm. There was nothing you could have done.

But it wasn't that, not really. It was more as if, through a magic mirror, she'd glimpsed her other half, her opposite, the dark side of herself. So clumsy, so shy, so frightened.

And so very, very thin. Julie frowned. Under her bulky coat the girl had been nothing but bones. Watching her go down those steps had been a kind of torture, like watching a fledgeling bird that had fallen out of its nest, all legs and trailing wings.

I don't like worrying, thought Julie. It doesn't do any good. And yet, as she plucked a tuft of cottonwool from the dispenser and began to clean her face she found herself, against all the odds, against all her better judgement, making plans.

CHAPTER THREE

'HELP DARLING JANA PLEASE COME AT ONCE I
NEED YOU TODAY REPEAT TODAY 1.15 VICTORIA
ARRIVES DENE 2.20 BLESSINGS JULIE PS BRING
PINS'

The capital letters milled disjointedly under Janna's gaze.

Above her the station indicator gave a sudden roll and clack
as it shuffled its pack of cards and dealt again. She looked up
in alarm. She could tell that people were staring at her as she
fumbled for her ticket, checked and double-checked the time
and platform.

'Darling Jana.' She tested the words in her mind. They
seemed to refer to someone else, not just because her name
was spelled wrong. The sort of person who made trips, caught
trains, had friends who sent telegrams . . .

Janna shook her head. Even now she could hardly believe
it, though she'd seen the evidence with her own eyes, this
morning, as she came up the basement steps. There they
were, dozens of them, scores – neat little official envelopes
protruding from each cracked and peeling door like so many
puppydogs' tongues. Julie had sent a telegram, not just to
Janna's house, but to every single dwelling in the whole of
Rose Alley.

And all because of the pins. Janna smiled involuntarily.
Thinking of that night two months ago, she felt a small thrill
of pleasure, almost pride. It had worked, hadn't it, her idea?
She'd seen it all from the basement window, seen the crew
pack up their equipment, load it into the pantechnicon with
much shouting and laughter and drive away.

She'd looked round then for her stack of wood, remembered
she'd left it somewhere out there in the darkness. She'd put

her hands in the pockets of her coat to keep warm and found three small packets. The scented soap. It smelled of summer. She held it to her face and breathed in the smell as if it could make her warm. And slowly, as she stood there, she began to realise that the soap wasn't the only thing that Julie had given her. Somewhere, deep inside, she felt different. The memory of her one small success was something no-one could take away.

The next morning, shaking not just with cold, she went to the sari shop. With the last of her train money she bought a length of primrose yellow silk, only a small piece, but it had to be the best. She was glad the sari man didn't speak any English. He was used to conversing in silent signals, with averted eyes, so all she had to do was point and pay.

She took the silk home, hurrying. She felt as if it was her whole future lying there, feather-light, in her hands. She washed the fabric in cold water, wearing cotton gloves so that it wouldn't snag, handling it very carefully because despite its strength silk tore like paper when it was wet. Having no iron, she pinned it smooth to dry. She worked over it all that day into the evening, checking each stitch to make sure it was invisible, re-doing each seam until it lay properly smooth. By the time darkness came she had it finished at last, a perfect miniature model of a woman's camisole, the tiny edges embroidered to indicate lace.

She reached the sari shop five minutes before it closed. The man behind the counter looked up as she entered but didn't smile. It was as if he'd never seen her before. Silently, she pushed her small tissue-wrapped package towards him, watched, every nerve taut, as his brown hands moved slowly over the silk. He turned the tiny garment inside out, held the stitches up to the light, tugged at each minute seam. Finally, he nodded, just once. Still no smile. But when Janna left the shop she had a commission for his wife, an identical silk camisole, with Brussels lace.

It was a beginning, only a small one, but slowly, gradually, more commissions came. Mostly Bengali women, recommendations by word of mouth. Silent referrals over the same counter, lists of measurements on scraps of paper, followed by a used note or two, carefully rolled, or payments in kind. A quilt, an enamel kettle for her fire, a bolt of remaindered fabric, strange fruits. Janna never met her clients. None of them so much as knew where she lived. But she liked to think of her minutely hand-stitched silk slips hidden like tropical plumage under the dun-coloured coats of women whose names she'd never know.

Not that there was much time for thinking. The work was hard. At the end of a day's stitching Janna's eyes ached and the muscles of her neck and shoulders were stiff. There was never quite enough light, even if she got up at dawn. Twice she completed a garment late in the evening and had to unpick all she'd done the next day. Quality work, that's what it had to be, not just for clients but for herself. No seam must rub, no loose ends offend.

And still no-one came. This was the East End, after all. No permits needed, no questions asked. They'd grown used to people like her, these small streets. Refugees.

Sometimes she ate, sometimes she didn't. There were other things she needed. Two brass bolts for the inside of her door. An oil lamp. A paraffin heater, second-hand from a stall in Brick Lane, so that she could have warmth while she sewed. The fan of sunlight that flirted with her basement window spread a little wider each day but never reached right in. The wood fire created too much dust and smoke, leaving particles of soot on the silk, so she saved it for last thing at night. That was her favourite time. At night the house became another place, very old, very small. Darkness softened its edges. With the silk safely tucked away in its nest of lead-free tissue, Janna could curl up inside her quilt and watch the embers, waiting for sleep to float out of the dusty old walls and spirit her away.

And that, finally, was why she'd answered Julie's summons, made herself face the crowds and noise. Without Julie, she would never have had them, those two long months of freedom and firelight. Now the days had lengthened into summer. This morning, like an omen, she'd seen the first dandelion seed and scatter, a milky puff on the city wind.

A few hopeful seeds still clung to Janna's dark brown pullover. Anxiously, she brushed them away. She hadn't known what she should wear to visit Julie. Fortunately she didn't have very many clothes to choose from. The pullover and matching trousers from the same market stall which had given her the heater were her best clothes. She liked the trousers because of their pleats around the waist, a sort of disguise. Only the leg length had needed altering. But she could be proud of her bag. That was a real find, almost new. There were a few scuffs on the outside but inside it was quite perfect, like a workbasket, with every pocket and compartment you could think of needing, plus a few more. Quickly, she checked its contents. Money. A clean handkerchief. Her return ticket. Last of all and most important, a packet of brand-new, extralength, stainless-steel pins.

The thought of the pins gave Janna courage as she shouldered her bag and climbed onto the train. Pins – they were always the same, always there when you needed them. You knew where you were with pins.

The train was small, almost empty. She was glad of that. But every few minutes it slowed down or stopped, often with no station in sight. Each time she had to fight down the temptation to throw open the carriage door and run all the way back to Victoria Station. Now that she was actually on her way her mind was flooded with unanswerable questions. Would she be met? Was she expected? Had Julie's telegram been just a whim, a gamble made on the slightest of chances, not meant to be taken seriously?

At last, Dene station, the name just visible under a curtain of overhanging leaves. Janna left the carriage with a sense of fear and relief combined. But the platform was deserted. The office, too, was empty. There was no-one to check her ticket, no map to consult, nothing. Everything lay quiet and still in the hazy midsummer sunlight. Janna had to reassure herself repeatedly that she'd come to the right place. Perhaps Julie had meant Dean, not Dene, in her telegram?

Luckily there was only one road leading away from the station, plunging deep into a cutting overfringed with trees.

Janna had never seen so much green. Lush, scented, over-powering, something from a storybook or a Sunday supplement. Some kind of winged insect danced in clouds above her head. She envied it its grace, prayed to survive the day without disaster. The air smelled rich and damp, warm pastry rising. On the left, to her relief, she spotted a white signpost that said 'Dene'. That must be the way to the village. She felt happier now. If only there were signposts for everything – 'Smile now', 'Look up', 'Look down'.

The lane leading towards the village was wider than she'd expected, in fact almost a road, flanked by great mounds of glossy-leaved shrubs. Janna hadn't imagined that Julie would live somewhere so quiet, so rural. She seemed too exotic for all this greenery. There was something strange about it, a little stagey. Ahead was an avenue, surprisingly straight. Tall trees marched on either side, their branches producing a filtered shade. Behind them unrolled a sea of emerald grass. Janna began to feel more and more out of place, as if she'd crossed the border into a foreign country, a looking-glass world. Or at least the next county, a million miles from that sleepy country halt with its deserted platform.

Ahead, the road swept authoritatively to the right. Janna noticed, half-hidden amongst the shrubbery, a sort of gingerbread house, with fancifully leaded windows and a mossy tiled roof. She hesitated. Julie's? No – it seemed to be deserted.

Janna paused for a moment to rest. She hadn't imagined it would be so hot, she could feel sweat beginning to trickle beneath her arms. She wondered whether she should take off her pullover. The checked blouse she wore underneath was full enough to hide her body, but even so she couldn't bring herself to do it. Discomfort versus shame . . . The question tormented her like the winged flies brushing at the edges of her vision. She walked on.

The road continued to curve in an achingly leisurely manner to the right. If there was much further to go, Janna knew deep in herself, she wouldn't be able to manage it. She'd give up, turn back, take her shameful, hot self back where it belonged, in the cool dim basement room where nothing happened and nothing changed.

And then, at last, she rounded the corner and saw, over a haze of smooth lawn, the house. No, not the house. The House. If ever a house deserved capitals it was this one. As her heart sank slowly into the pit of her stomach Janna knew at last why Julie seemed so different from other people. Here was the source of her golden self-assurance, her happy acceptance of whatever came. For no matter what happened in the outside world it could create barely a ripple on the surface of this great green pool. No matter where Julie went, she'd always have this to come back to.

Now, too late, Janna realised why Julie's address was simply The House, Dene. Dene *was* The House. The House *was* Dene. Solitary, splendid and perfectly white, its Palladian façade was wider than mere human eyes could take in at a single glance. Severe, symmetrical, self-contained. No need to advertise. Size alone spoke the message clarion clear. Pillars, porticoes, parapets. A fanfare of windows. A glimpse of espaliered pears, a fig tree. From somewhere the faint sound of a lawnmower, the click of shears, the humming of bees.

'Hey, Janna!' It was Julie, wading through a golden froth of spaniel, what seemed at first sight a pack of them but resolved itself into just one, all ears and tail. 'They saw you at the Lodge. You should have waited – I was going to send a car.'

'Oh.' Janna faltered to a halt. The train must have been early. Belatedly she realised how wrong it had been of her to arrive like this, unannounced. She hadn't even thought to let Julie know she was coming. She tried to smile but it wouldn't work. She felt her face freezing into a sort of grimace. And yet, underneath, despite her confusion, she couldn't help feeling a small bubble of pure pleasure at seeing Julie again. If anything she was more beautiful than ever, a rare bird seen in her natural habitat. Her loose cream cotton shirt might be crumpled and not over-clean, her snuff-brown cords covered in spaniel hairs, but she looked right, natural. Janna realised instantly that that was how people must dress in the country,

33

that was how it was done. She stood there, feeling large and awkward in her own neat, dull, careful clothes.

'Come on, let's go in. I've got so much to tell you!' Janna followed, anxious to get in out of the sunlight. Indoors she'd feel less conspicuous and out-of-place. My clothes won't matter there, she thought gratefully, only my pins.

But as she mounted the broad steps to the entrance door Janna couldn't help noticing that the portico alone was twice the size of her own front room. For a moment she was blinded by longing for her little house, its uneven bricks, her companions. Don't be stupid, she told herself fiercely. A wall is just a wall, anywhere.

But even that certainty was shaken as the big oaken doors swung wide. The hall that Janna entered seemed as dim and vast as Victoria Station had done an hour ago. And as for the walls, she'd never seen anything like them. Gilded, fretted, tinted, panelled, fluted and moulded like a wedding cake, they weren't walls so much as works of art. No homely brown bricks, no comforting dark wood, only stucco and marble, cool and pale. A marble fireplace, huge as a larder. More marble on the floor, alive with Persian rugs, and on the terrace-wide stair, sweeping round in a dizzying curve to more gilded heights beyond.

Julie, without so much as breaking stride, crossed to the fireplace, where despite the time of year an ample fire burned. She seemed to claim the room, to hold it up to herself like a mirror. As she turned her smile outshone the flames.

'Gray?' Julie lifted a hand. Suddenly, startling Janna, a man materialised out of the shadows.

'This is Janna.' Julie's voice, a merciful filling of the silence. 'Remember her, please, she's a very important person.'

'Of course.' The man inclined his head politely. He was very tall, very fair. The dark formal suit he wore made him seem oddly remote. Like a statue, thought Janna confusedly. Marble and gold, like the house. She was dimly aware of a pair of blue eyes, not as brilliant as Julie's, but much more penetrating. 'Here, let me take your things, Miss –?'

34

'Brown.' On the verge of handing over her bag, Janna remembered just in time. 'Wait a minute.' Gray's face was a study in polite inquiry as she dug frantically inside. Only a moment ago it had seemed so well-organised, but now . . . At last her hand closed round the box of pins. She surrendered the bag mutely, feeling her cheeks flame, as if she'd been caught picking someone's pocket. It was the way Gray stood there, so graceful, so still, as if he owned the world and everything in it, her bag included. Now she knew what they meant when they said butlers were chosen for their 'presence'. There was something mesmerising about Gray's deliberate restraint.

'Did you bring a dress?'

Startled, Janna tore her eyes away from Gray's dark-suited back to face Julie. 'No, I thought . . .' She heard herself begin to stammer, bit her lip. Had she misunderstood completely? Had Julie meant her to make up a dress in advance, without fittings, consultations, patterns? 'I've got the pins,' she finished, lamely. A faint rustle from behind her, where Gray was standing motionless. Could you hear a smile?

'I meant for you.' Julie put her hand to her mouth. 'Didn't I say? I meant to, really I did. I want you to stay for the ball.'

'The ball?' By now Janna was completely disorientated.

'I forgot, didn't I? Oh, dear.' Julie's expression was comical. 'I'm not very good on paper, I'm afraid. Will you forgive me?'

Janna was so relieved that she would have forgiven her anything, but Julie didn't give her time. 'Never mind, we'll find you something.' Janna opened her mouth to protest then closed it again. She was uneasily conscious of Gray's silent presence. She didn't like to talk in front of him as if he didn't exist, but to include him in the conversation would probably be wrong too.

Fortunately Gray resolved her unspoken problem. With a single impassive look in Julie's direction and a polite inclination of the head in her own, he withdrew, melting back into the shadows as silently as he'd come.

'Don't mind Gray.' Julie seemed to sense her discomfiture. 'You'll get used to him. Think of him as – oh, just part of the furniture. It's much easier that way.'

35

'I'll try.' Janna was doubtful. Whatever else Gray might be, behind that impassive courtesy he was very much alive.

Julie's eyes fell on the packet of pins. 'You brought them! Good.' She paused, her face alight with anticipation. 'But before we start there's something you've simply got to see.'

Janna followed her, through a winding, dimly-lit corridor and into a long panelled gallery hung with gold-framed oils. Gilded filigree couches waited haughtily on either side. As she hurried to keep up with Julie, Janna felt her vision begin to blur. She'd never seen such treasures this side of museum glass. Jade and ivory and porcelain, marble and ebony and precious stones. Every surface that met her eye was patterned and veneered and inlaid, every window swagged and festooned, every piece of velvet embroidered, every knob embossed. The dust itself, filtering through half-drawn blinds, seemed like pure gold. Even the summer green of the grounds seemed too new and brash for this mellow interior. And yet Julie hardly looked from left to right but forged on, her yellow mane bright as a torch in the dimness

'This is the Great Apartment.' Julie swept through another doorway, much taller, where cherubs played with serpents in a bower of vines.

'On your right, Presence Chamber . . . Drawing Room . . . Chamber of State . . . Anteroom . . .'

Now the scale had changed. Before there had been detail but now there was magnificence. A banquet hall forested with exquisite gold-and-white chairs, a room lined entirely with painted silk, Chinese ebony dragons coiling round the mantel, pearly fruits and flowers strewn across an inlaid marble floor . . .

'There.' Julie halted at last, under a final doorway so elaborately grained that it looked more like marble than marble ever could. 'What do you think?'

Janna looked in, cautiously. Her eyes were drawn instantly upwards to a huge vaulted ceiling where naked gods and goddesses reclined on clouds. So much rose-pink flesh, soft and roundly curved, an arrogant abundance. She looked away. Beneath, the room was curiously empty. Except for one thing. So large that Janna almost missed it. Familiar, yet barely recognisable. Enormous, overpowering, motionless in the dimness like some great carnivorous beast. A bed.

But what a bed. Janna was glad it was fenced in behind its own ornate brass balustrade, otherwise it might escape and engulf them both. Above it towered a vast canopy, blood-red silk fading to rust where the light had touched it, crusted with gold and silver embroidery, festooned and ruched, puckered and puffed, braided and brocaded, dripping with golden butterfly fringing now dark and tarry with age.

With a whoop Julie vaulted the balustrade and threw herself onto the priceless silk coverlet.

'You can't do that!' The words were out in a sort of gasp before Janna could stop them. She half expected the fabric to disintegrate before her eyes like the petals of a dried Mme Perrière rose.

'But I always do.' Julie grinned, unrepentant. 'Look, four mattresses. One straw, two hair, then swansdown. My cousin's a stickler for detail.'

Janna flinched. A cousin . . . It hadn't occurred to her that Julie would have family. She seemed so complete on her own. But now – Janna sent a quick panicky glance towards the doorway. It had no door, someone could come in at any minute.

But Julie didn't seem to care. 'He hates me doing this, of course.' Her smile took on a devilish gleam. 'But he can't stop me. Not yet.' She bounced up and down. 'I bring everyone here. Everyone likes beds. Don't you?' She didn't wait for an answer but threw herself backwards, stretched out full length as if on a grassy bank. 'It takes a lot of living up to, this bed,' she observed inconsequentially. 'But I've done my best.'

Janna stared, unsure how to react. So simple an object, a bed – and so complicated.

'Come on, then, it won't bite!'

Gingerly, Janna edged a little nearer. She'd love to see the stitching close to. How many people must have worked on that canopy – it would have taken months . . . Very gently she touched one of the folds. It was papery, stiff.

'Did people really sleep in this?'

'Oh, yes. Queen Elizabeth, for one. Though I don't think she can have been very comfortable.' Julie patted the mattress beside her. 'Come on, try it.' Janna sat down, as lightly as she could, and sank as if she'd stepped into a boat.

'I see what you mean.' Janna tried to keep her balance and failed. 'Not a lot of back support.'

Julie threw back her head and laughed out loud, Janna could feel the tremors reaching her through the four mattresses. With a dextrous movement Julie reached up, pulled something, and crimson darkness descended with a silken whisper.

'I used to hide in here when I was small. Pretend it was my very own house.'

'But why?' Janna found she too was speaking in a whisper. It was almost as if the two of them were in a church. 'All this space, and you hid in here? Why?'

'I don't know.' Julie's face in the rosy half-light looked younger, almost like the small girl she must have been. Then, suddenly, her face broke into that familiar grin. 'It meant I could get away from my governesses. They weren't allowed in the State Apartments. They knew I must be here, but they couldn't come and get me. I used to wait until Father came home. I liked that.' She looked around, sighed. 'I shall miss the State Bed.'

'Miss it?' Janna hesitated. 'Is it going to be sold, or something?'

'Oh, no.' Julie sounded shocked. 'It stays here. It's just that – well, it won't be mine any more.'

'I don't understand.'

'It's the entail, you see.' Julie smoothed the faded coverlet. 'Father wouldn't break it, even for me. Now if I'd been a boy . . .' Janna caught the hint of longing in her voice and was surprised. Maybe inside every woman, even one as beautiful as Julie, there was that sense of being dispossessed, excluded.

'You mean that none of this – the House and everything – belongs to you?'

Julie shook her head. 'Not now I'm twenty-one.' Her face was suddenly serious. 'I envy you, you know. Having a place

38

of your own, right in the centre of town. So sensible.'

'Not really.' Janna shook her head. 'I'm only – squatting, I suppose. I could get thrown out any time.'

'But not on your birthday.' Julie's tone was tragic. Janna was aghast.

'Today's your birthday?'

Julie nodded. 'Julie, July, get it? Father was a very organised sort of person. I think it helped him remember when my birthday came round. Anyway, that's what this ball is all about. Which reminds me.' She brightened suddenly. 'There's someone I want you to meet. My very favourite lady.'

Janna froze. This was what she'd been afraid of all along. But Julie knelt up on the coverlet and pointed at the panelled wall above the bedhead.

Janna relaxed a little. It was simply the portrait of an Elizabethan lady, elongated shoulders rising out of a ruff of silver lace, narrow blue-veined temples, a plucked hairline, stern heavy-lidded eyes and a nose long as an icicle.

'Isn't she beautiful?' Julie spoke with utter satisfaction. 'Isobel Le Franceys, on the occasion of her wedding. That's what I want to look like at the ball tonight. A virgin bride.'

'Impossible.' Janna coloured. That hadn't come out right. 'I mean –' she hurried to explain before Julie's amused glance, 'her clothes.' Isobel Le Franceys was a study in formal elaboration. Her intricately coiffed hair was laced with pearls and gemstones, her bodice meticulously crafted over layer upon layer of embroidered undergarments, her ruff boned, her puffed sleeves slashed to reveal more gorgeous brocade beneath. 'Look at them.' Janna offered her knowledge hesitantly. 'She wouldn't have worn them even to a ball, only to have her portrait painted.'

'Really?' Julie's confidence seemed undimmed. 'But you can do it, I know you can. Don't forget, I've seen you at work. If you can turn me into a butterfly in ten minutes flat, surely you can make me a virgin bride in an afternoon?'

Janna shook her head reluctantly. Julie's voice deepened, cajoling.

'Just wait till you see the bits of stuff I've found, I've been looting the attics for weeks. Lace, brocade, velvets – everything we could possibly need.' Janna bit her lip. She'd love to see them – Julie couldn't know how much. But there was no point in promising something that was impossible. She shook her head again. Julie took no notice. 'And look . . .' Delving in her pocket, Julie came up with a fistful of enormous costume rings. 'This one I got on a Campari ad, this one came out of a cracker. Clever, eh?' She spilled them with childish pleasure into Janna's palm. 'You'll do it, won't you?'

'I can't promise anything. It may not –' Julie cut her short.

'I knew you would.' She glissaded off the bed, grabbed Janna's hand. With the other, as they rocketed through the empty corridors, she was already unbuttoning her shirt.

CHAPTER FOUR

Silently, eyes wide, Julie approached the mirror. Silk rustled. She looked in.

Behind her, reflected in the glass, was a scene of chaos, clothes tipped everywhere, drawers rifled, the floor littered with lengths of fabric.

But Julie was transformed. Her wild hair was now pulled severely back from a brow powdered white as marble. Not a trace of gold showed through the liberal coating of starch, which, Janna had discovered, fixed hair almost as well as Allways hairspray. The pearls Julie's father had given her, three matched pairs every birthday since she was eleven, were looped at her hairline. All vestiges of her cinnamon tan were gone. Tiny ice-blue veins were painted at her temples. She looked delicate, fragile, almost tubercular.

Julie studied her face in the mirror thoughtfully, pursed her lips.

'Are you sure about the lipstick? Not just the littlest, littlest bit? I always wear it, even to answer the telephone . . .'

'Yes, I'm sure.' Janna couldn't explain why. It was a feeling, something she knew in her bones. With her hair powdered, a single beauty mark challenging at her cheekbone, the only colour in Julie's face came from her eyes. 'It would be too much. You should be like – a rainbow shining through an icicle.'

'Pretty.' Julie smiled.

'No.' Janna shook her head. Julie looked startled. Janna hurried to explain. 'The smile, I mean. You see, they never did, those Elizabethan ladies. Because of their black teeth.'

Julie gazed at her in fascination. 'Really? What a horrible thought!' She ran her tongue over her own perfect teeth with a

41

meditative expression. 'Maybe we should – no, perhaps not. But how do you know all this?'

Janna felt herself flush with pleasure. She gave an awkward little shrug. 'I get books. From the library.'

Julie touched her own glass image. 'I think that's wonderful.' Janna wasn't sure whether she meant the library books or her own reflection in the mirror, but it didn't matter. 'What should I wear on my feet, heels?'

Janna hesitated, then shook her head. Rummaging in the almost empty closet she came up with some flat white pumps. Julie looked doubtful as she slipped them on. One was stained at the toe. Inspired now, Janna added a small ribbon bow, clipping it on with a single mother-of-pearl ear-ring.

'Perfect! You're a magician, Janna!' Suddenly Julie leaned down and planted a kiss on her cheek. Before Janna could react, before she could even register more than the faint powdery smell of her skin, soft as a baby's or a little old lady's, Julie was up again, swooping, spinning, flinging out her bell of a skirt like a top, almost scattering the open box of pins. Janna covered it just in time.

'Just think!' Julie's eyes were alight. 'Tonight I'll be able to kiss whoever I like, as much as I like – no lipstick!' She halted abruptly, in an eddy of brocade. 'Now.' She stood there, hands on hips, head on one side, assessing. 'Now it's your turn.'

'What?' Janna stared up at her. 'I don't understand.'

'Your turn to get dressed up, of course.' Julie spoke with a trace of impatience. Already she was foraging through the clothes on the floor, her improvised corsets creaking. 'Now I see why they needed maids, these Elizabethan ladies – I can barely bend in the middle! Here, try this.'

Janna shook her head, alarm coursing through her whole body. 'I can't. I mean – you don't understand. I'm not coming to the ball.'

'But I need you, Janna.' Julie sat back on her heels, bunching her skirt in ringed hands. Her eyes were pleading. 'Who else have I got to carry my train? I won't be able to manage the stairs without you. Just think, I might trip, snag this brocade. It's priceless, you know, Spitalfields silk.'

'Spitalfields?' Janna stared at the tiny flower sprigs with new eyes. 'But that's where I live!' What connection could there possibly be between that exquisite brocade and the grimy, decaying streets which had given her shelter?

'Really? How extraordinary.' Julie's mind was clearly elsewhere. 'If you want to know about that sort of thing you should ask my cousin. French Huguenot weavers, that's the password. Just start him off and he'll keep going for hours.'

Janna drew in her breath. Thank god she hadn't been asked to cut into the fabric. Thank god the pins she'd brought had been stainless steel. She hadn't dreamed the material could be so old. Two-hundred-and-fifty years old at least, and yet the wreaths and festoons were as clear as if they'd been woven yesterday. Silk had that way of defeating time. It was only light it really feared. And yet it was strange to think that all those years ago, maybe in a street very near hers, some lonely Frenchman had sat at his loom in the grey foreign light and laboured over beauty to be free. That explained Fleur-de-Lis Street, Fournier Street, Brune Street, exotic names flowering as unexpectedly in those dark alleys as this silk had done.

'Hmm.' Julie was holding up a simple white dress. Her eyes scanned Janna's body. 'You're so slim – are you on a diet?'

'No.' Suddenly all the warmth seemed to leave the room. Janna felt herself shrink away from Julie's eyes. She couldn't talk about it. Too many memories. The feel of the cold rubber weighing mat under her bare feet. The clang of the little metal weights racing time across the bar. Her nakedness under the starched surgical gown. And questions, always questions. Questions and eyes. Spyholes in the door. No door at all on the lavatory. No hiding-place, no escape.

They'd tried to feed her intravenously. She'd felt like a pig being readied for slaughter. That's what they'd wanted her to be, a bag of lard, a smear on the face of the earth. She'd ripped out the drip at night, when she was alone. Her body had gone into shock. She'd lain there helpless, panting, a force-fed pupa, a twenty-year-old foetus. Let me go, she'd prayed. Let me go.

'We only want to help you.' No-one heard that voice inside

her. Help *me*. Not this body I hate that rules me. Help *me*.

'If you lose any more weight, Miss Brown, you will die. Do you understand?'

What did they understand about dying? There were living deaths too, prisons without bars. Janna felt her heart leap and shudder in her rib-cage like a trapped moth. There had to be something more than waking and eating and sleeping, a grub in the world's skin. There had to be.

'Lucky you.' The rushing in Janna's ears receded. She found Julie looking at her, not with that hospital look, that saw without seeing, touched without feeling. She was smiling, almost as if she understood. 'I have to diet all the time. Cameras have more calories than a cream bun.' She held up a pair of white satin trousers. 'You might even be able to get into these.'

Before she knew it, Janna found herself in Julie's bathroom, her arms full of clothes – the white satin trousers, cream tights, a full-sleeved white shirt with lace collar and cuffs, an old felt hat which with a bit of pummelling and pinching might pass as a pageboy's tricorne.

Slowly, feeling strangely weak and empty, Janna put them on. Julie hadn't left her any other choice. Because of that moment when Julie had looked at her body and seen, not the ugly flesh that still remained, but the longing inside. To be beautiful, to be free.

It was odd, wearing Julie's clothes. No transformation, but – a difference. Janna felt a small upsurge of confidence, as if something of Julie's beauty had rubbed off on her clothes. The shirt was much too long, dropping off her shoulders and falling over her wrists. but the fabric was so fine that it fell beautifully. Janna liked the way it hid her body. Her hipbones projected through the white satin like a young boy's. For a second, as she glimpsed her reflection in the bathroom mirror, Janna felt young, light, a stranger to herself. Quickly she looked away.

Julie greeted her with complete approval. 'I haven't worn those trousers since I was thirteen and thought I was Hamlet. They look great.' Janna felt herself grow tall. It was all right. It must be. Julie said so.

44

Proudly, almost eagerly, she took up her position holding Julie's train and they went out into the corridor. From the Great Hall below came a hum of voices, echoing. Janna fixed her eyes on Julie's upright back. She must blot out the people sounds, concentrate on what she had to do. There was no need to worry. She'd be safe in Julie's shadow. I make a good henchman, she thought with relief. It's almost like being invisible.

'Here we go!' A backwards hiss from Julie, incongruous above her haughty ruff. Slowly, majestically, accompanied by delicious rustlings and creakings of centuries-old fabric, they proceeded to the top of the marble staircase, timing their steps as carefully as a pair of Siamese twins. Julie was right. Alone, with her panniers and the ruff that prevented her looking down, she could never have managed both her train and the stairs. And the train was beautiful, worth every moment's labour. Now, in the flicker of candlelight from the Great Hall below, every gold thread, every gem, struck fire.

Julie didn't pause or turn. Janna felt her heart begin to beat a little faster. She was safe in Julie's shadow, but even so . . . She tightened her grip on the Spitalfields silk. Once Julie was safely down the stairs, her train unsnagged, she could slip away. No-one would notice her – Julie was dazzling enough to make sure of that. How graceful she was, even in her rigid bodice and encumbering sleeves.

Only a few more steps. Janna trod carefully. Her black pumps, three sizes too large, had cotton wool stuffed in the toes. At all costs she mustn't trip and spoil Julie's moment of glory. Out of the corner of her eye she caught sight of Gray, his silver head hardly a shade lighter though covered in powder. He looked perfectly at home as he moved amongst the guests, only the greater restraint of his livery betraying the fact that he wasn't one of them. And what a crowd it was! Powdered and patched, masked and monocled, a cast straight from the pages of the Rake's Progress. Silk and satin and figured velvet. Rouged cheeks and glittering eyes, a high, excited murmur of cultured voices, a sudden piercing laugh.

'There's my cousin. Watch his face!' Janna turned just in

time to catch Julie's whisper. Following her gaze she saw a florid, balding man wearing a gorgeous costume, turquoise and gold, the finest in the whole gathering. He was holding forth to a circle of charmed listeners.

Janna held her breath. What would he think when he saw Julie? What would he say? She looked magnificent. Suddenly her hands were shaking not just with nervousness but with excitement.

But wait a minute . . . There was something wrong. A subtle jarring, a sort of discord. Janna felt it before she saw it. A change in atmosphere, a thundery tension, as if somehow they'd come to the wrong place, on the wrong day, uninvited. She shrank behind Julie's wide skirt, trying to make herself as small as possible. Her mind raced with frantic questions. What could possibly have gone wrong? Had one of the pins slipped without her noticing? Had Julie's ruff come undone? Even worse, had something torn, despite her care? She waited, hardly breathing, desperate to see yet not daring to look.

Julie stopped, seemingly oblivious, three steps from the bottom of the stairs, and tapped the gilded baluster with her white fan. The small sharp noise carried like a gunshot. All heads turned upwards. There was a universal intaking of breath. Janna felt the silk brocade slip from her hands. Now, at last, she realised what it was they saw. Everyone else, right down to the last buttoned knee-breech and ribboned eyeglass, was in eighteenth-century costume, painstakingly matched to their surroundings. She and Julie, dressed as Elizabethans, were as conspicuous and out of place in that gathering as painted savages. An anachronism, a calculated insult, two whole centuries out of date.

The bottom step. 'Julie!' A mass of people thronged forward, eyes shining with curiosity in the candlelight. 'You look divine. But how on earth . . .?' Janna felt the heat of speculation on her face, turning her skin to paper. Questions, circling her head like flies, humming, buzzing, closer and closer. Soon they'd find out who was responsible, and then . . . Janna looked wildly from side to side. What would happen to her, the intruder, the outsider, the one who didn't belong?

Bodies pressed round her. Strangers' faces, moving behind the mask of make-up. Appraising eyes, red-rimmed, moist, raw, inside their black outline. Chalk-white powder furring every cheek, so men looked like women and women like dolls. And eyes, eyes . . . A pit of snakes, seething. A nightmare.

Escape. Janna turned to run back up the stairs to safety but Julie was surrounded, the route blocked. Head down, breathless, Janna plunged down into the mêlée. Bodies pressed round her. It was warmer down here, suffocatingly warm, with the July heat and the massed candles. The smell of hot wax mingled with a pot-pourri of clashing scents. Janna was suddenly dizzy. Her heart drummed, tattooing her ribs. She couldn't see any way through the press of alien bodies. She swayed, buffeted by panniers, jabbed by fans. Inside her borrowed clothes her skin crawled in terror. To be touched, jostled, crushed – she couldn't bear it. She had to get away.

At last she found cover at the base of the grand stairs. She leaned back against the ancient panelling, taking in great thankful gasps of air. But seconds later, with a horrifying noiseless lurch, the wall itself gave way behind her. She fell backwards, sure for one desperate moment that she was going to be plunged far below in the murky waters of the moat.

Only, of course, there was no moat, just a flight of stone steps leading innocently down. Janna drew a deep, shuddering breath of relief. It hadn't been a wall she'd leant against at all, but a double-hinged door.

She waited on the top step until her heart went back to its proper place. The stone felt cool and reassuringly solid under her feet. Best of all, there was no-one in sight. Even the buzz of noise from above was now muted by solid, close-fitting oak.

A breath of cool air touched her cheek, reminding her of home. She followed it down the little stair, feeling safer with every step. She rounded the corner, ducking her head to avoid an over-hanging beam, and stopped dead.

For a moment Janna couldn't believe what she saw. She'd come so far, survived the worst, only to fall into a trap. And such a trap, so cunningly baited, as if designed uniquely for her.

Desperately her eyes searched each corner of the room, but it was empty. She was alone, perfectly alone, just as she'd wanted to be. No-one there. No-one to protect her, no-one to come between her and that long, wide table crowded to its edges, almost overflowing with food.

And not just food – a banquet. A feast for the senses, fit to place before those gods and goddesses she'd seen above the Great Bed. Something out of a dream, her dreams. Syllabubs, perfect as baby flesh, each in its own silver sacrificial dish. Tarts, jewelled with summer fruit set in pastry so light it would dissolve in her mouth as innocently as a cloud. A whole ham, tender pink, studded with cloves. Golden glazed breads. Individual pats of butter stamped with the head of a fat little Franciscan monk, beaded with sweet moisture. A monumental Stilton cheese. A trifle veiled in cream. Whiskered raspberries piled on ice. Rum-soaked peaches edged with petit-fours. A summer pudding steeped in royal purple, one runnel of juice overflowing the plate to stain the white cloth beneath.

There was no turning away from that table. It drew Janna like an altar, an Eden tree. Threatening, promising, an ancient siren song. Come to me, surrender. Give me your soul and I will promise you pleasure beyond telling. Trust me. I am your friend, your lover, your reward. Forget everything but me.

In the centre, coal-black, moist, deceptively plain, a black wheel. Chocolate cheesecake. What would it contain? Menier chocolate, cream cheese, double cream to bind, egg yolks, nutmeg, dark soft brown sugar in an almond meal crust. So simple. So rich. So fatal.

There was a knife lying ready by the plate. It glittered. Ivory handle, delicate scrollwork on the silver blade. A beautifully balanced knife. Janna found it in her hand. Swiftly, precisely, she plunged the blade dead centre.

Once, twice. A perfect wedge. She picked it up. Her mouth filled with foreknowledge of taste and texture, a sort of death. Nothing else mattered. But she wouldn't swallow. She told

48

herself that, knew it was so. All she craved was the flavour, the explosion of pleasure far back on her tongue.

The mixture was thick, sticky. It clung to her teeth and palate. She struggled to hold it there, fix the sensation of a full mouth in her mind, make the satisfaction last. But she couldn't. Without meaning to, with a convulsive reflex action, she swallowed.

Janna knew, then, that nothing had changed. She'd failed, just as she'd always failed. She hadn't escaped them after all: Mother's high teas, those endless, heavy meals that under-studied love. Bread fried in dripping till it shone like marca-site. Pork pies glistening with white fat. Sausages chattering in their own grease. Scones piled high with cream. Innocent deadly cream . . . No, nothing had changed. It was all the same. The same taste. The same despair.

And there was no going back. She'd begun now and couldn't stop. Already her hand was reaching for the knife. But that was too slow, too safe. She reached out blindly with both hands, lifted the whole mass to her mouth, sank her teeth full into its black assassin's heart.

Then she heard something that turned the crumbs in her mouth to ashes. Steps on the stairs.

Janna froze, stricken. Looking round she saw evidence of her crime, her body's treachery, everywhere. Dark smears on her hands, the cloth, hospital-white, the plate. What could she do? She flew to the fridge, heart racing, and thrust the remains inside. Without pausing to draw breath she darted back to the double sink, turned on the tap and began, leisurely, to wash her hands.

'Good evening.'

Slowly, agonisingly, Janna turned, reaching with desperate casualness for the towel. When she saw who it was standing there at the base of the stairs she was hit by a wave of relief so violent it left her faint. It could have been worse, so much worse. It might have been a guest standing there, not Julie because she would have understood, but someone else, one of the nameless painted faces with jewelled eyes. Worst of all, it could have been her host.

But it was Gray. She might have expected that if she'd been able to think at all. He was the most likely person to come below stairs when the ball was in full swing. Janna leaned thankfully against the cold steel rim of the sink and half closed her eyes. Now the madness was over all she could feel was self-disgust.

'Are you all right?'

Janna nodded. She couldn't speak. What she'd eaten lay like a lump of lead in her throat. She could barely lift her head, let alone meet Gray's eyes. She wished she could simply leave, walk away, but that was impossible. He was standing between her and the stairs, effectively blocking her exit. To escape she'd have to go right past him, feel his eyes on her, close . . . She couldn't do it.

Gray moved. Janna flinched, busied herself with the towel to hide her alarm. Where was he going? What had he come to do? His face was turned away from her but his presence filled the room. In eighteenth-century livery, black knee-breeches over white hose, scarlet embroidered waistcoat under black-and-silver frock-coat, he looked cool as ever. Unreal, yet somehow more than real. An actor perfectly at home in his role.

Slowly, deliberately, Gray walked over to the table. Janna's heart missed a beat then seemed to stop altogether. She should have known. He had come down specifically to check on the banquet, make sure that everything was just as it should be for his guests. She froze, stricken. The empty space where the cheesecake should have been glared suddenly white, Alaska-wide.

Gracefully, with a practised motion, Gray flicked the Mechlin lace away from his wrists and ladled out a glassful of punch from the deep central bowl. 'Here.' He held out the glass, forcing Janna to look at him. 'This will make you feel better.' Awkwardly, Janna took the glass. She didn't know what else to do. As she did so she risked a quick glance at his face. It had the kind of bones that mastered any sort of light, even the harsh modern brightness of the kitchen. And yet she had no idea what he was thinking, none at all. If he'd noticed the absence of the cheesecake, not a flicker of suspicion showed. His expression was calm, courteous, professionally patient. Only a shadow of curiosity showed in his eyes, the way he was watching her, as if he, too, were waiting to see what she would do.

The silence stretched. Janna had to fill it somehow. Nervously she ducked her head to her glass, pretended to savour the bouquet, conscious all the time of Gray's eyes on her, assessing. The yellowish liquid was thick, almost syrupy, heavily scented with lemon peel and spices. It made her stomach turn. Unbidden memories, uninvited guests. Sweet sherry, biscuits from a tin. Her eighteenth birthday. 'You're grown-up now.' A net of words and smiles and other people's expectations, falling over her head, silk-fine . . . The next week she'd been admitted to hospital. No more sweet sherry, no more 'grown-up now'.

But there was no escaping Gray's eyes. Reluctantly, Janna took a sip. After the cheesecake the punch tasted sickeningly sweet. But what else could she do? She was trapped, by her own guilt.

'More.' Gray's voice, crisp, authoritative. 'Waste not, want not . . .' Janna shuddered inwardly. She tilted the glass, drained it in one swallow as if it were medicine.

'Good girl.'

That, never. Gray took her glass, set it meticulously on the drainer. He was an excellent butler, Janna could see that. He'd even been right about the punch. It had made her feel, not better exactly, but less. Around her everything seemed to have receded to a comfortable distance. Even her own thoughts had been replaced by a sort of vague, heavy warmth.

'Don't let me keep you.' She stumbled a little over the words, her tongue seemed twice its usual size. 'You must have lots to do.'

'Nothing that can't wait.' Gray inclined his head politely. 'Julia asked me to see how you were.'

'Julia?' Janna frowned, confused.

'Miss Le Franceys.'

'Oh. Julie.' Janna smiled in relief. Just thinking of Julie was enough to make her feel better. 'She's very kind, isn't she?'

'Don't be so humble.' Gray's tone held a hint of bitterness. 'She's kind when it suits her.'

Janna stared at him, startled. She didn't know what to say. And yet she felt driven to say something, anything, in Julie's defence.

·'She looks marvellous tonight, don't you think?' Belatedly Janna realised she must sound as if she was fishing for compliments on her own work, and blushed.

'Most effective.' Gray's tone was dry. 'You, too.'

'Me?' Janna blinked in surprise.

'Of course.' Gray spoke patiently. 'You make a most convincing page.'

'Thank you.' Janna's flush deepened. She could feel his eyes on her, moving lazily from hat-brim to pointed toes. She fixed her eyes on the floor and tried to curve her body inwards, hiding inside the full shirt.

'You're enjoying the assembly, I hope?'

'No. I mean . . .' Janna's voice tailed away. Faced with that penetrating gaze she couldn't think of anything else but the truth. Cold, graceless, uncomfortable, like the stone floor of her basement room.

'You intrigue me.' Gray spoke slowly, leaning back against the stair-well as if he had all the time in the world. Suddenly Janna wished she had somewhere to put her hands. The satin trousers had no pockets, not even a belt in which to hook her thumbs. 'You're different, aren't you?'

Janna bit her lip.

'Not like most of Julia's friends.' Gray smiled. 'A refreshing change, believe me.' Janna stared back at him doubtfully. The outline of his face was unclear. He looked golden, god-like, untouchable. She struggled to hold onto reality.

'I don't think . . .' Her thoughts were escaping her, straying away like so many sheep. 'I really don't think you should say things like that. About Julie's friends.' She halted, suddenly dismayed. She hadn't meant to sound so rude.

But Gray seemed unmoved. 'Perhaps not.' Suddenly another glass brimmed in his hand. 'More punch?'

Janna hesitated, torn between reluctance and the need to make up for her rudeness. At last she took the glass.

'Thank you.' Suddenly she felt giddy, almost reckless. 'I hope it's authentic.'

'It should be.' Gray didn't smile. 'I made it myself.'

'Oh, well, in that case . . .' Janna drank deep. The punch tasted better this time. She set her glass down, very carefully. Her own hand seemed small and far away. 'Tell me . . .' She leaned forward. Men liked to talk about themselves, she'd read that in a magazine. 'What is it really like, your job? Do you ever get bored?'

'Sometimes.' Gray smiled a little. 'But it has its compensations.' He shrugged. 'Living here. Being surrounded by beautiful things.'

'Oh, yes.' Janna let out her breath in one long sigh. She understood so perfectly that she felt almost faint. What she'd give to be a part of Dene, to belong, even just as a custodian. 'Sometimes I wish I was . . .'

'What?' Gray was watching her, quizzically.

Janna blushed. A lifetime of wishing had been in her voice, she'd said too much, gone too far.

'Well?' Gray prompted her, one eyebrow raised. Janna swallowed. She'd given herself away too thoroughly to go back now.

'I don't know.' She hesitated, then spoke in a rush, the words tumbling in the intensity of her need to make him understand. 'Something – beautiful. A Georgian teapot. A *cloisonné* vase.' Something small and smooth and perfectly hard, kept safe forever in a glass-fronted cupboard, beyond needs or feelings or memories, out of reach of any human hand.

'A woman?' Gray was still watching her, his expression unchanged.

'No.' Janna shook her head fiercely. 'Not that, ever.'

'But then . . .' Gray's voice was oddly gentle. His eyes held a trace of sympathy as he watched her, as if she were a foolish moth blundered in from the dark and caught inside a shade. 'It's hardly a matter of choice, is it?'

'Yes, it is.' Janna spoke quickly. She had to believe that, it was her rock, her lifeline. Without it she would be sucked down again into the maelstrom, where nothing was safe or known, even herself. 'I don't want to be a woman. I choose not to be. I want to stay just as I am.'

'I see.' Gray put his head one side, studied her, his eyes moving slowly from her legs in their white satin, over her body and back up again to her face. Suddenly Janna felt raw, vulnerable, as if he'd stripped her to her nerve ends. I'm not here, she wanted to shout at him, don't you understand? What you see is nothing, just a woman's body. I don't want it. I never asked for it. It has nothing to do with me. I disown it and all its demands. I refuse.

'Yes.' Gray nodded, unsmiling. 'A considerable achievement. You have my congratulations.'

Janna stared at him. Suddenly, foolishly, tears pricked at the back of her eyes. It's worked, she thought. I've done it. I'm safe at last, free. She waited for it to come, the pleasure of her victory, her job well done. But she felt nothing, only a sort of emptiness. It had taken so long, the struggle, consumed her every waking moment. Without it, how would she fill the hours?

'You know . . .' Gray's tone was meditative. He rose to his feet. 'I rather like the way you look. Especially now.'

Suddenly, terrifying her, he stepped forward, placed his hands on her shoulders. They seemed to burn right through the thin cloth and into her bones. Without a word, with one irresistible movement of his wrists, he pivoted her until she faced the stainless-steel-clad wall above the work surface. In the grey metal she saw a subtly distorted image of her own face, the lower half liberally smeared with chocolate.

'Guilt incarnate.' Gray's voice was in her ear. 'That is always interesting.'

Janna's face flamed. She threw off his hands with a convulsive movement, ran to the sink, scrubbed at her face with the damp towel. But it was too late. He knew. He'd known all along. Perhaps all along he'd been playing with her, drawing her out for his own amusement, a cruel backstairs game.

'May I help?' Gray's voice was calm, politeness itself. Janna buried her face in the rough linen. She shook her head. She couldn't speak.

'In that case I'd better get back to my guests. Are you coming?' Janna shook her head again.

'Just as you please.' Carrying the punchbowl, Gray paused halfway up the stairs. 'In that case . . .' Janna looked up just in time to catch the shadow of a smile. '*Bon appétit!*'

As soon as he'd gone Janna went into the pantry and bolted the door on the inside. She sat there, shivering, for an hour, maybe two. In the darkness it was hard to keep track of time. Through the crack in the door she saw movement as waiters appeared to ferry the rest of the banquet upstairs. She felt a wave of nausea, remembering the cheesecake. That was how it always went. First, the terrible desire, and afterwards, no trace of it, just the memory of madness, and the fear.

Perhaps, even now, Gray was telling her story, explaining to the waiters. They'd laugh. A whisper here, a whisper there . . . Soon everyone would know. Janna's ears burned.

At last the noise and music from above died away. Janna crept out, stiff and aching. She hadn't dared move. But she couldn't leave much later or she might have to stay the night. That would be unbearable.

Before the door leading out to the Great Hall she hesitated one last time. Silence. Her head ached, her mouth tasted sour. She pushed the door open just a crack. The guests hadn't gone, it was still too early, but at least the way was clear. They were all grouped against the walls, leaving the marble floor egg-shell bare. This was her chance.

Her heart drumming, her breathing ragged in her ears, Janna edged her way towards the grand stairs. It was darker there, she could slip away unobserved.

'Wait!' It was Gray's voice, crisp and clear. All eyes swung round, pinning Janna as surely as a searchlight. She froze, almost within reach of the bottom stair. Looking over her shoulder she saw Gray, striding towards her across the deserted floor.

He held out his hand. Janna shrank back. Looking up at

him in the dim light, she saw his eyes glitter and felt suddenly afraid. In the few hours since she'd seen him last he'd changed. Now his manner was less immaculate, less controlled.

'What do you want?' Her voice came out high and small.

'The last dance.' There was something strange in the way Gray spoke, loudly, head thrown back. At her, not to her. Janna felt cold. It was as if he didn't really see her, as if she were some minor piece in a game he was playing, a game without rules. Before she could frame an answer, before she even knew what he was doing, he pulled her towards him. 'I'm tired of women and all their ways. I want to dance with you.'

Everyone heard. It was if with those words he'd stripped Janna naked, bared her secret for all to see. There was nothing she could do. Two steps and she was on the dance floor, slow stately music imprisoning her as surely as Gray's arms.

Lost in her private shame it took Janna a few seconds to realise the full horror of what Gray had done. As the music swung them round she glimpsed Julie's face in the crowd. Her cheeks had a high colour under the powder. She looked beautiful, and very angry. As she has every right to be, thought Janna miserably. This is wrong, all wrong. Her head swam. She fought against a treacherous sense of unreality. It couldn't be happening, this relentless circling, it must be a nightmare. But she could feel her shoes catch on melted wax pooling on the marble, feel the velvet of Gray's frock-coat hot under her cheek.

'Please,' she whispered, achingly conscious of the watching eyes. 'Please stop.'

'Why?' From the tone of his voice Janna could tell that he was smiling. Somehow, that made it worse.

'For your own sake.' Unbidden, the face of Julie's cousin swam into Janna's line of vision. He looked shocked, florid cheeks pale, eyes staring. 'Don't you see? You'll get the sack.'

Gray spun her suddenly, frock-coat flaring wide. A deep laugh welled beneath his velvet.

'My dear girl, just who do you think I am?'

Janna's heart sank. It was as if he hadn't heard her.

'Well?' She felt Gray's hand press insistently at the small of her back. 'You haven't answered my question. Who am I?'

Janna closed her eyes. 'Gray.' Her lips felt stiff, her head ached.

Gray laughed again. 'I have other names you know. Most people do.'

Janna flushed. Of course, she shouldn't have called him by his surname, as Julie did. She had no right.

'Quite a selection, really.' Again it was as if Gray's attention was focussed somewhere else, out there amongst the startled faces and disapproving eyes. 'Perhaps one of them will please you. Let me see . . .' His tone was musing, utterly calm, as if he knew exactly what he was doing and simply didn't care. 'How about Francis, for instance?'

'Francis Gray.' Janna repeated, helplessly. She didn't know what to say. 'It's – it's a very nice name.'

'Francis Gray?' Again that sudden, disturbing laugh. 'Oh no – he's quite another fellow. Not to be confused with me under any circumstances.'

Looking up at his face in astonishment Janna realised that he meant exactly what he said. As they dipped and swayed in the rhythm of the dance she wondered if it were she who had forgotten who she was – she who had gone mad.

'Who are you then?'

He looked down. His eyes were very blue, very clear, very cold. 'I . . .' Now there was no trace of slurring in his speech. He spun her again, expertly. 'I am Gray Rowland Decimus Hartford Le Franceys of Dene.' His voice hardened a little. 'The tenth lord. You may call me Gray.'

The music swelled, beating in Janna's head like the blood inside her brain. She went on moving in the pattern of the dance, but if Gray hadn't been holding her so firmly she'd have fallen. Pieces of the pattern fell into place with agonising slowness, burning themselves into her mind's eye. Julie's cousin. Gray was Julie's cousin. She should have known. She should have suspected. The family resemblance. Julie and Gray, both so tall and golden and self-assured. The relationship between them – now, too late, she realised it wasn't that between mistress and servant at all. Gray's ease of manner, the way he looked . . . Fragments of their kitchen conversation surged into Janna's memory and she wished she could curl herself into a tiny ball and roll away.

'Are you enjoying the assembly?'

'No.'

What could he have thought of her? What would Julie think, when she knew?

At last the music ended. Gray's arm loosened a fraction as he turned to bow to the assembled guests. Quickly, before he could make any attempt to restrain her, Janna slipped out from under his arm and away, up the enormous stairs and along the endless corridor to Julie's room. No-one followed her. In the bathroom she found her clothes exactly where she'd left them, neatly folded. Hurriedly, nearly wrenching her zip from its seam, she dressed. It was only then, with her hand on the door leading out to the corridor, that she realised her bag, with her ticket inside it, was still downstairs. She sat down on the edge of the bath and buried her face in her hands. Her bag, her beautiful, almost new bag, with its many compartments, for all emergencies. She wanted it, she needed it, but now it, too, was lost to her, as far away as the moon. Her heart ached. I don't want to be beautiful any more, she thought. I just want to go home.

How much time went by Janna didn't know. She was roused by the murmur of voices.

'Julia.' Janna froze. A man's voice, throaty, yet oddly familiar.

'Don't call me that – you know I hate it.' No mistaking that warm, golden note.

The whisper of silk, a half-smothered laugh. 'Stop it, Gray!'

Janna rose to her feet. She didn't know what to do.

And then, she heard it, another sound, so small that only a trained ear would have caught it. It told her once and for all that she had no place there, none at all. She left, silently, by the bathroom's outer door.

She found her bag at last in a cloakroom off the Great Hall, let herself out of the big oaken doors. An hour later she boarded the milk train back to London. But the noise seemed to follow her all the way home. Tiny, delicate, appalling, charged with a meaning even she couldn't fail to understand – the dropping of pins.

CHAPTER FIVE ·

Bang bang bang. Janna's heart lurched. Her hand flew instantly to douse the lamp. The orange she'd been peeling rolled away unheeded. She crouched in the blue-black darkness, trying to make herself very small, very still.

Bang bang bang. There it was again. A noise she'd never heard, yet familiar. The door upstairs. Someone was knocking on it, insistently, repeatedly. Someone wanted to come in. Janna sent the lamp an agonised glance. She shouldn't have had it on. But it was late, and she couldn't sleep. In the darkness pictures haunted her, tableaux from a lantern-slide show. Every time she closed her eyes she found herself back there on the dance floor, revolving endlessly on its huge marble eye. She smelled the candles, burning low, heard the music, the same refrain over and over. She'd never forget it, she'd never forget anything that had happened that night, no matter how hard she tried. It was her own fault. She didn't belong, she didn't fit in. She was as out of place among people as a pin in a fine seam.

But someone was coming. Janna listened, straining her ears, almost deafened by the beating of her own heart. There was no mistaking what she heard. Tentative, remorseless. Steps on the basement stairs.

Bang bang bang. Her own door, near as her heart. They've found me, she thought. After so long. Slowly, she rose to her feet. There was a dull ache in the centre of her body. If only I'd left that rubbish at the threshold as camouflage. If only I hadn't lit the lamp. If only . . . But it's too late now. They're here. She looked round, once. There was no way out, no back exit. She was trapped, in the end, by her own beloved bars.

One by one, dismantling the dream, Janna withdrew her

beautiful brass bolts. No metal strong enough to keep out the world for ever. There would be two of them, she knew. Uniformed, probably. Uniformed faces for sure, something to hide behind.

The door swung open. Braced against unimaginable pain, for a moment Janna was blind. The light from the alley's solitary streetlamp outlined a figure, just one.

'Hi.' The figure spoke. Shadows and light resolved themselves into a familiar face, the last Janna had ever expected to see. 'Aren't you going to ask me in?'

Janna fell back, astonished. In the space she created, Julie flowed in.

'Heavens, it's dark in here . . . What happened to the light? It's a good job I saw it or I'd never have found you.'

'Just a minute.' Janna's voice seemed to creak, rusty with disuse. She hadn't spoken to anyone, not since the ball. How long had it been, two weeks, three? She had no idea. In the basement it was easy to lose track of time. She reached for the lamp, spilling oil in her haste, split one match, dropped another, managed finally to relight the wick without breaking the shade. She turned anxiously to see Julie looking round the room.

'Hey . . .' Julie's voice seemed to fill the small space, furnish it. 'This is wonderful.'

She likes it, Janna thought. She likes my room. Really. She's not just saying it. I can tell. Suddenly she was overcome with pleasure, a mother complimented on the beauty of her only child.

'I'm sorry.' Half-forgotten rituals of hospitality jostled in her brain. 'There isn't anywhere to sit down.'

'I know.' Julie smiled, her big watermelon grin. 'It's wonderful. You've simply no idea how wonderful it is.' Her eyes rested on the bare stone flags and crumbling plaster walls with childlike satisfaction. 'It's like – a tree house, the very best kind. The ones nobody knows are there.' She swung round, beaming. Her eyes fell full on Janna's face for the first time and her smile faded. 'What's the matter? Has my mascara run?' She whipped out an old-fashioned pressed powder compact and consulted it anxiously. It sported a huge plum-coloured jewel which might have been a trinket from a Christmas cracker or a cabuchon ruby.

'No.' Words spilled from Janna's mouth with sudden, disastrous frankness. 'It's just that I – I thought you'd never want to see me again.'

'Why?' Julie's round blue eyes seemed genuinely perplexed.

Janna's throat constricted. 'Gray.' She mustn't shirk it. 'I thought he was the butler!'

Julie laughed. 'Oh, that. You mustn't worry about Gray, ever. It was a fancy dress ball, after all. Serves him right, the superior bastard!'

'If only he were.' Janna spoke with feeling.

'Why, Janna!' Julie looked almost as surprised as Janna felt herself. 'You made a joke.'

Janna blushed. She felt ridiculously pleased. Julie perched on the table, legs swinging, chin resting on her hand. Janna's pleasure faded to be replaced by concern. She was worried for Julie's skirt, one of those frail Indian cottons shot through with silver thread, and her nylons too. The deal table was cleaner than it used to be, but chockful of splinters.

'Hmm . . .' Julie spoke half to herself, a contented, almost housewifely murmur. 'We'll have to get some closet space. And a telephone. My agent will get a migraine if she can't reach me.'

Janna stared at her. 'What do you mean, we?'

'Didn't I say?' Julie looked up. Her eyes were alight with anticipation. 'I'm coming to stay.'

Janna blinked in astonishment. 'But – but what about Dene?'

'I told you about that at the ball.' Julie shook her head with a trace of impatience. 'The entail, remember? As of last birthday –' she threw her arms wide in a dramatic gesture. 'I'm on the streets!' She gave a deep sigh. 'Twenty-one. That's old for a model, you know. I've been at it since I was sixteen, but of course I haven't saved a penny. I just sort of hoped that something would turn up. And now . . .' Her voice rang with satisfaction. 'Now it has. Don't worry, I've got it all planned out. Money's always coming in, and if I don't spend it on rent I'll only fritter it away on things I don't really want. Believe me, it's the best possible arrangement. I need a place to live, and . . .' Julie paused, frowning a little. 'I like you. We get on. We're – friends, aren't we?' The hint of anxiety in her voice was utterly charming.

Janna stared back at her, lost for words. Friendship, between Julie and herself? It seemed so unlikely, an impossible pairing. What could Julie see in her? And yet – she'd heard of thoroughbred racehorses that insisted on sharing their stables with the strangest creatures, goats and rats and one-eyed cats, refusing to eat or sleep unless their companion was there with them in the straw . . .

Even so she hesitated. For so long she'd pretended to herself that she didn't care about such things. Friendship wasn't for her, it was dangerous, fattening, the sort of food that once tasted she might not be able to live without. But now – Julie made it sound so easy, so natural. Suddenly everything seemed possible, like a dream. Afraid to break the spell, Janna nodded, just once. Friends!

'I thought so.' Julie smiled, gloriously. 'I'm good at friends, you'll see.' A note of quiet satisfaction. 'Yes, it's going to work. Very, very well.'

And to Janna's amazement, and delight, and daily pleasure, it did. Just as she'd claimed, Julie was good at friends, good enough for two. Janna watched and marvelled and did her best to learn the ropes. It was hard work, but worth every minute. By some extraordinary sleight-of-hand and a touch of judicious name-dropping Julie managed to get a phone installed inside the week. From that moment on life was one long round of activity. No time for Janna to think, or worry, or watch food sitting malevolently on the table. She took messages, braving the shrill ring and the stranger's voice on the other end of the line because she had to – it was Julie's work, far better paid and more important than her own sewing had ever been. She mended clothes, polished shoes, parcelled sheets for the laundry service Julie always used, paid parking tickets on Julie's battered white Mini, filed her receipts and invoices and cheque stubs in shoe-boxes stacked under the back room sink, scoured neighbouring shops to find one that stocked her favourite camomile shampoo, and marvelled at the kaleidoscope of Julie's days. She was always wanted somewhere, always late turning up, always forgiven. As the weeks went by, under expert instruction, Janna became an indispensable partner in Julie's double act. The secret lay not just in answering the telephone, but in how you answered it.

Phone rings. Julie blissfully asleep.

'She's already left. She should be with you in – oh, ten minutes at the outside.' Then the scramble.

And the things Julie ate! Overdone hamburgers. Soggy cornflakes. Tinned custard. Sauerkraut on toast. Anything that didn't need cooking, that came in a fluorescent package or could be eaten on the run. Julie simply didn't care. She blamed her taste in food on a lifetime of French cooking and estate-grown vegetables, dinners of such creaking longeur that she claimed her tastebuds had withered away from pure boredom.

Janna was relieved. She'd wondered how they'd manage, the two of them, over meals. She'd hated the idea of food in the house, left-overs. She couldn't live with temptation. But all that remained of Julie's meals was empty tins and polythene wrappers. Julie never planned ahead, she simply picked up what she fancied at the local shop on her way back from sessions, and if she couldn't be bothered with that, she ordered takeaway.

It was the same with the division of space. Julie seemed perfectly happy with the back room, even though it was smaller, because she could sleep late, undisturbed by the early morning sounds of the flower market, the rattle of trolleys over the cobbles, the barrow boys joking and cursing, the scrape and clatter of crates. As long as she had closet space and a telephone, Julie was content. She had the true aristocrat's lack of interest in household details. It was left to Janna to bag Julie's clothes in plastic because of the damp and put up a makeshift rail. In her spare moments Janna tried to sort them into outfits. They were such a motley collection, as gay and random as a diary. Indian cotton from a Vogue session in the Seychelles, studded leather jackets from a Suzuki ad, knitted lurex tops from a Leicester street market, all flung together anyhow. Julie tended to wear whatever was nearest. Janna tried, tentatively, to cure her of her passion for scarlet tights.

'Your legs are fine just as they are.'

Gypsy ear-rings were Julie's other great passion – but there was time . . .

Between them, they managed to rig up an improvised shower, using a length of hose, part of a watering-can and half an oil-drum suspended from the ceiling. Julie was very proud of the rickety construction and showered every day, cold water notwithstanding.

'It's fun. Like being a Girl Guide.' She scrubbed and sang, standing stark naked in the washing up bowl, seemingly oblivious to the chill. 'I much prefer showers anyway. Gray says it's in my blood. My mother was from Kansas City.'

Janna could only listen, amazed. Julie was only a few months older than herself but she seemed to have been everywhere, done everything. She brought things with her for the flat, messages from the great outside world. A Shiraz rug that would have been priceless if some careless nineteenth-century ancestor hadn't used it as a bathmat. Damp had rotted the fibres but the colours still glowed indomitably through. And then there were Julie's bottles, an amazing array of talcs and scents and lotions, which almost crowded out Janna's soap and well-boiled flannel from the back room window-ledge. Janna liked to see them there. She felt privileged that Julie had chosen her as a friend, trusted her with her bottles and her nakedness and her receipts.

Finally, and most importantly, at least from Julie's point of view, came her beaten-up transistor radio. It crackled like a forest fire, but when Janna tried to retune it for her Julie refused outright.

'I've had it on that frequency since I was thirteen. It's my family.' The tinny, fuzzy sound went on first thing in the morning and as soon as she came back at night.

If she came back at all. There were many occasions when Janna said goodbye to an immaculate Julie, band-box smart, only to get her back the next morning stained, rumpled but unrepentant. R and R, Julie called it, with an angelic smile.

And there were calls. Lots of them. Male voices, alternately anxious, baffled, hopeful, exasperated, wistful. Some Janna had to disappoint so often that they began to seem like old friends. She could tell they envied her proximity to Julie, and was proud. She became adept at dealing with them, on the phone at least, assuaging their wounds, reassuring them without promising them the impossible, persuading them, at least, to leave their names, just in case.

Except for Gray. He called, just once. The mere sound of his clipped, level tones, so light, so clear, froze the words in Janna's mouth. He seemed in no need of reassurance, or even explanations. He seemed to know exactly what Julie was up to without Janna saying a word.

'Tell her to be at the Savoy Grill at 1 pm. Sharp. I've only got an hour to spare.'

Julie went, even though it meant cancelling a long-awaited appointment with Hamidullah, who had been going to put a blue streak in her hair. She came back pale, mutinous, somehow diminished. She hurled her canvas bag into one corner of the room and leaned against the window surround, unusually silent. Janna wondered what she and Gray had been talking about. Family matters, probably. Or other things, that could be discussed only in whispers, alone . . . Resolutely Janna closed her mind to that. She still hadn't forgotten the pins dropping. She was determined never to be so obtuse again.

'I could marry him, I suppose,' Julie spoke reflectively, almost to herself. 'It would certainly solve my housing problem. But I think he'd like that a little too much.' Janna had no idea what she meant. She wondered for a moment what it must feel like, to be so much desired. Julie sighed, despairingly. 'I don't know. Anyone would think he was my father. He says I'm spoiled.' Suddenly she turned, fixing her blue gaze on Janna, her eyes so much more eloquent now that Janna knew they saw very little beyond the end of her splendidly straight nose. Julie hated wearing her glasses, but had to ration her contact lenses for work, so most of the time her world was a blur. 'Do you think I'm spoiled, Janna?'

Janna hesitated. Spoiled for choice Julie certainly was. Every man she met became her slave, apart from Gray.

'I don't think you're anything.' No matter what, Julie was her friend. 'Just you.'

'You're a darling!' Julie brightened like a freshly-watered peony. 'You wouldn't lie to me, would you?'

'I never lie.' Janna flushed a little, remembering the phone. Did that count? She wasn't sure. So much in her life had changed since Julie.

'I do.' Julie shook her head in mock regret. 'All the time. I can't help it. People seem to expect it of me, I don't know why. "Do you love me, Julie?" What do they expect me to say? I'm a nice girl, kind to animals, I don't want to hurt anybody's feelings if I can help it . . .'

'So what do you say?' Janna was fascinated. Julie's problem was so far outside her own experience that until now she hadn't thought it could be a problem at all.

'Well . . .' Julie grimaced. 'Sometimes I pretend I haven't heard. Sometimes I say "Mmm". Sometimes I say "Of course I do", as if it didn't matter. Sometimes, if things are getting really difficult, I say "I don't think I know what love is". The only problem with that is they will try and show you. Sometimes I say "Goodness, is that the time?".' She heaved a sigh. 'The trouble is, I like them, I really do. Men, I mean. I like the way they look, their hairy wrists, their big feet . . . Their little ways. But sometimes, I must say, I wonder if it's all worth it. They get so sad . . . Unless they're married, of course.'

'Julie!' Janna was shocked, right down to the marrow of her bones. 'You mean to say you go out with married men?'

'They're men too, you know.' Julie looked mildly put out. 'And at least they don't ask me to marry them all the time.'

'That's not the point.' Janna struggled to put her thoughts in order. 'It's wrong . . . I mean, think of the children!'

Julie shrugged. 'They never even see their children, half the time.'

'All the same.' Janna was shocked again, but did her best to hide it. 'It's not fair.'

'Oh, Janna . . .' Julie gave a rueful smile. 'All right. Just for you, I promise. No more married men.' Her face darkened. 'But I warn you, I'll hold you responsible for the consequences.' She sighed again. 'Oh, dear.' Her expression was comically resigned. 'The other ones are so much more demanding. Maybe I'd do better to give up men altogether . . .'

She looked up, gazed short-sightedly around the room. 'You know something . . .' Her tone was meditative. 'I think this is the first real home I've ever had.' Janna followed her eyes. Peeling plaster, stone floor, lighting that could hardly be called sympathetic – and yet she knew what Julie meant. She felt the same, though she'd never have dared put it into words. The floor might be stone, the water clay cold, but between the two of them there was warmth and to spare, at least till winter came. What the basement might be like in January she didn't like to imagine. With an effort Janna banished the thought from her mind. Julie was teaching her to live more in the present. Anyway, it was always summer when Julie was around.

'I know!' Julie's face lit up, her eyes sparkled. 'Let's get married, you and me! We've got everything we need, a house, a car, a telephone . . .'

'Some car.' Julie's Mini was as scarred and pock-marked as a returned moon capsule.

'Don't be bitchy.' Julie's tone was chiding. 'Just think . . . two little old ladies sitting by the fire, talking about old times. We could move to the country, maybe . . .'

'Not likely.' Janna spoke more sharply than she intended. Some nerve in her was triggered by the image, some superstitious fear. Things were going so well, she shouldn't dream of more, it was asking for trouble. She hid behind sarcasm. 'Not since they've cancelled all the bus routes.'

'I'll still be able to drive.'

'With your eyesight?' Janna forced a smile. 'You'll be lucky if you're still alive. I don't know how you managed to pass your driving test in the first place.'

'The examiner's glasses were all misted up.' Julie gave a throaty giggle. 'His hand was shaking so much he could hardly sign the certificate. But seriously, Janna,' Julie's face was suddenly earnest, 'don't you think it's odd, you and me? Living here, just the two of us, perfectly happy?'

'Only till the phone rings,' Janna reminded her.

Julie wriggled. 'Oh, Janna, why do you have to be so truthful? You'll never get a man that way.'

'I don't want one.' Janna tried to shrug it off. 'I wouldn't know where to put him, now you've taken up all the closet space.'

'Don't talk rubbish, Janna.' Julie wasn't going to be put off so easily. 'That's like saying you don't like caviare before you've even tasted it. There must be someone you've liked the look of. How about Gray?'

Janna shivered. Just hearing Gray's name made her feel suddenly cold. Yet the cold was all mixed up in her mind with something else, the way his body had felt under the velvet, warm and hard. Against her will an image of his face swam up in her mind's eye. It frightened her. It was so clear.

'Now who's talking rubbish?' Janna banished the image with an effort. 'Gray's yours, you know that. And, anyway, he wouldn't be interested in me.'

Julie sighed in exasperation. 'You could be very attractive if you tried, you know.'

' "Oh, Miss Smith, without your glasses you're almost – beautiful!".' Janna shook her head. 'Don't forget, Julie, I've got 20/20 vision.'

'No need to be so proud of it.' Julie wagged a finger at her. 'And men haven't either, that's why they're so easy. It doesn't take much, honestly. A change of clothes, a new hairdo, just to show willing. I mean, look at you. You've been wearing the same colour ever since I met you, that's if you'd call it a colour at all. And what about the money I give you? You never seem to spend any of it on yourself. You hardly eat, you never go out . . . you even wash in two inches of water.'

'I can't help it.' Janna bit her lip. She wasn't used to criticism from Julie. She could feel herself freezing over again, her body stiff. 'It's the way I was brought up.'

But Julie wasn't deterred. Now she was looking at Janna as if seeing her for the first time.

'You're so slim – you'd look wonderful in the right clothes. It's so much easier to dress if you're small. Just think, all those belts and buttons and tiny prints – men love them, but they make me look like a rag doll. And your hair – why do you cut it so short? You should let it grow, it's beautiful.'

'I like it like this.' Janna heard her voice go high. 'It's neat.' Don't you see, she begged inwardly, if I don't try, I don't fail. It's so much safer that way. Please, please understand. Please, in this, too, be my friend.

Julie smiled, shrugged. 'OK, I get the message. I don't know why I bothered. I like you just the way you are.'

Janna looked up, shaken. No-one had ever said that to her before. But then, before, no-one had been her friend.

She stood up, suddenly, fired with energy. She wanted to jump or shout or sing or run five times round the world in a minute – but of course she'd do none of those things. Still, she must do something, something really special to celebrate this moment, a sort of commemoration. Like her first day in the house, when she'd blackleaded the fire.

'You know what?' She turned to Julie, inspired, her eyes wide. For weeks now they'd been reproaching her, mutely, like so many children with dirty faces, noses that needed wiping. Now was the time. 'I'm going to clear those stairs!'

As she scraped away at the dried-on plaster with the one knife she and Julie possessed between them, Janna knew that what she was doing made no sense. They were stairs that led nowhere, and yet . . . She couldn't help thinking about those two little white-haired old ladies, one rather tall and beautiful, the other small and dumpy and plain, tucked up snugly before their shining fire. Tea in the pot, a cat by the hearth, maybe rain falling outside. Not real, just a pipe-dream which couldn't come true, yet the image persisted. It meant something – faith in the future, acceptance that there might actually be a future, that the promise of happiness didn't have to disappear like hot water down a drain.

The house. It was as if the house, with its old bricks, was talking to her. I didn't expect to be here either, after all this time, it was saying. But here I am. Use me. Janna found herself looking at those bricks with new eyes, noticing their different sizes and shapes, some no bigger than a child's hand. The way they were laid, eccentrically, with no plan or pattern except the desire to become a wall. Their different colours, from sooty black through grey to deep rose. A plain house, a small house – but not empty any more.

Janna rested her hand on the newel post. She remembered touching it that first night, how it had frightened her. It had seemed too close, too much like the clasp of a warm wooden hand. But now, despite herself, she had grown fond of it. Often as she went down the corridor to knock on Julie's door she let her hand brush over it in passing. At night it was a sort of landmark, letting her know exactly where she was. Who she was, too. That's what friends were for.

She stared at it. For some reason, today, because of Julie, because of Gray, the small carved newel post reminded her of Dene.

Now that was a foolish thing. What possible link could there be between great, white, gilded Dene and this dingy little corridor? Yet there was something deeply satisfying about that post, its irregularities, its barley-sugar twists and turns. The way it stood there, upright, almost jaunty, a soldier on guard duty, defending for ever its non-existent stair. She wished she knew more about newel posts.

The next morning, greatly daring, Janna deserted her own post by the telephone to rush down to the nearest public library. She pored over architectural books for much longer than she'd intended, raced back to look at the house with new eyes. Her brain buzzed with newly-acquired knowledge as she craned her head back to take in the façade. Yes, the wood-framed windows were flush with the brickwork. That meant the fire regulations brought out forty years after the Great Fire of London hadn't come into force when this house was built. And surely, up there on the top floor, those large windows meant it had once been a silk-weaver's loft? Maybe the silk for Julie's train had been woven right here, on a loom set up by those very windows, facing due west to catch every last beam of light . . .

Breathless with haste, Janna clattered down the basement steps.

'Julie!' Julie, pale and heavy-lidded after a night so late it really deserved to be called a morning, looked up from her seat at the table where she was lazily consuming a tin of cold baked beans. 'Did you know . . .' Janna careered to a halt on the stone flags. This was important news, it must be delivered with dignity. 'Did you know you've been living in one of the oldest Georgian houses in the whole of England?'

'Dene, you mean?' Julie foraged deeper into the tin. 'I'm afraid so. 1740. That's one date I was never allowed to forget, believe me.'

'No, not Dene, not even Dene!' Janna was triumphant. Somehow what she'd learned this morning made up for Dene, just a little. 'This house, yes, our house, is older by a full twenty years! Pure Georgian. Completely unspoiled. And you know what? From the look of the windows on the top floor I think it's something special – a silk-weaver's loft! There's only a few of those left in the whole of London! Just think, there were mulberry trees in Shoreditch . . .'

'So?' Clearly Julie couldn't understand Janna's enthusiasm. But then she hadn't been brought up in a bleak, purpose-built semi-detached, walls as bare as the day they were first plastered because her mother didn't want to spoil the wallpaper.

'Come on.' Janna levered a protesting Julie to her feet. 'We're going to explore!'

It took a combined effort to ease open the main front door.

'Careful!' From the look of the leaded light above, the door, too, was original. These weathered planks had seen ten generations of hands come and go . . .

'Really, Janna.' Between pushes Julie managed a note of school-marmish reproof. 'It's just a door after all.'

At last the lock gave and they were in. Ahead was a dark

narrow hallway and a stair leading up.

'Look!' Janna flew to the stair-rail. 'A barley-corn balustrade, just like downstairs! Three uprights – and a corbel – the best!'

'I don't know what you're talking about. You sound just like Gray.' Julie stepped gingerly over what appeared to be a heap of rags. But Janna could tell she was intrigued despite herself.

'Can you feel it?' Janna whispered, awed. 'The atmosphere?'

'I don't know about that.' Julie sniffed doubtfully. 'But I can certainly smell it.'

She was right. There was a smell – not just damp and decay but something else.

'I hope we're not going to find a three-hundred-year-old tramp festering away somewhere.' Julie's tone was uneasy.

'Don't worry about that. Just follow me.'

Janna tiptoed up the narrow stair, edged open a door. She wasn't frightened of the house at all. Bricks and mortar might smell bad, but they'd never hurt you.

Julie followed gingerly just as Janna folded back the shutters, letting sunlight and an onrush of fresh air into the room.

'Isn't it beautiful?' Janna stared round, delighted. The whole room was not plastered, like the basement, but panelled, little cupboards and shelves built in round the fireplace, each shutter supplied with its own diminutive casement. Above, a dental cornice, well-embroidered with cobwebs, below, pine boards.

'Perfection.' Very, very gently Janna prised open one of the tiny cupboards. A row of little knobs met her eyes.

'Periwig pegs!' She sighed, a small, exhaled breath of pure satisfaction.

'Janna!' Julie's horrified voice dragged her abruptly across two and a half centuries. 'Don't touch anything!'

'I don't see why not.' Janna felt defensive. She'd been careful, very careful. 'I'm not doing any harm.'

'But haven't you *noticed*?' Julie's voice was a squeak of revulsion. 'The whole place – everything – it's simply dripping with pigeon droppings!'

It was true. Janna had been so lost in the past that she hadn't seen. The room looked like an action painting and smelled a great deal worse.

'That's because of the broken windows.' Suddenly Janna burned with sympathy for the little room, open and defence-less. It wasn't its fault it wasn't clean. 'It's all right though. It'd come off with a bit of scrubbing.'

'I'm glad to hear it.' Julie's tone was dry but Janna hardly heard her. She laid her hand lightly on the whitened panels, warm and old and dry.

'Yes,' she spoke in a whisper. 'This must have been the parlour. The ladies' drawing-room. For sewing and writing letters, maybe playing the harpsichord . . . Yes. A coal fire. A bit of paint on the panels – pale green, I think. That was very popular. Like sitting on a bank under trees . . . Velvet cur-tains, some books. Rushlights. Firedogs and a fender – steel for up here, I think, not so grand as downstairs, no need for brass. A clock, maybe. And a spinning-wheel with an ivory mount. A big gilded mirror above the fire. Lots of pictures. A settee, some stools –'

'There are quite enough of those already.' Julie's tone was tart.

'Isn't it unbelievable?'

'Absolutely.' Julie spoke with feeling. She seemed reluc-tant to step any further than strictly necessary into the room, her eyes fixed on the stained floor.

'That should be sanded, I think. Not polished, they liked a white-wood floor. With just one rug in the middle.'

'A Shiraz, no doubt.'

'Perfect!'

In the long pause that followed Janna met Julie's eyes.

'You're crazy.' Julie spoke at last. 'Look at this place. It's a wreck.'

'Only on the surface.' Janna spoke staunchly in defence of her vision. 'All it needs is a new hairdo, a change of clothes.' Oh, how it needed her, this house. She could make it better. She knew how to sew and clean, mend and make-do. She turned to Julie in sudden anxiety.

'Do you really think I'm crazy?' Already in her mind's eye Janna could see it all fading away, the pale green paint, the stripped floor, the shelves shining with blue-and-white china. She'd been a fool to think she could create such a vision. She hadn't the means, or the talent, or the nerve.

'I think . . .' Julie paused, shook her head weightily. 'I think you should stop thinking about it altogether.'

'Oh.' Janna's face fell. Julie was her friend, she wouldn't lie to her.

But then Julie's face split into that wide cat-burglar's grin.

'Just do it. No ifs, no buts, just do it.'

That night Janna tossed and turned, unable to sleep, unable to make up her mind. Could it be done? Should it be done? It was such a risk. It would mean – committing herself, going public, inviting officialdom into what had been her and Julie's private world. And they might lose everything. At the moment, two girls camping in a basement, they were invisible – but once they moved above ground it would be a very different matter.

Janna shivered under the bedclothes. It was all right for Julie to say go ahead. It wasn't the same for her. This wasn't her only home and she'd soon find another. But these four damp walls were all that stood between Janna and the dark. Supposing they told her she would have to leave – she had no right to be there? What would she do? Where would she go? There was no place out there for someone like her.

And yet – the house called her. Empty, loveless, dying. A thin house, a plain house, a house that no-one wanted, it spoke in a language only she could understand. It wanted her.

In the small hours, silently so as not to wake Julie, Janna got up and began to make calculations, lists, endless dolls-house plans and drawings on scraps of paper that she could hardly see in the amber darkness. In the end, one image and one only made up her mind. The two old ladies by their fire. Permanence, security – terrifying, but worth fighting for, and fighting very hard.

Even so, during the weeks that followed, if it hadn't been for Julie, Janna would have given up the struggle a hundred

75

times. Julie was a clerk-dazzler, a swash-buckling slicer through red tape. She wouldn't take no for an answer. She flirted with planners and inspectors and housing officials, took them to lunch, darlinged them to death, entrusted them with her life-story, remembered their first names and where they planned to go on holiday, plied them with best Columbian coffee and cognac, asked them to interpret her dreams . . . She wasn't so keen on the avalanche of forms, but that was Janna's department. Plans, permits and correspondence, photocopies, certificates, deeds, regulations, bye-laws . . . Janna pored over small print till her eyes ached. Now they'd begun there was no turning back – it was win or lose.

And there was a chance, just a small one, that they might win. For the council the house was a liability. They'd been saddled with it as a compulsory purchase after conservationists had halted a slum-clearance programme over a decade ago. Since then it had succumbed, gradually, to planners' blight. No-one wanted it, but no-one could knock it down. It was a nuisance, cluttering up agendas, occasionally the subject of accusations in the press, a prey to every passing vandal. Suddenly, after weeks of stalling, the council offered Janna and Julie a lease. Rent free, as long as all rates were paid.

But there was a snag. Before they could become the house's legal tenants they must guarantee to put it into habitable condition inside six months. And habitable didn't mean spinets and green-painted panelling – it meant fire-proofing, an indoor lavatory, through ventilation, a damp-proof course, and a great deal of money. Up to eighty per cent would be refunded by the council if the renovations came up to their approved standard, but not a single penny until all the work was done.

Clearly, at this point, the council expected them to back down, to fight shy of taking on such a awesome proposition. How could two young girls cope with such a commitment, let alone finance it? They'd be living on the premises too, while the house was torn apart about their ears. And the deadline was tight, very tight. Bad weather, illness – anything could see them back a week, maybe two, and there'd be no house waiting at the end of all their labour.

It was a terrible decision to make. Janna worked frantically over the shoeboxes, preparing endless cash-flow outlines, lists of assets, expenses, earnings, outgoings, matching them up with builders' estimates, biting her nails over the gap between them, gritting her teeth, starting again. There was no point in involving Julie. Every time Julie saw her coming with an armful of facts and figures she waved her away. 'I don't need to know all that. Just tell me who to charm.'

In the end, Janna managed to make the sums come out right. With Julie's income and all the fine seams Janna could sew, providing they did as much of the work as possible themselves and a world shortage didn't double the price of plaster overnight, they might, just, be able to afford the necessary repairs. They'd have to. No-one was going to lend them any money on a two-hundred-year-old property that had been empty for a decade, and even Julie's trust fund didn't come into operation until she was twenty-five.

At last Janna signed her name on the dotted line, sent Julie off with a brand-new file containing all she'd gleaned from the shoeboxes, neatly written out in longhand. The wait was agony. But even when Julie came back there was still no firm decision. 'Don't worry,' Julie assured her blithely. 'If you really want the house you're bound to get it in the end.'

Janna wasn't so sure. She was almost sick with worry. It was no trouble not eating – she had no appetite. She wanted the house so much she could think of nothing else.

And then, one September Saturday, when she'd almost given up hope, it came. Formal, official, signed, sealed and delivered – the lease. The promise of a future. Janna could have kissed the duplicated sheets. The house was theirs. Dank, decaying, infested with pigeons and more than a touch of dry rot, hedged about with restrictions and mortgaged to the hilt, but theirs at last, to love and cherish to their heart's content.

Janna could hardly believe it, even now that she held the paper in her hands. How could it be that someone like her, with no money, no connections, no prospects, could become the legal tenant of a house, a real live house? Without Julie she could never have done it. What a difference it made, just having a friend. She couldn't wait to tell her. Somehow it wouldn't feel real until Julie knew too.

But of course it was a Saturday. There was as much chance of finding Julie home on a Saturday as finding a butterfly in the icebox. If you had an icebox, that is. However, today was a little out of the ordinary, even for Julie. A South American financier and landowner had seen the Allways ad as far afield as Brazil and flown specially to London to invite her to lunch at Claridges. Janna had seen her off that morning, even worried a little. After all, it was lunch with a complete stranger.

'You don't understand, Janna.' Julie explained patiently as she stood in front of the mirror, discarding first one necklace then another. 'Millionaires are different. Anyway, Claridges is hardly the Casbah. I shall flirt with him of course – that's only polite – but I think he's got more important things on his mind.'

'What sort of things?' Still Janna felt dubious.

'Well . . .' Julie dropped her voice, frowned as forbiddingly as it was ever possible for her to frown. 'Don't breathe a word to anyone –' (whom Janna was likely to tell she didn't make quite clear) – 'but rumour has it that he's thinking of backing a play!'

Janna stared back at her blankly.

'Don't you see?' Julie's eyes were wide. 'This could be it – my big chance! I've always wanted to be an actress. There's no point in being a model much past twenty-five. It's time for me to move on.'

'What kind of play?'

'Perfectly respectable, I'll have you know.' Julie pursed her lips, shook out her blonde mane. 'There are two wonderful parts in it, the Virgin Mary and a nun. Even you can't find anything wrong with that!' She picked up a multi-coloured voile blouse, held it against herself. 'He's Catholic, of course. And rolling, simply rolling!'

'Then you'd better give me that.' Quickly, before Julie could protest, Janna repossessed herself of the blouse, folded it neatly. 'If you want to be cast as a nun you'll have to dress like a lady, at least.' She took out a claret-coloured skirt, pale grey cashmere sweater, sheer stockings and burgundy pumps. 'No jewellery, I'm afraid. Just the pearls.'

'You can't be serious!' Julie's voice was a wail. 'I look positively middle-aged!'

'I know.' Janna sympathised with all her heart. 'But if you want the role . . .' She sat Julie down, twisted her hair into a smooth pleat at the back of her head and spiked it firm. 'He'll want to see your profile. Nuns are all profile, you see.'

Julie's face was a study. 'Janna! How on earth do you know these things? Surely it doesn't say that in the library?'

Janna blushed a little, pleased. 'I don't know how I know. I just do.'

'Ear-rings?' Julie's tone was hopeful.

'Sorry.' Janna shook her head regretfully.

'Nuns don't have pierced ears, right?'

Janna nodded.

'Oh, well.' Julie's gaze in her powder compact was worthy of a tragedy queen.

Janna watched her go, feeling proud and protective as a sparrow with a cuckoo chick.

'Don't be late!'

She might as well have shouted at a passing cloud. With a crashing of gears and a racing driver's revving of the Mini's long-suffering engine Julie was gone.

But she'd be back later this afternoon. Janna leapt to her feet, suddenly inspired. This was a red-letter day. It deserved a celebration. She glanced at her watch. Yes, there was just time.

She set to work like a whirlwind, expecting any minute to hear the Mini bumping up the alley. Arms full of cloths, brushes, pails of cold water, she hurried up to the ground-floor front room. Luckily the pigeons hadn't penetrated this far down; no droppings to clean away, just good honest antique grime. After an hour's hard work the room was – well, not exactly transformed, but at least recognisable as a room. Janna raced downstairs, ferried up first the kitchen table, then the two chairs she and Julie had picked up early on

Sunday morning at the market in Petticoat Lane. They seemed to settle into the room with a sigh of relief, home at last. Janna hugged herself. She'd never known such happiness was possible, allowed. She still couldn't quite believe it, even looking at the table and chairs. But she would, once Julie was home.

And now that she'd started on the room, ideas flowed, fountaining up in bubbles of pure joy. A clean cloth – they had none, but a folded sheet fresh from the laundry would do beautifully. Flowers for the table – dandelion heads, torch bright, from the yard, propped in a glass. Perfection. Candles, they had plenty of those, but they looked different, special, on the white cloth, beside the flowers. Ceremonially Janna placed this afternoon's all-important letter beside Julie's place. She hesitated a moment, then lit the candles. She wanted Julie to see the table like that, a surprise, a sort of foretaste of what the house could be like – would be like one day.

Wait a minute. She rushed downstairs, came back with Julie's radio and a new bottle of ketchup. There. Everything that Julie liked, to celebrate the beginning of a new life.

For it was going to be a new life, for both of them. We'll eat together, Janna thought. A proper meal, with table-cloths and conversation. My first time. But I can do it now, she told herself. I can be strong. For Julie and the house.

She perched on the window-sill beside the open shutters facing the alley. That way she'd see Julie in time to turn on the radio. It wouldn't do to waste the batteries. She debated for a moment. Perhaps she should go out to Macdonald's and get the takeaway now? She knew just what Julie liked. Two straws, an extra packet of salt . . . She decided against it. She felt strong now, but there was nothing worse than cold hamburger and the smell of greasy paper. She would wait.

Time passed, slowly. It got dark. Janna began to feel strange, sitting at the window in the dark. When she stood up her movements seemed very loud in the empty room. She snuffed the candles. A little melted wax had spilled on the cloth. She scrubbed at it with her fingernail but it wouldn't come off. Seeing how far the candles had burned down worried her. It was getting late. Macdonalds would be shut soon. Why hadn't Julie come back? She'd have rung if she was going to be late, surely?

Suddenly Janna felt cold. Caught up in her preparations, she'd forgotten all about the phone. Up here, she'd never have heard it. And Julie never rang twice. She'd have assumed Janna had gone to bed early and decided it wasn't worth coming back tonight. Who knows – perhaps she'd got her part. In that case she'd have better things to think about, celebrations of her own.

Of course. Janna stared at the table and chairs. She'd better put everything back, quickly, before Julie came back, just in case. She didn't want to embarrass her, make her think she'd let her down. Manhandling them down the stone steps she scraped her knuckles on the railing. They seemed so much bigger and heavier this time, all corners. By the time everything was back in its usual place she felt exhausted. She threw the dandelions away. They'd wilted anyway.

Some of her excitement had faded too. She felt empty. Hunger gnawed at her. She was glad it was too late to get any food for dinner, glad too that no one had seen her laying the table, lighting the candles. She wouldn't tell Julie, she decided. Well – maybe one day, a long time from now, when they could laugh about it together.

At midnight the phone rang.

'Julie!' Relief made Janna's voice come out halfway between a squeak and a croak.

'Hi there!' Julie's suspicion of a Transatlantic accent sounded much stronger over the telephone. 'Hang on a second.' Janna didn't mind waiting. What did a second more or less matter? There was a pause while Julie appeared to be talking to someone else. 'I rang you as soon as I could, honestly. Now.' Excitement bubbled even through the bad line. 'Guess where I am?'

'Rio?'

Julie's laugh rippled out, suddenly clear as if she was in the next room.

'Good try!' Another, longer pause. 'Sorry, love, I'm in a booth at the airport, and there's a queue.' Another throaty giggle. 'Or maybe it's me they're waiting for!'

Of course. She'd gone to see him off, her millionaire. Julie loved airports, and duty-free shops, and waving goodbye.

'What do you need – petrol, money?' She'd probably run out of both. It wouldn't be the first time.

'Hardly.' Julie sounded like a cat whisker-deep in cream. 'I'm not at Heathrow, I'm at Kennedy.'

'Kennedy?'

'Kennedy airport, fool. As in New York!'

For the first time since she'd picked up the phone Janna felt a stab of unease. Was this one of Julie's jokes? And yet it was possible, she knew. Like all international models, Julie never went anywhere without her passport. And because of her Kansas-born mother, she could flit across the Atlantic almost as easily as breathing . . .

'What about your millionaire?'

'Carlos? Oh, he's here too. He wants me to meet the director, just to be sure. I can't wait. Oh, Janna –' Julie's voice dropped to a whisper. 'I think this is it. I think I've got it!'

'Oh.' For some reason Janna couldn't think of anything else to say. Her mind had gone cold and empty, full of echoes.

'They've got the set half-built already . . .' Despite its excitement, Julie's voice suddenly sounded very far away. New York. Another world. 'Carlos is taking me to see it first thing tomorrow, to get me in the mood, he says. I'm so lucky – Equity can't object to me being cast because it's a non-speaking role! It must have been made for me, Carlos says . . .' Julie rattled on. Janna felt the receiver grow unbearably heavy in her hand. Her eyes ached. She was tired, tired.

'So you won't be back for a while?'

'I guess not.' Julie sounded surprised, as if the thought had only just occurred to her. 'Listen, Janna, are you going to be all right, for money and everything? Maybe you should let my room?'

'Maybe.' The word felt like a stone in Janna's mouth, hard and strange. She wouldn't tell Julie about the lease, not now. It wouldn't be fair.

'I know.' A note of triumph and relief. 'You can have Snowdrop! I've left her outside Claridges. The keys are under the bonnet. I was going to ask you to collect her anyway.'

'But, Julie –'

'No buts. I mean it.' Muffled voices in the background again. 'Listen, Janna, I've got to go. I'll speak to you soon, OK? And Janna –' For the first time there was a hint of anxiety in Julie's voice. 'You understand, don't you?'

'Of course.'

And the trouble was, she did.

Only too well. Janna sat there for a long time, long after the receiver had begun its high-pitched wail of protest. Now, too late, with nightmare clarity, she understood. No Julie. No repair. No lease. No house.

For Julie wouldn't be coming back, not now. Julie didn't need this little house. She never had. The world was her oyster and she'd just found her pearl, the one thing she'd always wanted. Something really big, really important. It would have to be, to make her leave behind her radio.

As for letting Julie's room . . . Janna pressed the receiver against her forehead. The small print on the lease put paid to that, even if she could have found anyone to take Julie's place. Most people would see the lack of plumbing as an insult, not an adventure. But how could Julie, brought up in country-house splendour, know that? No-one had ever told her.

And there was something else no-one had told her. The car, Julie's parting gift. Such a generous thought, so very Julie. The only problem was, Janna couldn't drive.

Oh, Julie. I'm going to miss you so much. The thought pressed, leaden, dull, a promise of pain. And I didn't even say goodbye. Janna closed her eyes. I let her down, she thought. She sounded so pleased, so happy on the phone, and I didn't even say 'Well done' or 'Good luck'. Maybe that was the best moment of her life too and she wanted me to share it, just like I wanted her to share dandelions in a jar.

Slowly, carefully, like someone returning a captive animal to the wild, Janna replaced the receiver in its socket. Without the little high-pitched noise the room seemed suddenly very dark, very quiet.

'Oh, Julie.' She spoke aloud. It didn't matter now. She was alone. 'What am I going to do?'

CHAPTER SIX

Janna laid her scraper aside, pulled down the scarf that covered the lower half of her face, rose stiffly to her feet and went to the window to take in a deep breath of fresh air. Tentatively, she stretched. Her joints grated. She'd never ached so much in her whole life, as if the grit and plaster dust and ancient soot had become part of her, sunk into her very bones.

'Of course, if you had any sense you'd rip the whole lot out and start again from scratch.' The planning officer seemed to think she was mad, trying to scrape decades of pigeon filth and old paint off the pine panelling. 'It's not worth saving – look, softwood keyed straight into brickwork, just asking for trouble.' There was no encouragement to be had from that quarter. He saw Janna's struggle to preserve the old house as a piece of romantic wishful thinking, a conservationist's pipe-dream, like saving the whale.

And what lay behind the panelling hadn't been the only unpleasant surprise. After three weeks of hard labour Janna was beginning to feel she knew the builder of her beloved No. 3 Rose Alley like an elderly, charming but not altogether reliable friend. He'd put all his effort and money into the façade, with its lovely window arches and doorcases, but hadn't bothered to fasten it firmly to the rest of the structure. Now, according to the council's surveyor, it was bidding a long, fond farewell to its underpinnings.

'Built to last a hundred years, tops,' said the surveyor sourly, dusting off his hands. He didn't seem to see the fact that the house had survived this long, against such heavy odds, as a miracle – simply a mistake. He implied she'd be lucky if the roof didn't fall in on her while she lay in bed asleep. I don't care, thought Janna to herself. Just as long as it falls in after February. That was the council's deadline, a race against time.

But everything that went wrong, every new fault that was discovered, every setback, only made Janna more determined to carry on. In a funny sort of way she was working for Julie too, even though Julie might never set foot in the house again. It was Julie's faith in her, Julie's friendship, that she cemented into the brickwork. Friendship meant – trying to be your best self, trying to grow. Painful, hard. Not a cosy retreat for two but a branching out, reaching for the light. Julie had taught her that and she'd never forget it. Without Julie there wouldn't have been a house at all. And maybe no Janna, too.

That thought got Janna up early and to bed late. When she had time to think about it, she realised she'd stopped worrying about what she ate or why. There was no room in her mind to worry about anything else but the work in hand and the pile of steadily mounting bills.

Janna winced as a deafening noise erupted from the basement two floors below. She could feel her precious old bricks trembling, an old lady's ruffled petticoats. The builders she'd had to bring in to install the damp-proof course had turned her and Julie's refuge into a scene of chaos, dust and rubble, and even, to her horror, bare London clay visible where the flags had been wrenched up. She'd stopped going down there to look. She couldn't bear it. That and the thought of how on earth she was going to pay their bill.

Janna looked at her hands, cracked, blistered, with torn nails and calloused palms, and wondered if they'd ever sew a fine stitch again. She was doing as much of the work as she could herself, but even so she couldn't see how she was going to meet the deadline. There was still no bathroom, no flush toilet, no power points. Plumbing, electric wiring – they were still mysteries to her, no matter how many books she got from the library, and yet how was she ever going to be able to afford qualified help? At the end of the day the future seemed like an ever-narrowing black tunnel, lavishly papered with twenty-pound notes.

And yet, despite her exhaustion, despite the ever-present fear that she might never sit in the panelled parlour or sleep in the bedroom under the eaves, the house was still a passion. Whenever she could, in the evening usually, when it got too dark to work inside, she scoured the neighbouring skips for period fixtures and fittings – pieces of architrave for a damaged door surround, blackened knobs that polished up butter-gold. At night, in the camp bed she'd set up here on the second floor, she dreamed of brocaded walls, gilded mouldings burnished with agate – and woke to find her bedclothes covered in a film of two-hundred-year-old dust.

Janna turned away reluctantly from the window. A quick splash in the bucket of cold water, a cheese sandwich. Her teeth grated on fragments of old plaster as she chewed. Welcome silence from below indicated that Marlon and Jerry, too, had stopped work for the day. It was almost dark, time to light a candle or two. Then swiftly to bed before it got too cold, so she'd be ready to rise at dawn.

Her eyes fell on the neatly-stacked, polythene-armoured boxes containing Julie's clothes. She'd had to move them up here from the basement. They got in her way while she was working, but she didn't mind that. They were a sort of company.

Especially now. Because, she had to admit it, nights were no longer her favourite time. In the basement, behind the friendly bars, with her grate and the glow of the fire, she'd felt safe, but up here she felt much more vulnerable. Partly it was because there was so much more light, the streetlamp casting long shadows on the panelled walls, but there were also noises, much louder than any she'd heard in the basement, creakings of the old timber floor and rattling window-frames. Sometimes they even woke her up and she had to convince herself there was no one actually in the house except herself. It was surprising what night-time and solitude could do to the imagination.

Resolutely Janna snuffed the candle – after all her hard work there was no point in letting the house burn down about her ears – and lay down on the bed. She didn't know why she'd bothered to change her clothes. Everything, from night-dress to sheets, was stiff with plaster dust. Including her hair, which had taken on a dry, brittle look all its own. But it didn't matter, she told herself. There was no one to see her, only the builders, and they looked much the same . . .

Creak. There was that noise again. Janna's body tensed, refusing to listen to all the sensible things her mind had to say. There's someone in the house, her beating heart insisted. Right now, right here. Ghosts, burglars, assassins . . . Much more likely to be death-watch beetle, she told herself sternly, and hid her head beneath the covers.

Noises and suspicions of noises kept her in an uneasy half-sleep most of the night. Dawn came at last, and with it a little more courage. Without even pausing to dress she picked up a heavy wooden mallet and went upstairs. Whatever was lurking up there she was going to confront it, find out once and for all. She couldn't take the strain a moment longer.

But the top floor was deserted. Janna looked round, per-plexed. Up here the air was still foul. She hadn't begun clean-ing these rooms yet. Her plan was to move up the house one storey at a time, otherwise the thought of all the work that still remained would drive her mad. All she'd done up here so far was replace the broken window glass to keep out more pigeons.

Pigeons? It was a possibility. Janna glanced doubtfully up at the ceiling above the stair-well. The noise, whatever it was, had certainly come from above. Maybe the attic? There was a trapdoor, but when she'd tried it before it had refused to budge. She'd left it alone after that. The attic was last on her list of priorities. But now – she dreaded to think of a bird trapped in there, alone in the dark . . .

Creak. This time the noise was definite as a pistol-shot in the dawn silence. Definite and, at close quarters, instantly recognisable. A footstep on the floor above. No bird, no mouse, no cat on the tiles ever made a sound like that.

Janna was momentarily paralysed by shock. After shock came fear, hard on fear came anger, a pure white bolt of rage that terrified her even more. It made every nerve and muscle in her body shake. She hadn't dreamed she could feel like that, ever. It was as if the house was part of her, as if she herself had been invaded, violated. She didn't need to ask how he'd got in. Half the window-frames were rotten, the rest had faulty catches, it would have been child's play, an open invitation. She found herself praying that he hadn't broken one of the few remaining pieces of eighteenth-century glass.

There. There it was again. Janna's heart hammered so hard she could barely breathe. She looked up at the trapdoor. Knowing her house, that wood would be paper-thin. She tested the mallet's weight in her hand. One solid blow and the trapdoor would give way. But did she dare? Shouldn't she be sensible, call the police? She bit her lip. No, that wouldn't work. By the time they sent anyone the intruder would be gone, she'd never be able to put a face to that footstep, it would always haunt her.

She had to know, now. Slowly, moving as quietly as she could, wincing at every creak of the boards beneath, Janna edged an empty crate under the trapdoor. Silently she mounted her wooden castle, measuring the distance and the mallet's weight. She'd have one chance and one only. Quickly, putting all her weight and all the tension in her body behind the blow, she struck.

The trapdoor opened with a deafening crash. Light rushed down in a waterfall, confusing Janna momentarily. Weren't attics supposed to be dark, light-starved places? She stared upwards through narrowed eyes. Something moved, outlined against the brightness. She tensed. A human figure, whether man or woman she couldn't make out. Then, like a reflection on water grown suddenly still, the shape resolved itself. A man. Quite, quite definitely a man. Janna felt the blood rush into her face. No, not so much a man, more an anatomy lesson. For beneath a shock of dark hair he was stark naked.

At that point, dazed, she must have leaned too far backwards, because she felt the crate begin to rock dangerously beneath her feet. She reached out for the edge of the trap but it was too late. In the split second before her castle toppled she heard the mallet, falling from her hand, drop right through the fragile boards below.

'Are you all right?'

Bruised and shaking, hurriedly pulling her nightdress back into some semblance of respectability, Janna clambered back to her feet. A shaggy head was peering down at her through the trapdoor. 'You disappeared like a Jack-in-the-box!'

Janna glared fiercely up at him, feeling very much at a disadvantage. She'd cricked her neck in falling but her dignity hurt more. He seemed so – matter-of-fact, almost at ease. 'Who on earth are you?'

Adding insult to injury, he didn't reply. The black head simply disappeared.

'What are you doing?' Janna's voice cracked with frustration and fury. The head reappeared, halfway through the neck of a dark blue fisherman's jersey. 'Getting dressed, of course.' The voice was mildly reproachful. 'I'll be with you in a moment. Unless you'd rather come up here?'

'Certainly not.' Janna pulled her nightdress together at the neck. Now the heat of the moment was past she felt cold and distinctly vulnerable. 'Very well. I'll see you downstairs in the parlour in five minutes.'

Stiff with outrage, Janna made her way downstairs, retrieving the mallet on the way. Luckily it hadn't broken any balusters, just chipped the wall. Her hands shook as she scrambled hurriedly into her work-clothes. She could feel her eyes wide with fury, as if the lids had been pinned back by some Oriental torturer. Her throat felt tight, her face burned, her teeth chattered as if she had a fever. Her house, her little house. She'd thought it was hers, but what did they prove, her documents, her callouses? How long had he been there, without her knowing? She shivered. At any moment she'd hear his step on her stair . . .

She flung back the shutters in the parlour. She wanted to be within shouting distance of the street, just in case.

'Good morning.' Janna spun on her heel. He'd crept up on her as silently as a cat. His feet were still bare and very white on the dark boards. She averted her eyes hastily. No gentleman, no gentleman at all. Looking up she was subtly pleased to see that he was possibly the ugliest man she'd ever set eyes on. A big head, made to seem bigger by the shock of coal-black hair, set above powerful shoulders. A big nose, comically uptilted at the end, between eyebrows as thick and dark as caterpillars. A wide, muscular mouth, unsmiling. If it weren't for his very blue eyes and his white skin he'd have been almost grotesque, a sort of gnome.

'Well . . .' He was looking round the room, half-frowning, with a relaxed, almost proprietorial air which infuriated her. 'Whatever in the world has become of Mrs Jarvis's sitting-room?'

'I don't know what you're talking about.' Janna felt stiff and artificial, like a whey-faced Victorian doll. A faint memory stirred in her all the same. What was it – something the council officer had said? 'I live here now.'

'So I see.' He spoke slowly, with a deliberation that was almost foreign. For the first time she noticed his voice. It was very deep, dark, warm as black velvet in the sun. It set up vibrations in her, made her forget what he was actually saying. It didn't match his face at all.

'So . . .' He was smiling at her, not with his mouth but with his eyes and voice. A sort of trick. She wondered how it was done. 'You're my new landlady.'

Memory flickered once again. Mrs Jarvis . . . the council officer had said an old lady used to rent the upper floors two years ago, but she'd been moved out into an old people's home as the house advanced in squalor. She'd had a lodger about whom she'd been most concerned, but that had been a girl. Diane, that was the name. Elusive Diane – no-one had ever found any trace of her. She'd turned out to be a figment of the old lady's imagination.

'I am nothing of the sort.' Janna spoke with dignity. No sub-letting. She knew her ground, none better.

He said nothing, just looked at her. Not stared, simply looked, gravely, quietly, as if looking was the thing he did best in the whole world. Janna was suddenly conscious of her matted hair, her unwashed face, the deplorable state of her clothes.

'There is room in this grand house for the both of us,

91

surely?' Oh, that voice. Janna searched it for sarcasm but found none. It was warm and sweet as honey, and as transparent.

'That's not the point.' Her own voice sounded thin and hard by comparison. She resented the role in which she found herself, it seemed suddenly ungenerous.

'Is it not?' He smiled for the first time, wide and full, a real shout of a smile. No Englishman ever smiled like that. His face was instantly transformed, the map redrawn.

'The point is . . .' Faced with that smile, beguiling as a child's, Janna felt herself losing track of what she meant to say. 'The point is you have no right to be here at all.' She wavered. She was beginning to sound exactly like the council official.

'Oh, you're a hard, cruel woman indeed.' His voice was a lament but his blue eyes glinted. 'Not like Mrs Jarvis.' Janna had the impression he was laughing at her. It was as if he'd seen her naked, not the other way round.

'It's no use hiding behind Mrs Jarvis.' Janna controlled her voice with an effort. 'I can check with her any time. I know where she is.'

'So do I.' He seemed faintly surprised. 'I saw her only last week.'

'At the Home?' Suddenly Janna felt a little faint.

'Where else would she be, at her age?' His voice was oddly gentle.

'Oh.' Janna's mind raced. Oh, how badly this was turning out. It couldn't be worse. How come she'd never heard of him? Why hadn't anyone told her?

'You're welcome to ask her about me if you like. My name's Dion, Dion Malloy.' He held out his hand. Numb with shock, Janna took it. It was very warm.

'Janna Brown.' Politeness ruled, but her heart was sinking like a lead weight. Diane, Dion – such a simple error, the easiest thing in the world. She stared at him, wishing that he would suddenly, magically, disappear. Now, truly, he was a problem. If only he'd been a tramp, a burglar, even an escaped lunatic. Anything but Mrs Jarvis's lodger. What on earth was she going to do with him now?

'I'm glad we've met at last.' He was smiling at her. 'Many's the time I've walked down the alley late at night and thought, who is that beautiful girl in the basement, sitting all alone.'

'That was Julie. It's no use pining after her, she's gone to New York.'

He seemed about to say something, then thought better of it.

'So be it.' He shrugged, turned away suddenly to the back window, leaned out. 'Is this your waste, Janna Brown?'

For a moment she hadn't the slightest idea what he was talking about. Then he tapped one of the down pipes and understanding dawned.

'I've no idea.' At the back of Janna's mind the faintest, most fragile hope began to stir. 'Do you . . . by any chance . . . understand about plumbing?' She spoke as cautiously, as delicately as if she were inquiring about his love life. This, to her, was a matter of life or death.

He shrugged, a smooth, boneless movement. 'There's not much to understand. What goes in must come out. Eventually.' He pulled his head back in. 'I need to tap into it, really. At the moment my water drains into the roof gutter and that's faulty, it's leaking into the brickwork. Bricks don't like water, do you see.'

Janna stared at him. Suddenly, in the space between one heartbeat and the next, he had become as desirable, in her eyes at least, as a goldmine.

'I like what you're doing to the house.' He nodded gently. 'Yes, I approve.'

'Then – would you help me? I was going to do it all myself, but . . .' Something of her desperate need must have showed in her face because his eyes were suddenly serious.

'Every plumber needs a mate?'

'Something like that.' Janna didn't like the sound of the word 'mate' at all. 'I mean, it's in both our interests.'

He looked at her long and slow, then seemed to make up his mind.

'We'll work something out.' He yawned, quite suddenly, as neatly and inoffensively as an animal, stretched luxuriously, then made for the stair down.

93

'Where are you going?' Suddenly Janna felt panicky. Would she ever see him again?

'Back to sleep.' Dion smiled. 'I think it's best to keep the trapdoor for – emergencies, don't you? My entrance is up through the house next door. The roof's seen better days but the stairs are fine. It's easy to get through from that attic to this one, all I have to do is step over the wall.'

'Step over?' Janna was horrified. 'You mean . . .' Her voice tailed away. There was no need for him to explain. Bricks were expensive in the eighteenth century, she could follow her elderly builder's reasoning exactly. What did any attic need but half a wall?

'Single course brick?' She hardly needed to ask. Dion nodded, solemnly. Janna sighed. These little houses seemed to share everything, even their walls. Dion turned to go.

'Wait.' Janna craned over the banisters. Before he went, there was one more thing she simply had to know. 'If you want more sleep, what on earth were you doing up at 5 am?'

'Nothing, nothing at all.' He smiled at her obliquely, a flash of white teeth in a three-day growth of blue-black beard. 'Simply watching the morning grow.'

Within a week Janna knew she had made the right decision. Dion Malloy was just the man for the job. He might be ugly enough to shatter glass but he could make a copper pipe bend to his will with just a stroke of those long fingers. She'd been struggling to refit a skirting, using hard old seasoned wood she'd found on one of her evening forays, and had ruined three saw edges – but when he tackled it the tough old fibres parted as meekly as butter.

And he worked hard and long, with a concentrated intensity that surprised her. He never lost his temper or despaired when things went wrong, simply laid down his tools and disappeared for half an hour. When he came back, miraculously, the problem would often have cured itself, as if the house were a living entity with its own capacity for healing. Nothing was too dirty or too difficult for him to tackle. By some mysterious process the dirt was always on his clothes, never on him. She was half afraid of him, as if he really was some kind of leprechaun.

He certainly looked the part. She'd never forget the first time she saw his ears, usually hidden under the shock of black hair. He was showing her a rough diagram of the proposed hot water system, a pencil shoved casually behind one ear. She looked sideways, and there it was. Perfect, close-set, neat – but with an extraordinary point at the top, just like a pixie's. She felt a ridiculous impulse to stroke that ear, as if it were a little animal. To see if it were real or made of wax, like Mr Spock's. She could have – she was sure he wouldn't have minded – but she didn't, because she was terrified of his hair. It was so wild, so thick, so . . . hairy. Yes, he really was an ugly man. He was so black and white, there was too much contrast. His two front teeth at the top overlapped slightly, giving his wide grin an element of devilry. He moved so quietly that she could never be quite sure when or where he would appear next. And yet . . . his hands and feet were beautiful, like those on a marble statue, and he moved like smoke, with an unselfconscious grace she would have found remarkable in a woman.

But that was the sum total of her knowledge of him. What he did for a living, where he'd come from, how he spent the rest of his time, were all a mystery.

'How did you manage to . . . you know . . . before all this?' She gestured at the shining copper pipework. She would have known if he'd been using the rickety shed in the garden, as she did. It might seem a personal question, but in some respects she knew him better than a wife. Plumbing was a great leveller.

Dion looked up, two nails hanging at the corner of his mouth rather like fangs, and smiled a mysterious, lop-sided smile.

'Self-discipline.' With that she had to be content.

They had a system for contacting each other. It was vital, working all day and spending each night in such close proximity, to respect each other's privacy. If she needed to see him out of working hours she would clamber painstakingly up the ruined house next door, skirting the holes in the floorboards with the aid of the warnings he'd chalked on the wall. But she never went into his attic. If he wanted to contact her he'd leave a message on her side of the trapdoor. If he didn't want to be disturbed at all he left an enigmatic note saying 'Gone to the races'. That happened fairly frequently, though she suspected he hadn't gone anywhere at all. If she bothered to strain her ears she could hear girls' voices, muffled laughter, little shrieks. Occasionally, purely by accident, she saw visitors going in next door to follow the chalk-marks up the rotting stair. Girls, usually, sometimes more than one at a time. She tried not to feel shocked, but once, after a particularly busy sequence, she tackled him about it.

'How do you get away with it?'

'What?' His eyes were innocence itself.

'All those girls.'

'Such an ugly devil as myself, you mean?' He laughed. 'I don't invite them, you know. They just come, and who am I to turn them away? I think it's my secret weapon that brings them.' He grinned outrageously. 'Word gets around and curiosity does the rest.'

'Your secret weapon?' Janna could feel her cheeks getting hot.

'The stairs, of course.' She bit her lip. 'None of them can resist the challenge. You know what females are.'

Janna wasn't sure that she did. She didn't feel happy with his tone either, very much man-to-man. It should have pleased her – hadn't she been aiming for that sexless camaraderie all her life? But for some reason it didn't. She found herself wondering how Dion really saw her – as employer, landlady, workmate? Responsible positions all of them, but somehow unappealing.

'Do women just – fall into your lap?'

'Oh, no.' Dion stood up, effectively putting an end to the conversation. 'I fall into theirs.' And he disappeared, just like a stage Irishman.

Janna didn't see him again for two whole weeks. By the time he came back she was in enough of a panic to know that she mustn't ask any more questions. But it seemed to her that the stream of giggling bright-eyed girls diminished to something more like a trickle.

And one day, wonder of wonders, there came a voice from the trap-door. Janna rushed upstairs, thinking at least there'd been an accident. But it was Dion, his face alight with sheer blazing excitement.

'Look what I've found!' It was something on a plate, a strange, whiskered, multi-coloured object, unearthly greens and blues mingling with scarlet and black.

'What is it?' She eyed it, half fascinated, half repelled. It looked like nothing she'd ever seen, but it had a strange lunar beauty of its own.

'A red pepper.' His voice held utter satisfaction. 'I left it under the bed and forgot about it. Have you ever seen anything so beautiful?'

Janna handed it back to him. A cloud of lime-green fungus spores drifted down over her face, together with a damp, earthy scent. She couldn't think of a word to say. But Dion didn't notice her silence, he was in a world of his own.

'You never see that nowadays, you know . . .' He raised it tenderly as if it was spun glass. 'And they say there's no life after death!'

The trap-door closed on his transfigured face and Janna was left standing there, the phosphorescent dust falling on her face like a blessing.

But even Dion couldn't protect her from Marlon and Jerry's bill. The fatal day came. The day of reckoning. No matter how Janna added up the figures they always came out the same. She owed them, give or take a few pence, two thousand pounds. Terms net, thirty days.

If only Julie were here. Julie could earn two thousand pounds in as many minutes, just by smiling. Wild schemes chased themselves round Janna's head. She hadn't heard a word from Julie, she didn't even know where she was staying, but perhaps she could find out? Julie would help. Julie would lend her the money without blinking an eyelid, she knew that. If . . . Janna's heart sank. If she had it. Which she wouldn't.

Julie was no saver, and anyway she wouldn't have worked for months now, because of the play.

Terms net, thirty days. Janna dug her nails deep into her palms with pure frustration. For the house, if it would help, she would give every last drop of blood in her body. But blood and sweat and tears weren't legal tender nowadays. Oh, for a South American millionaire of her very own . . .

'Janna Brown.' Dion's lazy voice from the hall. 'Someone for you.'

'I'm not here.' How could she think of anything else at a time like this?

A murmur of voices. Dion appeared to be hanging out of the window and talking to someone in the alley beneath.

'He says don't be so silly.' Dion's tone was quizzical. 'He says he's come to take you out to lunch.'

Janna sighed. She understood now. Another of Julie's admirers, one low down in the pecking order, who still hadn't learned that the bird had flown.

'All right, I'm coming.' She'd better break it to him gently – she hated to see their faces fall. She leaned out of the window. In the alley below was a long, low, silver-grey Bentley, complete with green-uniformed chauffeur. 'I'm sorry, she's not here. Really.' The door at the back of the Bentley swung open and a man stepped out. He tilted his head back and Janna caught her breath. No mistaking that pale hair, that etched profile. Without speaking a word he raised the tone of the alley by several points. He was almost enough to put up the rates single-handed.

'Gray.' Janna hated the way her voice changed, softened, betraying her. 'What are you doing here?'

'Is that you, Janna?' She realised she must be barely recognisable in her working gear and wondered why she minded. There was no reason for her to mind – it wasn't important. 'I know you're never hungry, but I am.' Was that a touch of irony in Gray's voice? Janna remembered the chocolate cheesecake and her ears burned. But she'd changed since then. Hadn't she? 'Hurry on down, there's a good girl, and I'll take you to lunch.'

'Me?' There it was again, that other person's voice, a foolish squeak.

'Who else?' Gray began to look impatient, in a graceful sort of way. 'That is, if you're free?'

Janna was speechless. Lunch – with Gray? Impossible. Out of the question. And yet, from the look on his face, he was clearly expecting her to accept. He was used to getting his own way. Desperately she racked her brains to remember any one of Julie's sheaf of excuses – but most of them only worked on the telephone. Face to face was – different. It made it hard for her to think at all. Suddenly Janna was acutely aware of the triangle of sunlight at the corner of the alley, much narrower than it had been only last week. Autumn had come, abruptly, the days were racing in. She hadn't seen much of the summer. The air smelled good, as it always did between rush hours . . . And there was Gray, in her alley.

'I'll be down in a minute.' She'd heard Julie say the words so often that they tripped neatly, almost convincingly, off her own tongue. Flustered, she ducked back inside the window so suddenly that she banged her head on the sash. When the stars faded she saw Dion, waiting on the half landing. His sky-blue eyes seemed clearer than ever as they rested on her.

'Now who'll be needing chalkmarks?' His expression was quizzical. Janna hadn't a clue what he was talking about. Her mind was on other things. She turned to him distractedly. 'What on earth am I going to wear?'

He eyed her up and down. 'You look fine to me. Go as you are.'

'How can I?' Janna's voice rose to a wail as she looked down at her paint-spattered trousers and dust-encrusted pullover.

'Radical chic – it suits you.' Dion's tone was innocence itself, but a spark of mischief danced in his eyes. Janna shook her head. This was no time for jokes, couldn't he see that? This was serious, the most important day of her life so far. Suddenly, for the first time in years, clothes mattered.

'But if it's not to your taste . . .' Dion smiled, relenting. 'Why don't you change? There's no sense in not feeling

99

comfortable. I'll entertain the big fellow, just leave him to me.'

Janna eyed him doubtfully. The thought of Gray and Dion together was – uncomfortable, to say the least. What they would make of each other she had no idea. But one thing she was suddenly very sure of. She didn't want them to meet now, this minute. She had quite enough on her plate as it was.

'It's all right. I won't be long. Just – keep an eye on him for me. Make sure he doesn't go away?'

But as she raced up the stairs to her bedroom Janna found herself wondering which would be worse, to come down and find Gray gone, or still there. She rummaged frantically through her clothes. It was like searching for a unicorn – the outfit which would transform her into a vision of elegance and sophistication in Gray's eyes simply didn't exist, and never had. She leaned back on her heels, racking her brains to remember what Julie used to wear for her many lunches. But it didn't really help. No-one ever noticed what Julie wore, she was too beautiful for that. If she looked at all odd everyone simply assumed she was one step ahead of the fashion.

And there was so little time. At any moment Janna dreaded the sound of Dion's voice, inviting Gray (and the chauffeur, oh horror of horrors, he'd be sure to include the chauffeur!) up to the dust-filled parlour for a cup of liquorice-black tea and a sing-song. She wouldn't put it past him, not at all. That tea was enough to shrivel your tonsils, but Dion could always sing . . .

At last, in desperation, her eye was caught by the polythene-wrapped parcels containing Julie's abandoned clothes. She ripped one open, grabbed the first thing she saw. Crisp cotton, navy and white, with a squared white collar. It was far too loose and long, so she belted it at the hips and did what she could with the surplus fabric. Luckily her own dark blue shoes were enough of a match to pass. Flushed with triumph she clattered down the stairs, smoothing down her hair as she went.

'Oh, no!'

Her cry of anguish summoned Dion. He took the stairs in long strides, two at a time.

'Now, now . . .' his voice soothed. 'What's the matter?'

'My hair!' Janna tugged at it frantically with both hands. 'Look at it!' Cold-water washing and cement dust had left it the consistency of wire wool. Not for the first time Janna was glad there were no mirrors in her house.

'Never you mind about that.' Dion brushed her hands away gently, checked her over with a critical eye. A tweak of her collar here, an adjustment of the folds at her waist, skilful, light, like a groom currying a nervous horse before the big race. 'Here.' He reached up and untied the scarf from his own neck. It was red silk, a fetching pattern of dots and squiggles and little ladies' faces. 'A Malloy original,' he explained as he tucked it over her treacherous hair and knotted it securely at the back of her head. The silk smelled of him, musky and faintly sweet. He adjusted the fit, stepped back, nodded with approval. The warmth of his smile lighted Janna's way down the stairs.

It was only after Gray had shown her into the sofa-sized back seat of the Bentley that Janna realised what Dion had meant by his crack about the chalkmarks. She was glad of the darkness.

As the car glided over the cobbles, every tremor soaked up by its cottonwool suspension, Janna could hardly believe it was herself and not Julie sitting beside Gray. Julie's dress, Julie's cousin – she only wished she had Julie's charm. At the moment she felt paralysed, unable to think of a word to say.

'You've changed.' Gray's voice, light, almost expressionless. Janna felt her body tense, as if he'd seen right into her soul itself. Suddenly, sitting beside Gray in her borrowed dress, the first dress she'd willingly worn for years, she realised it was true. Six months ago, before she'd met Julie, she could never have done it – accepted his invitation, worn the dress, entered the car. It would have seemed like the worst form of torture. The mere thought of eating in public, or being seen not eating, would have made her feel faint with terror. But so much had happened to her since then. First the house, the first place where she'd ever felt at home, then Julie, her first friend. Even Dion had helped, in his way. Looking back at the last few weeks Janna realised with surprise that she'd eaten with Dion without actually registering the fact. Quick snacks while they pored over scale plans, a sandwich here, a mug of coffee there. But eating with Dion had been part of the job, a sort of mid-air refuelling. This, with Gray, was different. Something special, public, an occasion. Janna tightened her hands in her lap. She wanted so much to get it right, to make up for Dene. At least, this time, she was wearing the right clothes.

'What a pretty dress.' Janna blushed. Of course, Gray hadn't been referring to her at all, but to what she was wearing. Maybe – awful thought – he'd recognised the dress as one of Julie's? Her blush deepened.

'Thank you.' When in doubt, say as little as possible. Stick to the rules. Janna risked another quick sideways glance. A faint smile curved Gray's mouth. Had she sounded – suburban, prim? Julie would have done so much better. You only had to exchange two words with Julie to feel you'd known her all your life.

Janna bit her lip. She must try harder. She'd have to, she had so much catching up to do. She concentrated hard, trying to take in every detail of what was happening so that she could replay it later, in the safety of her camp bed. What Gray was wearing, the exact amber shade of the leather-covered seat, the purr of the engine, the faint, fresh smell of Gray's cologne, the strange, weightless feeling at the pit of her own stomach. She wriggled her toes inside her shoes. If she ever had any money to spare she was going to go right out and buy herself a new pair. White, maybe. Reckless, extravagant, sinful white.

'Where would you like to go for lunch?' Janna felt her eyes grow round in sudden panic. This was a test, she knew it – and she wasn't prepared, not at all. Julie could answer 'Macdonald's' and be acclaimed as a wit, but on her own lips it would sound like a bad joke, almost an insult. She thought frantically. Why hadn't she listened more closely to Julie when she'd told her where she'd been and where she was going, all those strange and incomprehensible foreign names? Now she couldn't be certain of remembering one correctly.

'Er – how about Claridges?' That was one name at least

she'd never forget. Out of the corner of her eye she glimpsed Gray's expression. Not shocked, thank goodness, or disappointed, but more than a little surprised.

'It's a little late to book, I'm afraid, but we can try if you like?' His eyes rested on her with a curious expression, as if he couldn't quite make her out.

'No, no.' Janna waved the suggestion away hurriedly. 'Why don't you decide?' Another of Julie's lines, and a very useful one.

'How about the Tate?'

Now it was Janna's turn to feel surprised, but she did her best to hide it. She'd been prepared for food on the menu, not art. She nodded bravely, but the thought of walking round a gallery with Gray, who was probably an authority on painting as well as everything else, filled her with dread. She sank back into the leather seat and tried to summon up everything she'd ever read about Braque, but her mind was a blank.

By the time they reached the Tate Janna was wishing she'd never come. The broad flight of sunlit steps overlooking the Thames seemed all too short, the dim entrance hall like a medieval torture chamber. She waited meekly for Gray to lead the way. But as they walked through the corridors she became more and more confused. Gray was moving at such a pace – and he didn't seem to be looking at the paintings at all, only the merest glance from time to time. Surely, surely that was a Picasso print? She cast him an anguished glance. He probably only liked painters she'd never heard of . . .

Gray must have noticed her expresssion because he stopped in mid-stride.

'Do you want to look at the paintings?'

Janna could feel her eyes darting nervously from side to side. Another tricky question. She loved paintings, she really did, but she certainly didn't want to look at them at the moment. She was far too worried about liking the wrong ones. Maybe, finally, honesty was the best policy?

'No. Thank you,' she added, belatedly.

'Good!' Unexpectedly, Gray's face split into a broad smile. 'In painting as in port, vintage is best.'

Janna gave a deep inward sigh of relief. She should have known that Gray and modern art were incompatible from the start – but at least she hadn't said the wrong thing, yet. She averted her eyes from what would have seemed only five minutes ago a glorious splash of colour. In Gray's company she could see how vulgar and careless it really was.

But if Gray didn't care for modern art, why had he brought her here? At last, down a flight of stairs, the mystery was solved. For the first time in her life Janna felt almost relieved at the sight of white napery and crystal glasses. A restaurant. That at least was one message that spoke clarion clear. A lovely place too – silky black tables and chairs set between smooth white pillars, walls a blue-green haze of mural, summer trees and cloudless sky under which gambolled hunters and hounds.

'The Expedition in Pursuit of Rare Meats.' Gray smiled as he settled her in her seat. 'Somewhat similar to our own, I think?'

Looking at the menu Janna understood instantly why he had brought her here. The art might be modern but the food was purely period, in fact almost antiquarian. Umbles paste, a wonderful pin-striped pâté made up of layers of dark chicken-liver mixture alternating with slices of white meat. 'Not completely authentic,' Gray explained to her gravely. 'The original medieval recipe in the British Museum was much more spicy, but in these days of refrigeration . . .' Janna detected in his voice a note of real regret. Then there were hindle wakes, boned rolled capon plumped out with prunes and served with a tangy lemon sauce, veal kidneys Florentine, a favourite dish in the Court of Elizabeth I, and Old English trifle, an extravaganza of sherry-drenched macaroons, citron and orange zest sprinkled with ginger and cinnamon, sauced with redcurrant and raspberry preserve and topped with syllabub and tartlet cream.

'From a recipe set down by Oliver Cromwell's wife,' said Gray. Hardly Puritan, though. Even less so was Janna's Grand Sallet, which turned out to have raisins, almonds, minced chicken, shrimps and even sturgeon amongst the olives, pickled cucumber and shredded lemon. Exotic, a rare meat indeed – and packed with calories, even if she declined the dressing.

But somehow, with Gray there on the other side of the table, Janna was able to pace herself. She ate carefully, consciously, feeling as if with each mouthful she was breaking new ground. There was so much taste that she could almost think herself satisfied, and so many distractions that the food could never take control. The other diners, her own excitement, the look of the place, the airy painted walls, so detailed she felt they were eating in the open air under an Italian sky, and most of all – Gray. He was the rarest of the rare meats, and the most satisfying. If she could watch him like this for the rest of her life, she felt she'd never feel hungry again.

Being with Gray was an education in itself. Everything he did was so graceful, so assured. Janna felt as if she were in a dream, the best kind, the ones you wish would never end. She could hardly believe she was there, talking and eating as if she went out to lunch every day of the week. She had to keep checking on herself, to make sure she was sitting up straight, not eating too fast or too slowly, using the right cutlery. It was so long since she'd been anywhere that wasn't inch-deep in debris that she felt like some sort of cavewoman spirited into the light. She saw that Gray was studying her too. Perhaps she was as strange and fascinating to him as he was to her. That was unlikely – but still, childishly, she longed for someone he knew to see them lunching together and jump to all the wrong conclusions.

For, as became clear over coffee, Gray simply wanted to talk to her about Julie. Janna fought to rise above her disappointment, determined not to let it spoil what might be left of her time with him. What had she expected, after all? It was hardly likely to be her company that interested him. There must be a hundred girls in this city of pretty women who would have jumped at the chance to have lunch with Gray – just as she had herself.

'You mean you don't know where she is either?'

Janna shook her head. For a moment she wondered how

105

many similar conversations went on every day all over the capital.

'Where is Julie? How is she? What is she doing? Is she ever coming back?' Julie was a subject of passionate, almost ritual interest, like the first spring cuckoo.

'I thought she'd write, but . . .' Janna felt driven to defend her absent friend. 'I'm sure she's been much too busy.'

'Julie's not a great one for the written word.' Gray's tone was preoccupied. He shook his head. 'I shall have to marry her one of these days, just to keep her in one place.'

Janna understood only too well what he meant. She, too, liked continuity, tradition. The English style. But she couldn't let Julie be disapproved of, even by Gray.

'It's not her fault. It's just that – everyone likes her. She has so many friends.'

'That's what I mean. Too many friends – and none of them the right kind.' Gray's gaze rested on Janna's face thoughtfully. 'Except yourself, of course.' Janna had no idea whether he was complimenting her or simply being polite. 'In any case . . .' How authoritative that clear, clipped voice sounded. 'Being liked is not the be-all and end-all of existence.'

Suddenly, he signalled for the bill. Janna felt bereft. She didn't want to leave this table. She didn't want to let go of the dream.

But the afternoon wasn't over yet. Gray seemed for some reason to want her company, almost to enjoy it. Perhaps because they both knew Julie, perhaps because, with Julie gone, he was even a little lonely?

This was such an astonishing thought that it reduced Janna to silence. Fortunately Gray didn't seem to mind. He was apparently happy to have her standing by quietly while he collected a pair of the most exquisite handmade shoes from Lobb's of St James', and a tub of his favourite clove-scented shaving soap from Floris. Together they walked under the arches of Burlington Arcade, where Gray instructed her in the art of sauntering – essential there, for top-hatted beadles still enforced the Regency law against whistling, singing or hurrying – but almost impossible for Janna. She couldn't relax, knowing that these were things Gray would rather have done with Julie.

But she felt a little better in a Piccadilly auction room, where a collection of eighteenth-century paintings caught Gray's eye. To Janna the prices he suggested seemed extraordinary. Some of the paintings were badly damaged. Many needed cleaning. Others were so roughly executed that a child might have done them. Gray smiled at her surprise.

'It's their age, you see, their rarity value.'

'I wouldn't hang any of them in my house,' she answered, almost ashamed to think that just one of these pieces was worth more to someone than the whole of No. 3.

Gray's smile deepened a little.

'Which one would you choose, if you had to?'

Janna looked round doubtfully. But in the end the choice was relatively easy. There was only one painting she might have hung in No. 3, and that was very small, very simple, almost naïve, a picture of a small brown bird on its nest. Gray laughed. Janna blushed. The painting was probably worthless, but it pleased her.

'You have a good eye,' Gray informed her casually. 'Those twenty square inches of canvas should fetch in the region of fifteen thousand pounds.'

Janna blinked in amazement. Gray left bids for several of the pieces. Obviously he was known to the attendants, and too well-known to bid for himself.

As Gray escorted her back to the car Janna wished suddenly he could see No. 3, not as it was now, but as she saw it in her mind's eye, in all its recreated glory. Her creation, her dream come true. He of all people would appreciate it, understand what it meant to her, just as she'd understood about Dene. And not only that. If he saw No. 3, transformed, perhaps he'd also feel that inside Janna Brown there was someone worth knowing too, under the dull surface a brush-touch of gold.

'Goodbye.' Gray smiled at her as he shook her hand. His touch was firm and cool. Janna barely felt it. Her mind was spinning with memories and impressions of their afternoon together, as if she'd packed a whole lifetime's experience into a few short hours. She felt exhausted yet strangely buoyant. In a sort of daze she accepted a chauffeur-driven drive back home. As she sat in the back of the Bentley it felt very different without Gray beside her. She tried to work out why, but couldn't seem to complete a single thought. Images kept flicking behind her eyes. The way he turned his head, the glint of rare October sunshine on his hair, the colour of his skin against the snowy whiteness of his linen shirt.

Suddenly it struck her, a revelation. White lightning on an autumn afternoon. She felt rocked, and lost, and old, and new, unsure of the past and the future, unsure of everything in the world except one thing. Something had happened to her, something she'd never wanted or expected, a stranger at her door. She didn't know how to greet it, what to say.

I'm falling, Janna thought, with a sort of disbelief, all her solitary certainties crumbling away. Now I know why they call it falling. But why? He doesn't care for me. He hardly knows I exist . . . and yet I'm falling still, heavy as a meteor, light as a dandelion seed, falling in love with Gray.

CHAPTER SEVEN

'Are you *sure* you can drive?' Janna cast an anxious glance at Dion as he flung the Mini into the whirlpool of Hyde Park Corner.

'Surely!' Dion's voice was blithe. 'There's nothing to it. Of course, if you'd asked me about a licence . . .'

Janna closed her eyes and hung onto her seat for dear life. Why had she ever agreed to this? She had her reasons, two thousand of them – but maybe she should have left Julie's Mini safe in the police pound where it had been taken. Even if she managed to find a buyer for it, it was hardly likely to fetch more than a few hundred pounds. It was the kind of car most people would pay to have taken away.

But Dion said he had a plan. What exactly it involved he wouldn't tell her, but she was rapidly running out of alternatives. Terms net, thirty days – and there were only ten days left.

'Good little car, this.' Dion accelerated ferociously into the right-hand lane.

'I'll take your word for it.' Janna could only hope they wouldn't be stopped by the police.

Dion dropped her off outside No. 3 but left the Mini's engine running. Janna hardly had time to shut the car door before he was off, toy-sized wheels jiggling alarmingly over the cobbles. At least she knew better than to ask him where he was going or when he might be back. It could be ten minutes or ten days.

Ten days. With Dion gone they seemed like so many years. Janna started half a dozen jobs around the house but always, before she'd managed to get very far, she ran up against some knotty technical problem which needed Dion's advice, the sort that couldn't be found in library books. He had a knack of making things sound easy even if they weren't. And the house seemed very empty, very quiet, without Dion's humming and hammering. Janna didn't miss him exactly, but after three days of quietness and emptiness she wrote out a note addressed to herself saying 'Gone to the races' and pinned it to Dion's trap-door. Foolish, but it made her feel a little better.

Because he was the only person she could talk to about Gray. And it helped to talk, even to Dion. It helped to let the words bubble out, the fear and joy and confusion. Dion was a good listener, sympathetic. He seemed almost pleased for her, as if she'd crossed some sort of bridge.

'It's only natural,' he observed, almost paternally. That wasn't quite the reaction Janna had expected. The idea that anyone could feel as strongly as she did about Gray, be spell-bound and weightless and transformed just by the sight of one face, the touch of one hand, didn't seem possible. Gray was special, unique.

'Yes, a good-looking fellow, a prince among men,' Dion agreed, but somehow Janna had the feeling he was teasing her. He must feel disadvantaged by comparison with Gray, after all.

By the tenth day, the day of reckoning, there was still no sign of Dion. Janna didn't dare go out in case she came face to face with Marlon and Jerry, who were still in the basement packing up their tools, spinning out the last few little jobs. She suspected they didn't intend to leave without the rest of their money. She couldn't make up her mind which one to confront with the awful truth – Jerry, the elder, a married man with five children to support, or Marlon, young and unattached and given to studded leather jackets.

An extraordinary noise, half trumpet, half Swiss yodel, took her mind off the decision for a moment. She leaned out of the window. Beneath was Dion, beaming broadly. Behind him, gleaming in the autumn sunlight, was a ten-foot-long naked lady.

The Mini. Janna stared at it, appalled. Whatever had happened to it? She rushed down the stairs and into the alley.

Marlon and Jerry had come up from the basement too, summoned by that clarion call. Now Janna saw where it had come from – a huge brass serpent horn coiled by the driver's window.

But as for the rest – as Janna looked at what Dion had done to Julie's Mini words failed her. Right across the bonnet and roof, legs braced, hands on hips, wild hair streaming, was the figure of a woman, painstakingly painted in every detail. Not quite naked after all, but giving entirely that impression. And what a woman. A goddess, a Valkyrie. She had everything, and to spare. Curves galore, peach-pink flesh on a sky-blue ground, gleaming, smooth, a triumph of matter over mind. And yet – she'd been painted so skilfully, with the cunning of an eighteenth-century *trompe l'oeil*.

'This yours, mate?' There was no doubting what Marlon thought of the new visitor. Very, very delicately he ran a grimy finger down the giantess's immaculate shin. Dion paused long, his face a mask of regret.

'Sorry, mate.' Janna observed that his accent had subtly changed. 'It belongs to the lady here.'

Marlon turned on Janna eyes of liquid desire. His hand now rested proprietorily on the painted woman's knee.

'Ever thought of selling?'

Janna opened her mouth but before she could get a word out Dion smoothly intervened.

'Out of the question, I'm afraid. It's a work of art.' His expression was sympathetic, almost pitying. 'You couldn't possibly afford it.'

'Why don't we let the lady decide?' Marlon's resolve was clearly strengthening.

Janna looked from one to the other, completely confused. 'Well . . .' The faintest suspicion of a wink from Dion's left eye. 'I could do with the money, I suppose.'

Dion shook his head. 'You're making a mistake, Miss Brown, a big mistake. A customised car like this, it's going to appreciate with every day that goes by. It's a one-off, this is.'

So are you, thought Janna in amazement. We're all in your play and you've written the parts. The tiniest jerk of his head gave her her cue.

'You deal with it, Mr Malloy.' She spoke out with as much dignity as she could muster, given the circumstances and the roll of the naked lady's roguish eye. 'I have other things to do.' She retreated into the house but couldn't resist peeking from the upstairs window. The three men were still standing there, almost motionless, hardly saying a word – cagey as cattle-dealers. Then, suddenly, it was done. Money changed hands, she couldn't see how much, and then she heard Dion's step on the stair.

Without a word Dion thrust a bundle of stained five pound notes into her hands. It looked a lot but couldn't be more than a few hundred pounds. Janna's heart sank. He'd tried so hard . . .

Dion took one look at her face and laughed out loud. 'Where's that bill?'

Puzzled, she handed it to him. He tore it neatly into four pieces and threw it into the fireplace.

'You mean . . .'

'Exactly.' He beamed at her. 'A fair exchange is no rob-bery. That –' he indicated the money in Janna's hands '– that's extra, a bonus. The icing on the cake.'

Janna shook her head in amazement. She still couldn't quite believe it. Down below Marlon and Jerry were still admiring the car.

'Who did it?'

'I did.' Dion smiled. 'One of my lesser talents.'

Belatedly, revelation dawned. So that's what Dion did up there in the attic, with his fungus-covered peppers. All was explained.

'You're an artist!'

'I paint.' His tone was suddenly guarded, his eyes shuttered.

'So I see.' Janna looked down at the Mini with new eyes. Very, very gently, with the care that befitted an Old Master at least, the two men below opened the car doors and got inside. 'A successful one, too. Marlon's going to enjoy driving that car.'

'Marlon?' Dion was back to his old self, his eyes alight with laughter. 'You couldn't be more wrong. It was Jerry who

bought it in the end, just as I thought. For his wife!'
Dextrously, while Janna still stared at him open-mouthed,
Dion helped himself to a couple of five-pound notes. 'For the
paint,' he called back over his shoulder as he bounded down
the stairs. A few minutes later, through the trap-door, Janna
heard the faint sound of whistling. A friendly, busy, impersonal sound. She smiled involuntarily. Everything was fine
now, just as it should be. Dion was back.

And only just in time. That same evening the long dry
autumn ended with typically English abruptness. Rain fell
heavily all night, while Janna hugged to herself the thought of
her newly completed, newly paid-for, damp-proof course. All
the next day it still rained, softly, a grey curtain in front of the
light. The house felt warm and safe. Janna found herself
looking forward to her first winter here, a sure, confident
feeling, like wearing all the right clothes on a snowy day.

All that day, while the rain fell, at the back of her mind was
the thought of Dion. She owed him so much, but he wasn't
the sort of man who'd like speeches and prize-giving. Nevertheless she wanted to do something for him to show how
grateful she was. A gift, maybe? For a man with so few
worldly goods there seemed to be very little he needed – and
without having seen into his attic she couldn't be sure what
his taste might be. He dressed exotically in a mixture of
self-designed originals and junk-shop cast-offs. He'd probably appreciate a pair of hand-knitted socks for those elegant
feet, but there wasn't time for that. She wanted to give him
something today, before she lost her nerve.

And yet Dion wasn't the sort of man who'd be happy with
anything. She had a strong idea that the reason he didn't own
much was because he hadn't found anything much worth
owning. If only she knew what kind of pictures he painted –
there was nothing worse than giving an artist almost the right
kind of brush. And her own dress-making skills weren't much
help in his case either. She hardly dared to think what use
Dion might make of a pair of lace-trimmed briefs . . .

Janna hesitated and debated while she swept out her parlour drawing-room properly for the first time. Now Marlon

113

and Jerry had stopped work there should be much less dust and grime. When it was done she found herself unpacking the Shiraz from its calico roll, just to see how it would look. Dion would like that as a present – who wouldn't – but it wasn't hers to give. Almost immediately, with the rug at the hearth, the room looked furnished, lived in. The dim grey light suited it, glossed over the raw edges that remained. Come the dark and candle time it would look warm and bright as a Christmas card, the ones she'd always liked best, with open fires and chestnuts roasting in the embers . . .

That's it! The idea came to her out of the blue. She'd only eaten chestnuts once before, at a Guy Fawkes' party, before she realised how many calories they contained. But she'd never forgotten the taste of them, warm, rich, mysterious. Yes. Suddenly her mind was made up. It would be hard, but she would do it. For Dion, and Dion alone, she would eat chestnuts.

She flew round the parlour, dusting and polishing, one step ahead of her second thoughts. She wouldn't let memories of the last time she'd prepared for a guest deter her. Dion was different from Julie, he was on the premises. Even now the creak of his footsteps on the floor above was a comforting background, a sort of companion.

It didn't take long. There was nowhere to sit but the rug, but Dion wouldn't mind that. A glass crammed full of apricot-coloured Virginia creeper furnished the mantelpiece. Candles on the shelves, not forgetting the matches, kettle at the ready to make tea, chestnuts overflowing their brown-paper bag, and it was done. Janna went upstairs to put on her best pullover and a clean pair of trousers. Squinting down at herself she wondered with a twinge of real surprise why she'd ever liked the colour. She'd thought it subtle, flattering, slimming. But it wasn't, it was simply – inconspicuous, dull. A sort of indeterminate grey-brown, not a colour at all. In the dimness of the parlour Dion would have to strain his eyes to see her at all. But that didn't matter. She and Dion were used to each other, clothes didn't make any difference.

Strengthened by that thought, Janna went to knock on the

trap-door. By the sudden silence on the other side she knew Dion was surprised at her break with tradition. But after a moment his shaggy black head appeared in the square of light in an almost exact replay of their first encounter. Only this time there was no fear, no embarrassment. He was so plain, so very, very safe.

'I've come to invite you to tea. In the parlour.' It was an important announcement. Janna savoured it, and the pleasure on Dion's face, to the full. 'Are you free?'

'Never freer.' Dion smiled broadly. He took hold of the edge of the trap-door and with one easy, graceful movement, slid through to land on his feet as neatly as a sailor. Wafting through the open trap and clinging to his clothes was a sweet, buttery smell. Oil paint. Of course. Janna resisted the temptation to peek further into the attic. She didn't want to see any of his paintings, especially one in progress. Suppose he wasn't any good? She didn't like to think of that. It was better if he stayed a mystery man.

'Follow me.' Janna's heart gave a small flutter of excitement as she led the way grandly down. Her first visitor to the new parlour. It was by way of being an occasion, a sort of house-warming. She only hoped the fire wouldn't have gone out.

Dion's reaction to the room was all she could have hoped for. He stood there, quite silent, a half smile on his face, simply looking, in that way he had, as if everything he saw was beyond his wildest expectations. Then he turned to her.

'You're looking very nice today, Janna Brown.'

'Oh.' Expecting compliments on the room Janna was a little flustered, felt her cheeks go pink. 'Thank you.'

Without being told where to sit Dion made his way straight to the Shiraz. Janna felt his eyes on her as she lit the candles, one by one, then sat down beside him, suddenly glad that it was quite a big rug.

Dion looked at her quizzically. In the firelight his eyes were much darker. His hair had reddish glints. His presence completed the room, rather like a cat on the hearth. She resisted an impulse to stroke him. Strange . . . Dion was ugly only if you compared him with other people. Seen as himself alone he was neither ugly nor beautiful, just . . .

'You're a great home-maker, Janna Brown.' The deep voice held an amused undercurrent. 'But as a fire-maker you have your weak points.'

Janna tore her eyes away from his face just in time to see her fire send up one last distress flare of flame then collapse from the middle outwards like a badly-built house of cards.

'Of course . . .' Dion's voice was meditative. 'These fireplaces were made for coal, not wood – but I think we'll get a good blaze going in a minute.'

Swiftly, skilfully, he rebuilt the fire. Just as he'd promised, it was crackling vigorously inside the minute. Dion sniffed the smoke appreciatively. 'There's nothing like a good fire.' A dramatic pause. 'Except, possibly . . .' His eyes rested momentarily on the brown paper bag. 'Except possibly one with chestnuts in it?'

Smiling, Janna handed him the one sharp knife and the brimming bagful. With practised skill he scored the shiny brown cases and stacked them neatly at the base of the blaze.

'They say you should wait until the blaze dies down.' His eyes twinkled. 'But I never could, could you? I'd rather eat them half raw, half burnt, than wait a second longer than I must.' There was in Dion's eyes so much rueful, amused acceptance of human frailty that Janna felt all the invisible knots in her body loosen and slip free as if by magic. Yes, she would be able to enjoy her chestnuts, this time. The hot, floury flesh wouldn't stick in her throat and threaten to choke her. This wasn't a test or a confrontation, one more skirmish in a battle that had no end. This was simply chestnuts, no more, no less. Chestnuts by the fire.

They were good, too, warm and sweet inside their scorched shells. She liked the way Dion swept the debris neatly into the grate, without fuss or officiousness.

'We never had an open fire at home.' Dion nodded, apparently neither surprised nor concerned. 'My mother . . .' Janna's voice died away. Still, after all this time, the word stuck in her throat. But she forced herself to complete the

116

sentence. 'My mother said they made too much dirt.'

'She was not wrong.' So calm, so accepting his voice. 'It's like the dust in this old house. Half the time, when it settles on a painting before the oil has dried, I hate it, it's my sworn enemy. And then, when the sun catches it and makes angel's wings, it's more beautiful than anything I could ever set down on canvas. It's the same with an open fire. No matter how well you lay it, there comes a point when it gets out of control . . .'

'That's what I've always felt about food.' Janna could hardly believe it was her own voice speaking. She felt strangely calm, as if she were talking about another person, not present, someone who could be discussed openly, honestly, with ease. Was it a false calm? She couldn't be sure. She'd never told anyone how she really felt about eating, not even the hospital doctor. What was the point? She'd known, somehow, that he wouldn't understand. Why should he? She didn't deserve it. Understanding was for other people, the ones who could make themselves clear, who could cry neatly, acceptably, with a smile. Rainbow tears. She couldn't afford them. If she once began to cry, really cry, she knew she'd never stop. It would all come out, the ugliness, unbearable, accusing, a whipped dog's howl.

But now . . . Slowly, gradually, as she stared dry-eyed into the flames, hardly seeing them yet feeling their warmth on her face, she sensed something moving in herself, a door opening, not wide, just a chink, letting light into a small dark room. Whether it was the fire, or Dion's silence, not tense or solemn or preoccupied but simply – waiting, or the fact of the house, her own walls that held her safe, she wasn't sure, but suddenly she could speak, say what she meant and have it heard.

'I hated it. I hated the way it made me feel. Not just hungry but – out of control. I was so frightened. I thought – I thought –'

'You thought it was going to eat you up.' Janna blinked. Whatever she'd expected it wasn't this, a brisk, matter-of-fact nod of pure agreement. 'It's the same with me. Each time I begin a painting I'm terrified that I won't finish it – instead it will finish me.'

A long pause, while fear went up the chimney with the flames. Then he turned to her, firelight shining in his eyes.

'So tell me, Janna Brown, now that we know all there is to know about each other, what is your real name?'

Janna shivered. Such an innocent question but so full of pitfalls. Memories, old shames, playground voices, her mother's disappointment, never stated but flowing deep and chill as a river underground.

'My full name, you mean?' She played for time. 'What's wrong with Janna?'

'Nothing, nothing at all.' Dion turned away, still smiling. Janna knew then that she didn't have to tell him, and that was why, with an effort that dried her throat, she made herself say it.

'January. My christened name is January.' She gave an awkward shrug. 'I hate that too. I always have.'

'Why so?' Dion's eyes were on the fire but somehow she knew he was listening with his whole attention, in that way he had, like a child with his ear to a shell.

'Because . . .' She hesitated, then plunged. 'Because it's an ugly name, cold and ugly.' Like me, too much like me. 'The worst month of the year. I think –' Now the words came in a rush because she knew if she didn't get them out quickly she'd never say them. 'I think my mother chose it because that was the month I was born, and my being born was the worst thing that ever happened to her in her whole life.'

'Oh, mothers – what a hard furrow to plough!' Dion turned to her, his eyes sympathetic but unshocked. 'January . . . well now. A good month – for an artist the best in the whole year. No leaves, no grass, no lies. You can see so clearly when there is snow. Black and white, the truth at the heart of the world.' He smiled. 'I like your name, January. It suits you.'

'Yes, I'm afraid it does.' Janna sighed. 'My mother was right, you see. She always said I was a cold sort of person. She had terrible trouble with me when I was a baby. I wouldn't feed, I cried all the time. "You'll never find a man to take care of you," she used to say, "with no flesh on your bones." '

Janna shuddered a little. 'But I don't want a man, anyway. I'm not – a pillow.'

'What about Sir Lancelot?' Dion's voice teased. 'Him of the Bentley and the sea-green chauffeur?'

'Gray, you mean?' Janna blushed. Trust Dion to go straight to the heart of the matter. For Gray she'd do anything, be anything. Yes, she'd changed, more than she'd realised. At the sound of Gray's name, yearning rushed back, salty, painful, sweet. 'It's no good.' She spoke gruffly, defending herself against that painful pleasure. 'He's not interested in me and never will be. I'm just – well, no good with men.'

'And proud of it.' Dion reached forward unconcernedly and stirred the fire. 'Don't worry, it's just a phase.'

Despite herself, Janna was stung. How like a man. Patronising, careless, confident that everything in a woman's life could be put right once she buckled down to her proper task, pleasing men. 'Go on!' Her tone was as caustic as she could make it. 'Tell me I haven't met Mr Right yet!'

'Far from it.' Dion reached over and very gently touched her hand. 'I'd say you haven't yet met your Mr Wrong.'

Silence. A flicker of candle-flames, a whisper of smoke. Janna stared at him, numb with shock. How could he, after all she'd told him about Gray? How could he? Who had she invited to sit on Julie's Shiraz, in all good faith, the Devil himself? There was enough hair on that ugly black head to hide a couple of horns. If she touched him, maybe she would catch fire and burn, burn till there was nothing left of her, burn for his delectation and desire . . . A shiver ran up her spine. She felt her soul shrink inside her. She should never have confided in him. He wasn't to be trusted after all. He didn't understand. How could he ever have thought she'd be one of those girls who trekked so eagerly up the chalk-marked stair? Or perhaps, because she was the landlady, she'd deserve the trap-door? She winced, every nerve stiff with outrage.

Then, he looked at her. With Dion's eyes, laughing, grave, but Janna didn't know him at all. Or herself. What was happening to her? She could feel her strength draining away, her body softening, melting. If she went on looking into his eyes

119

she'd become nothing, a wraith, a shadow on the wall. Whatever he did then, whatever movement he made, would find its echo in her bones, pull her limbs with it in dark undertow, a mirror dance, make her one with the dying fire, the falling rain, the candle-flames.

She couldn't let that happen. She mustn't look. She mustn't. But there was no way to escape those eyes. Helpless, Janna looked, and lost, and felt all the known world melt away like smoke, leaving nothing but emptiness, warm, heavy, waiting to be filled.

'Well, January.' Dion rose, in one long fluid movement, held out his hand. 'Coming to the races?'

Silence, echoing, endless. No words would come. Janna's body weighted her, swollen, drugged. It was impossible to move or speak. Only in the depths of her mind, panic-stricken, alarm bells shrilled. Don't ask me. Please don't ask me. It's too much. I can't bear it. Let me go. Let me go.

The alarm bells went on ringing, piercing, making the air vibrate.

'The telephone.' Janna grasped at the sound like a drowning man in a pitch black sea. Sharp, familiar, it snapped the tension, cut her free. Dion regarded her steadily, unmoving, unspeaking. The bell went again, ringing for ever and ever. 'I'd better answer it.' Slowly, stiffly, Janna turned away, picked up the receiver, blessedly cool and impersonal in her hand.

'Hello?' For a moment she didn't recognise whose voice it was on the line. It seemed a million miles away. But she clung to it, her rescuer. 'Yes. Yes. Have I? No, not really, it's just – there's someone here. No. Well – not a lodger exactly, but – yes. I did. Now? Today? I don't know. Look – wait a minute.' Carefully her heart hammering, Janna covered the receiver with her hand just as Julie had taught her, and turned. It felt as if she was dragging the whole planet's weight with her, but she made herself turn, turn and face Dion once again.

'It's . . .' Her voice tailed away. The room was empty. He'd gone, her black cat by the hearth, as swiftly and silently as if he'd never been, a shadow fading into the night. The fire still whispered, the chestnuts gave up their golden earthy scent, but all the warmth had gone out of the air.

Slowly, Janna turned back to the phone. She felt dazed and disorientated, but she had a great deal to be thankful for. 'Yes.' Little by little, now, she could feel life returning. 'Yes. If you're really sure. It'll be good for me to get away.'

CHAPTER EIGHT

The hall was vast, seats in their thousands ranged flight upon flight, tier upon tier, as far as the eye could see. A huge bowl, a sounding shell, the ceiling so far above it was only visible by its lights. Impressive enough in itself, but there was more. In the shadows Gothic arches soared upwards, stained glass windows scattered rainbow shards on stone flags. Through fretted arches a glimpse of cloisters, stone statues set in carven niches. A pool of light on the raised altar, flanked by milky candles, child-high.

And yet it wasn't just the detail, marvellous as it was, that tipped the balance into awe, but the sheer scale of the enterprise. How could anyone, even someone crazy and determined and very, very rich, ever hope to transform an entire auditorium into the interior of a medieval cathedral?

And yet, it had been done, and in mere months instead of generations. That was why the audience, despite their first-night finery, moved about so quietly in the pillared aisles. They were stunned into solemnity. The atmosphere breathed incense and expectation. No-one spoke above a whisper, no-one cared that the pillars might be hollow, the niches one-dimensional, the candle-flames special bulbs with a computerised flicker. The illusion, the moment, lived.

When, suddenly, church bells rang out from high above in an unseen steeple it seemed both startling and altogether right. A call to faith, a call to grace. Take your seats for eternity. A subdued rustle as the audience found their places facing the high altar.

Janna leaned forward, breathless, amazed. Her head was spinning, she could hardly believe she was actually here, in a strange land, in a strange city, in a front-row seat labelled with her name. So many firsts in almost as many hours, starting with that international call, with its haunting pauses and delays in which she forgot everything she'd meant to say. Then, her first airport, her first plane journey, her first visit to a theatre, a real live theatre full of real live people like herself. She felt as if she'd barely touched solid earth since the 747 took off from Heathrow. Ever since then she'd been breathing different air, dry, scented, rarefied.

And all because of Julie. Because of Julie, because she was Julie's friend, Janna had been met at the airport, whisked to the theatre in a limousine, greeted personally by the director's assistant, ushered to her seat complete with a glossy full-colour programme, assured at least half-a-dozen times that her own presence in the audience would make all the difference to the night's production, Julie's performance especially . . . Flattery, of course, but Janna knew she wasn't immune. The sensation was so new she almost forgot about No. 3 and the ashes of her chestnut fire. Now she knew why Julie loved travelling so much. It put the past into a sort of cold storage. No time to think, or feel, or worry about the might-have-beens, the almost-dids.

Janna bit her lip, remembering. She'd have liked to clear up a little before she left, but by the time she'd written three differently-worded notes to Dion and torn up two she was in danger of missing the midnight plane. 'Gone to New York.' She liked writing that. It sounded so cosmopolitan, sophisticated. Not at all like running away. 'Back soon.' Vague enough, she hoped, for Dion to lose interest in the prospect of her return – even, knowing Dion, to put her out of his mind completely. 'Please take care of No. 3.' That was the important part. She hadn't known how to sign herself. 'Love' was wrong but 'Yours' sounded false too, so in the end she put, simply, 'Janna'.

It would be all right. The ashes of the chestnut fire would be cold in the grate by now. Nothing to worry about, nothing at all.

Except for one thing. Even now, Janna wasn't sure quite how she'd reached the decision. She'd put it off a hundred times, told herself a week more couldn't possibly make any difference, since it was something she should have done so long ago. But at the airport she'd passed a row of mail slots on her way to collect her ticket. That line of patient, empty mouths reminded her, unwillingly, of something Dion had said. 'Mothers . . . What a hard furrow to plough.' It was then that she made herself a promise, a sort of trade-off bargain with the future. If there really was a ticket waiting for her at the counter, then she'd do it. Just a card. That wouldn't matter. No-one could ever trace it, posted from the airport. She'd be gone before it was even collected from the box.

The ticket was there. Quickly, not giving herself time to think, Janna picked out a card with a clean white aeroplane small as a child's toy against bright blue sky, scrawled the address and three words. 'Everything fine. Janna.' Meaningless, empty words, and yet as she posted them into the mail slot she felt a moment's panic, as if she'd tempted fate.

But it didn't matter. She was safe now, far away.

Faint strains of music, then silent and graceful as swans on water came a file of robed nuns. Forewarned, Janna knew that among them would be Julie, black-cloaked for invisibility. She would glide behind the gold-embroidered banner that obscured the Madonna's statue, slip into the fibre-glass stone shell, put on her crown and take up the figure of the baby Christ. There, for an hour, motionless, she must wait. Janna knew that, with one half of her mind. Perhaps the audience knew it too, but in that timeless grey hush all disbelief was suspended. In its way, a little miracle.

No curtain, no applause, not even a word spoken, a quiet unfolding. A simple story, black and white as the habit of the rebel nun. A woman's story, of love and the corruption of love, seduction, betrayal, disgrace. Old as the hills, new as tomorrow's papers. Poignant, terrible – but Janna ached only for Julie, her friend, marooned in her stone niche like one of her own ancestors on a marble tomb, powerless yet all-important. All eyes upon her, radiant, beautiful.

But beauty alone wouldn't be enough. Singly, without words, Julie must complete the circle, clothe the miracle in flesh. And how could she possibly do that – Julie of the cold baked beans and endless phone calls – how could anyone? Surely it was too much to expect?

At last the moment came. Slowly, gracefully, the statue of the Madonna woke from her stone, descended from the niche to lay aside her jewelled crown. In silence she gathered up the betrayed nun's discarded veil and cord, lifted the abandoned child into her arms, looked up, just once, towards the cross. Light fell on Julie's profile, transfiguring. Mute, almost without expression, yet it spoke volumes. No-one breathed. Carefully, carrying her lost human child, the Madonna ascended to her niche.

The Miracle was complete. Not one word spoken from beginning to end, but no soul left unstirred. There were tears in Janna's eyes. How right the director had been to choose Julie for the role, unlikely though it might have seemed. Without her, without the authority of her beauty, unique and yet somehow universal, the play's conclusion might easily have failed. But Julie, and Julie alone, worked the miracle. She belonged there, centre stage, in the faint haze of perfume and cigar smoke, the warm midnight hush. And the audience loved her.

Backstage Janna found Julie still in her vestments but without her veil, the centre of an adoring crowd and a lightning storm of flash photographs. Champagne corks popped. Flowers filled every corner of the dressing-room. Telegrams covered the noticeboard, overflowing onto the make-up table, circling the mirror. Janna's eye was caught by one signed simply 'Gray'. She tried not to read it but it was so short she couldn't help it. Two words only, mysterious, stern. 'Be good.'

Gray would have been proud of Julie tonight. She'd been more than good, she'd been – miraculous. And Janna wasn't the only member of the audience to think so. Everyone wanted to speak to Julie, tell her how wonderful her performance had been. Janna hovered on the outskirts of the group surrounding her friend, unsure what to do. She didn't like to push forward, but she couldn't leave without telling Julie how good she'd been, thanking her for the plane ticket and the front-row seat.

At last the crowd thinned momentarily and Janna was able to edge her way through. Close to, she could see that Julie's face was flushed, her eyes rapturous. She looked happier than Janna had ever seen her.

'You were wonderful, Julie. Thank you.' Janna could barely hear herself in the hubbub. How did these theatre people make their voices carrying so clearly? She braced herself to try again, then her courage failed her. Half reluctant, half relieved, she turned to go. When she got home she'd write Julie a long letter, put down on paper all the things she couldn't say in person.

'Janna!' Julie swung round suddenly and caught her arm. 'Where are you going?'

Janna felt all eyes swivel, blushed.

'Home.' She gave an awkward smile. 'Winter's coming – I've got pipes to lag.' A ripple of laughter. Janna's blush deepened. She hadn't intended any joke. This was purely serious to her.

'But you can't leave now!' Julie's warmth enveloped her. 'You're my mascot, my good luck charm!' She paused dramatically. 'I told them, if I couldn't have you here for the first night, I wouldn't go on at all!'

'Really?' Dizzy, breathless and exhausted as she was, hardly able to keep her feet in the backstage crush, Janna felt a glow of pride. To be needed – and by Julie! It was an extraordinary sensation. 'At least –' Now Julie's voice cajoled as only she knew how. 'At least wait up with me for the notices. The Sundays will be out by 5 am at the latest . . .'

'5 am?' Janna stared at her. 'You mean you're going to stay up till then?'

'Of course.' Julie beamed at her, radiating energy. 'This is my first first-night. I want to do it properly. It's like getting married – it only happens once!'

'Theoretically.' Buffeted by elbows and dazzled by the ring of light bulbs round Julie's make-up mirror Janna spoke without thinking. Another ripple of laughter, stronger this time, made her blink in surprise.

'I like your friend, Julie.' The director, hovering at his protégée's shoulder. 'She's got style.'

Janna blushed again. What an extraordinary country, what

126

extraordinary people! They seemed to laugh as easily as breathing. She risked a look round. Smiles everywhere, large as life. For some reason, foolishly, from excitement and fatigue, she felt tears come to her eyes.

'Style?' As always Julie pounced on the key word. 'What about me?'

The director grinned. 'You don't need style, Julie. You're going to wake up famous.'

It happened just as he'd predicted, a climax as irresistible as the conclusion of *The Miracle* itself. After a late, later supper at Sardi's, the rush for the newstands. Janna found herself with a lapful of newsprint. 'You read them to me,' whispered Julie. 'I don't want to wear my glasses in public!'

Pride and pleasure made Janna forget instantly how tired she was. As eager as Julie herself, she thumbed through for those all-important, make-or-break reviews. They were good, very, very good, even she could tell that. For once, the critics were in perfect agreement. From across the table, underneath the photographs and caricatures of a century of Broadway names, Julie glowed.

'Just think – there'll be queues three times round the booth in Times Square!' She winked at Janna, irrepressibly. 'Looks like no-one wants to offend the Virgin Mary round Christmas-time . . .'

And that was only the beginning. In the weeks that followed *The Miracle*'s revival sparked off a whole nostalgia boom for simpler, less cynical days. Janna couldn't pick up a paper without finding favourable comparisons between Julie and Lady Diana Cooper, who'd first taken the role in the Twenties, fashion columns proclaiming the revival of the wimple and the no-make-up look, pieces on Julie's privileged background, her ancestral home where according to some sources she ate off gold plates and raced prime bloodstock for a hobby.

Julie laughed with glee. 'If only they could have seen me at No. 3!' Janna felt a small chill. Had it been so bad for Julie in the basement room? Everything was changing so fast in her friend's life, that sometimes Janna felt they were further apart than when they'd been separated by an entire ocean. Julie was so busy, so much in demand. And she thrived on it – the photo sessions, the interviews, the jammed phone lines, the admirers, the armfuls of madonna lilies. Her stone habit was even featured in *Women's Wear Daily*.

By the end of the first week it seemed as if everyone in the city knew Julie. She'd become a symbol, a totem, a landmark. She was deluged with gifts, and accepted everything she was offered with one of her brilliant, short-sighted smiles, whether it was a free ride from an adoring Italian cab-driver or a free suite at the Regency for the duration of *The Miracle*.

'Don't worry, it's good publicity for them,' Julie assured Janna when she ventured a doubting word. 'No room at the inn, and all that . . .' Julie glanced vaguely round at their palatial surroundings. 'Louis XVI – it makes me feel quite at home.' Janna said nothing. French tapestries, Italian marble floors, an elaboration of gilded mirrors – why, there was even a gold-and-white telephone in the bathroom . . .

'Poor Janna.' Within a few seconds Julie had her cases open and her clothes distributed over the floor, just as she liked them. 'You'll get used to it.'

She didn't, of course. Every day, thinking wistfully of No. 3, Janna decided that she really must go home tomorrow, but every day Julie managed to find some way to delay her.

'Janna, should the Virgin Mary endorse eyeliner?'

'Julie, you really shouldn't have to ask that.'

'I suppose you're right.' A melancholy sigh. 'You've got such good taste.'

'But look . . .' Janna hated to see Julie look sad. 'Julie Francis can.' Julie's expression brightened instantly. Janna shook her head. 'You need a mother, Julia.'

'I know.' Julie dimpled. 'But you'll do, for the moment.' She eyed Janna appraisingly, her head on one side. 'You've grown your hair, haven't you. Who is he?'

'What do you mean?' Janna felt her cheeks grow hot. She wasn't used to Julie's scrutiny. If Julie looked anywhere it was usually in a mirror. 'It just grew, that's all. I've been too busy to cut it.'

But Julie was relentless. 'Your lodger – it's a man, isn't it?' Her eyes went wide. 'That's it! That's why you keep wanting to go back home – you're living with a man!'

'No I'm not.' Janna bit her lip. Now she was on shaky ground. But no matter what she said Julie was bound to jump to all the wrong conclusions. She'd better distract her with at least a small part of the truth. 'But you're right, I'm in love.'

'Janna!' Clearly Julie was thrilled, all curiosity about Janna's mystery lodger forgotten. 'Who is it?'

'I'd rather not say.' Janna felt a pang of regret. There was nothing she'd rather do than talk to Julie about Gray – it would be such a relief to confide in her, such a pleasure to discuss Gray with someone who knew him so well – but of course she couldn't. If she so much as mentioned Gray's name Julie would sense, just from her tone of voice, exactly how she felt.

'How about him?' Julie was frowning now. Janna could tell she was rooting for her, all her partisan instincts roused. 'Does he feel the same way about you?'

'I'm afraid not.' Janna attempted a casual shrug. 'He's hopelessly in love with someone else.'

'Oh, that's good.' Surprisingly, Julie's expression was relieved. 'That'll keep him going nicely till you get him.' She leaned forward, full of enthusiasm. 'I can help you do that, no problem. First of all, a little make-up –'

'I'm not going on the stage, Julie.' Janna felt suddenly nervous. This was getting complicated. She began to wish she hadn't so much as mentioned the fact she was in love. 'I'm just – a plumber.'

Julie shook her head disparagingly. 'That house – it's as if you were married to it! Don't you see? If you get the right man, he'll buy you all the houses you need.'

But it wouldn't be the same, thought Janna. I need that house, because it's mine. It's my – shell. My chance to start again. Without it I'd be nothing.

'Yes.' Julie's mind was clearly made up. 'You'd better start practising, fast.'

'It'll take more than practice.' Janna sighed. Why was it

that beautiful girls, who'd been born that way and would die that way, thought that plain ones could be made-over with a wave of a magic wand? 'Look.' Hands on hips she tossed back her hair and paraded across the room in a deliberate parody of Julie's head-turning glide. She wouldn't have dared do it in front of anyone but Julie, but she had to show her how ridiculous such airs and graces looked on someone like herself. Beauty was for beauties – it was a natural law.

But instead of being shocked or offended Julie seemed delighted, almost flattered. 'Janna, you clever thing! Why, it's even better than watching myself on video!' She ran to the wardrobe, dragged out a red vinyl hatbox. Janna watched, bemused, as Julie dug inside, came up with an armful of bouncing curls the exact honey blonde shade of her own.

'Try this on.' Julie dropped the confection into Janna's lap. The hair felt soft, warm, almost alive. Janna touched it gingerly. 'Go on,' Julie encouraged. 'I only use it when my roots are dark.'

Janna looked up. 'I didn't know you bleached your hair?'

'Of course not.' Julie grinned. 'That's why I got the wig, so no one would know!' Now she was pulling out drawers, scattering their contents far and wide. Janna winced as a fresh powder compact hit the old rose carpeting and disintegrated. But at last Julie found what she was looking for, a small rolled-gold container in which swam two tiny transparent circles.

'Soft lenses,' Julie explained. 'I never wear them. They make my eyelids puffy – some kind of allergy I guess. But if you put on some of this blue stuff . . .' Julie added a few drops of liquid and the circles went a delicious azure. 'Here, I'll help you put them in. You won't be able to see much but you might get the general effect.'

Janna hesitated. Julie's enthusiasm was infectious. Despite herself, hope stirred. A different country, a different city – maybe a different Janna too? But could she risk it? She hadn't looked in a mirror for so long, she hardly dared. Mirrors were her allergy. Looking at her own reflection made her feel sick and faint and strange. She remembered turning endlessly in front of the glass, trying to find one forgiving angle, but all that stared back at her was the truth. Flesh, clumsy, useless, unsightly, pads and pockets of it that, no matter how hard she tried, refused to go away. To see it, to see her own weakness reflected in the mirror, was a sort of crucifixion. She had no courage for it any more.

But this would be just her face. Maybe, after all this time, it wouldn't be so bad? Janna took a deep breath, leaned forward, opened her eyes. The lenses, corrected for Julie's short sight, blurred her vision, but she saw enough to give herself an extraordinary surprise. Her face, in the flattering soft focus, looked quite unrecognisable. Staring out of it, forget-me-not blue, were Julie's eyes. Even her view of the world seemed different, framed by dancing blonde curls glimpsed at the edges of her vision. The reflection in the mirror, on a dark night, in a snowstorm, might have been Julie herself.

Julie squealed with pure delight. Her face swam up beside Janna's in the mirror. Four blue eyes, two sets of honey-blonde curls, a beguiling vision.

'Oh . . .' Julie gave a pleasurable little wriggle. 'If only Gray could see us now!'

'That's enough.' Suddenly frightened, Janna pulled off the wig. She wanted her 20/20 vision back quickly. She didn't want to think that Gray might be hers for the price of a borrowed wig and a fleeting resemblance to Julie. It was too dangerous a temptation.

Yes, New York was a dangerous place. Janna was learning fast. In this city, even in the depths of winter, everyone worked on the premise that anything was possible, tomorrow if not yesterday. If by the end of the day you hadn't gained your heart's desire you could send out for it, any hour of the day or night. The streets might be cold, the sidewalk black with half-melted snow, but your foot never needed to touch concrete, if you were rich enough. That was the dream.

The city was full of wanting. That was why no-one ever stopped walking, with a rapid, weaving, dancing gait, like a well-trained boxer limbering up for the big match. Temptation lurked on every corner. Delicatessens, windows chockful of bagels as shiny as boot-buttons. Hot-dog stands steaming in the icy air. Counter shops hardly wider than a bookshelf where lunch-hour patrons downed skyscraper sandwiches as fast as they could be constructed.

But little by little, Janna found herself adjusting to the pace. There was so much choice, so many claims for her attention, that there was no time left to worry. And in Julie she had an expert guide to the intricacies of the machine. Julie showed her the patient queue of Japanese that lined up every lunch-time outside Gucci's Fifth Avenue outlet, Oriental inscrutability severely tested by Italian siesta. Julie gave her courage to taste chocolate velvet with hot minted sauce at The Four Seasons. Julie rang Gray from a pagoda-shaped telephone booth in Chinatown while Janna squeezed in beside her, breath misting the cold glass. Julie let her in on the all-important secret that whatever the blandishments of Bloomingdales and Bonwit Teller, no real New Yorker ever bought so much as toothpick there that he could get on the Lower East Side, wholesale.

New York was a wholesale kind of a place altogether. Janna wondered sometimes what Gray would make of it. Vulgar, pushy, money-hungry, with no time or space for the subtle elegancies of living. And yet – the women were so perfectly turned out, the street vendors so enterprising with their monkeys muffled up in wool under their picturesque Victorian lace, the vest pocket parks so determinedly cheerful despite the leafless trees and a dandruff sprinkling of snow, that Janna couldn't help admire. So much effort, so much energy, so many plans and projects rubbing up against each other in the chilly air that by sheer force of friction they made it glow and spark, a winter firecracker, a brazier of dreams.

And Julie the dream princess, deluged with offers, gifts, invitations, all fitting tributes to her beauty. She played her part to the hilt, revelled in it – so when, one afternoon, she returned to the Regency drawn and white-faced, Janna was seriously alarmed.

'What's the matter?' As far as she knew from Julie's crowded timetable her last appointment had been with her agent. What could have happened?

132

'An audition.' Julie dropped into a chair. 'For a film. This afternoon.'

Janna hesitated. 'Would you rather not go? If you like I could ring Ellen, tell her you're ill or something?'

Julie shook her head. 'You don't understand. I want to go, I really do. It's just that – well, I can't.'

'Why not?' Now Janna was genuinely perplexed.

'They haven't sent round a copy of the script.' Julie's voice held a note of desperation. 'They swore to Ellen that they'd get me a copy in time, but they haven't. It's not at the desk downstairs, I've checked and double-checked. Oh, why, why hasn't it come?'

'Well –' Janna hazarded a guess. 'Maybe they haven't finished writing it yet?' But Julie didn't seem to hear. Now she was up and pacing the floor.

'A screen test – just think of it! My big chance . . . And not just anyone, it had to be Fernand Kim, of all people. *A Dangerous Woman* – the best film ever. And he wants me. Ellen said so. He was at the first-night – oh, I can't bear it!'

Janna laid down the ruffled petticoat she was mending and watched Julie with concern. In all the long run of *The Miracle* she'd never once seen her friend show any outward signs of stage fright, yet here she was shaking like a leaf and wringing her hands. Why was she so troubled? It was a mystery.

'Look, Julie . . .' Janna hesitated. 'I don't know much about films, but surely if this Fernand person has seen *The Miracle* and liked you enough to contact your agent specially, then you're practically home and dry? All you have to do is turn up, read for him, and –'

'But that's the whole point!' Tears trembled in Julie's eyes. 'I can't, I simply can't – not unless I see the script first!'

'So you said.' Janna waited patiently. 'But you didn't say why.'

'Oh, Janna.' Suddenly Julie looked exhausted, shrunken, so unlike her usual radiant self that Janna was seriously worried. 'Even you don't understand. Believe me, I'd spell it out for you if I could.' Her shoulders drooped. Her voice dropped to a whisper. Suddenly she looked like a little girl. 'I

133

can't read. I never learned. I can't do it. That's all.'

'What?' Even as Janna felt her eyes grow round in disbelief she knew it made sense. It explained so much. Julie's skill at avoiding menus, so charming – 'You order for me, darling, you know just what I like' – her bad driving, her addiction to the telephone, or, if that failed her, the Juliegrams, dictated to a friendly anonymous voice that also knew how to spell.

'Not even a little bit?' Janna kept her voice steady with an effort. She knew this sort of thing happened – but to other people, surely! Not Julie, not golden, confident Julie . . .

Julie gave a shaky laugh. 'I'm afraid not. Oh, I've got pretty good at guessing, over the years. Enough to get by, but not to be sure.' She gave a little shiver. 'That's been the worst part, never being sure. It's such a strain. I have to be so nice to everyone, just so they won't notice anything's wrong.'

'But how on earth did it happen?' Suddenly Janna was angry for Julie. It must have been so hard, missing out on something most people took for granted. Being beautiful couldn't make up for everything.

Julie shrugged. 'My eyesight. No-one noticed I couldn't see properly until it was too late. I didn't know I was any different – I just thought I was stupid. That's why I bluffed all the time, pretending I could read. I wanted Father to be proud of me. Whenever one of my governesses began to suspect I'd persuade Father to give her the sack.' She laughed, unsteadily. 'I got through a lot of governesses!'

'And you've managed to keep it secret ever since?' Janna marvelled. It must have been so difficult.

'Well . . .' Julie gave a watery sniff. 'Gray knows. He used to cover for me when I was younger. But I hated always depending on him, always being in his power. That's why I had to get away, in the end. It was hard managing on my own, but Ellen dealt with most of the paperwork, and then there was you.' She smiled at Janna. 'You're so lucky, you know. You can read, just like that! Remember the shoeboxes?'

There was such a look of longing and admiration on Julie's face that if it had been on film it would have won an Oscar. Janna was touched, more than she dared to show. No wonder

Julie's accounts had been in such a state. Poor Julie. She was only glad she'd been around to help.

'Listen.' Janna folded up the petticoat neatly, gave it a brisk little pat. 'Would you still like to learn to read?'

'Oh, yes.' There was no mistaking Julie's sincerity.

'Well, then,' Janna took a deep breath, 'I'll teach you.' She looked up at Julie a little shyly. 'I'd be proud to.' It would be some recompense for the chocolate velvet and the suite at the Regency and the glimpses of a life beyond her wildest imaginings.

'Now?' Julie leaned forward, suddenly eager. 'In time for the audition this afternoon?'

'But . . .' Janna's voice tailed away. Faced with the enthusiasm in Julie's face, the utter confidence that she, Janna, could solve all her problems with a wave of a magic wand, she was suddenly speechless. How could she begin to explain that learning to read wasn't something you could do as easily as putting on a wig? And yet, Julie deserved her chance, after all these years of struggling. She'd come so far on her own. Janna wished with all her heart there was something, anything she could do, to help her on her way.

They stared at each other for a long time, unspeaking. Slowly, Janna saw unfolding in Julie's eyes the beginnings of an idea, foolish, reckless, impossible, the mirror image of her own.

'It wouldn't work.' They spoke simultaneously, surprising each other. Then Janna heard another voice, her own, timid, questioning, rash. 'Would it?'

CHAPTER NINE

'Number five. Miss Julie Francis.'

Fernand Kim leaned forward very slightly and tapped the shoulder of the man in front. 'This is the one I told you about.' His voice was quiet. He signalled to his assistant waiting patiently by the door. 'One moment.'

Fernand waited, just as patiently, for his small inward surge of elation to disappear. It was better so. He must hold himself alert yet detached, in a sort of meditation. It was important, this first view. The girl's beauty – it had stirred him, but he must not let it touch his judgement. He must remain high above, far away, for the panorama, the eagle's eye view. And yet be ready to focus in, lightning swift, on the slightest shadow, the faintest stir of movement in the grass below.

That was how it was with him now, after twenty years. Once seen that panorama was impossible to forgo. For him, on his seventh major feature, there was no longer a choice. No grey area, no middle zone. With each project he lost a little more of what other people called self. Each time he set up camp, a shifting nucleus of uncertain souls, a little state bound by its own fragile rules, the end was implicit in the beginning. Like the films he made. Between today and tomorrow, between two beats of the heart, there might be a different film, two films instead of one, no film at all. He'd grown used to that. He had struck camp so often that now he travelled light.

It was that settled look of hers that had first attracted him. The English. Everyone knew that they were made of stone. It had been extraordinary, in *The Miracle*, to see her step down from her wall. Oh, these English. How sulky they looked, as if the world had not played fair, had stolen their ball and run away. But behind the pique, centuries of confidence. Look how they travelled – their maps, their woollen underwear, their implements for tea . . . He admired that. He'd always admired the creation of a role from nothing. Professional.

Though he, himself, preferred to work with amateurs. Occasionally, perhaps, one big star, ageing, cross-cast. Stars worked so hard, on the way down, and that effort made good cinema. You could see every vein.

Fernand frowned. He wondered sometimes if he might one day go too far. But there was nowhere else for him to go. Last year he'd been back to China for the first time. It was strange to think his French missionary father had only been posted there because his wife spoke fluent Chinese. Maman had been second-generation, San Francisco born and bred. She could pass for Chinese in a cheong-sam but when she smiled it was another continent. Fernand learned very early that nothing was quite what it seemed.

China too. They seemed like a mirage now, those days in Peking. Backdrops from a flimsy paper theatre, images from a willow pattern plate. The Lycée, where the French of France sounded stranger than birdsong. The garden with its green pavilion. He remembered a tree hung with lights, silence, rain. That China was gone now, everything changed. And yet, perhaps, not everything. He was a child of three continents, a hybrid, a gypsy, but still, like his maternal grandfather before him, a taker-in of other people's washing, a launderer of hopes and fears.

'Send her in.'

The door swung open. Prepared for Julie, Fernand frowned. 'There must be some mistake. You're not Julie Francis.' Hair and eyes were similar, but this was a different face altogether, a different presence. No poise, no marble calm. This girl was shaking.

'I never said I was.' Her voice was small. He could barely catch what she was saying, and yet she stood her ground, with the same panicky insistence he'd seen in birds confronted by a snake.

'In that case . . .' Fernand inclined his head politely but dismissively. 'We are wasting each other's time.' Whoever she was, she was quite wrong for the part, there was no point in going further.

'I've come to read for you.' He saw how pale she was and felt an instant's sympathy he suspected he was going to regret. 'I'm Janna Francis. My agent made the appointment.'

Fernand hesitated. It was an easy error to make. And he must be careful. Her agent might be one of the big ones. It could be a mistake to turn her away. He shrugged, passed across the well-thumbed single sheet of paper, carrying his best midnight thoughts. Let her massacre them. It would be good for him, a sort of test.

'The parts underlined in red, please. My assistant will read the rest.'

'Is this the only copy?' Fernand blinked, taken aback. The girl didn't seem to have heard. Her voice, as she studied the paper intently, still shook but held a note of what he could only interpret as criticism. He began to regret his moment's sympathy.

'If it's not good enough for you, then –' He held out his hand.

'No, no, it's fine.' She clutched the paper as if it were a lifeline. 'May I have a moment to prepare?'

'Certainly not.' Mentally Fernand cast his eyes skywards. 'This is not the *Comédie Française*!' He shook his head. A method actor, no less. This was ridiculous, a complete waste of time. She was blatantly unsuitable for the role. She looked so – odd. Everything she wore seemed slightly too big for her, as if she was a child in her mother's clothes. The effect was sluttish yet curiously innocent, a sparrow tricked up as a peacock. On an impulse Fernand signalled quietly to the video cameraman. What was ten minutes of wasted tape in this business? It would be intriguing to have a record of this street urchin in her hand-me-downs.

Just as he'd expected she read badly, so badly that he found it impossible even to interrupt her. Mercifully, the scene was short. But before he could dismiss her she was in with a

138

question of her own. 'Tell me, Mr Kim . . .' Quaint, that combination of hesitation and determination. 'What kind of woman is she, this Claudia?'

'A provisional name only.' Despite himself Fernand was seduced into discussion. No. 5 might read the lines as if they came straight out of an obituary but there was no mistaking her interest. It burned in that pale face, those blinking, probably short-sighted eyes. 'Claudia is a woman of society, privileged, beautiful, even a little spoiled. A type. And yet, being a woman, she is always wanting something more, something beyond her reach – that's what makes her interesting.'

'Oh, I see.' No. 5's gaze fell back to the page in front of her. Before he could stop her she began to read again. This time her rendition was even worse, a halting monotone, slurring some words, hurrying others, completely without rhyme or reason. Fernand's assistant, so used to the dialogue that he barely had to glance at the page in front of him, struggled to keep up, lost his place and never found it again. Fernand himself could hardly follow what the girl was saying. He'd never heard anything like it. It was as if she was reading a foreign language, writing reflected in a mirror. He made a quick mental note of the effect. It might be useful one day. And relatively easy to arrange. Words could be projected onto a mirror just above the camera, the mirror itself acting as a fill-in reflector. Yes, it might be interesting. One would catch an authentic confusion in the speaker's eyes . . .

Lost in his own thoughts Fernand was barely aware that No. 5 had finished the scene. His assistant coughed, recalling him.

'Thank you, Miss Francis.' Quickly Fernand removed the script from the girl's hands. She seemed strangely reluctant to let it go. And yet she said nothing, simply turned to the door, her face set, her body stiff, as if she were carrying a full container of some precious liquid, not a drop of which must be allowed to spill. For some reason, now, she was in a hurry to get away. He was even more surprised to see, as she closed the door behind her, the shadow of a first, small smile.

*   *   *

Outside, Janna hurried from the co-ordinator's desk, past the row of other girls waiting on the banquette, and into the relative safety of the corridor. She glanced quickly to left and right, then made straight for the ladies' lavatory. It was empty, just as they'd hoped. She entered the first cubicle on the left-hand side, shut the door and bolted it. Taking off her wig she stuffed it unceremoniously into her big sackcloth bag. She took out a piece of paper and a pencil, sat down, and concentrating furiously, began to write.

'Janna?' A knock sounded very faintly on the door. Janna slid the bolt back to let Julie in. There was barely enough room in the cubicle for both of them.

'Did you get it all?' Julie whispered. Her face was very pale.

'I hope so.' Janna bit her lip. 'There were two parts though, a man and a woman, I didn't expect that somehow. I didn't manage to memorise both of them, but I think I got your cues. Here goes.'

Slowly, whispering still in case they were overheard, Janna read from her precious piece of paper. Julie listened intently, her lips mouthing the words. She was a quick learner, Janna realised. Over the years, she'd had to be.

'OK.' Julie's eyes were shining now, her cheeks pink. 'Shall we run it through, just to get the timing? You be the man.'

Janna nodded. It felt strange, the two of them crammed into the tiny cubicle, talking in whispers, like some sort of childhood game. Exciting. And yet she'd be glad when it was over. The tension had left her feeling weightless, empty, as if she might blow away. In Julie's clothes she'd felt like someone else. The audition seemed to have gone by like a dream, outside her own volition.

' "But Eden, I wanted to talk to her!" '

The words seemed to come to life as Julie spoke them. Suddenly Claudia was a real person, not just lines on a page.

' "Don't be ridiculous, Claudia." '

' "Admit it, you're jealous!" '

' "Of a woman like that?" '

' "I thought at night all cats were grey?" '

140

' "There is always the morning after." '

' "Eden! You mean you've . . .?" '

' "That's none of your business, Claudia." '

' "Oh, don't be so stuffy, darling. This is the Twentieth Century, after all." '

' "I don't want to discuss it, Claudia." '

' "But you'd discuss it with that woman outside, wouldn't you? Why not me?" '

' "Because you're a lady." '

' "And she's not? Why are you so sure? If she was wearing my clothes and I was wearing hers, I don't think you'd be able to tell the difference!" '

Janna looked at Julie in admiration. She'd have applauded, only there wasn't enough room.

'Word perfect!'

'Yes . . .' Julie still seemed doubtful. 'But what does it mean?'

'I don't know.' Janna shook her head. 'I asked the co-ordinator but she was very vague. She said he always works like this. He doesn't like to start cooking until he knows what he's got in the cupboard. That's why you didn't get an advance copy of the script. I think this –' Janna indicated her piece of paper, 'is all there is. Outside Fernand Kim's head, that is.'

'What's he like?' Julie bent forward eagerly.

'I'm not sure.' Janna cast her mind back. It was difficult, she'd been so nervous. All she retained was the impression of a small man, rather crumpled, with slanty eyes so black they reflected no light at all, and yet seemed to see everything. 'He's sort of –' She tried to find a word for that quality. Not ruthless exactly, that was too strong. Determined? Not strong enough. 'Preoccupied, I suppose.'

'Did it help, looking him up in the library?'

'Not really.' Janna had memorised the entire list of Fernand Kim's films, from his first short 'film noir', *Le Chat*, to his last, a musical set in South America and entitled *The Beach*. But face to face with him she'd had the odd impression that if she mentioned one of his previous films by name he might not even remember it.

141

'Listen, I'd better go.' Julie slid back the bolt, peered round to check no-one was watching. 'They'll be calling me soon. Wish me luck!'

Janna nodded. 'Break a leg!' She'd been well-trained. When Julie had gone she folded the piece of paper carefully and stowed it in her bag, along with the black-leather jacket and stiletto heels. She waited five more minutes just to be safe, then, transformed and she hoped completely unrecognisable, went down to the lobby to wait for Julie.

'Well, what did he say?' Julie came down at last, smiling.

'The usual.' Julie shrugged but Janna could tell she was very pleased. 'He said I read well. Imagine that!'

Janna smiled, relief flooding through her body. It had worked, after all. All the planning, all the worrying had been worth while.

'But maybe I was a little young, he said. He asked me to frown, and he tested me twice, that was why I was in there so long. Once with my hair up. And . . .'

'Yes, yes?'

'He asked me to lunch.' Julie tossed her head. 'I said no, of course.'

'Why? Don't you like him?'

'Like him? Without my lenses I could hardly see him. But that's not the point. You should never say yes at once – I thought everyone knew that.'

'So what did you say?'

'Call me Wednesday, I'm at the Regency.' Julie dimpled. 'It sounded great.' Her eyes narrowed a little, meditatively. 'Let me see now. Half French, half Chinese . . . I wonder which half is the French bit?'

Janna blushed. Julie seemed to have met a different Fernand Kim altogether. That was always the way with Julie. Quickly, she changed the subject.

'I wonder where he'll take you?'

'I don't care.' Julie gave a little skip of pure joy. 'I'm so relieved I could eat *filet mignon* and enjoy it.' She paused in mid-flight, a little concerned. 'Say, Janna – could you teach me to read by Wednesday?'

Janna did her best. She spent a day in the reference library photocopying every last newspaper review of *The Miracle*. Julie began by picking out her own name, then that of the play, then the various bits of hyperbole that had been so lavishly applied to her own performance. 'Magnetic.' 'Miraculous.' 'A triumph of timing over time.' 'Silent sorcery.'

Julie loved it. Soon she knew the reviews by heart and Janna would find her chanting them away to herself, one lacquered finger moving carefully along the line. By the end of that week she had mastered the reviews and was lusting for stronger meat. They moved on to back copies of *The Stage*, gossip columns in magazines, even a portion of the *New York Times*. They snacked on theatrical posters and newspaper headlines, Julie's eyes wide as she found out for the first time what the rest of the world found so interesting. She became a newspaper addict. Her first action after taking off her nun's veiling every evening after the performance was to pick up her copy of the day's newspaper left ready by her dresser. Julie called it, importantly, keeping in touch. For the first time Janna heard her say, 'Turn off that radio, I'm trying to read.'

Janna was so proud of her. That Wednesday, primed with a morning's menu practice, Julie went off to lunch with Fernand Kim 109 floors up at Windows on the World, and for the first time in her life chose what she wanted to eat. She came back jubilant.

'To think I used to pick lunch with a pin! Oh, Janna, the things I've seen on plates you wouldn't believe. I'll never forget that pig's trotter – you could count its toenails! And then there was the calf's head – can you imagine, they'd left the eye in? It kept staring at me as if it knew me – horrible! At least at Macdonald's they show you a picture of what you're getting at the door . . .

'Talking of pictures, there was this at the desk.' Julie handed Janna an opened envelope. 'Sorry, I shouldn't have looked inside, but I thought it was for me.'

That was only natural. The mail always was. And Julie always liked to open her own now, to see if she could read

143

what it said. Janna took the envelope with a strange sense of foreboding. Only Dion knew where she was staying – and why were there so many Air Express stickers?

Inside the envelope was a single sheet of very thick white paper. No message, just a drawing. In a few deft black lines Dion had managed to convey everything he needed. He'd sketched the house from above, as a passing pigeon might view it. Only the house was barely recognisable as itself. Where its roof should have been, a jagged, gaping hole. A litter of slates on the attic floor, the angry edges of partly rotted joists. Inside, a small figure kneeling on the attic floor so suddenly and rudely opened to the sky, Dion had drawn himself, under a torn umbrella on which he'd drawn a large black question-mark.

'What is it?' Julie was staring at her. Janna shook her head, unable to speak. She felt as if that large black question-mark had been burned into her heart. Her body felt hollow and cold, just like her poor little house, open to the worst winter could do. She should have stayed, she knew that now, no matter what. The house had missed her. It was as if she'd been holding up those rickety joists with her own body. And now, the worst had happened, at the worst possible time, only three weeks before her deadline, in the middle of winter. What the rain and frost didn't ruin, the pigeons would. Roofless, the house was doomed.

'Janna!' Julie's voice was concerned. 'You've got to tell me. What's the matter?'

'Dry rot.' Two words for a sentence of death. She handed Julie Dion's drawing. It was her own fault, she knew that. She could have gone back to No. 3 any time in the last month, Julie would have let her. Oh, there'd been the audition, teaching Julie to read, important things, but they weren't really why she'd stayed. Somewhere deep inside herself she'd been afraid. Of going back. Of Dion. How foolish that fear seemed now. Compared with this, what could Dion have done to hurt her?

'You mean this is No. 3?' Julie stared at the paper, appalled. 'Hadn't you better get it mended?'

144

Janna shook her head. There was so much Julie didn't understand, she didn't know where to begin. 'A new roof would cost a lot of money, Julie. Not just materials, but labour. To get it done quickly, at this time of year, they'd need extra men, lights, platforms, a tarpaulin . . . It would cost thousands of pounds, maybe more than the rest of the house put together.'

'Oh, dear.' Julie made a sympathetic face. 'I just wish I'd landed a part in that film.'

'You mean you didn't get it?' Concern for Julie took Janna's mind off her own disaster, just for a moment.

'I'm afraid not. Fernand told me over lunch, in the nicest possible way.' Julie's expression brightened. 'But I could try and change his mind. There's always the casting couch . . .'

'No, thank you!' Janna felt her cheeks colour. 'I couldn't let you do that. I don't think it would work.' Julie looked a little offended. Janna hurried to explain. 'I mean, I'm sure he likes you enough to want to change his mind – but he wouldn't. Not about his film.' Janna halted, knowing she wasn't making much sense. And yet, for some reason, she felt that she was right – she felt she understood Fernand Kim in a way that Julie hadn't. How could she? Men always behaved differently when Julie was around, trying to impress her, hide their real selves. But she, Janna, had seen Fernand Kim thinking of anything and everything but herself. Having seen that, instinctively, she knew what it must feel like to make films. Not how it was done, but why. She'd felt something like it herself. She'd sewn in fading light, for no-one's eyes but her own, because that was all there was. She'd stripped layers of ancient paint off hand-planed skirtings, for nothing but hope that beauty would be there, scrubbed grimy floorboards till her knuckles were raw, in a sort of blind faith, a deep unspoken need for there to be something worth saving, some vision worth seeking, some honest end. A shelter, a shrine, a signpost in the desert, saying, 'This is where I live, this is my home.'

'Well.' Julie still sounded offended, an expert challenged in her speciality field. 'If you're so sure you know what makes him tick maybe you should go and see him yourself. He's staying at the Plaza.'

Janna bit her lip. Julie was right. Her one small insight into the way Fernand Kim's mind worked was useless. All the understanding in the world wouldn't change the fact that she had nothing to offer a man in his position, nothing at all.

And yet, she had to do something.

'Where are you going?' Julie's voice, startled.

'Nowhere.' Janna picked up her coat and bag but didn't turn. If she did she might realise what she was doing and change her mind. 'Just out.'

CHAPTER TEN

'Yes?' The clerk behind the reception desk looked up. Janna felt her voice die in her throat. His expression was as easy to read as one of Julie's banner headlines. You, it said, are not the sort of person who stays at the Plaza. You, with your sackcloth bag and undistinguished coat, have no place here. Our mouldings are burnished with real gold, it said. Yours are not.

Janna swallowed. She'd spent an hour and more money than she could afford riding round and round Central Park in the same taxi, trying to find the courage to come through these doors. She couldn't give up now.

'I've come to see Fernand Kim.'

'I'm sorry.' A small impervious smile from behind the desk. 'Mr Kim has given us express instructions that he is not to be disturbed.'

Janna's heart sank. She'd spent so long trying to think of something she could say to Fernand Kim that it hadn't occurred to her that she might not see him at all.

'Are you sure?' She heard the note of desperate entreaty in her own voice and was ashamed.

'Under no circumstances.' The clerk shook his head. 'Mr Kim's own words.' His tone told Janna quite clearly that there was nothing she might say or do which would change his mind.

And yet Janna couldn't bring herself to go. It would mean turning her back on No. 3 forever. The roof, her roof. At this very moment rain might be swirling in, bringing with it black London dirt to rot her little joists. What would Julie do now?

'Call him.' Janna tried hard to mimic Julie's casual authority. She lifted her head, straightened her back, almost tossed an imaginary golden mane.

A long pause. Janna's heart thundered. She held the clerk's

gaze with an effort. Be Julie, she told herself. Just for five minutes more.

The clerk hesitated, shrugged, then pressed a button.

'Who shall I say, Miss?'

'Julie Francis.' Almost as soon as the words were out Janna wished she could take them back. It was such a risk. Julie's was a well-known face, a household name. She could only pray that the man behind the desk was one of the few remaining New Yorkers who hadn't seen *The Miracle*.

And yet the effect of Julie's name alone was almost miraculous. After a few words on the telephone the clerk's expression changed. Now he was all deference. From that moment bells rang, escorts materialised and well-oiled machinery swept Janna up to a suite at what must be the very top of the building.

Slowly, every pace silent in the velvet carpeting, Janna made her way to the door indicated. It was so quiet that she might have been the only person alive in the whole city. But her heart was beating hard enough for a hundred. The roof, the roof, she thought. Just a little bit of roof, a few tiles . . . but life or death for No. 3.

The door swung open. It was Fernand Kim, slight and rumpled yet somehow forbidding, despite his open-necked shirt and rolled-up sleeves. He stared at Janna for a long moment, almost as if he recognised her, even without the wig and the make-up and Julie's clothes. Janna held her breath, too frightened to say a word. Now, truly, she felt like an impostor. Would he be angry? He had every right to be.

'Who are you?' His eyes were narrowed, as if he'd tried to place her face but failed. 'And, what is more to the point, why are you pretending to be Julie?'

Janna was silent. Everything had happened so fast, she'd had no time to think. It had been a last-minute gamble. She hadn't expected to get so far. But she must say something, anything.

'I'm – er –' She cast around frantically for a convincing reason. Suddenly she remembered all those telephone conversations, when she and Julie had been almost interchangeable.

Under Julie's instruction she'd played so many roles, and no-one had seemed to mind. 'I'm – acting for her.' That at least was true, and always had been.

'Her agent?' Fernand's voice was suddenly sharp. 'I thought she was with Ellen Berne?'

Janna bit her lip. Of course, Julie would have told him that.

'Yes. She is.' Panic stirred inside her. What could she say now? 'I'm – er –' Her voice tailed away, the words sticking in her throat like broken glass. 'I'm – Julie's other agent.' Lies and more lies. Janna felt Fernand's eyes on her, knew she was floundering deeper and deeper into quicksand. 'She has two.' She struggled on, knowing she was talking too much, giving too many explanations. 'It's – it's better that way. I specialise. In films.'

'Well . . .' Fernand turned away at last, releasing her from that all too perceptive gaze. 'In that case you'd better come in, Miss – er?'

'Brown.'

'Yes. But I'm afraid you're wasting your time, Miss Brown. Diana is not for Julie.'

'Diana?' For a moment Janna wondered if she'd heard right. 'But I thought she read for Claudia?'

Fernand halted, swung round. Behind him the panorama of Central Park spread out dark and mysterious in the fading light. He hadn't drawn the drapes, Janna had no need to wonder why. 'The name has changed – didn't Julie tell you? Wait a minute . . .' He took a step closer, flicked on a lamp. 'Haven't we met before?'

Janna backed away from the unwelcome brightness. 'I don't think so.' But Fernand didn't seem to hear her. He went on studying her in the light of the lamp, his eyes looking as if he were in another galaxy. As if, any minute, he might put two and two together to make No. 5. There wasn't much time. Anxiously Janna searched the room, wishing she had a clearer idea what she was looking for. Her eyes fell on Fernand's desk, strewn with papers, littered with small unidentifiable pieces of equipment. Amongst them, at last, she saw it – small, battered, its casing scratched and dulled, but recognisable even so – a television.

149

That meant he must have the tapes here. Janna steeled herself. It was her only chance.

'Julie's tape . . .' Julie had said he'd made a recording of her audition, but had refused to show it to her. 'Could I see it?' Janna prayed that her voice sounded cool, businesslike, an agent making a bona fide request on her client's behalf. So much depended on Fernand's reply. Without seeing for herself how Julie had performed at the audition, Janna couldn't hope to change his mind.

At last, to her relief, Fernand turned away, reached up to a shelf above his desk and slotted a video tape into the playback machine. The image flickered, then steadied.

'Oh.'

'What's the matter?'

Janna coloured. She wished she knew more about video tape. 'What about the sound?'

'Why bother?' Fernand's eyes rested on the screen, abstracted. 'We both know Julie. Don't we?'

'Yes. Of course.' Janna concentrated hard on the silently mouthing image. It was distracting, the absence of sound, but now she realised why Fernand had turned it down. To prove his point. To show, with the clarity of mime, exactly what it was that Julie had done wrong. It was simple, in the end. She'd tried too hard. Moved too much, smiled too wide, forced the mood. In silence, with her golden voice removed, she was almost painful to watch, a netted fish, gasping and straining in a medium that wasn't its own. Overacting. Permissible on stage, in real life, but clearly not on film.

I wish I'd been there, Janna thought. Maybe I could have helped. Maybe I could have persuaded Julie out of that gypsy hoop of a performance and into something more discreet.

The tape flickered out. Janna searched desperately for something she could say.

'The lighting.' She cleared her throat, trying hard to sound professional, detached, when every nerve ached for Julie. 'It's not right for her.'

'I know.' Fernand nodded slowly. 'But it doesn't make any

difference in the end. Julie is simply wrong for the part. She is too beautiful.'

Janna frowned, trying hard to understand. How could anyone be too beautiful for a film? It was difficult to believe – but maybe he'd given her a clue, just a small one, how to proceed.

'Did you know . . .' She took a deep breath, hoping Julie would forgive her. 'Did you know that Julie bleaches her hair? And puts coloured drops in her eyes?'

'Really?' A flicker of interest crossed Fernand's face. Janna felt a small stir of hope.

'I'm sure she'd agree to stop, just for the film . . .'

'Even so.' Fernand shook his head. 'She is not – how shall I put it? She is not lucky with the camera. Film broadens her face, flattens it.' He smiled a small smile. 'The camera is no respecter of pedigrees, I'm afraid.'

Having seen Julie's tape, Janna knew exactly what he meant. Julie on film was somehow smaller, less alive, than Julie on stage or in a still photograph.

'Couldn't you do something about that?' She looked at Fernand hopefully.

'Such as?' Fernand's expression was mildly amused.

'Well . . .' Janna struggled gamely on. 'Something technical. Special lighting maybe, or make-up?'

'Of course.' Fernand shrugged. 'But why should I bother?' He flicked on the video machine again, slid in another tape. 'Here, let me show you what I mean.'

To Janna's horror, what swam out of the black-and-white snowstorm on the small screen was a full-colour close-up of her own face, framed in borrowed blonde curls. She stood rooted to the spot, utterly silenced, all her worst fears realised. How long had Fernand known she was No. 5? How long had he been playing with her, in lazy anticipation of this moment?

And yet, despite her horror, Janna couldn't seem to take her eyes off the screen. The camera was pulling out now, away from the close-up of her face to a full-length shot. And what Janna saw then was so amazing, so much a revelation that the shock of it trembled through her body like the first tremor of an earthquake. She knew that looking back on this moment she would see a huge chasm, a massive San Andreas fault, open up between the two halves of her life. Before and after. Already she could feel the change, an explosion of relief and astonishment and disbelief forced up from the centre of her body, spilling out to harden into certainty.

The camera did not lie. It might insult, as it had done with Julie, but it would not lie. It would simply state what it saw, incontrovertibly. That image on the screen was herself. Forget the wig. Forget the halting delivery. Forget the overdone make-up and ill-fitting clothes, stripped away as mercilessly as Julie's charm had been. None of that mattered.

For she was thin. Janna looked, and looked again, but try as she might to find traces of the hated flesh that had haunted her for so long, it wasn't there. I'm thin, she thought. My arms, my legs, my face. Thin. Even, she saw with a secondary wave of astonishment, a little too thin. The hollows beneath her cheekbones, her neck, almost too fragile to support her head, her narrow wrists. If Julie looked like that, she thought, bemused, I'd think she was ill.

It was as if the world had been turned upside down. A whole new view of herself, utterly different from anything she'd seen in a mirror or a photograph. Movement, three dimensions – a revelation. Had she all along, when she looked at her own body, seen only what she'd expected to see, the reflection of her own self-hatred? Even now she could hardly believe that puff of thistledown on the screen bore any relationship to herself. She stared till her eyes burned with looking. She wanted to take that image in, make it part of herself. If she could do that, if somehow she could marry the way she felt and the way the screen told her she looked, then surely, at last, she'd be set free.

'Well, No. 5?' Fernand sat quite still in his leather chair, poised as a cat. 'Do you realise we've been looking for you everywhere? Don't you ever read *The Stage*?'

'Only the back numbers.' Janna's sense of release was still with her. She could scarcely tear her eyes away from the screen, now blank. When Fernand reached up to turn it off she felt as if a friend had died.

'Who's your agent? Not, I suspect, Ellen Berne . . .' Fernand's tone was dry.

'I'm afraid not.' Janna swallowed as she began to realise what she'd done. Would Ellen ever forgive her? And yet, it had been worth everything, just to gain this knowledge. She felt light as air. If she breathed in deeply she might float off the floor and straight up. How long would it last? Would she still feel like this new, thin self out in the street, in the real world? If she could just remember, fix the image in her mind . . .

'Do it.' Brief, brisk, commanding.

Janna frowned, momentarily brought back to earth. 'What do you mean?'

Fernand's eyebrows went up. 'You've seen the tape. You're just what we've been looking for.'

'Me? Claudia? I mean Diana?' Janna stared at him in astonishment. What could he be thinking of? Thin she might be, but a society beauty? Never.

'No, no . . .' Fernand made an impatient gesture. 'Diana is far from being the only part in the film. There's another female role, much smaller, non-speaking, but well worth having all the same.'

'And you want me?' Still Janna couldn't believe it. Then she remembered that image on the screen. It wasn't herself that Fernand wanted, but that other girl, the one she hardly knew, with her strange thin face, her shadowed eyes, mysterious as water glimpsed in the bottom of a well. She made you want to know the end of the story – where she went, what she did, what happened next. You felt you could see right through her skin to her small, bony soul.

'This role –' Janna hesitated. She was almost afraid to ask, almost afraid to look at the innocent cassette lying on Fernand's desk, in case it disappeared. Black magic. Was it possible that she might have her roof after all? 'Would you – would you pay me anything for it?'

Fernand's eyes gleamed with amusement. 'That is customary.' Janna paused. This was almost too much to take in. She breathed deep, testing the air. No, she hadn't died, no, she wasn't dreaming.

153

'Enough for a new roof?'

Fernand's eyebrows rose. 'How should I know? I'm no architect.' His tone was dismissive.

Janna bit her lip. 'And I'm no actress, I'm afraid.'

There was a long pause while Fernand studied her. Janna wondered if she'd lost everything. But she couldn't lie any more.

'So I'm beginning to realise.' Fernand spoke at last. 'You haven't even asked me what kind of part I'm offering you.'

'It doesn't matter.' A small part, non-speaking. She could manage that, surely, for No. 3. 'Just so long as I get my roof.'

'I see.' A smile twitched the corner of Fernand's mouth. 'In that case, if you give me what I want, I will make sure that you do. You may send the bill to me. Is it a deal?'

Yes, oh, yes, thought Janna, drunk with relief and happiness. Yes, yes, yes a million times. The best deal in the world.

Except for one thing. A chill ran over her as she remembered Julie. How could she ever go back to the Regency and tell Julie that instead of persuading Fernand to star her in his new film she'd accepted a part, even a small one, for herself? There was no way she could do that to Julie. It wouldn't be fair. Unless . . .

'There's just one condition.' Janna took a deep breath. It felt as if she was throwing No. 3's future away, but she had no choice. 'I can't possibly take the part unless Julie's in the film too.'

Fernand eyed her thoughtfully. 'What are you two – sisters? Cousins? Lovers?'

Janna blushed. How very French. She shook her head. 'Just friends.' She saw from his eyes that he was already losing interest. Already, brick by brick, No. 3 was slipping away. What could she do to change his mind about Julie? What could she say?

'I was wondering . . .' Janna's voice shook. She struggled to control it. 'Did Julie mention her house when she saw you? Dene – perhaps you've heard of it? More of a stately home than a house, really.' Fernand looked suddenly attentive. Janna took heart. Maybe that one small insight she'd had about him was right after all. 'Two-hundred-and-fifty acres of Capability Brown, deer in the park . . .' Her own feeling for Dene spilled over into her voice, giving it the ring of absolute truth. She would make him see it, she must.

Fernand stiffened. Janna held her breath. For an interminable moment everything rested in the balance.

'This Dene –' Fernand's eyes narrowed. 'Would Julie let us use it, as a location?'

'Well . . .' Janna's every instinct was to say yes, promise everything and anything, but she knew she mustn't. This was Fernand's work, as important to him as No. 3 was to her. 'It really belongs to her cousin. But I think she could persuade him. Provided –'

'Provided she was cast in the leading role.' Fernand paused. Janna could hear beads rattling on his internal abacus.

'No bleach?' He shot the question at her lightning swift. 'You would see to that?'

Janna nodded, fervently.

'No – funny drops in the eyes?'

'I guarantee it.'

'No – acting?' He made it sound like the worst form of perversion.

'Not if I can help it.'

'Hmm.' Fernand eyed her with a trace of sympathy. 'That last – I suspect it may not be so easy. This roof must mean a great deal to you.'

'Everything.' Janna put heart and soul into the one word.

'In that case . . .' Fernand extended his hand, took hers in a cool, firm grip. 'It's a deal. A house for a roof – I think I have a bargain there, don't you? Including mademoiselle Julie. Have her agent ring me in the morning.' Already he was escorting her to the door. 'Tell Julie she must be out of *The Miracle* by – let me see, the third week of February by the latest.'

There was no doubting Julie's reaction when Janna got back to the Regency and told her the news. She was thrilled, absolutely and unconditionally.

'Just think!' She threw herself backwards on the bed, kicked

155

her legs in the air for pure joy. 'I'm going to be in a film! Oh, Janna, it's the answer to everything . . .' She sat up, stared down at her long glossy legs. 'It's been such a worry, you know, trying to decide who to bequeath myself to. It seems a shame to waste all this on just one person. But now, everyone will have a chance to see me. I'll be immortalised on celluloid!'

'I don't think they use celluloid any more, Julie.' Janna sat down rather suddenly on a spare corner of Julie's bed. Now the tension was over she felt exhausted. And Julie's reaction seemed to make her own doubts loom suddenly larger. A film role – what had made her think she could handle it, even a small one?

'Why not?' Julie looked affronted.

'Something to do with the fire risk, I think.'

'How dreadful!' Julie's eyes went wide. 'I do hope they've got something better now. I don't want to go to all this trouble just to go up in flames.' She smiled a faint, faraway smile. 'I want to last and last. I want to be a national institution, just like Dene. Open to the public every afternoon between 1 and 4, reduced rates for pensioners and the disabled . . . Which reminds me.' She turned suddenly, rumpling the figured-satin quilt. 'This part he's given you – what's it like?'

Janna shrugged. 'I don't really know. It can't be very important since I don't have any lines to say.' She wouldn't dream of telling Julie how she'd come to get her own role. Even now, it seemed hardly credible.

'Perfect!' Julie looked relieved, smiled her most brilliant, Jack-the-Giant-Killer smile. 'You'll be able to help me learn mine.' She put both hands to her cheeks as if discovering the softness of her own skin for the very first time. 'Just think of it, Janna – I'm to be Diana!'

'I wouldn't be too sure.' Janna tried to make a joke of it, to cover her own doubts and fears. She mustn't spoil Julie's pleasure. 'Fernand may have changed the name again by the next time we see him . . .'

It wasn't only the name that had changed the next time Janna and Julie saw Fernand. Suddenly he'd decided to set the film back half a dozen decades.

'The last golden age . . .' It was probably the Edwardian ambiance of the Plaza that had inspired him, Janna thought. 'Which do you prefer, 1890 or 1912?'

Julie and Janna exchanged doubtful glances. Janna suspected that whatever they said, the decision would be governed by other considerations. And so it turned out to be. The 1890 fashions, ornate, covered in beading and embroidery and using yards of material, would be far too time-consuming to make up. 1912 proved more amenable. Fernand liked the look of all the Oriental exotica inspired by the *Ballet Russe*. The colours, strange and mannered as a Japanese print, the Poiret turbans and small pointed shoes, the ribbons and tassels, the harem trousers and Chinese tunics . . . Janna found them fascinating, but Julie wasn't so sure. She'd wanted to be a Gibson Girl. She had the height to carry off puffed sleeves and wide skirts to perfection.

But it wasn't to be. And that was how Janna and Julie came to find themselves shivering in identical white on white muslin afternoon dresses on a deserted Atlantic City beach at 9 am in the middle of February.

'Julie, Janna, remember, this is the most important scene in the whole film.' Fernand's voice, drifting down to them through the loud-hailer, held infinite authority. Janna knew without having to be told that for Fernand every scene he was currently directing would be the most important. She and Julie had no way of judging, since neither of them had yet seen a script. That was the way Fernand worked. Janna had heard the story of an actress, now well known, who'd starred in one of his early films, only to discover at the première that she'd been playing twins. 'No wonder I had problems with motivation,' she'd said. 'I just thought he was being avant-garde.'

But Fernand had his reasons, clearly well thought out. He wanted the freshness, he said, the purity of ignorance. In real life, he said, people didn't know what was going to happen, so why should they? And truly, in this scene, what he wanted did seem simple. All she and Julie had to do was walk down the beach, arm-in-arm.

And for that, such a simple, even tenuous thing, there were in attendance two crews, countless lights and reflector screens, a main generator, a secondary generator in case the main one failed, a refreshment caravan and a crowd of busy people hung around with clapperboards and walkie-talkies, discussing cutaways and zip pans and other techniques so mysterious they could only be mentioned by their initials.

'But what are we supposed to be doing?' Julie had asked. 'Admiring the view?'

'Nothing.' Fernand had smiled his enigmatic smile. 'Just being.'

But that was the most difficult thing in the world. Janna had been up since dawn, listening, observing, trying to find out exactly what went on when you made a film. But it was very hard to pin down. She could see lots of activity, but hardly any action. It seemed to be all preparation, helpless waiting and unfocussed tension, interspersed by short moments of silence and calm where, it seemed, something might be about to happen, but never did. She noticed that everyone, not just Julie and herself but every member of the crew and even the few hardy fishermen who'd braved the cold, hung on Fernand's every word. No-one seemed to know when they'd done well, unless it was affirmed by his nod of the head.

But even Fernand wasn't all-powerful. There was always something – a hair in the gate, sunshine where no sunshine should be, condensation on the lens, a vapour trail in a supposedly Edwardian sky. Each time Janna and Julie had to halt their progress down the beach and return to their marks, followed by two assistants with special brooms who swept away each footmark from the sand. And if it wasn't something technical that went wrong, it was the hats, scratchy wide-brimmed golden straws which were awkward to manage in a brisk Atlantic breeze, even though the way the ribbons fluttered must look very pretty. In fact it all made sense, in a crazy sort of way, right down to the decision to do the beach scene now, in February, because by summer every beach in the world would be crowded.

Yet again Fernand called 'Cut!' The cameraman, frowning

and looking rather like a mole in his fingerless gloves, searched through his black case of filters.

'I feel like the asterisks in a swearword,' Julie whispered. Janna tried not to smile as they clung together for warmth under the unwieldy yellow-lacquered parasol. Fernand wouldn't want to lose the mood.

'No smiling!' She'd been right. Fernand's voice could sound stentorian when he wanted to. Julie sobered instantly.

'God, I'm nervous, aren't you?' Janna could feel Julie trembling as she'd never done before going on stage.

'Not really.' Janna surprised herself. Having a small part helped, of course, and knowing that everything she did was simply for the roof, a straight-forward business arrangement. But that wasn't all. The fact was, she felt no different. Being in front of the camera was no more difficult than real life. As far back as she could remember she'd felt awkward and ill at ease when anyone looked directly at her – but now, at least, she was under direction, with someone else responsible for the end result of what she did. It was a strange feeling, almost comfortable. Fernand's loud-hailer would tell her instantly if she did the wrong thing. And everyone else had so much to do, so many responsibilities of their own, that she knew they barely saw her at all.

But of course, she was with Julie. She had no idea what might happen if she had to do a scene with a stranger. Hopefully, there wouldn't be any. If there were, she'd try and think about No. 3 instead.

'Once more, *mes enfants*. Action!'

They set off once more, the difference in their heights, the weight of the parasol and their odd-shaped, low-heeled shoes making progress a slow affair. Janna shot a quick sideways look at Julie. She was still beautiful, even without her blonde curls. The hair that showed under the broad-brimmed hat was now a smooth pale brown ripple, setting off her Grecian profile to perfection. Walking beside her Janna was very conscious of her own lack of grace. She'd almost forgotten how to manage a dress, especially one that flared at the hip and drew in at the ankle like this one.

'Slower, slower!' It had taken a while to get used to the fact that Fernand talked non-stop throughout the take, though no-one else was permitted so much as a clearing of the throat. Apparently all the sound would be added later, with the aid of wild tracks and a dubbing studio, where the right effects could be mixed properly. Post-production, they called it, a vitally-important stage where the film could be perfected or ruined, according to Fernand. That knowledge made Janna's role easier. All she had to do was follow orders, to the letter.

'Now! No, not both at once, Julie first this time.' Julie bent for the twentieth time, slipped off her shoes. Janna watched her. Next, the hat. With a flick of her wrist Julie sent it flying to join the gulls overhead. Janna watched it go with some concern. Already they'd ruined three hats, one in the water, one stained with tar, another with a broken brim . . .

'Good, Janna. Hold that expression . . . *ce petit air somnambuliste, c'est ravissant.*' Fernand's voice cajoled, commanded. 'Now, Janna, your turn!'

Slowly, struggling with the awkward pins, Janna took off her own hat, eased off her shoes. She placed them neatly side by side, covered them with the hat. Julie tugged at her arm.

'Now, both of you!'

Lifting their white muslin skirts to the knee they approached the edge of the waves.

'Go on – you're enjoying it!'

Obediently they paddled. The water was very cold. After so many takes Janna's feet were almost completely numb. She splashed a little, trying to restore the circulation. Julie responded in kind, showering her with water. They began to leap about in the shallows, laughing out loud. It was so pointless, so ridiculous – so cold!

'OK, that's a wrap.' Fernand's nod sent them hurrying for their coats, wet muslin clinging to their legs like a second skin. 'Hot soup in the van!'

Fernand didn't want them to see the day's rushes, but Julie managed to persuade him, pointing out that he was already making use of her own name for the leading role – Julia – not to mention her ancestral home, so he owed her something in return. Grudgingly, Fernand agreed.

'Just this once. But afterwards – no discussion!'

After she'd seen the results of the day's shoot Janna realised why Fernand had been so reluctant. Even unedited, without a sound-track, interspersed with flashes and false starts, innumerable repetitions and brandishings of the clapper-board's black-and-white jaws, what Fernand had made out of a small stretch of grimy Atlantic City beach had to be seen to be believed. That flat, grey, February light turned out to be the most flattering fabric in the world, transformed by some optical wizardry into a golden heat haze. The sand, painstakingly raked clear of beer cans and candy wrappers and cigarette stubs, looked as if it had never so much as dreamed of a human footprint. And the sea – well, the sea had movie-making in its blood, one could tell.

Julie came out of the theatre exhilarated. And why not? She'd looked beautiful this time. Fernand had done exactly what he'd promised. But for some reason Janna felt heavy-hearted, almost oppressed. Not by how she looked – though it had been clever of Fernand to dress herself and Julie alike, it helped to emphasise the difference between them – but by the image itself. The two girls in their filmy white dresses, the yellow parasol, fragile and hopeful as a rain-heavy flower, the two sets of footprints smoothed over by the tide. It troubled her, that image, reminding her of something lost or never found . . . She glanced at Fernand nervously. What were his plans for herself and Julie? What kind of film was he making? And how was it that the sight of those two girls on the sand had made her want to cry?

'Julie.' Fernand's voice was solid with satisfaction. 'You are going to be good, very, very good. And you, Janna . . .' He turned to her almost as an afterthought. 'You are going to get your roof.'

Suddenly, instinctively, Janna realised that right up to that very moment in the viewing theatre Fernand had not been completely sure. Despite everything, contracts and bookings and fittings and signings on the dotted line, they'd both been on trial, Julie and herself, until now.

Remembering how she'd felt on the beach, settled, almost at ease, safe in the knowledge that workmen had already started repairing the roof of No. 3, Janna felt a chill. Even now, it seemed, she couldn't be sure of Fernand. At any moment, if her performance didn't please him, he might change his mind. The good of the film was all he cared about, just as all she cared about was the future of No. 3. She knew then that the honeymoon was over almost before it had begun. She could never afford to feel so much at ease in front of his camera again.

But for the moment at least, Fernand was all charm. He threw an arm lightly about their shoulders.

'Pack your cases, *mesdemoiselles*. We shall be in Nice for the mimosa.'

CHAPTER ELEVEN

'*La Baie des Anges*.' A swift, guttural aside, over and despite the taxi-driver's wrinkled Gauloise. Janna looked out and was dazzled by a stained-glass sea, a promenade white as a matelot's smile. Nice was wonderful, just as Fernand had promised. Palm trees feathering an Italian garden, white columns and cypress trees, sugar-pink villas along winding roads fringed with Aleppo pine. And mimosa, mimosa everywhere, great golden clouds of it under a cotton-crisp sky.

Janna ducked her head away. So much light, so much colour, she'd never seen anything like it. There was so much beauty here, naked, brilliant. Stone, sea and sky, carved out of nothing but light.

The hotel where she and Julie were to stay was another bright, white place, with the same indefinable air of having a neatly pressed crease in its trousers and a jaunty angle to its hat, unmistakably Continental. They'd been allotted a room each, complete with sprigged and valanced counterpane, blue and white for Janna, green and white for Julie, a sheaf of white marguerites, a litre bottle of Perrier, a list of essential telephone numbers that ran to two pages, a welcoming note from Fernand, and a heavily annotated copy of the script for the next week's scenes.

Janna sat down on the bed, hardly able to believe she was actually there. It was all so strange, and new, and unreal. But becoming more real with every passing second. Real flowers, real bubbles in the Perrier, the real sound of some Frenchman revving his real Japanese motorbike in the courtyard below. In the next room she could hear Julie moving about, humming to herself as she scattered her belongings over the floor as usual. She wouldn't wonder at the marguerites and the Perrier – she'd simply take them in her stride.

Janna put down her case. She didn't feel ready to unpack, not yet. She picked up her copy of the script. Having it in her hands reassured her a little. Work at least was always the same. And she needed to acquaint herself with Julie's lines so that she could rehearse her later.

But it was difficult to make sense of what she read. The script wasn't set out like a book, with descriptions and conversations, in logical order. Even the dialogue, what there was of it, was buried amongst a lot of stage directions and technical data. It was hard to follow the story.

And yet, despite the difficulties, Janna found herself becoming interested. It was a challenge, to piece together a storyline from all these unrelated bits and pieces, rather like doing a jigsaw or working on a crossword. As she read she kept an eye out for any mention of her own character, Jeanne. She had no words to say but she should figure somewhere among the directions.

There! Janna felt a small glow of pride and pleasure. Jeanne, no mistaking it, bold black capitals. That's me, she thought. My very own part.

Wait a minute. Janna read the directions, rubbed her eyes, read them again. That couldn't be right, surely? Maybe she'd mistaken the name? No, the directions were underlined in red in her copy, specially for her. The lines seemed to dance and blur in front of her eyes. She read on in growing horror.

'Julie!' Julie must have heard the shock in her voice because she came almost instantly.

'What on earth's the matter?'

Janna gestured helplessly at the script. 'The third scene – have you read it yet?'

'No.' Julie smiled. 'I was hoping you'd give me a rough outline first. But what's wrong with it?' Her face was suddenly anxious. 'My part – has it been cut or something?'

'No, no, nothing like that.' Janna shook her head. 'Your part's not the problem at all – it's mine. I just can't do it.'

'Why not?' Clearly Julie was relieved. 'It can't be that bad, surely – you haven't got any lines to learn!'

'I know.' Janna swallowed hard. 'I only wish I had.'

It took Janna a long time to find Fernand on the back lot of the Studios de la Victorine. Even when she'd found him, it was difficult to attract his attention. He was constantly on the move, trailing a flutter of urgent questioners like a kite with an overlong tail.

'I'm sorry, Mr Kim –'

'Fernand, please.' His tone was abstracted.

'Fernand.' His first name stuck in her throat. He was going to be so angry with her when he knew.

'Yes?'

'It's Jeanne.' Janna hesitated. He seemed so busy. She couldn't be sure he was even listening. But she had to tell him now. Tomorrow would be too late. 'I just can't play her.'

'Why not?'

'I – I –' Janna felt her cheeks go red. Of course, Fernand was half French, why should he understand her reluctance? 'I don't approve.' She realised, uncomfortably, that she sounded like a maiden aunt.

'So?' Now Fernand's tone was impatient. 'Script approval is not your responsibility. Haven't you read your contract? Constructive suggestions I appreciate, but disapproval . . .' He shook his head sternly. 'It's not what I expected from you, Janna. What about your roof?'

'I know.' Janna bit her lip. How could she explain? 'It's just that – you've got the wrong person. I simply wouldn't know where to start.'

'But you've started already.' Fernand gave a little chuckle. 'What do you think you were doing in my hotel room at the Plaza?'

'That was completely different!' Indignation untied the knot in Janna's throat at last. One of the studio riggers looked up with a twinkle in his eye and she dropped her voice with an effort. 'That was work!'

'And what is Jeanne's line of business, a form of recreation?' Fernand's tone was dry. 'Don't waste my time, Janna. Jeanne – all she wants is a roof over her head, just like you and me.'

With that, Fernand was gone. Janna watched him go, despairing. He couldn't possibly suspect the depth of her

165

ignorance or he'd never have chosen her for such a part. If only there was a library book she could consult. If only she could find someone who knew.

Julie was sympathetic.

'Hmm. There's not very much you can do about it now – you've signed all the contracts. Maybe you should just – well, walk it?'

Janna shook her head. She couldn't help wishing Julie had chosen another word. But it wouldn't work, in any case. Fernand wasn't going to be satisfied by anything less than total commitment.

'What would you do, Julie, if you were me?'

Julie thought for a minute. 'What I always do, I expect – send a telegram. It usually works.'

Yes, thought Janna a little ruefully. If your address book's full of shining knights, it probably does.

'I could ask Gray?' Julie volunteered helpfully.

'No!' Janna heard her voice rise in panic just at the thought. 'Please don't.' She saw doubt in Julie's face and tried to sound firm. 'It'll be all right. I'll think of something, I'm sure.'

She went to her room and looked at her case, still packed. If only she could simply pick it up and leave, it would solve all her problems. Fernand would find another Jeanne, easily, she'd only shot one scene. But would she find another roof? Her heart sank. Monday seemed to yawn at her feet like a bottomless pit. There was no-one who could break her fall, no-one.

Unless . . . Janna lifted her head, faint hope stirring. It was a long shot, but worth a try.

'January.'

Janna spun round. There he was, hair on end and grin in place, looking as if he caught the dawn flight to Nice Côte d'Azur airport every other day of his life. She'd forgotten since she'd last seen him how solid his physical presence was. Even the early morning air seemed warmer under the influence of that open-ended Irish smile. Janna felt a ridiculous impulse to throw herself headlong into his arms, bury her face in that rumpled cotton shirt. It would smell so clean . . .

'Dion.' Janna controlled herself with an effort. 'I want you to tell me how to be a fallen woman. By Monday.'

'Now then, January.' Dion's voice was deep and soothing as he steered her gently through the airport crowd. 'Let's first of all have a touch of breakfast and talk this over sensibly, just you and me together.'

'I don't mean for real.' Janna didn't know whether to be flattered or insulted. She suspected Dion would greet both with the same philosophical smile. But just the sound of his voice made her feel better, like the thought of a warm bath after a hard day. Already, his hand at her elbow, she felt safer, paired off, cancelled out. A restful feeling. As they walked towards the exit she noticed that both men and women were looking at her differently, eyes flicking from Dion to herself and back again. She glanced sideways at him. In this chic Continental setting he stood out like a shaggy pony amongst ferociously well-groomed thoroughbreds, black yeasty beer amongst delicate table wines. Somehow he made the sky seem bluer, the mimosa woollier, shapes and textures clearer and more defined. As they emerged into the wider air Janna caught the scent of magnolia. Was it too late, she wondered with a sudden pang of homesickness almost as sharp as hunger, to plant a windowbox full of hyacinths for No. 3?

In the winding streets of the old town, between the flower market and the terraced gardens of Castle Hill, covered with aloes and umbrella pines, they found a small café which had just opened its doors, and sat down at one of the minute white tables while a postage-stamp of an awning was unrolled above them.

'Black coffee for the lady. For me, whatever you have to eat, in plenty!' Which meant crusty southern bread, with the gold of the sun in it, little foil-wrapped tablets of butter and apricot jam, and a bowl of black Provençal olives the size of small plums. Janna watched Dion eat, copiously, neatly, and was troubled by memories only for a moment. How long ago that seemed, tea by the fire, ancient history. Nothing to worry about, nothing at all. She might have known. Dion was far too interested in the taste of today's olives to remember yesterday's chestnuts.

'Now, my lady of the night . . .' Dion licked the last crumbs from his fingers, pushed away his burial mound of olive pips. 'Tell me everything.'

He listened quietly, thoroughly, didn't say a word until she'd finished. No questions, no comments, not so much as a raised eyebrow. He didn't call her a fool or a prude or a coward – he even gave her suggestion of the seafront at Marseilles weighty consideration.

'I think not, January. The waterfront is only for amateurs, casuals, and women on the way down. Too many risks.'

'Really?' Despite herself Janna was interested. There was so much to learn. 'How do you know?'

Dion smiled. 'Artists and street-women have a lot in common. Love or money, it's a choice we both have to make, sooner or later. But one thing I know for sure – you won't find the best painting on the pavement. The good ones retire early if they can. Or get married.'

'Married?'

'And why should they not?' Dion's smile broadened. 'You make marriage sound like some kind of perversion. They were babies once, just like you and me, so why shouldn't they be wives too, in the end?' Dion gave his coffee a leisurely stir. He'd added so much cream that it would have floated a spoon. French cream, too, which tasted as if it had never seen a cow. Janna didn't know how he could bear it. But then, Dion had an astonishing appetite for new experiences. 'Talking of which, there's one sitting right next to us.'

'What?' Janna swung round in amazement. 'At this hour in the morning?'

'Especially at this hour in the morning, I thought every girl knew that!' Dion's eyes were mischievous. 'But for heaven's sake, January Brown, didn't your mother tell you it's rude to stare? Anyway, you've got the wrong woman. Look at all those buttons – far too many of them, and much too small. A mere man would get dizzy just looking at them. The last thing she'd want is for him to change his mind.'

'Oh.' Janna felt discomfited. 'I didn't realise it was all so – well, technical.'

Dion sighed lugubriously. 'Nothing is easy in this modern world. But it's just so much commonsense really. I'll give you some pointers. The trick is, to see everything from the man's point of view. That means – bare legs, for instance, no tights to snag, no time wasted. Eye shadow, the more the better, especially baby blue – but not too much lipstick, men hate to come away looking like a circus clown. Such shy creatures they are, and clumsy – best give them a dress with just one fastening, easy to understand. No belts or buckles or pins, nothing sharp or hard, unless it's a heel. And never, but never a hat. Why, under one of those wide brims a man would be lucky to recognise his own mother! As for fashion, it's better to be ten years out of date rather than one step ahead – a man likes continuity. He needs to know where he stands.'

'I've got her!' Janna was positive this time. Sultry, dark, full-lipped, glowing with youth and promise, she wore black fishnet stockings and a short leather skirt. But Dion shook his head.

'Probably an ambassador's daughter straight out of convent school. Try a little to the right.'

Janna followed his eyes to a plump, jolly-looking woman with an affable smile and a gold tooth, sunning herself in a doorway and swinging one loose shoe.

'But she must be forty!' Even as Janna spoke a car drew up, the woman moved forward, whispered at the window, got in.

'But she looked so – ordinary! And, well – cheerful!'

Dion laughed out loud. 'All the better. No man wants to spend Saturday night and a large part of his hard-earned wages mopping up tears. Men like simple things – a smile, a bit of nice pink flesh, curls, a walk that wiggles. Not so difficult, surely?'

'I couldn't do it.' The horror of it struck Janna all over again. The indignity. A bit of nice pink flesh indeed. She'd rather die. 'Could you?'

'Hmm.' Dion drained the last of his coffee with a thoughtful expression. 'I see what you mean.' He pushed his cup resolutely aside. 'Yes, I think this is the moment to call in the experts. How much money have you got on you?'

'About £100'. That included all of Fernand's allowance for incidental expenses. 'And a few dollars.'

'I just hope it's enough. Good advice comes expensive nowadays.' Dion stood up, his face a comical mask of resignation. 'January Brown, the things I do for you. When will it ever end?' Shaking his head, he strode into the café.

Five minutes later they were sweeping down the coast road through eucalyptus forest and carnation fields, vineyards and olive groves. Bravely, Dion declined the temptation to take in Picasso's old studio in the disused scent factory at Vallauris, the bathing beauties on the beach at Juan-les-Pins, the subtropical gardens of Cap d'Antibes. They pressed onwards towards Cannes.

'We're not going in there, surely?' Janna was aghast as the taxi drew up outside the glittering white façade of the Carlton Hotel, overlooking the silver sands of La Croisette.

'This is the place, all right.' Dion led the way up the road-wide path between the palms and parterres set with lemon trees and magnolia. 'Look up there.'

Janna followed his eyes up the cliff-face of snowy stucco. At each end of the lofty sweep was a rounded cupola outlined against the sky.

'You can't miss them,' he said. 'They were modelled after a famous Edwardian courtesan, la Belle Otéro.'

Janna blushed and dropped her eyes. No mistaking what they were meant to be – but what kind of immortality was that? Heart sinking with every step, she followed Dion into the merciful dimness of the bar.

'Look friendly, for heaven's sake,' Dion reproved her as she perched uneasily on her stool, a fresh-squeezed orange juice freezing her fingers. By rights, considering what it cost, it should have been liquid gold. 'She's got some sort of special arrangement with the management – if we don't pass muster they'll tip her the wink and she'll leave us stranded!'

Janna did her best, but glancing sideways she saw that Dion was trying hard enough for two. She wasn't at all sure she liked the expression on his face – expectant, excited, even a little smug. And he just couldn't take his eyes off the entrance.

'Anyone would think we were meeting the Queen,' she observed a little tartly.

'We are.' Dion's eyes were alight with anticipation. 'The Queen of the Night! Party manners, please – remember, we need her a great deal more than she needs us.'

Obediently Janna sat up straight. What a time of day to be bar-hopping! It was barely 10 am. All right for Dion, with his feckless habits, but not what she was used to at all . . .

And then, swimming up out of the dimness, came the most delicious scent, pure jasmine. Exotic, lingering, so sweet and heavy she could almost touch it. A rustle of silk and there she was with them, the Queen of the Night.

A moment's silence, appraising on her part, stunned on theirs. Janna's first thought was that never in her entire life had she seen anyone, man, woman or child, so perfectly turned out at 10 o'clock in the morning. Even her accessories were accessorised. She was as intriguing and as one-dimensional as a photograph in a newly-printed magazine. And yet she was alive, no doubting it. Every last hair on her glossy red head looked as if it would be warm to the touch.

Janna's second thought, a heartbeat behind the first but even more of a revelation, was that this woman, despite her immediate impact, wasn't actually beautiful at all. Her nose was fleshy, her teeth overlarge, her shoulders too wide for her height. Without heels she might be short, even dumpy. But how her matte black dress accentuated the honey tones of her skin, the warmth of her fig-brown eyes. How bold the fact that round her perfectly turned neck she wore no jewellery at all, not so much as a gold chain. Only, in her ears, two minute seed pearls.

'*Bonjour monsieur, mademoiselle.*' A voice like an autumn leaf, a sigh of a voice. '*Je suis Liane.*'

'Liane.' Dion was the first to recover himself. In an instant he was off his stool and bowing low over the vision's apricot-tinted fingernails. 'This is indeed an honour. May I say that you are even more beautiful than I'd hoped?' Janna winced. Suddenly Dion was courtly, graceful, more French than any blue-eyed Irishman had any right to be. Surely, this time, he'd never get away with it? But the Queen of the Night inclined her head, smiled a small, secret smile.

'You may. *Merci du compliment*.' Janna bit her lip. He'd pleased her. Damn!

'*Champagne!*' Dion summoned the bartender with a lordly wave. The Queen of the Night shrugged, a liquid movement of her shoulders like a snake shedding its skin, and accepted the stool Dion proffered. She perched, like Janna, only somehow she had no trouble with the arrangement of her arms and legs. Everything fell into place, naturally, inevitably, water finding its own level. By comparison, Janna felt like a clumsy child, all bones and corners. Sitting like that might look easy, but she knew better – it was no more or less than an art form. From nowhere a little rhyme that Julie had taught her drifted into Janna's mind.

> 'Menton's dowdy,
> Monte's brass,
> Nice is rowdy,
> Cannes is class.'

And how, as Julie would say. Looking back on her own thoughts of fish-net stockings and peek-a-boo corsets Janna could only blush.

'You would like to speak English, I expect?' Liane's eyes creased, just a little, her mouth quirked upwards, revealing a little gap between her upper two front teeth. Such a gap seemed instantly the most desirable thing in the world.

'May I compliment you on your accent?' Dion again, his charm like a fourth person in the room.

'*Merci, monsieur*.' From somewhere in that honey-gold, smooth skin Liane produced a dimple. It might as well have had Dion's name written on it in letters of fire.

'Liane's English is excellent, don't you agree, Janna?'

'Oh, yes.' Janna gritted her teeth. She might have reverted to childhood, but Dion was clearly stuck fast at adolescence. Liane's eyes rested on them both, thoughtfully. 'Now then, *mes enfants*. Let us not waste any more of my time or your money. Tell me exactly what it is that you desire?'

CHAPTER TWELVE

And so it was that Janna found herself, barely ten minutes later, parading up and down a room overlooking the most elegant and sophisticated promenade in the whole of Western Europe, dressed in nothing but her underwear. Once the door was shut behind them Liane turned from siren to martinet in the blink of an eye. Briskly impersonal as a good doctor, she had Janna stripped to the essentials without so much as a word spoken. The merest gesture, a small jerk of that smoothly coiffed head, was enough.

'First lesson.' Liane's voice was stern. Janna paused, her jumper up around her ears. 'Never pull your clothes over your head when you undress. A woman with her head in her petticoats looks ridiculous, like a badly-risen soufflé. Your man wants to see your face, not your umbilicus.'

More than a little flustered, Janna couldn't help protesting.

'How on earth am I supposed to take off my jumper without pulling it over my head?' She half expected Liane to produce a pair of giant scissors.

But Liane merely smiled. 'Exactly. Therefore, no jumpers. The bedroom is not a polo field, after all.'

'I suppose not.' Uneasily Janna folded the offending garment neatly and laid it aside.

'No, no, no.' Liane was shaking her head, exasperated. 'Where is the passion, the drama? You are not a washer-woman. Let your clothes lie as they fall, as if you have lived only for this moment, as if there is nothing in your mind but the overwhelming desire to be rid of them, to be naked, for his eyes! Kick them away, if the fancy takes you. Here, I will show you what I mean.'

With one fluid movement Liane unfastened her black dress

173

and let it slip to the floor. She emerged as radiantly unconcerned as a lovely statue, seemingly just as fully clothed in her underwear as she had been in her street clothes.

And what underwear. Not girlish skin-pink, or obvious black, or garish red, but a wonderfully flattering true beige, as rich with pale lace as an Irish coffee is with cream.

'*Viens, chérie.*' There was no disobeying that command. Janna edged closer, overwhelmingly conscious of the fact that her cotton underpants had lost whatever shape they'd once had in the wash. But that didn't seem to trouble Liane half as much as the new elastic Janna had put round the waist.

'*Quel crime!*' Liane shook her head disparagingly. 'It leaves such an ugly mark on the skin, one might as well have been run over by a tractor. Everything you wear should be tailored, to fit only you – then you will have no need for such barbarities.' She smoothed her own hips with the air of an experienced schoolteacher demonstrating a simple mathematical equation. Not a wrinkle, not even a gather in sight, it was as if the glossy fabric had been grafted on. But Liane wasn't finished yet.

'What is this?' With one delicate apricot fingernail she hooked up a portion of material.

'A vest.' Janna felt her cheeks grow pink. Why should she be ashamed of her vest? It was a splendid, practical object, clean on that very day.

Liane's eyes grew round with wonderment. 'A vest – but that is a garment for *les tout petits, n'est-ce-pas*? With a little bonnet, tied under the chin, so?'

'It keeps me warm.' Janna spoke up staunchly in defence of her vest. Common sense was on her side, after all – this might be Cannes but it was still February, the evenings could be chilly. Warm underwear was a sensible insurance policy, and everyone knew the hygienic properties of pure cotton. And yet . . . why did she feel so thoroughly outmanoeuvred by Liane's lace-fringed cami-knickers, so lustrous and fine they might have been spun by spiders on the moon?

'You have men for that.' Liane slid back into her black dress with a shrug and a shimmy, leaned gracefully backwards to check her seams. 'And money.'

Janna bit her lip. This was one of those moments in life when discretion was definitely the better part of valour.

'Now, stand straight.'

Janna jerked obediently to attention. It took all she had to stand still under Liane's scrutiny, it was almost worse than a school medical. But at least there was no mockery or disapproval in those purple-brown eyes, simply straightforward, professional appraisal.

'*Zut!*' Liane permitted herself a small frown. 'You are so thin. A man might cut himself just looking at you. Where is your *brassière?*'

'I don't wear one.' Janna had never been able to bring herself to try them on before she bought them, and the ones she took home unseen never fitted properly.

'But that is a scandal!' Liane was as shocked as if Janna had proposed walking down the street stark naked. 'You may go without, but what about him? Would you offer an honoured guest fine wine straight from the bottle? Think how much better it would taste from crystal, a little Lalique . . .'

'But . . .' Janna blushed, hunching her shoulders protectively, 'I don't actually need one.'

'That is easily remedied.' Liane snapped open her snakeskin clutch bag and took out a foil-wrapped container of small yellow pills. 'I take them myself, not to improve my figure – I am fortunate in that respect – but for their other benefits. You should be able to get them from your doctor quite easily.'

'But what are they?' Janna picked up the packet gingerly.

'The contraceptive pill, *chérie.*' Liane's expression was surprised and a little concerned. 'Where have you been living all this time, in a nunnery?'

'I didn't realise . . .' Janna looked a little closer. The pills were so small, so pretty, so innocent-looking. So light in the hand. She could hardly believe they could be powerful enough to change anything. 'You mean taking these would give me –' She gestured tentatively in the region of Liane's beige lace.

'Maybe. In time. But let us not expect miracles.' Liane glanced down, clearly well-satisfied with what she saw. 'They

175

will give you enough to justify a bra, that much is certain.'

'Really?' Janna watched as Liane stowed the golden container back in her bag. It seemed wrong somehow, too easy. A sort of cheat. And yet, she was tempted. 'Are you sure it wouldn't make me fat?'

'Believe me, *chérie* –' Liane gave her that formidably French once-over. 'Nothing in this world could make you fat.' Briskly, with surgical precision, she inserted two lace-trimmed handkerchiefs down the front of Janna's despised vest, stood back to assess their effect, squinted slightly, nodded once. '*Ça ira.*' Janna quailed as that relentless gaze moved upwards to her face.

'No, you are not pretty.' A definitive pronouncement – and yet it came as a relief. Whatever else, Liane told the truth. '*Tant pis!*' A philosophical shrug. 'But then, if you were merely pretty, you would not have come to me, *n'est-ce pas*? Life would already have taught you all you needed to know. But now –' The fig-brown eyes were intent. 'Sit down here, in front of the mirror. It is time to decide upon your style.'

'My style?' It was the first time that Janna had seen herself in a mirror since that time in the Regency with Julie. She forced herself to look. It can't be as bad as it seems, she thought. Remember the video. She tried very hard to see herself impersonally, as Liane did. Liane's commentary helped.

'Good eyes.' Liane frowned in concentration. 'Did you know that one is slightly darker than the other? No, I thought not. You can accentuate that with make-up, *ce sera charmant*. But nothing too sophisticated – you are young and look younger. Not always an advantage, you must make it one. A little uncertainty, a little *élément fantaisiste*, boy/girl, woman/child . . .' Nimbly she whisked up a portion of Janna's hair, leaving the rest to trail and tickle. 'Never give him time to notice that you are not pretty. Distract him. Never be entirely still, not for so much as a minute. Make him notice your breathing, the way you cross your legs. Tuck one foot underneath you as you sit so that he can study the one that is left – your ankles are excellent.' Liane's hands moved over Janna's head, like a conjuror making magic passes. Janna tried to touch one trailing wisp of hair but her hand was smartly returned to her lap. 'No fidgeting. Never touch your face or your hair, that is for him to do.' Deftly the hands turned her head sideways on.

'Hmmm – your profile is interesting. Use it. Never let him see all of you at once. A little cinema, a little mystery . . . your hair neither completely up nor completely down, tears that never fall – high heels or bare feet, nothing in between. Provocation. You may even make him angry. You must be his city, his season, irresistible. He must say, "Whenever I am with you, I am in Paris." He must think, "This woman is all women. Only this woman will do." '

'It sounds wonderful.' Despite herself Janna let a sigh escape her. 'And impossible.'

'Why should it be?' Liane's voice held a trace of indignation. 'You should be able to attract any man.'

'Any man? Janna felt suddenly breathless. 'Any man at all?'

'But of course.' Now Liane was truly affronted. 'That is your right, as a woman.'

Janna said nothing. Was this what it felt like to be a woman, to have a mind teeming with sudden possibilities? Gray, and the roof . . . Could they both depend on something so negligible, so apparently frivolous, as the way she wore her hair? But before she could so much as frame the question Liane had moved on, ticking off items from her mental list with a practised, almost housewifely air. Clothes. Shoes. Jewellery. Accessories. Perfume. Half a lifetime's experience, distilled.

'There is one problem, of course.' Liane paused at last, permitted herself one small frown. 'Men are tediously clannish creatures. To attract one, unfortunately, one must attract them all. Getting rid of the ones you don't want is a great deal more difficult.'

I wouldn't mind that, Janna thought. It would be worth anything to have Gray look at me, just once, as I've seen him look at Julie. Round-eyed, she gazed into the mirror as if, all of a sudden, it might become her ally if not her friend. She saw

177

that her eyes had dilated, darkened. Now at last she had an insight into what it might be like to be Jeanne – to need, to want, to be willing to pay any price . . .

'Remember.' Liane was leaning back now. 'There are two kinds of woman for every man, the ones who can be bought and the ones who cannot. The second kind, of course, is much more expensive. You must be that kind if your currency is not to be devalued. You must make men work to love you, but not too hard. Men are fragile. They depend on you to lead them safely into port. You must never fail to do so. You must never even admit to yourself the possibility of failure. If – and it should never be allowed to happen – a man you have selected escapes you, you must leave him convinced that in you he has missed the greatest experience of his entire life. And you –' Liane tapped Janna smartly on the top of her head – 'You must believe that too. Not just when you are with a man, but all the time – in the bath, on the telephone, asleep . . . You are the best. Remember that. You are the best, the very best, at what you do. And now, my pigeon . . .' Liane paused, weightily. 'Before we go any further I have one very important question to ask you. I want you to think very hard before you give me your answer.'

Janna's heart sank. There would be no lying to those melting brown eyes, she knew that.

'Why?'

Janna blinked. For a moment she couldn't think what to say. She had the feeling that for some reason her answer would be the key to what followed. Should she talk of art, or invent an ambition to become an actress, or the desire to communicate, or . . .

'I need the money.' It sounded bald and very inadequate. 'For a new roof.' That was even worse. Liane stared at her for a long moment then, surprisingly, her face split into a broad, almost boyish grin.

'I approve.' Liane stood up, decisively. 'I have a farm, myself, in Normandy. Almost paid for. For when I retire, you understand. No more men. I shall wear big boots and grow apples for a living. So.' She crossed to the bureau, rested one hand on its lacquered surface. 'I shall entrust you with one more secret, the best of all. It is not something to be trifled with, but I know you will use it wisely, because you are a sensible girl, and you need it, for your roof.'

Janna watched Liane nervously. What was this astonishing woman going to offer her now?

'Watch me.' Liane's voice was crisp but a little far away. 'Your last lesson, remember it well. I will show you once, and once only. The Walk.'

Wordlessly, she turned, walked to the window and back again. Janna's eyes widened. It was extraordinary, that walk. Just so must the Little Mermaid have walked on knives of fire to win the heart of her prince. And yet what exactly was Liane doing? What equipment did she possess, that other women didn't? The same two legs, the same bony cradle of the hips, the same shoulders and arms, all put together in the same order. And yet, and yet . . . Somehow she made the air move. She held herself so straight, still as a guardsman from the shoulders up, which meant that there was nowhere else to look but the hypnotic figure of eight rotation of her hips and thighs. It was indeed a lesson, as fascinating and revealing as a film in slow motion. Liane sitting might be an art form, but Liane walking was a breach of the peace. No – more than that. A revolution.

'Now, you.'

The walk was even more difficult to do than it looked. For a start, how was it physically possible to move so slowly, without looking up or down, left or right, without overbalancing?

'How do you feel?'

'Uncomfortable.' Janna wavered, nearly fell. This was as hard as walking a tightrope without looking down. Each foot had to be swung round and placed with geometrical accuracy exactly in front of the other, making the ligaments of hip and knee sing with the strain. How on earth had Liane managed to make it look like water flowing downstream?

'That is irrelevant.' Liane was merciless. 'Men are not interested in how you feel, but in how you make them feel. Now turn.'

179

Janna obeyed. She couldn't have spoken anyway – it required all her concentration merely to stay upright.

'Good.' Liane's voice was flat, completely without emotion. 'No, don't look at me. Eyes straight ahead, like a soldier on parade. He is your commanding officer. It is up to him to look, not you. No matter how much you may want to see the effect you are having, no matter how difficult it is to pretend you haven't seen him, that this is how you walk every day, you must not catch his eye or all will be lost instantly.' Obediently Janna fixed her eyes straight ahead, unblinking, till her vision began to blur with the effort. At last, Liane took pity.

'Very well, you may look now, just once. Bend your head slightly to one side. Look slanting under your lashes. No staring, you are not a policewoman on patrol. He must think your first sight of him is a surprise, the most delightful, unexpected surprise. Good. Now count to five, slowly. No, not aloud, you are not a machine! Not bad . . . Now you may look away. No, not down, straight ahead. Don't stop walking. You want him to believe you are going somewhere interesting. You want him to follow but he must think it is all his own idea. But relax those hands – you look as if you're wringing laundry!'

Janna stopped, exhausted despite the fact that she'd only walked twice the width of a hotel room. How was she going to remember everything?

'*Alors*.' Liane glanced at her watch. 'Time's up. You know everything you need to know. Now you must practise, practise, practise.'

Stiffly, Janna began to dress.

'I will. I promise.'

'No, no.' Liane shook her head reprovingly. 'I mean now. Theory is worth nothing without a practical examination. So. You are to obtain a client, using the walk and the look, within, let us say – fifteen minutes from now. May I suggest you try first the lobby, then the bar? I will be watching you. Arrange to meet him in Room 31 – I will take care of the rest.'

'But –'

'Of course, it is up to you.' Liane shrugged. 'But in the time

I have spent with you I could have seen two clients, at least. If you do not succeed I shall have to charge you double.'

Janna swallowed hard. She felt as if every thought in her head had been turned upside down, shaken hard, and put back in a different place. Maybe that was the effect Liane had on all her clients. Like being born all over again, tugged kicking and struggling and protesting into a different world by a particularly determined midwife. As she reached the door her brain was buzzing with new impressions, startling glimpses of what life might be like if only half of what Liane had said was true.

If. Janna tried a few steps of the walk in a sheltered bend of the stairs, stumbled and nearly fell. Panic stirred as she heard the lift above whir into motion. Her examiner was already on her way down. What would happen if Janna failed her test didn't even bear thinking about. Between them, she and Dion had hardly enough cash left to pay Liane a single fee, let alone a double one. And if they defaulted?

Horrid thoughts of the Mafia – Italy was only a train ride away, and hadn't the barman seemed a little swarthy? – stiffened Janna's spine and sharpened her perceptions. A murmur of voices came from the direction of the lobby. The hotel was filling up with early evening visitors, returning guests.

'To attract one, you must attract them all . . .'

She lifted her head, fixed to her face a smile like a postcard with no return address. One deep breath, eyes straight ahead, and then the walk. As she entered she was dimly aware of heads turning, the faintest hush. Suddenly the lobby seemed all too small. She couldn't allow herself to reach the exit without snaring a client. Someone, anyone. She had one chance, and one only. Though her every instinct was to bolt and run, down the steps, between the palms, over the sands and into the sunlit safety of the sea, she must carry out her self-appointed task. Panic drummed in her ears, the air burned her lungs, the effort of taking smaller and smaller steps was so extreme it was like a physical pain. And the eyes . . . she could feel them settling on her like flies.

How much longer? Janna gritted her teeth behind her

Mona Lisa smile. Straight ahead, in the small area of anonymous space she'd reserved for her gaze, she saw Dion, leaning back in a milky white leather-covered sofa, looking rumpled, disreputable and disgracefully at his ease. A half-filled glass was at his elbow, plus a well-streaked ash-blonde with a suspect tan and one too many gold bracelets.

Janna's head lifted. How dare he? Anger rushed through her, loosening every sinew. Here she was, working harder than she'd ever done in her whole life, and all Dion could think of to help was lie back and enjoy himself. How like a man! Wasn't it his roof too? Had he seen her? She didn't care. He was welcome to his weathered blonde.

There. A ripple on the surface of the pool, a shadow glimpsed out of the corner of her eye. She'd snagged one. She hadn't expected the rush of warmth, the flare of triumph that ran through her body. It was a dizzying feeling. As if simply doing the walk had changed her into a different kind of person, someone with power of her own. She could feel every moment crackling with electricity.

The bar. With difficulty Janna brought herself back on course. She mustn't forget her instructions. She must steer him safely into port, her unknown passenger. Regally, gracefully, she glided through the tall mahogany doors. Now, at last, the look.

Oh, no! After all that walking it was a grave disappointment. In the dimness of the bar after the brightly-lit lobby she couldn't see his face. Never mind – her moment would come. Wherever she chose to lead him, he would go, she knew that now, with a bemused, incredulous certainty. It had worked, just as Liane had said it would.

With careful, eggshell elegance Janna slid sideways onto the stool. She could feel him at her side, her nameless quarry, waiting, waiting for her. She looked under her lashes.

Why, he was quite young! Janna almost forgot herself enough to stare. And even attractive. Surprise, and pleasure, and pure gratitude rendered her speechless. But the expression in his eyes was unmistakable in any language. Intense, yet impersonal. No light. Just heat.

She almost said it to him, outright, just to see. 'There's nothing under my jumper but handkerchieves.' But that wouldn't be fair. She held his eyes, two dark stars. Oh, the power . . . it flowed through and over her, a warm, honeyed wave, making her skin tingle, her hair lift.

'Room 31, in ten minutes.' He looked a little blank. Inspired now, Janna dipped her finger in the ice bowl on which floated three perfect camellias and drew a sweeping figure 31 on the polished surface of the bar. He gave a little nod, then walked away.

Janna watched him go. Now it was over she felt strange, almost – bereaved. He'd been hers, after all, just for five minutes, but now she'd given him up. Not a smile, not a sound, not a single word. Now she'd never know if he was married or single, happy or sad, clever or foolish, not even the colour of the socks he wore. She wouldn't have wanted to go to Room 31, of course not, but all the same she'd have liked to get to know him just a little better, the first man who'd ever picked her out of the crowd and wanted her, only for an hour maybe, or a day, but wanted her, really wanted her for his own.

CHAPTER THIRTEEN

'OK, you can open your eyes now.'

The make-up artist slipped Janna's protective plastic cape expertly off her shoulders. Janna tensed. This was the moment she'd been dreading, when she'd know once and for all whether all yesterday's efforts, her own and Dion's, had been worth while. She willed herself to face the mirror. Only this time she was looking, not for herself, but for Jeanne.

There, in the mirror, was a face she hardly recognised. Wide, overbright eyes glittered above twin spots of rouge, startling in the white-powdered pallor of her skin. Underneath her eyes were violet stains, beneath her cheekbones greyish hollows – but her lips were pure scarlet, one shade deeper and darker than blood.

And the dress . . . As Janna touched her soiled white fichu of guipure lace she knew that Dion had been right. What else would Jeanne wear but a turn-of-the-century hand-me-down, ten years out of date, but cosseted and patched to the last shabby aigrette plume, to pass, on a dark Riviera night, for loveliness? And remind her clients, for an evening, an hour, of the years when they were young . . .

Janna had fought hard for that dress, harder than she'd ever dreamed she could. She had to get Jeanne right in every detail, or she'd never be able to play her. She had to make her real. Fernand had been first surprised, then angry, then dismissive, but desperation had made Janna strong. In the end a frantic last-minute search by the costume girl had produced this shabby theatrical cast-off, which no-one had even bothered to have cleaned since it was last worn on stage. But it was just what she'd wanted for Jeanne. The puffed sleeves and heavily padded bustline accentuated the slenderness of her arms and shoulders. Formal, elaborate, the rose-pink and green shot silk made her look almost grotesque yet oddly charming, like an abandoned marionette. With it she was to wear a fraying straw hat trimmed with fabric roses, and carry a matching parasol trimmed with shot-silk ribbon bows.

Janna looked. In that moment, as Jeanne looked back at her, she seemed as real as the girl next door, a chance acquaintance glimpsed across a café table. Strange yet familiar, distant yet close – close as her own heartbeat.

Janna looked away. It was too close, too near, what she'd seen in that white face, too much a reflection of her own unspoken hopes and fears. And yet, perhaps, that was the secret, just as Fernand had said. Perhaps, to make Jeanne live, she must do nothing, step aside, let that inner Jeanne take over. Dangerous, difficult, the most difficult thing in the world. A sort of death. But Jeanne was there already, inside her, her mirror image, waiting only to be freed. A plain girl snatching her last chance at beauty, a guttering candle burning high and bright before it died.

'Now the hair.'

Janna waited nervously as make-up artist and stylist changed places in the cramped confines of the location caravan. Janna watched Marcus's face as he busied himself untying the knots in the silk scarf she'd wound around her head. Jeanne would approve of what she'd done to her hair, but would he?

In the mirror she saw Marcus's eyes widen. He picked up two handfuls of hair, spread it reflectively with his fingers, rubbed a few strands, looked more closely to examine it.

'What did you use?'

'Er . . .' Janna cleared her throat. 'Just something I found hanging around. A – natural product.' She paused anxiously. 'What do you think?'

'Well . . .' Marcus piled her hair on top of her head, considered it. 'It's weird – but I like it.'

Janna breathed an inward sigh of relief. She'd been bracing herself to tell him how in period it was, how someone like Jeanne wouldn't have had access to the powerful new bleaches that were sweeping through fashionable society in 1912, so she'd have been forced to resort to home remedies – but now she wouldn't have to. The contrast between the chalky pallor of her skin and that extraordinary shade of red spoke for itself. It was just what Jeanne would have chosen – eye-catching, even startling, a flame-red beacon in the dusk.

Janna had Dion to thank for that idea too. After her session with Liane she'd been fired with enthusiasm, a whole new way of looking at herself and the part. Now, somehow, she was determined to do Jeanne justice, to make her live. But there was so little time . . .

'What can I do about my hair?' Liane had set her imagination running. For Jeanne, she needed nothing less than a transformation. 'It's so – ordinary!'

'What women do, surely – go to the hairdresser?' Dion sounded a little cross. Janna suspected he hadn't liked being torn away from his blonde to pay Liane. By the time he got back the blonde had turned her attention elsewhere.

'How can I go to the hairdresser? It's Sunday!'

Dion thought, then a slow smile spread across his face.

'You should do what the Irish gypsies do.'

'What's that?' Janna was intrigued.

Dion gave her a conspiratorial look. 'I'd rather not say till we get back.'

Fortunately the hotel was almost deserted. No sign of Julie – just how fortunate that was Janna didn't realise until Dion disappeared into the bathroom with a grin, came back with a toothmug full of amber liquid.

'What have you got there?' Janna eyed the container suspiciously. The liquid smelled strong and spicy, not unpleasant exactly but – familiar.

'Dion!' Janna recoiled in shock. 'Is that what I think it is?'

'Beggars can't be choosers.' Dion grinned at her cheerfully. 'The idea is to put it on and leave it as long as you can bear it, then wash it off and there you are.'

'Oh, no!' Janna closed her eyes. 'Do I have to?'

'It won't do you any harm to try.' Dion's expression was limpid innocence. 'You like Persian carpets, don't you?'

'What's that got to do with it?'

'They're washed in it – that's what makes the wool so lustrous. And not just the human kind, either – goats, camels, donkeys, you name it, they use it. Consider yourself lucky you've got me.'

Reluctantly, Janna edged closer to the mug. 'But couldn't I use my own?'

'It wouldn't work, I'm afraid.' Dion's expression was solicitous. 'Not strong enough. One of those unfortunate cases of male superiority.' His grin took on a faintly wolfish gleam. Janna suspected he was taking a belated revenge for the blonde. 'Of course we should really boil it up a bit, concentrate the ammonia . . .'

'No, thank you very much.' Janna took the mug from him with as much dignity as she could muster. 'This will do nicely.'

It did, too. Dion leaned on the door jamb, issuing a stream of helpful directions, while Janna dunked her head then wrapped it into a steaming aromatic parcel. 'The hotter the better,' Dion advised sagely. Janna had to take his word for it. She sat down, very careful not to let the towels come undone. She'd be all right, just so long as she didn't let herself dwell too long on what exactly lay underneath. The smell you got used to. After a while. There was many a hairdresser's solution that smelt worse, after all. It was just – well, a difficult situation. Unusual, intimate. She didn't quite know how to handle it. And Dion showed no inclination to leave. He seemed to be enjoying himself.

Janna steamed in uncomfortable silence for ten minutes, then made up her mind. 'Thank you, Dion, for everything you've done. I couldn't have managed without you.' For no reason, she felt herself blushing. 'But now – well, you haven't much time before your flight home. Why don't you go sight-seeing, or something? Don't worry about me, I'll be fine now.'

'Maybe later.' Dion smiled broadly. 'I'll stand by for a little longer, just in case of – well, need?'

The expression in his eyes was so comical that in any other circumstances Janna would have laughed out loud.

It was almost a relief when, moments later, a knock sounded at the door, followed by a vigorous rattle.

'Janna!' Julie's voice, eager, impatient. 'Why have you locked your door? Listen, I want you to come with me to the Carnival this afternoon . . . Come on, I know you're in there!'

Janna looked doubtfully from Dion to the door and back again. It was an awkward situation. She didn't really want to explain herself and what she was doing, not right now, with Dion actually here in the room.

'I can't, Julie . . .' She reached up one hand gingerly to her towelling turban. 'I'm washing my hair!'

'Don't give me that, Janna.' Julie rattled the door again, sounding injured. 'It'll dry in minutes in this sunshine, you know that. Come on! I haven't got forever.' Her tone was suddenly plaintive. 'I can't go on my own, really, I'll get pinched to death . . . You know what these Frenchmen are like . . .'

Janna hesitated, looked a little desperately at Dion. He said nothing, simply winked, and gestured at the bathroom door. Leave this to me, his expression said. Feeling deeply relieved, Janna retreated. Dion would deal with it. Dion would sort it out.

He did, too. Muffled voices at the door, then receding down the corridor. Janna listened for Dion's returning steps, but they didn't come. She ran to the bathroom window overlooking the courtyard, looked out. There, walking side by side down the path leading to the road, were Dion and Julie, deep in conversation.

It came as a shock. She'd thought Dion was simply going to explain to Julie, make some excuse, not volunteer himself as an escort. And yet why was she so surprised? She'd wanted him to go – she'd made that quite clear. And what man in the world wouldn't want to accompany Julie to a carnival?

Janna didn't get much sleep that night. It was uncomfortable in the towel, but that wasn't all. She kept listening for some sign of life next door to show that Julie had come home. She had lines to learn for tomorrow, after all. But she heard nothing. In the end she couldn't even listen any more. She put her head under the pillow and held fast the one consoling thought of Dion's booked return flight home.

In the morning Janna felt a little better, especially after she'd washed her hair. It was changed beyond recognition, full and smooth and lustrous, the colour lifted to an amazing golden red, like a courtesan from a Titian painting. She wrapped a scarf round her head and went to knock on Julie's door. She'd need waking if she was to get to the set on time.

'Mmm?' From past experience Janna knew that meant 'Come in'. She put her head round the door, a little uncertain. Normally she would have gone in without hesitation, but today was different. Julie was still in bed. As usual her clothes from the night before were scattered over the floor. Janna picked them up, automatically, and hung them over the back of a chair.

'Hi.' Julie yawned and stretched luxuriously. 'What time is it?' Janna looked at her watch. Now all the clothes were tidied up she wasn't sure what to do with her hands. For the first time in Julie's presence she felt a hint of constraint. She cleared her throat, trying hard to behave as if everything was just as normal.

'It's late.' It was always best not to tell Julie the exact time, because she tended to underestimate how long it took her to get dressed. 'I think you'd better get up.'

'Oh, there's no hurry.' Julie smiled. 'They'll be late starting this morning. It's the first day.' She sounded as if she'd been making films all her life.

'But what about your lines? I didn't get a chance to rehearse you.' Yesterday evening. When you went out with Dion. The unspoken words seemed to hang in the air between them.

'Don't worry.' Julie ran her fingers through her hair, stretched again, easy and graceful as a cat. 'I know them already. It's the same scene as the audition, remember?'

Janna blushed. Of course. She'd forgotten. There'd been no need for Julie to come back early at all. Only wishful thinking, on her part.

'Did you . . .' Janna hadn't meant to ask any questions, but somehow she couldn't help it. 'Did you enjoy the Carnival?'

'Mmm.' Julie smiled. 'You should have come, Janna, really you should. Brass bands, confetti, dancing in the streets . . .' Janna waited, anxiously, for Julie to say more, but that was all. Julie wasn't a great one for describing things.

189

'Did – er – did Dion catch his plane all right?' Janna hoped Julie wouldn't notice anything strange about her voice. I have to know, she thought, because of Dion's plumbing. I've got a deadline to work to. I can't have Julie putting him off.

Julie blinked. 'I've no idea.' She smiled her vague, whipped-cream smile. 'It was pretty late by the time he left. Which reminds me.' She sat up slowly, reached for the bedside table, picked up a toothmug. 'Oh, dear.' She frowned down at it. 'I guess I forgot to put them in water. I was so tired when I got in . . . But, anyway . . .' She held out the glass. 'These are from Dion. For you.'

'Oh.' Janna looked at the extraordinary objects in the tooth-mug with misgiving. Was this one of Dion's jokes? They could have been carrot tops, seaweed, almost anything. 'What are they?'

'Carnations. From the carnival. Dyed green, specially.' Julie leaned over, patted the drooping heads, tried to make them stand upright, failed, gave a rueful shrug. 'Don't you like them? We were so sure you would.'

We. Such a small word, so casual, and yet a chill ran over Janna's skin. She saw a sudden image of Julie and Dion together at the Carnival, laughing, talking . . . They would have enjoyed it, she knew. They both had that gift. Suddenly she wished she'd run after them, wet hair, towel and all. But it wouldn't have been the same if she'd gone too. She'd have been out of place in the noisy crowd, like a child at a grown-up's party, wishing she'd never come.

'He's nice, your lodger.' Julie looked thoughtful. 'How did you happen to meet him?'

'I didn't, exactly.' Janna wasn't sure what to say. 'He – came with the house.'

'Really?' Julie's voice warmed with interest. 'Sort of built-in, as it were? All mod. cons.?'

'You could say that.' Janna looked away. For some reason she didn't feel like explaining, as if somewhere between think-ing and speaking the truth might end up twisted into some-thing else entirely. There was an awkward silence. Janna picked out one withered blossom from the toothmug, sniffed it.

The petals were rough and dry, there was no scent. Green carnations. Irish green. Dion would have liked that.

And then, because she didn't want to think any more, because she wanted it all to be over, cut and dried like the carnations, she said it. 'He always wanted to meet you, you know.' Once she'd begun it was easier. 'He used to look at you in the basement, he told me so. "The beautiful girl in the basement", that's what he called you.'

Julie laughed. Clearly she was pleased. The atmosphere between them lightened momentarily. Janna was glad of that, glad, too, that she'd said what she had, faced facts. The truth at least held a measure of safety.

All the same, it was a relief to get to the set and enter Jeanne's unreal but immediate world. There at least she knew how she was supposed to feel – what she was supposed to do. It gave her pleasure to hear Marcus humming happily to himself as he swept her hair into a full, soft mass over cunningly hidden pads, with a twist on top of her head and kiss-curls over her forehead. Probably he wouldn't be quite so pleased with the colour if he knew what caused it. But then she herself might never feel quite the same about Julie's Shiraz.

Marcus pushed in one last ebony-headed pin and settled the straw hat on her head with the utmost care. Janna was now complete. No, not Janna, Jeanne. That sad little white face under the summery hat could belong to no-one else.

Janna stood, feeling the creak of whalebone. Her waist was tightly cinched into the right *fin-de-siècle* S-bend. She hoped she'd still be able to do the walk. At the moment it seemed difficult even to draw her breath. Julie would be luckier. Playing a lady, she was allowed to wear the much looser, freer fashions of 1911.

Very carefully, because of her kid laced boots with their bows and tassels, and the wide ruffled hem of her ankle-length skirt, Janna went down the trailer steps. A familiar sight met her eyes – the immaculate wide promenade of the Boulevard de la Croisette. It was ironic that she should have been here with Dion only yesterday. She pushed the thought away. She needed all her concentration, for Jeanne.

'Time for your lighting check, Miss Brown.' A production assistant led her to her mark. Janna felt her heart flutter against the whalebone. No matter how many times she'd rehearsed this scene, blocking it out step by step under Fernand's eagle eye till she knew it by heart, every position, every movement, she wouldn't feel safe until it was over. It was an important scene, introducing Jeanne, Julia and Eden, the three elements of Fernand's eternal triangle, almost simultaneously. That was why, just as Julie had predicted, the shooting schedule was already running late. They'd had to wait for Julie's male co-star to fly in that afternoon. Janna wondered for a moment what he would be like. Many different actors, famous and unknown, had been suggested for the part, and as usual Fernand had kept his final decision secret to the last minute. Only Lisa, the make-up girl, had seen him so far; all she could say, with a faraway look in her eyes, was that he was very good-looking.

Quickly Janna ran over the forthcoming scene in her own mind. On the surface it was simple, a case of mistaken identity. Jeanne, half starved and desperate, accosts Julia, taking her for a young buck about town in her fancy-dress disguise. But it was all a question of timing. Janna had to remember exactly when to pause, when to turn, to synchronise her movements with the arrival of the white Hispano-Suiza outside the gates of the Casino. That meant counting paces, measuring them against the distance between lampposts, keeping one eye on Fernand, listening for his instructions and all the while remembering to do the walk. It was very complicated, especially now, with her costume and parasol.

A final shout, the whip-crack of the clapperboard. Janna's mouth went dry. Fernand had said he wanted this scene done in a single take, she didn't know why. Perhaps because they were running late? But in any case, it was too late for speculation. Lights blazed, a cruel high noon despite the fact that this was a night scene. From beyond the wall of light came a silence deeper than death. Janna stood frozen, rooted to the spot. It was as if the air had turned to stone. Then Fernand's voice at last. 'Cue rain!'

A sudden shower of droplets descended on the bare skin of

Janna's neck and wrists, shocking her out of immobility. Automatically she lifted her parasol for some protection. There'd been no mention of rain in the script, at least not in her copy. Now, too late, she realised why the ground under her feet seemed so damp. She'd assumed it had been sprayed with water for some technical reason, perhaps to keep down the dust.

The rain fell, heavier now, weighting the ruffles of her skirt, forming puddles underfoot. Her parasol was getting heavy, soaked. As Janna stared into the camera for Fernand's count of five the breeze from the sea blew rain straight into her face, bringing tears to her eyes. She could feel powder running on her cheeks, damp strands of hair clinging to the back of her neck. Then, because she had to, she walked. Small steps, little frozen halts, sidelong glances. A little play with the parasol, a futile attempt to lift her muddied hem from the ground, then on, on, hunted by the second camera on its silent rails. Seven more paces and the long white Hispano-Suiza swept up behind her, spraying black water from the gutter in a tidal wave.

'Smile, Janna!'

Janna did her best. Through the curtain of the rain she saw Julie get out of the car, tall and elegant in her fancy dress costume of top hat and tails. She'd added a small blond moustache and looked as if she might be Gray's younger brother. Suddenly Janna realised why Fernand needed this scene shot in one take. Soon Julie would be as wet through as she was herself. Urgency made Janna's vision suddenly crystal clear. Everyone, from the youngest clapper-boy to Julie's co-star, now standing quietly beside the car with the relaxed elegance of a born actor, depended on her. She had to get it right. It seemed to take all the energy she had left to smile at Julie, haughtily, as Jeanne would have done. Water dripped from her parasol edge onto her bare neck and she shivered. Her heart thundered, her hands shook. She lowered her lashes as Liane had taught her, looked from one to the other, sidelong, her eyes lingering on Julie. She flirted with her parasol, paused a moment, then walked on, luring her with her eyes, her small uncertain steps.

'Cut!' The lights shut down. The rain ceased, magically. Fernand strode forward, his face wreathed in smiles. 'Good.

That's a print.' He turned to Janna. 'If I had told you in advance, *ma petite*, we would never have got it in one take. And I did not want you to catch your death of cold.'

Janna furled her parasol with relief. Rain or no rain, she knew that if Fernand hadn't been satisfied with her scene he'd have made her do it all again. Quickly she unpinned her wide-brimmed straw. It was so wet that it was still dripping.

'Hey, Janna!' Julie was smiling at her. 'I like your hair . . .' Janna blushed. She was only too conscious of how she must look, with her kiss-curls plastered in rat-tails on her forehead, her make-up streaked, rain-darkened fabric clinging to every inch of her body, weighting her down so thoroughly that she could barely move. But it didn't matter now – nothing mattered. She felt herself smile in return, a smile of pure joy and relief. The scene was over, the one she'd dreaded. She'd ruined her shoes, snagged her lace petticoat on the fourth lamp-post, nearly forgotten which hand she was supposed to use for the parasol, but all that was over now. She'd survived. With Liane's help, and Dion's, Jeanne had come to life for her at last. Even now the scene was over Janna felt something of her still in her movements, in the way she held her head as she risked a quick look at Julie's co-star. He hadn't said anything so far, but then, he didn't need to. He looked magnificent, tall and broad-shouldered in his gold brocade and pleated turban. He wore the luxurious caftan with the ease and arrogance of a Mogul prince. His disguise extended to the brown-stained skin and the golden hoops in his ears.

'Good afternoon, Janna.'

Janna froze. It was impossible. But that voice – she would recognise it anywhere. Now the Mogul prince was smiling at her, with Julie's eyes. The world spun. 'Gray!'

CHAPTER FOURTEEN

'But all the same – fainting!' Julie reached forward and helped herself to a handful of Muscadet grapes from the fruit basket Fernand had had delivered to Janna's room.

'I know.' Janna bit her lip. She'd never fainted in her life before. 'I think it was the corset – it was a bit too tight.' She hated lying to Julie, but didn't know what else she could do.

'Ah.' Julie nodded knowledgeably as she crunched the grape pips whole. 'Vanity – it always gets you in the end.'

Janna nodded, remembering. It was her vanity that had been hurt most of all. Why couldn't Gray have seen her before the rain? At least then there'd been something almost impressive about Jeanne, nothing to be ashamed of. But hatless, dripping, streaked with powder and eye-black – she'd seen how she must look from the expression in Gray's eyes.

'Did you know, Julie?' Janna cleared her throat with difficulty. 'About Gray playing Eden, I mean?'

'Only yesterday.' Julie smiled. 'It was kind of a last minute thing. I was going to tell you, but first there was the Carnival, and then this morning I was so tired – I completely forgot.'

'But . . .' Even now Janna could hardly believe it. It seemed like a nightmare. How was she ever going to complete her work on the film with Gray standing by? She'd never be able to concentrate. She'd never be able to lose herself in Jeanne. Even if Gray wasn't there she'd be thinking of him constantly, expecting to see him at any moment, round any corner. And when she did . . . Every time that happened her heart seemed to come loose inside her body. She forgot everything, who she was, what she was supposed to be doing. Her face burned. Her hands went icy cold. Half of her longed for him to look at her, the other half longed with equal violence to run away. It was an

195

impossible situation. She didn't know how she was going to survive it without being torn in two. 'How did it happen?'

'Well, it's obvious, isn't it?' Julie shrugged. 'Fernand went to check out Dene, of course, and after one look at Gray – well, who can blame him? Gray's so terribly goodlooking.'

'Yes.' Janna swallowed. Even with his skin stained brown and his hair hidden in a turban Gray had a presence, an imperturbable, masculine confidence, that shone through every move, every gesture. 'But how on earth did Fernand manage to persuade him?'

'You don't know Gray!' Julie laughed. 'Dressing up, charades, he loves all that sort of thing. There's not much else to do in the country. He'd have –' Julie broke off in mid-sentence as her gaze fell on the big bouquet of tuberoses overflowing Janna's dressing-table. 'Those are pretty.'

'Aren't they?' Janna felt herself blush. 'Gray sent them.' It had been kind of him to send her roses. He must have felt sorry for her. He'd probably guessed, by this time, how she felt about him. Knowing that, she could hardly bear the sight of his roses. Yet how could she get rid of them? If she did, Julie would know too.

'Mmm.' Julie bent to sniff the china-pink petals. 'Heavenly.' She glanced at her watch. 'Which reminds me, I must rush. Gray's taking me to lunch at Cap d'Antibes. Hope you're feeling better tomorrow, in case . . .' Julie paused with unaccustomed delicacy. 'Well, in case you're asleep when I get back.'

Janna leaned back against the pillows. Julie's kindness only made her feel worse. It was clear that she didn't intend to return home tonight.

When Julie had gone, Janna's eyes fell on Fernand's basket of perfect fruit. Somewhere between her head and her heart was a small, hard knot of pain. What was it, nausea, hunger? A sort of emptiness . . .

It was then, lying between the flowers and the grapes, that Janna knew she couldn't go on a moment longer. There was no use fighting any more. She threw back the covers and reached for her clothes.

*   *   *

The telephone. Janna struggled up from sleep.

'Hello?'

'Hey, Janna!' Julie's voice. 'I'm glad I caught you in time. You're on, this afternoon.'

'What?' Janna's mouth felt swollen, as if it was full of earth. Knowledge of what she'd done last night weighed on her like a crime. It had been so long, she'd forgotten what it felt like. How much, how many? She'd eaten and eaten until she could eat no more. And then, after she'd hit that pitch of reckless, self-destructive passion, half anger, half despair, she'd gone on eating. Ice cream, it was always possible to get that down, chocolate bars . . .

'Yes. We've switched scenes, something to do with the light. We're up at Cap Ferrat today. Fernand's sending a car.' Julie paused, with that new, uncomfortable tact. 'I thought I'd better call, just in case.'

'Thank you.' It sounded cold, formal. Janna bit her lip. She didn't want to feel grateful to Julie any more. Did that mean she was a horrible person? Yes. Looking at herself in the mirror, between Gray's tuberoses, she saw herself as she really was. Pale, swollen, ugly. Janna closed her eyes in shame.

Down in the courtyard a car horn sounded, authoritative. Janna dressed hurriedly, cinching her trouser belt so tight it cut into her skin. Why had she done it? Why did she ever do it? That first taste of sweetness – it was never the same again. And yet she never learned.

As the car bowled away down the Lower Corniche towards the narrow promontory of St Jean–Cap Ferrat, the kingfisher sky accused her. So clear, so fresh, the smell of pine and salt, the sunlit air. Up here the light was too bright, the colours too perfect. That blue – it promised too much, far more than five miles of atmosphere. Janna could almost smell crushed thyme and marjoram, knew the burnt sienna earth would be warm as human skin. But that warmth couldn't reach her, cold and alone in the back of the car.

At least lunch was over by the time she reached the set. As soon as Lisa spotted her she was hurried away to the safety of the trailer.

'Are you better now?' Lisa's voice was solicitous. 'You're still a bit pale. Never mind, it's in period.' She hovered over her palette. 'It's the crowd scene today. I've got to get everyone matching.'

Janna nodded. She couldn't do more. She felt so – heavy, defeated. She'd thought she was better too. 'Do you mind if I close my eyes?' If only she could fall asleep for a hundred years, wake to find every temptation gone.

'Go ahead.' Lisa's voice was preoccupied. 'This will take a while.' It was soothing to be just an object, a surface, stroked and patted by little brushes. Halfway through Marcus came in and set her hair in pincurls. Then, there was an important-sounding knock at the door. Janna froze. Who could it be, Julie, Gray?

'Do you think that's it?' Marcus's voice.

'Must be.' Lisa's voice, excited. 'You go and see.'

Janna relaxed a little. She heard murmurs and important rustlings, the click of a catch, then a long silence broken by one slow indrawn breath.

'I've never seen one, not for real.' Marcus's voice again, wistful. Janna felt a faint flicker of curiosity. What could it be? Something studded with twenty carat diamonds at least, from the sound of it. But she'd never been interested in precious stones, unless they were part of No. 3. Oh, if only she was back home right now, raking out old plaster, mixing paint . . .

Suddenly her chair was swung round, a long light box laid carefully across her knees.

'Go on!' Janna opened her eyes to see Lisa and Marcus's excited faces watching her. 'Have a look!'

For a moment Janna wasn't sure exactly what it was that lay inside the black velvet-lined box. Twisted into a loose spiral roll it seemed to glisten and pulse with a life of its own, like some strange umbilical cord. Very gently, Janna lifted it, and it unfurled at a touch, a long liquid slither of shining silk, wrinkled and slippery as a newborn baby. Janna had never seen silk like that in her whole life. It seemed to move and breathe.

But before she could take a closer look it was whisked away.

Lisa wrapped a chiffon scarf round her newly-made-up face and pin-curled head.

'Face to the wall, Marcus!'

The towel dropped away from Janna's shoulders and she felt the silk shiver down on her skin like night air. Marcus busied himself with her hair, unpinning, but instead of brushing out her curls as she'd expected, he ran his fingers lightly through them and a rich, exotic smell filled the small space of the trailer.

'What's that?'

'Pomade. Don't worry, it's –'

'– in period, I know.'

'There.' Two pairs of eager hands pulled and patted her round to face the mirror.

And then there was nothing left to say or do or think. And no need. What was she, that girl in the mirror? A high priestess, a sorceress, the lady of the oracle? The silk clung like running water to the outline of her body, pooled at her feet in an iridescent sea. She was treasure trove five fathoms deep, in a dark net the glimpse of mermaid's scales. Bronze, copper, gold – butterfly dust, ore in a mineshaft, tiger's eyes. Slave, empress, figurine . . . Above the Grecian neckline, edged with bronze Venetian beads, her skin was purest mother-of-pearl.

'What is it?' Janna moved, tentatively. The dress moved with her, a shimmer of light on water kissed by a dragonfly. The web of pleats was a second skin, utterly seamless, light as air. It was like wearing sunset.

'A Fortuny Delphos.' Satisfaction and awe beyond envy were in Lisa's voice. 'You could wear it anywhere.'

It was true. Such a dress was its own law, outside time. Eternal. Wearing it, each woman would be herself, and more than herself. A dream, a vision, a legend. Janna searched her own reflection for traces of the girl she thought she knew, and found none. For the first time in her life she was tall, like a candle or a pillar, and graceful. The minute pleats softened every angle yet accentuated her slimness, the breathtaking hollows beneath her collarbone, the bone-white narrowness of shoulder and wrist. Her neck seemed almost too fragile to carry that crop of thick, close curls, penny-red, threaded through by a single gold-kid band. Half boy, yet all woman, she stood poised on the steps of a temple, her eyes the only darkness in her white face, serious and a little afraid.

Time to go. In silence Janna turned away from the stranger in the mirror. She felt numb, almost stunned. And yet – she could feel the power in the room, nudging into her hand like a great golden cat, unsolicited yet impossible to deny. The tickle of its whiskers, its warm breath, its deep, commanding purr . . . Would she come away unscathed?

Walking with a lion. Janna felt the beast at her heels as she emerged into the perfumed air. It was only then that she realised that she'd left behind her copy of the script.

But nothing set down on paper in mere black and white could have prepared her for the sight of the Villa Ephrussi de Rothschild, perched like a reckless butterfly high on its rocky platform overlooking the dancing waters of the gulf. In a dream Janna followed the production assistant through the Baroness's garden, past cypresses and lily ponds, the Temple of Venus with its panoramic view across the Bay of Villefranche to Mount Boron, magnolia and eucalyptus trees with sly faun's heads peeping between the waxy leaves. A jewel of a place, emerald set in sapphire, with below, in what had once been the private harbour of the Dukes of Savoy, a scattering of white-sailed yachts like so many seed pearls.

Through the hanging garden and under the mulberry trees Janna walked in crystal air. The shade of the villa's wide Italianate verandah welcomed her into another world, a sultan's vision of paradise. Round an improvised courtyard, where hookahs bubbled and a rainbow-tinted fountain played, milled a kaleidoscopic crowd, trailing the gilded silks and flaming parrot colours of a Persian bazaar, sherbert lime and sugar pink, acid turquoise and minted green, Bakst blue and brilliant tangerine. Ostrich plumes and gold lamé, cummerbunds and turbans, curled toe slippers and wired tunic hems, all the Oriental exotica inspired by Diaghilev's Ballet Russe that had dazzled Paris in the last peacock years before the war. Under striped and tasselled awnings sweetmeat-sellers held trays strewn with tiny pastries, pistachios, Turkish delight, while across the Persian carpets pink ibis strolled, and slave-girls, half-naked under golden-gauze harem pantaloons, reclined on silken cushions, toying with tiny marmosets on jewelled chains.

'*C'est bien, n'est-ce pas?*' Fernand welcomed Janna. His simple cream jacket, amongst all that magnificence, looked very modern, almost alien. 'I would have liked incense, but they feared for the Della Robbias.'

As Janna followed him through the multi-coloured crowd she felt almost as conspicuous as Fernand. Surely her Fortuny, so simple, so ageless in its elegance, its restrained classic lines, had no place in this gathering? A thrill of unease ran through her as Fernand pointed to a tall enclosure suspended from an overhead gantry by three slender chains.

'You want me to go in there?'

The giant gilded cage swung gently as if it had heard her.

'Of course, *ma petite.*' Fernand smiled. 'You are to make an entrance *par excellence.*'

Janna felt a chill of dismay. 'But I thought I was – an extra? Just one of the crowd?'

'An extra?' Fernand looked horrified. 'In a Fortuny Delphos? Absolutely not!'

'Then I'm Jeanne?' Janna felt utterly confused. She glanced down at herself. Nothing could have been further removed from her shabby guipure lace on the Boulevard de la Croisette. 'But what's happened to me, in between?'

'Is it not obvious?' Fernand ran his hand impatiently through his hair, making himself look like a fledgeling blackbird. 'A transformation, from street-girl to lady, from chrysalis to butterfly.'

'Yes, but . . .' Janna steeled herself. She knew Fernand hated to reveal plot and motivation, but she had to know more. Poor Jeanne had no-one else to speak for her. 'Why?'

Fernand sighed. 'So distrustful, you amateurs. Very well, then. Julia, to tease Eden, her fiancé, has decided to dress Jeanne in her own clothes and pass her off as a Russian countess at the Thousand-and-One-Nights Ball.' Fernand turned to go. Janna only just managed to catch him by his cream linen sleeve.

'Yes, I see.' She swallowed. 'But why?'

Fernand looked surprised to be asked. 'Because she is a woman, of course. She wants to test Eden, to see if what he says about the difference between a street-woman and a lady like herself is really true. Like all women, she is not content with the simple knowledge that Eden loves her. She wants to know how much, exactly. Ah, poor Julia.' Fernand paused reflectively.

'Why?' Janna didn't dare let go of his sleeve.

'Because, of course, Julia's plan works too well. Eden is intrigued by Jeanne, almost tempted, even after Julia has done her best to give him clues. "Look," she says, wishing she'd never begun the masquerade, "the countess is wearing a Fortuny just like mine." But Eden is blind, as all men are blind. All he sees is the woman, not her clothes. "Surely not," he says. "It looks completely different." And so, pride forces Julia to play out her charade to the end, to test her lover to the limit and beyond.'

Janna listened, fascinated. She was beginning to realise why Fernand had such a reputation as a director of women.

'So what do you want me to do, in this scene?'

Almost as soon as she'd said the words Janna knew what Fernand's answer would be.

'Nothing. You simply – exist. A pawn in someone else's game, a bird in a gilded cage. Bait for the tiger.'

With a last enigmatic smile Fernand disappeared into the crowd. An assistant ushered Janna into the golden cage and fastened the door behind her.

'Hold onto the bars now, you're going up.'

The cage lifted, rocking under her feet. As Janna looked down at the festivities beneath she felt as if she was in a dream, floating, flying. Even the air up here was warmer, because of the banks of massed lights. She steadied herself against the bars. She had to be careful not to unbalance the cage.

Janna's heart missed a beat as she caught sight of Gray's golden turban, Julie by his side. She couldn't see his face, but that made no difference. It was as if he'd reached out and touched her, as if he was with her, inside the cage. Suddenly all her boundaries were melting, her skin on fire with awareness. Yes, Gray was there with her, under her skin. She was carrying him inside her like a smuggler with a cache of stolen diamonds.

Janna felt her cheeks burn under the powder. For a moment she wished she was still wearing the guipure lace with its wasp-waist corseting. In the Fortuny's spider silk, he'd be able to see every beat of her heart.

The cage trembled, swung, recalling Janna to herself. She must concentrate, not on her own feelings, but on becoming a Russian countess. But how could she? She had no more idea of how a countess might behave than Jeanne herself would have done. And that, she thought suddenly, with a chill of revelation, is why Fernand chose me.

Then, at last, she was on her way, swinging slowly down like a great bell, in a tremendous silence. No-one moved. No-one so much as breathed. What did they expect, a vision, an apparition, a Della Robbia Venus come to life? Janna drew herself up to meet that battery of unblinking eyes. She was cold now, every ounce of hope and courage drained from her body, leaving it a shell. The golden cage touched marble, sound-lessly. A negro page in scarlet-and-gold livery stepped forward to release the catch. Slowly, achingly conscious of the need not to snag her priceless silk, Janna stepped out. She felt utterly lost in that motley crowd, all faceless eyes. Where to turn, what to do? Fernand was unaccountably silent. Stiffly, a compass needle searching for its pole, Janna turned to find herself look-ing straight at Gray. Her heart jolted, every red hair on her head seemed to stand out in electric awareness while the rest of her body stayed frozen, motionless. She held his gaze for a second, a century, then dropped her eyes as if the air between them burned. Hardly breathing, concentrating her whole energy on the effort to stay upright, not to shiver into a million pieces, she walked past him. Julie, her face serious, almost sardonic, under her gleaming top hat, waited. Their eyes met, a long, silent look.

'Cut!'

The tableau melted away like frost in morning sunshine. Around Janna the technicians lost their tense, motionless posi-tions, began to smile and talk. But Janna couldn't relax. If anything she felt more tension now the lights were off and the camera had stopped running. Every movement, every breath she took felt enormous, thunderous. She was achingly conscious of the bare skin on the back of her neck, the tiny hairs on her upper arms, the involuntary muscles of her lips. She could feel Gray staring at her, with a surprised, thoughtful expression, as if he'd never seen her before. Perhaps it was the Fortuny? Gray's eyes seemed to surround her, cutting her off from the normal world. It was as if she were standing on top of a snow-capped mountain on a clear day with nothing to focus on but blue, blue sky. Heady, exhilarating, rarefied. And precarious, she felt that too. The merest breath of air might push her over the brink and down the mountainside. She hardly dared move in case she broke the spell.

But Fernand broke it for her.

'Lisa? Get that Fortuny back where it belongs, now. And don't forget the docket. Julie – the studio bus leaves in twenty minutes. I want you on it, please, for the scene in the hotel corridor. Gray – your next scene is scheduled for Friday, but please call in to check tomorrow morning. And you have a costume fitting. Fix a time with Lisa, please.'

With difficulty Janna managed to attract Fernand's attention.

'What about me?'

'You, Janna?' Fernand's tone was vaguely reproving. 'Have you not consulted the call-sheet? This is your last location scene here – you've been booked on the 9 pm flight. You have nine weeks' holiday when you get back but, please, keep yourself available, just in case. And no sitting in the sun – a tan would not be –'

'I know, in period.' Suddenly Janna's heart felt like lead. Back there, just for an instant, in this enchantment of a dress, she'd felt like someone else, a woman who made things happen, whose dreams took wing.

'A pity.' Gray's voice, light and lazy, echoing her own feelings exactly. 'I was going to ask you to have dinner with me.'

'Oh.' Janna had forgotten how beautifully he spoke. No wonder Fernand had snapped him up for Eden. His eyes were resting on her with that same expression, appraising, intrigued, as if he were seeing her for the first time. She could feel herself changing even as he looked at her, unfurling like a flower in the sun.

'But Janna doesn't eat dinner.' Julie answered for her, an odd note in her voice, almost challenging. Janna sensed the tension in the air. Only Gray appeared unconcerned.

'We could make it lunch.' His eyes crinkled at the corners, making him look much younger. 'A very late, late lunch? I know just the place.'

Janna hesitated. It was obvious what her answer should be. Gray was only asking her to provoke Julie, as one more skirmish in the power struggle between them. And yet, even though she had a multitude of excuses ready to hand – tiredness, lack of appetite, a plane to catch – Janna heard herself say quite clearly, with only the faintest tremor in her voice, 'Yes, I'd love to.'

Even with the words out and hanging in the air Janna could still hardly believe she'd said them. It must have been Jeanne who'd spoken out so brazenly, or her fictional Russian countess. And yet, wearing that Fortuny, she couldn't bring herself to take them back, any more than she could have deliberately drawn curtains on a sunset. This was too glorious a chance to miss, it would never come again.

From that moment, everything seemed to happen very fast. Gray had a way of getting what he wanted without seeming to exert any effort at all. He insisted that Janna should be allowed to wear the Fortuny. When Lisa demurred, he countered all her objections with a smile.

'But a Fortuny is virtually indestructible. I thought everyone knew that.'

Whether it was the smile or the hint of aristocratic hauteur in Gray's voice that persuaded Lisa, Janna didn't know. In any case, as Gray pointed out, almost as an afterthought, if the Fortuny wasn't back in its velvet-lined box by the stroke of 9 pm, he personally would guarantee not only the hiring fee but the entire cost of its replacement. From the look on Gray's face as he said that Janna could tell that he was enjoying himself. This was a novelty for him, an escapade. Janna wished Julie could have been there to see that for herself. Then, surely, she would have understood. Gray's invitation meant nothing, it was just another charade for him, a pleasant way of passing the time.

Even so, as Janna waited, half frightened, half exhilarated, in the Baroness's neo-classical garden she hardly expected Gray to return. He'd think better of it, change his mind, make some graceful excuse. She'd end up back in her hotel room where she belonged, in her little box, like the Fortuny . . .

But Gray came back, and far from empty-handed. Somehow he'd managed to persuade Lisa to surrender the exquisite silk-velvet cape designed to accompany the Fortuny, a glorious swirl of molten bronze and gold, mellowed by the years into a sumptuous chiaroscuro.

'In case you feel a little cold, later.' Gray smiled that enigmatic smile, and Janna wondered how it was possible to shiver and burn at the same time.

Gray had his own car, a pale blue Mercedes that floated up the rocky incline of the Grande Corniche, overlooking the hanging gardens and pastel villas of the bay, as if it were so much thistledown. Janna had no idea where they might be going, and couldn't bring herself to ask. She wanted to make the most of her borrowed finery, stolen time. She was riding on a magic carpet. The normal rules didn't apply.

And it was so beautiful, beauty so generous, so perfectly in tune with her own state of mind that the rose-red hills themselves seemed to be nodding their heads in Belle Époque approval. In the late afternoon sunlight every colour was deepening, mellowing, the fire of the morning become an ember, more warmth than light. The sky soft as figured velvet, the rocks fading to old rose. Coral and midnight blue, milky jade and violet. Fragile, fleeting, rare . . . Sitting in that car, perfumed air on her face, half-way between tender sky and crystal sea, Janna felt a yearning so acute it was almost a pain. If only this ride could last for ever she would be made new, all thoughts of herself, past and future, banished like dust beneath the noiseless wheels.

Gray drove expertly, as if every inch of the road was known to him. On they went, and down, flirting with that melting, translucent sea. A glimpse of snow-capped mountains to the north, delicate as clouds. A last, triumphant bend and then before her, laid out blue and white and silver as so much enamelled Fabergé, was her destination. No, her destiny. Maybe it had always been here, just round the corner of a winding road. Buried treasure, a child's surprise. A birthday party, a wedding feast, a fairy kingdom, spotless and bright on its tiny flood-lit stage. A blue square of harbour with the white wings of yachts, a dolls' house palace on a hill, a curve of snowy beach dotted with coloured parasols, and everything glittering, timeless, irresistible as a first-day issue, a newly-minted coin.

'Monaco.' Gray turned, and smiled, and for a heart-stopping instant Janna was Grace Kelly, in dark glasses and chiffon scarf, swooping down on her private kingdom with her prince at her side. No formalities, no frontiers. Monaco opened its arms wide and smiled too. Stucco houses pink as candy-floss, narrow Italianate streets striped with sun and shadow like seaside rock. A palace to end all palaces, just the right size, but extravagant beyond its size, crenellated beyond reason, capped with fishtail towers enough to delight the most exacting child. A wedding cake of a Casino, pillared and storeyed, sugar-white, overlooking terraced gardens starred with great cacti, the girth of oak-trees.

Gray parked the Mercedes by the harbour, where luxury cruisers and slim sailboats bobbed and curtseyed.

'Let's walk.' His smile took Janna's breath away. 'I want to show you off.'

Janna felt herself glow, with pride, and amazement, and fear. Could it be that she was here at last, with the right man, in the right place, at the right time, wearing the right clothes? At any moment she expected the sky to darken, for a giant voice to speak from a thundercloud and tell her this was all a mistake, not meant for her. She took a deep breath. She mustn't let Gray down, or the Fortuny, or this perfect place, where maharajahs and Grand Dukes had paved the way. Her whole body might be stiff with tension, but she mustn't show it. Gray turned to her.

'What would you like to do?'

Janna hesitated. She wanted so much to do the right thing,

but this was outside her experience.

'What does one do, in Monte Carlo?'

Gray laughed. 'That's an easy question to answer. One plays.'

I'm not sure I know how to do that, Janna thought, her anxiety returning. If it was work, I'd know, but play . . . Suddenly the prospect seemed terrifying. What would it involve? Perhaps, if she kept her eyes on Gray, she could take her cue from him . . .

It seemed to work. As they walked slowly up towards the old town Janna felt she was beginning to understand. If she thought of herself as a character in a play it made it easier. Everywhere she looked there were admiring eyes, resting on either herself and the Fortuny, or Gray, with his splendid English good looks, that casualness that was never remotely crumpled, relying on genes and grooming and pure grace for its effect. First of all they went to the Casino, as, Gray advised her gravely, they must, because it was one of Monte's unique experiences, denied to the natives, who were never allowed beneath Garnier's magnificent marzipan door. It was early yet, but already there were players at the tables under the frescoes and chandeliers. Gray told her about the *Salons Privés*, where evening dress was mandatory and millions rolled with the dice and the wheel, and about the Empress Eugénie, and her famous green silk parasol, and the white imperial reins of the Grand Dukes, one of whom loved the smell of strawberries so much that he had a dozen baskets brought to him each morning after a night at the tables, crushed their contents, inhaled just once then sent them away untasted. Janna listened, trying hard to take it in her stride, but the thought of the strawberries was too much for her. Such a waste . . .

'Maybe his valet ate them later – puréed?' For a moment she wished she hadn't spoken, but then, to her relief, Gray smiled.

'Perhaps so.'

Janna had the uneasy feeling that there was something she hadn't understood about the Grand Duke and the strawberries, but it was all right, just so long as Gray smiled. She decided

208

she'd better say as little as possible, just look, and follow, and remember.

And there was so much to remember. Insisting that she was hungry, Gray took her to the Café de Paris, and ordered something he said he knew she'd like. He was right. A silver tray of delicate butterfly sweetmeats, so light, so tiny they couldn't count as food at all. Pralinée flowers from nearby Grasse, the petits fours from Aix known as *calissons*, little ring-shaped anise-scented cakes from Albi, round yellow counters of dried almonds perfumed with orange flowers called '*soleils*', all the way from Marcillac-Vallon, crystallised violets from Toulouse, Carpentras figs, Remoulins cherries, a scatter of pistachios . . .

They melted on Janna's tongue. Food of the gods, ambrosia – and yet she hardly tasted them. The food she'd eaten the day before haunted her still. She dared not let go, forced herself to toy and pick while Gray told her that the ground under her feet was worth more today than its own weight, pound for pound, in solid gold, that the fine white sand on the beach below was imported specially each season, that for once in her lifetime she was on the other side of the window, the right side, where people laughed and played and were beautiful.

'That dress, Janna.' Gray leaned forward, touched the fabric very lightly with his fingertips. 'It is you.' Janna shivered, the expression in his eyes inseparable from the taste of the violets on her tongue.

'Shall we dance?' She nodded, speechless. He took her to the Sporting Club d'Hiver on the Larvotto peninsula overlooking the bay. There, in the Star Room, they danced, under the huge curved roof which opened like a giant mother-of-pearl-lined shell to reveal the purple sky.

'It's getting dark.' Janna met Gray's eyes and felt cold inside again. She didn't want this to end, not ever. She didn't want to think of the world outside. She wanted to spend the rest of her life walled off, like one of the gamblers in the lovely windowless Casino, with Gray. In the white marble foyer they laughed a little as they found themselves eased down a subtle incline towards the green-carpeted gaming salon. Janna felt suddenly reckless, a heady mixture of happiness and unhappiness that she'd never known before.

'Let's go in!'

Gray shrugged indulgently. From his eyes Janna could see that somehow, without knowing why, she'd pleased him. For once, she'd said the right, the expected thing, behaved like – a woman. Captious, greedy, frivolous. Suddenly she saw just how attractive that might be. I will do it, she thought, with a sudden leap of the heart. I will be like that, for Gray.

But at the threshold she was brought to a standstill. She recoiled, almost bumping into Gray, her resolve shattered.

'What's the matter?' Gray looked intrigued.

'Nothing.' Janna smiled, as brightly as she could. 'I've changed my mind. Let's – let's go somewhere else.'

'Very well.' Gray's light eyes darkened suddenly. 'Where would you like to go?'

Janna shrugged, with an effort at bravado. 'I don't mind. You choose.'

In silence they walked down to the harbour, now a jewelled net of light on inky waves. White boats danced on a sequinned sea. Music and laughter drifted out from Jimmy'z, just opened for the night, but off the water the breeze was cool. Janna shivered and pulled the folds of her cape a little closer. How much more of the night was left, for her? Gray leaned towards her, cupped her elbow lightly in the palm of his hand. Beside her he felt very tall, very silent. But she couldn't speak.

Just before the end of the Marina he turned, stepped onto the deck of a large yacht riding at anchor, its white sides so smooth that they reflected the waves beneath, chuckling against her hull.

'What are you doing?' Horror released Janna's powers of speech for a moment.

'Come on. It's perfectly safe.' Gray held out his hand. Mesmerised, she stepped onto the glass-smooth deck, then froze as a white-uniformed figure materialised out of the dusk.

'Good evening, sir.'

Gray nodded. The figure disappeared on silent feet.

'You mean –'

'Of course.' Gray's eyes caught the light. 'I always sleep well on water, don't you?' He held out his hand. Janna hesitated. A little impatiently, Gray indicated her narrow-heeled shoes. Mystified, she slipped them off, held them, wondering what she was supposed to do next.

'Here.' Now she noticed the edge of the deck was hung with small woven baskets. 'To protect the deck,' Gray explained, a little drily. Janna felt herself blush and was glad of the dark.

The yacht was huge. It rocked gently under her feet, as Gray led her to his suite, pointing out on the way the swimming pool which could be raised electrically to become a dance floor, the poop deck smoking room with its full-size billiard table and grand piano, the bar with its open fireplace and walnut panelling . . . Janna followed, awed, amazed, wondering if this was some kind of dream. Gray noticed her confusion and reassured her gently.

'In Monte landspace is at a premium, so –' he made a gesture towards the harbour, glinting through the saloon's panoramic window. 'A yacht is simply – sensible.' He paused. 'Hungry?'

Janna shook her head. She felt different now. Somehow being on a boat, even one as large as this, was – intimate, private. Up till now, all the afternoon and evening, she and Gray hadn't once been alone.

'Thirsty?'

She shook her head again.

'It's no trouble.' Gray's eyes rested on her quizzically. 'I can have someone bring you something. All I have to do is pick up the phone.'

'No, thank you.' She realised she was sitting bolt upright and tried hard to relax a little. Her stockinged feet on the deep-pile carpet felt strange, almost sinful.

'Then tell me.' Now Gray's eyes were curious. 'What happened back there, at Le Sporting?'

'Oh.' Janna coloured. Being on the boat had almost banished the shock of that glossy red head bent over the green baize from her mind. Supposing Liane had seen her? 'I thought I saw – someone I knew.'

Gray frowned. Janna blushed again. 'A woman, I mean.'
This was getting worse and worse.

'The blonde or the redhead?'

'Does it matter?'

'Not to me.' Gray shrugged. 'Women like that are too –
easy.' His eyes rested on Janna with a meditative expression.
'What could be less attractive than the determination to
attract?'

Janna's mouth was dry. She didn't want to meet Gray's eyes,
but somehow, she couldn't look away. What was he trying to
tell her? Had he sensed how desperately eager she was herself to
please him, to do the right thing? Was there, in the end, any
difference between herself and Liane? And it was getting late
. . . The brass clock on the bulkhead told her it was past eight,
surely too late for her to catch her plane back to London, too
late for the Fortuny to return to its velvet-lined box. Had Gray
realised the time? If only she could ask him, if only she could
say, simply, as she'd said to Fernand, 'Why, why have you
brought me here?' She'd thought it had been just a whim on his
part, but there was that expression in his eyes . . . If only she
knew more about men. If only she knew what to do, what to say.
If only the Fortuny could speak to her, with its long experience
of beauty, tell her all it knew. Now, wearing it, she felt like an
impostor for the first time. It would be shed so easily, that
silken skin, but underneath it she was still the same.

Silence. Gray held her eyes. Janna's heart missed a beat. Did
he really mean her to stay, here on the boat, with him? But if she
did – wouldn't that make her easy, forgettable, just another
girl?

At last, unable to bear his gaze a moment more, she looked
away. Then, she heard him pick up the phone.

'A taxi, please.'

Janna fixed her eyes on the carpet and wished she was somewhere else, someone else. Liane, or Julie, anyone but her own
frozen, awkward self. It had been so perfect, but now the
moment was gone.

'Don't worry.' Gray leaned back, still watching her. 'You

won't have missed your plane. I said I'd get you back in time, and I will.'

Janna stared at him. It was almost eight-thirty. How could he do any such thing?

Gray laughed as he saw the expression on her face.

'The heliport. You'll be back at Nice Côte d'Azur in six minutes.'

Janna blushed. She hadn't even known there was such a thing as a heliport. Of course, Gray hadn't meant her to stay. Why had she ever thought so for a moment? A few minutes later she heard the taxi draw up outside. Gray escorted her on deck. The night air was soft on her face as he lifted one hand and kissed it. Confused once more, she turned away.

'Wait!'

She waited, spellbound. If he said the word, she knew, she would stay, as long as he wanted. If the boat left its moorings during the night she'd go too, with him, anywhere in the whole darkened world.

'Your shoes, Cinderella.' He held them up to her, moonlight mocking in his smile.

'Thank you.' Stiffly, glad of the darkness, which laid cool hands over her hot face, Janna took the small bronze-satin mules. 'Goodbye.'

Gray reached forward to cup one hand under her chin, turning her face to the light. His hand was cool and dry.

'Till Dene.'

CHAPTER FIFTEEN

Till Dene. Gray's parting words echoed in Janna's mind as she caught the 9 pm flight back to London with only minutes to spare. Had they been threat or promise, simple courtesy? She replayed them endlessly, trying to pin down his exact inflection, the exact expression in his eyes, but still she couldn't tell. Gray was an enigma to her. Being with him was like being in a different world. She wasn't sure she would ever learn how to breathe its air. Perhaps you had to be born to it, like Julie.

And yet, she'd never forget a single minute of the time she'd spent with him. Every moment was locked in her memory, crystal clear, like flowers in a glass paperweight, tiny, perfect, unchanging. Could it have been her, that girl in the Fortuny? Looking back she seemed hardly real, something from a fairy tale. But that wasn't Gray's fault. Whenever she was with him she felt driven to play some kind of part, to try and be someone else. She had never dared show him the real Janna. How could she? She cared too much. And for him, she'd be willing to change herself into anyone or anything, if only he'd tell her what he wanted, who she was supposed to be. If only, just once, he'd allow her past that reserve of his, as deep or even deeper than her own.

It was a relief, in a way, when the plane touched down. Dealing with tangibles – currency, baggage, documents – was easy by comparison with Monte Carlo. It was a relief too, after blue skies, to see London rain. It was democratic, the rain. It fell on everyone alike.

To Janna, as she turned into Rose Alley and saw the cobbles shining like river pebbles under the solitary streetlamp it was as if she'd never been away. After all the uncertainties of film-making Rose Alley seemed very safe, very real. No fibre-glass lampposts here, no artificial rain. No brightly-lit scenario masquerading as the night, but the real thing, silent, velvety, cool. Janna stopped outside No. 3. Not a light shone. It was as if it was the first time.

Looking up, letting the rain fall on her face, Janna smiled. The house seemed very small, compared with Manhattan's glass towers or Cannes' ivory boulevards. But home. Whatever happened, No. 3 would always be that.

Her first thought was for the roof. Craning back, narrowing her eyes against the rain, she could just see the dark sheen of wet tiles, a section of smooth replacement guttering. She breathed a sigh of relief. It looked as if all the work had been completed just in time for the council's deadline. Dion had worked his magic once again. She wondered how many pots of tea it had taken. Roofers, Dion said, liked their tea thick enough to stand a spoon in, strong enough to blister skin.

On a sudden impulse Janna went down the basement steps. She told herself she needed to check on the damp course, but that wasn't all. As the door creaked open onto the small dim front room she felt strange, almost solemn. It was like entering a sort of shrine, a mausoleum – the shell of the girl she'd once been. She remembered sitting by the window, sewing patiently, waiting, always waiting. For darkness, for dawn. Afraid of both of them. Afraid of the future, herself. Afraid of everything.

In the back room Julie's collection of bottles on the window-ledge had acquired neat little epaulettes of cement dust. Janna felt a pang of loss. She wished she'd been able to say goodbye to Julie, but there'd been no opportunity. Gray had thought of everything. Her case, already packed, had been waiting for her at the airport, along with an escort for the Fortuny. She could only hope Julie would understand. The two of them had been happy, living down here together. Two fugitives . . . But Janna hadn't known that then, any more than she'd realised that Julie bleached her hair, or put blue drops in her eyes, or lived in fear of a printed page.

So much had changed since then, and not only the colour of

Janna's hair. Janna wasn't sure how it had happened. She'd been a child and now she was a householder, a landlady, a film actress even. And yet, inside, she felt the same. It was just her outside that had been refashioned, worked over by a bevy of experts, Fernand, Dion, Liane . . . She'd been made over, just like No. 3. Now they were stronger, both herself and the house, and yet they were still – unfinished, empty. A shell, waiting to be filled.

Slowly, a little heavily, Janna went up the newly reinstated internal stairs to the ground floor. Now she had proper electric light, ready at the flick of a switch. The unshaded bulbs were merciless to the dust and debris in the hall above. But there was no going back, she knew that. Her underground life was over now. Those little low-ceilinged rooms held only memories. From now on she belonged up here, in the light.

And there was so much still left to do. As Janna worked her way up through the house she noticed a window-frame that needed caulking, treads with splinters and protruding nails, a loose floorboard, cracked and sagging plaster where rain had got in before the new roof. They'd all have to be dealt with before she even thought of re-decoration or furnishing. Not that she had the money to spend in any case. Until the council inspector approved the work that had been done, and processed her application for a refund, it would be hard even to make ends meet. And it might take months for the money to come through.

But even so, she was glad, very, very glad, to be back. She lingered in the parlour, trying hard not to think of figured wallpaper and decorative friezes. She'd make this room her command centre, she decided, wondering if it was easy to extend telephone cable. Dion would know, but of course he wasn't here. He'd moved out to stay with a friend by the river until all contact with officialdom was over. But he'd be back, he'd assured her earnestly – he'd left his paints behind. And probably, thought Janna, half-a-dozen whiskered peppers under the bed into the bargain.

Dion had left the trapdoor open, knowing she would like to see the bright yellow wood of the new joists and rafters. Janna climbed up the stepladder just far enough to close the trap once more. She didn't want to go in. The attic was Dion's private space. And if he was satisfied with the roof, that was good enough for her. As she came down the ladder her eye was caught by a tangle of shining copper pipe leading from the new watertank. It wore, proudly, almost cockily, a big red ribbon bow. And to think I worried that Julie might put him off his plumbing, Janna thought, a little guiltily. She could almost hear Dion's voice saying, 'I told you so.'

Yes. In a way she was glad that Dion wasn't here. She was grateful for all his help, especially with Liane, but she needed a respite, a breathing space. Time to think.

Because in nine short weeks she would see Gray again. That thought shone like a beacon in the uncertainty ahead. It was – a fact, an appointment, something real to hold on to. Whatever happened, whatever doubts she had, whatever decisions she made, Gray would be there.

Janna took a deep breath. She wasn't sure whether she wanted the time to fly by or take for ever. She wanted to see Gray again more than she'd ever wanted anything, but she knew she wasn't ready. What would it take to transform her into the kind of girl Gray wanted, the one who'd caught his interest in Monte Carlo? She didn't know. She didn't even know if such a thing was possible. But she had to try. Because after Dene there would be no more Gray. Dene was her last chance.

That night Janna lay awake for hours, making mental lists of everything that needed to be done, crossing them out, starting again. Her priorities seemed to shift and change with every passing minute. When she fell asleep at last it was as if she and the house had become inextricably intertwined. She dreamed of Gray, arriving on her doorstep with the council's list of specifications, while she worried desperately because the pilot light on the central heating had gone out and she so much wanted the house to be warm. She ran through the house, searching, searching, up and down stairs, down corridors that only existed in the houses of her dreams, trying to locate the boiler, trying to remember where Dion had installed it, cursing him under her breath because he never put anything in its proper place . . . She woke, sweating with anxiety, still unable to remember. In the pre-dawn darkness she finally realised with relief that there was no central-heating boiler, never had been. Central heating was anathema to little old houses, cracking their plaster, drying out their wood.

In the morning, thankfully, her mind was steadier. Quietly, over breakfast, dry biscuits and three cups of Dion-strong tea, Janna made her decision. It was easy, in the end. The real decision had been taken long ago, outside her own volition, almost without her knowledge, when she'd first seen Gray in the Great Hall at Dene. It had drawn her then like a magnet, his ease, his sense of belonging. He was all the things she'd never been, never thought she could be. Looking back she could see that everything that had happened to her since that moment had been simply a preparation, for Gray. No. 3, Julie, Fernand, Dion, Liane – she'd learned from them everything that she could. But the rest of the way she must travel alone.

First of all, because she dreaded it most, Janna made an appointment with the doctor. It wasn't easy. There were questions, personal, probing, examinations, tests. Worst of all, for her, was being weighed. But as she stood barefoot on the executioner's rubber block she said silently to herself, 'For Gray', and the moment of panic passed. At last, when the ordeal was over, she had them, her small foil-wrapped packet of yellow pills, tiny golden apples off a magical tree. She took her first that same evening before she went to bed. The doctor had said she must choose a time and keep to it. She knew she would. What she was planning was much too important to leave to chance.

Each evening, after she'd taken her pill, she studied herself in her new mirror. It was as if she was packing all her growing up into a few days. She made herself wait a week, then another, to be sure. Then, proudly, she went out and bought herself her first real bra, a froth of lace in the Liane tradition. She was so proud of the fit that she hardly liked to dress

218

herself again. She found herself wishing that Dion would come back so that someone at least could see her new outline, and then again she didn't, because there was so much left for her to do.

The second part of her plan was harder than she'd expected. There was so much choice, the shop windows of Knightsbridge and Bond Street were full of it. She'd never set out to look for clothes for herself before. Every evening after finishing work on No. 3 she took a tube to a different destination, always waiting till the shops themselves were closed. She didn't want to go in, didn't want to be tempted to spend money she couldn't afford. It was knowledge she wanted. That could be had from the way the clothes were displayed almost as much as the garments themselves. She looked and looked, analysing the details of cut and styling and above all presentation.

Janna was glad to notice that money wasn't the answer, or even designer names. There was as much to learn from the girls in the street, the way a scarf was tied, eye-catching accessories – a feather, an unusual brooch, lacy socks under combat trousers – the matching of hair-style to heel-height and sleeve-length to skirt-length. Detailing without fuss, originality without stridency. Flair. Some had it, some hadn't. And it wasn't the prettiest girls who were necessarily the most striking. Some wore perfect outfits, but too consciously, some wore what might have been rags, but created fashion with every step.

Janna looked, and thought, and tried to remember everything Liane had said. Colour – clear and plain, men were confused by pattern. No brown, that was for country squires. No white, men hated to think of weddings. No green, because of lawns and football fields. But beige with enough pink in it, apricot and cream, innocent blue and shouting red, true yellow and pansy black . . .

Slowly, she narrowed down her choice. One outfit was the most she could afford, and she had to plan for everything, variable English weather, different occasions, times of day. She needed a dress for all seasons, which would be at home anywhere, like Gray.

But she mustn't let herself be taken in by a pretty face. High fashion, striking though it was, was for girls like Julie, with the height and presence to carry it off. What Janna needed was clothes that took second place, silent publicity agents, faithful servants, trusty friends. Nothing small, or approximate, or cheap – she couldn't afford it. She had to be careful, so careful, to spot a bag just that all-important fraction too small, a yellow with too much aniline green in it, a lining that should have been silk but wasn't, a neckline a millimetre too high, a skirt that creased in the wrong place, material skimped in the setting of a sleeve.

Slowly, carefully, Janna bought. It wasn't a pleasure, it was too terrifying, too testing for that. Remembering Liane's advice she began with accessories. A dress could always be found to match shoes, scarf, bag, but very rarely the other way around. 'You must never be tempted to compromise,' Liane had said. 'Bare feet are infinitely better than the wrong height of heel.'

At the end of three weeks of dedicated searching Janna laid out everything she'd chosen and studied it anxiously. One pair of small black patent leather shoes with winged heels, glossy as only real patent leather could be. They drew attention to her slender ankles, as Liane had advised. A wide, soft black bag of the smoothest Florentine leather – no compartments this time, but a lining of moiré silk that shone like oil on a pool. A silk dress, deceptively simple, the pure, dazzling blue of a Monte Carlo sky, so well cut that it would need only the finest adjustment at the shoulder line. A three-inch leather belt, in a blue two shades darker, with a butter-gold buckle, to emphasise her tiny waist. And finally, to celebrate, the smallest possible bottle of perfume, because Liane said perfume should be worn for herself alone, never for a man. 'If he asks for its name, never tell him, even if he promises you a litre flagon. It is your fragrance, and yours alone.'

Then came the hardest part of all. Practice, practice, and more practice. The art of applying the finest black line round her eyes, a hint of silver grey shadow, lipstick that gave colour without cover. The art of wearing new clothes as if they cost nothing, could be replaced in a moment, of cultivating a hair-style that was just half-way between hairdresser stiffness and casual tousle. Janna was glad she didn't have to rely on human agency for her colour any more. A little bleaching with a henna treatment gave her a red that was almost as good, though, looking at herself dripping with greenish mud, Janna realised that what Liane had said was all too true. You had to suffer to be beautiful, and it was as well to have a bathroom with a lockable door.

Then it was time to rehearse. Each morning, after she'd showered and combed her hair, Janna made up her face, then put on her new clothes. She wanted the dress to lose its shop-bought stiffness, fall into natural folds, so that it looked neither old nor new but simply right. Her shoes needed breaking in, very gently, so that they were comfortable to wear but unmarred by a single crease or crack. She practised slipping on the unfamiliar stockings, tried to emulate Liane's supple twist as she checked the spider-thin, coal-black seams. Then she experimented with different ways of standing and sitting. The dress governed the way she moved, gave her clues as to what she should and should not do. It turned out that Fernand was right. The less she did, the better she looked – but it required great poise to hold a position without fidgeting, face her own reflection with Liane's Mona-Lisa smile.

As the day grew nearer Janna felt more and more uncertain. There was such a difference between solitary rehearsal in front of the mirror and the real thing. She could see her own image was attractive, but that wasn't enough. Gray must have known many women, each of them more beautiful and sophisticated than herself. No amount of advice from Liane, no amount of peacock-blue silk, could cover up her lack of experience, the long empty years.

I want to learn so much, thought Janna, but I don't know where to begin. I've never even kissed a man before. I won't know what to do. Supposing my awkwardness offends him, supposing . . . She swallowed hard. Supposing he indulges me, out of politeness, out of pity. He would do that, being Gray. Her face burned. I couldn't bear that, she thought. If only I didn't care so much – if only it didn't matter, I could get through it somehow. But Gray's too important to risk that way.

Janna sighed. If only it was Dion she loved, instead of Gray. There'd be no problem then, no danger, no tension, no sickening tightrope walk between ecstasy and humiliation, just a comforting safety net of laughter. Dion's so – easy. I can say anything to him. He's safe, in a way Gray could never be. I could go to him right now and say, 'Please teach me how to kiss,' and he'd say, 'Certainly, when would you like to start – today?'

As she polished her shoes with milk and hung up her dress on the specially padded hanger she'd sprinkled with scent, Janna began to think maybe that wasn't such an outrageous idea after all. In fact, it was almost – sensible. A kind of research, like the careful window-shopping she'd done for her new clothes, trying on outfits she knew she would never buy, because each one had something to teach her about cut and colour, pattern and harmony. She'd learned as much, maybe more, from the ones that didn't fit as the ones that did.

Slowly, she folded her cobweb stockings and slid them carefully inside their cellophane. The idea stayed in her mind, a little stronger now. Dion wouldn't mind, she knew that. He was the sort of man who'd be – not flattered exactly, but glad to help. Willing. Janna felt herself flush, remembering the girls on the chalk-marked stairs. She didn't want to be just one of a number, but for Gray . . . She'd do anything to deserve him, to be a little more his equal, to fit a little better into his graceful, polished world. And at least with Dion she'd feel more in control of herself and the situation, there'd be no danger she'd get carried away.

On an impulse Janna went downstairs to the parlour, picked up the phone. Dion had left his friend's number, chalked on the underside of the trapdoor. As Janna listened to the ringing tone she decided the decision was out of her hands. If Dion answered, she'd ask him to come back. If there was no reply – well, she'd have to manage as best she could. As always, holding the phone, she felt like a different person, cool, confident, in control. It was so much easier when no-one could see her face.

A female voice informed her briskly that Dion wasn't there. Janna hesitated, momentarily taken aback. She didn't know why she'd assumed Dion's friend would be male. She decided to leave a message, though from the girl's tone of voice it seemed doubtful that Dion would ever get it.

'Is it urgent?'

'No, not really. Just tell him the inspector's been round and he's welcome to come back whenever he wants.'

Two days went by, then three, and there was no sign of Dion. Janna didn't ring again. Fate had taken its decision.

The next day Janna varnished her nails, washed and set her hair. There were still two days to go before she was due at Dene, but she didn't want to look too stiff or planned. In any case, she needed to start her preparations early. If she left everything until tomorrow night she'd be so nervous that she'd forget something vital. Even now her hands shook as she equipped her bag with pale blue tissues in a fabric cover, a fresh lipstick, pills, miniature scissors in case she snagged a nail, needle and blue silk thread, her tiny vial of perfume, five brand-new ten-pound notes, chequebook and card, passport, address book, in which she'd written a few extra imaginary names, her tortoiseshell backed hairbrush, a clean lace handkerchief and a small enamelled powder compact. She'd already forwarded her case to Dene, so that she could arrive unburdened, looking casual, free . . .

It was then, as she fastened the catch on her bag, that Janna heard a noise. She looked up, listened hard. Yes, there it was again. Familiar, unmistakable. The sound of Dion's footsteps on the attic floor.

Janna looked at her blue silk, hesitated just once, then made up her mind. Quickly, her blood racing, every nerve strung tight, she dressed, brushed out her hair. She'd practised so often that it hardly took a moment. She snatched up her bag, hurried out into the hall. Looking up at the trapdoor she realised she couldn't risk her stockings on the stepladder. But there was no time to lose. It might be early, but on a fine May morning Dion couldn't be relied on to stay indoors for more than five minutes together. She clattered down the stairs, opened the front door on a blaze of sunshine. It was a day cut by a master jeweller, brilliant, flawless, a hard edge of light to every surface. Janna locked the door behind her, just in case. She didn't know long she might be. But there wasn't far to go now. She took a deep breath, turned right. No need to hurry any more. If Dion was going out, she'd meet him on his way. Up the steps, through the ever-open door. The chalk-marked stair. Janna trod carefully, concentrating hard, to avoid the cracks and gaping holes. But there was no need for her to be nervous, not really. This was no monster's lair she was heading for, just Dion's attic.

And yet, even though she'd climbed slowly, Janna felt oddly breathless by the time she reached the top. It was the door. She'd never really studied it before. It was so umistakably Dion's, with its unexpected splits and doodlings and spatterings of paint. Phone numbers too, lots of them. Janna was almost tempted to turn back, but it was ridiculous to come so far only to change her mind.

The door opened so abruptly that Janna was caught off-balance, her hand upraised for a second knock. For a panicky moment she wondered whether Dion was alone.

'January.' Clearly Dion had only just woken. Surprise battled with drowsiness on that familiar face, so reassuringly ugly, so black and white. 'My, you're looking lovely today. But what brings you here?'

So simple to answer, and so difficult. Janna swallowed. 'It's such a beautiful day, I thought . . .' Her voice tailed away. Dion blinked at her. All the phrases Janna had been preparing on her way up the stairs fled instantly from her mind. Suddenly what she was proposing seemed preposterous, impossible. But she couldn't go back now. Flustered, uncomfortably aware of her flushed cheeks, her perfume, her clean hair, she went on.

'I thought we could go to the races.'

Janna watched Dion's face anxiously. She'd used his own code, so that he could say yes without compromising himself, no without hurting her feelings. But had he understood?

Slowly, superbly, Dion's eyes lit up. Janna felt a wave of

relief. Why had she ever doubted him? It would be all right now . . .

'I know the very place!' Dion ran a hand through his hair, grinned beatifically. 'How much money have you got?'

Janna looked at him, doubtful once again. Had he taken her literally? Or had he, perhaps, chosen to misunderstand?

'Enough.' She rallied, trying not to think of her bank account, now dangerously low. As long as she was with Dion, she'd find a way somehow. It was early yet. There was time.

'Good.' Dion's smile was undimmed. 'I wouldn't ask, only I've just bought three new sable brushes and five yards of canvas.'

An hour later, as they boarded a train headed for Liverpool, Janna felt that she'd made the right decision. It was better for them both to be on neutral territory. Aintree might not be Monte Carlo, but that didn't matter. In fact, though she was reluctant to admit it to herself, Janna was more than a little relieved that the next three hours would pass peacefully in public. She could relax, forget her plans and worries for a while. What with her early start that morning and the rhythmic rocking of the train she'd be hard put to it not to fall asleep . . .

Sometime later, her mouth dry and her neck stiff, Janna awoke to find that the train had stopped moving and Dion was nowhere to be seen. She sat up in sudden panic, looked wildly round the compartment. Dion's newspaper was still there, opened at the racing form, but that was all. Looking out through the grimy window she could see they'd arrived at Liverpool. Had he gone and left her sleeping?

'That's better!'

Janna spun round. It was Dion, running his hand over his freshly-shaven chin. He'd taken advantage of the amenities, as usual. Janna felt her cheeks flame. Why had he shaved, for the horses – or for her? Had he understood her after all? Caught off balance, she stood up so quickly that she forgot to check the fastening on her bag. Keys, passport and perfume fell out with a resounding clatter. Dion handed them back to her without so much as a raised eyebrow.

'Ready for anything, I see.'

'Why not?' Janna's blush deepened. Why was it so hard being a woman of the world? Maybe she'd get used to it, in time . . .

Ceremoniously Dion handed her down from the train.

'Just like being back in Nice, isn't it?'

Janna looked back at him a little doubtfully. Perhaps those blue eyes were a little short-sighted, like Julie's? Anywhere less like the Côte d'Azur than this grubby station platform she could scarcely imagine. And yet, walking beside him in the dusty sunlight she got an inkling of what he meant. He was the same, from the top of his inky head to his battered soft-soled shoes that made his walk as silent as falling snow. Yes, she'd chosen well. Whatever else Dion might be, he was an easy companion. No need for goodbyes and hellos and formal invitations with Dion. He was the perfect squatter, the cat that walked by himself.

A taxi took them on a long roundabout tour of what seemed the whole of Liverpool's backstreets and ended up at the docks. Janna got out, a little confused. A cool breeze off the water made her wish she'd ignored Liane's advice and brought one of her pullovers, just in case.

'I thought we were going to the races?'

'We are.'

Dion pointed over the harbour where one of those big ugly wide-bellied ferries was throbbing noisily against the quay, obviously on the point of departure. Suddenly Dion grabbed her hand and began to run. Before she knew it Janna found herself up the oily ramp and into the evil-smelling gloom. Around her towered the high cabs of juggernauts, chains clanking as the ferry rocked from side to side. A deafening noise roared under her, making the steel plates shake. She stared at Dion in dawning horror.

'But – but –' She had to shout to make herself heard above the din. 'I haven't brought anything, I didn't realise . . . Why didn't you tell me?'

'Because I only just thought of it, January darling! Don't you worry, you'll be fine, just fine.' Dion's smile was confidence itself. 'Leave everything to me.'

Janna shook her head, utterly dismayed, but she had no choice. The ship was moving now, steadily, relentlessly, heading for the open sea.

CHAPTER SIXTEEN

'Well, what do you think?' Dion let down one of the two upper bunks with a flourish to demonstrate the mechanism. 'Cunning, eh?'

Janna nodded. She didn't know what to say. Everything had happened so fast. One minute solid tarmac underfoot, the next – this. She glanced round the cabin, doubtfully. It was simple, white, almost monastic. And yet they'd managed to fit four beds into the tiny space.

'Please put it back.' Janna tried to speak as calmly as she could. But with the bed swung out from the wall there was barely room left to stand. As it was, each movement of the boat seemed to send her bumping into Dion. Dion shrugged, sent the bed back with what seemed a flick of the wrist. Janna looked up to see the Jolly Roger flying from his smile.

'Thank you.' Janna sat down on the lower bunk, thought better of it, stood up again. 'Why don't you – er –' Janna cast around for inspiration. She needed a little time to herself, to sort out her thoughts, recover from the surprise. 'Why don't you wait for me in the bar?'

'A fine idea.' Dion nodded, almost sagely. 'But don't be long. I might get waylaid by some lady pirate.'

Before Janna could think of a suitable reply he was gone, swinging jauntily up the narrow corridor like a born sailor.

Quickly, Janna washed her hands, brushed her hair, renewed her lipstick, trying to convince herself that the faint, rapid tremor that shook her body was due to the engine's vibration. She looked round the cabin, still doubtful. It was so – bare, so functional. Not what she'd imagined at all. And all those beds . . . She tried to pretend they weren't there. Casting her mind back to Fernand's lighting team she doused the central globe and the fluorescent tube above the mirror and switched on the two tiny bedside lamps. Dimmer, the cabin looked a little less austere. One last check in the mirror, and she was ready to go.

Except, perhaps, it was a bit too warm, even for May? Janna took out a tissue, blotted away the moisture from under her eyes and across her upper lip. The heating must be turned up too high. But the regulator was above the door, of all places. The effort of reaching it made her feel slightly faint. She sat down on the bunk bed for a moment to recover. It was then, for the first time, that she really felt the movement of the boat. An uneven roll, difficult to predict, a long deceptively smooth interval followed by a sudden sideways plunge. She found herself waiting for it, every muscle tense, and yet when it came it always took her by surprise.

For some reason, once she was on the bed, Janna found it difficult even to think of getting up again. She felt so tired. Travelling was tiring, everyone said that. If she just sat here for a few moments and closed her eyes she'd feel better soon.

But closing her eyes was a mistake. It made the corkscrew rolling of the boat even more obvious, as if the whole weight of the vessel was anchored somewhere near the pit of her stomach. And yet, when she tried to open her eyes again she couldn't seem to raise the lids more than halfway.

Very, very slowly, as if her skull was made of a glass so thin it might crack at any moment, Janna lowered her head to the pillow. She felt better lying down, just a little. In this position she could almost persuade herself that she was back on solid ground. Apart from her stomach. That seemed to have taken on an independent life of its own. It rolled and turned inside her, long irregular somersaults, one sickening beat of time behind the movement of the waves.

Dimly, from another life, Janna remembered that lying like this would crease her blue silk, that Dion was waiting for her in the bar, that really, truly, she should get up. But those thoughts weren't real. Nothing was real except the dryness in her mouth, the feeling that she'd been turned inside out, bled dry. The smell of diesel oil. Now that was something she'd never properly considered, not until this moment. It seemed to fill the cabin, overpowering, insistent, racking her with nausea. That was it – she was being poisoned by diesel fumes. Why else would she feel she was dying? It didn't trouble her, the thought of death. She welcomed it. The idea was so refreshing, clean and final and cold.

Then, suddenly, a convulsion gripped her body. Her stomach rose inside her, twisting, scalding. Janna struggled up, only one thought left in her mind. She reached the basin just in time.

Bent double, barely conscious, she didn't notice the door opening behind her until she saw Dion's face reflected in the mirror. Their eyes met in a look of perfect comprehension, a complete union of thought and feeling. Cautiously, like a very old man, Dion felt his way to a bunk bed and sat down.

No words were necessary. They lay down, as far beyond etiquette and inhibition as two statues side by side on a marble tomb. There was no past, no future, no possible escape. They took turns at the basin. Without turning her head Janna could tell from Dion's groans, the perfect echo of her own, exactly when need for the safety of the basin overrode longing for the comfort of the bunk.

And it was a contest without end. Long after there was nothing left inside her Janna's stomach went on contracting, uselessly. The cramps were all the more exhausting because they made no sense. She'd wanted to die before but now she knew she was going to. All the cells in her body seemed to be dissolving. She was being reduced to nothing, a mindless amoeba scooped up by the tide only to be cast away again, over and over.

She lost track of everything, even Gray. All her ideas about herself and the world were stripped from her. She was lost in an ancient nightmare, naked, terrified, a foetus tortured by a labour without end, tiny and helpless, unable to move or breathe and with no voice to scream. Nothing was as it should be, nothing could be trusted. She was deafened by the thunderous beating of the engine's heart as the world closed down on her in suffocating waves. There was no air, no life, no hope. She tried with her waning strength to push back the walls but they swooped in on her again, crushing her ribs, bruising her flesh, squeezing her till the blood pounded in her head. She was alone. No-one could hear her, no-one would save her. There was no-one and nothing but herself in the whole convulsing world. She was alone. She'd always been alone. She would die alone with no-one knowing that she'd ever lived. Her back arched, searing pain knifed through her spine, her throat filled with salt and a shrill internal scream of pain and loneliness that went on for ever.

Something touched her burning head, anchoring her in space. Little rivulets of cool water trickled down her temples like tears, defining her. Through half-open eyes she saw a shadow, a blur of movement. She could not turn her eyes to follow it but slowly, in the wreckage of her mind, a thought was born. There is someone there. Hold to that. There is someone beside me, almost near enough to touch. My twin beyond the barrier of eyes, the stronger one. I am not alone. Someone knows that I am here, shares my pain. I am not alone.

The ferry was two hours late into port. That didn't matter to its passengers as they wavered up from the depths like ghosts, pale and shrunken. Janna and Dion, two bodies with a single thought between them, joined the silent queue for disembarkation without a word spoken. Nothing mattered but to be off the ship – still rocking mutinously against the rubber-tyred quay – and onto solid ground.

Morning. The first and best morning of the world. Sunlight a miser's hoard of copper pennies. Sky a blue-and-white patchwork, newly-laundered. The smell of coffee brewing, bacon frying . . .

'If I don't have breakfast soon I shall blow away.' Dion's voice was hoarse, like a convalescent, a man returned from the grave. Janna nodded. She would too, on one of those starchy white clouds.

Gulls hovered over their rose-pink bacon and steaming rolls. Hot plates, a curl of breeze and butter the colour of a primrose. Paradise. Janna felt reborn, every slate wiped clean, every plan forgotten. Nothing would ever look or taste the same to her again. She wasn't sure where she was, who she was even – all she knew was that she was alive. She could have sat there for ever, listening to the silence, smiling like a baby. The peace. The cessation of pain. The surprise of it.

'A pet day.' Colour was returning to Dion's face. They exchanged a look of mutual sympathy and respect, like two survivors from a war. Janna knew exactly what he meant, though she'd never heard the phrase before. A pet day, a perfect day, the kind you'd want to take home with you and keep by you always. In the new-washed light she could see little specks of green and amber in his eyes. He leaned forward.

'To the journey back.' He lifted his coffee cup in a toast of impossible bravado.

'Don't.' Janna shivered. The horror of it was too much to contemplate, let alone mention casually over breakfast. And yet, from here, the blue-grey sea looked innocent as a school-girl's mackintosh.

'A bit of a twister, was it not?' There was a note almost of pride in Dion's voice. 'That's the Irish Sea for you.'

'Ah.' Realisation came to Janna slowly, like milk swirling into a cup of hot coffee. 'So this is Ireland.'

'No, no.' Dion's smile had survived the shipwreck too. 'This is Dublin. I will show you Ireland.'

Janna might have known that Dion's way of showing a visitor the sights wouldn't be like other people's. He talked his way onto a yellow-and-white Bus Scoile taking its cargo of children on a Saturday outing, and kept the driver in fits of laughter as they bounced down the narrow road, narrowly avoiding a herd of black-and-white china cows, heavy udders dripping into the dust. From the window Janna saw a water-colour landscape, every shade of green from viridian to moss. Cottages with buttermilk walls and fudge-coloured thatch, a stream like Dion's tea, rocks furred with grey lichen, clouds like huge pearls.

The bus dropped them on Dion's request in a sea of green

and silence. It was so quiet Janna could hear the wind in the grass. The air tasted sweet, almost good enough to eat. There was something soft and melting and creamy about it, cool and warm at the same time. How strange to see a landscape that was two-thirds sky, like a huge painting.

Dion set off across the dew-darkened grass like a red setter scenting partridge. By the time Janna caught up with him her patent leather shoes were soaked through.

'Where are we going?'

'To the horses.' Dion forged on, black hair lifting at every step. He'd obviously learned to walk on these slippery rounded hummocks that looked soft as feather pillows but turned out surprisingly firm. Janna scanned the horizon for a race-course but saw nothing. Dion hopped over a dilapidated stone wall and headed towards a long low building, walls bellying with layer on layer of lime, roof tiled with slates the colour of London rain. Tacked onto it with a sublime disregard for aesthetics was a much more recent structure with a hideous corrugated iron roof. Dion swung wide the five-barred gate fronting the yard and presented Janna with what looked rather like a section of the moon's surface complete with miniature craters, each filled with a baleful little pool of greenish water.

'You wait there.' Dion sprinted across the yard with obvious expertise, his feet leaving the hardened ridges just before they crumbled under his weight. He picked up something outside the cottage and came back as if he'd collared the Crown Jewels.

'This will do the trick nicely.' He held up a huge grey-green pair of Wellingtons, well-daubed with mud. Janna looked at them in horror.

'But I can't wear those!'

Dion shrugged. 'As you please. The choice is yours.' He set off across the yard again. Janna hesitated. Not the most seductive footwear she'd ever seen, but then Dion wasn't Gray. Did it matter after all? One more look at the depth of the moon craters decided her. Choice indeed. It was no choice at all.

The boots were cold and damp and seemed to weigh a ton. Walking across the soggy yard Janna felt like a prehistoric monster emerging from the slime. The mud made rude primeval noises at her and the boot tops cut disobligingly into the backs of her knees. Even Liane wouldn't have been able to do the walk in these, she thought ruefully.

But when she rounded the corner of the ugly barn she forgot everything – her boots, and the mud, and the fact that she'd hardly slept since yesterday afternoon, and the calorific content of fried bacon and buttered bread, and where she was and why she was there. For out of the half-rotted door with its rusty hinges and coating of green mould came the most perfect, beautiful creature, pale as an angel, dainty as a unicorn, stepping lightly and delicately over the mud ridges with hooves that seemed too tiny for its height and size.

'Mickeen, you devil.' Dion's voice, soft, a long, low whistle of pure delight. From behind the glossy bulk of the horse a face peeked.

'And it's the devil's own surprise you'd be giving me, Dion Malloy.' A high, soft voice, almost high enough for a woman's, but no woman would have worn that crumpled corduroy cap or that peculiar assortment of blue office-worker's shirt and hand-me-down hacking jacket.

'So this is January.' Janna felt her cheeks turn pink. How did he know her name – by some sort of Irish necromancy? Suddenly she felt very English, stiff and a little foolish. But the beautiful creature rescued her, swinging across her shining neck and dropping into Janna's palm a muzzle as soft as cottonwool. Janna found herself confronted by a large, brown, trusting eye, felt on her hand a puff of sweet breath like a child's kiss. She felt sudden foolish tears spring into her eyes. It was so big, but so gentle – and like Julie, all curves.

'What's her name?'

'Ah, there you have me.' Mickeen swung round to Dion. 'Have you thought?'

'Of nothing else.' Dion's voice was deeply serious. 'It is a matter for great thought, giving a name to beauty.'

'It is so.'

Seemingly aware of their scrutiny the horse stood motionless, ears pricked forward, nostrils flaring a little.

'She's such a lovely colour.' Tentatively Janna reached out to touch that shining skin. Grey – all colours and no colour, smoothed and blended by a master hand. Not dappled, nothing so vulgar, but air-brushed until she looked as if she would blow before the wind like thistle-down.

'Galway Gray was a thought I had . . .' Mickeen lifted an eyebrow in Dion's direction. Janna felt a little chill. Gray and this beautiful filly – thoroughbreds the both of them. Such beauty was unassailable, beyond the reach of mere mortals like herself.

'Gray she may be . . .' Was there a twinkle in Dion's eye? 'But Galway this is not, by a matter of miles.'

Slowly Mickeen nodded. 'You have a point there, and a good one. Still a name she must have, and quickly.'

But there seemed very little haste about the two of them as they stood there in the pale morning sunlight, feasting their eyes on the horse as it nodded and shifted in front of them.

'I have the answer. We shall leave it to the lady, the queen in her big boots.' Mickeen spoke with sudden, alarming certainty.

'Me?' Janna was as surprised as if the filly herself had spoken.

'Ladies know about such things.' Mickeen nodded his head wisely. 'You'll bring her luck, it stands to reason.'

Janna blinked. She could hardly believe it. Surely it was only given to princesses and millionaires' wives to choose the name of a thoroughbred racehorse? Yet here she was, plain January Brown, standing knee-deep in Irish mud and being consulted as if she was some sort of world authority. She was deeply, absurdly flattered. The only problem was, her mind was a complete blank.

'I have the answer.' Dion's voice, slow and considered. She was glad to be rescued, but very sorry to have missed her chance. 'Let her be called January, for the lady. January Girl.'

'January Girl . . .' Mickeen mused. The filly's ears pricked forward, she nudged him with her nose. 'It has a fine ring to it.' And it did, the way he said it. All three looked simultaneously at the horse and knew that it was her name. Janna felt suddenly dizzy, as if it were herself that had been re-christened, her own name given back to her transformed.

'What better gift could there be, from one pretty lady to another?' Mickeen was smiling as if a race had been won already. 'For she is the colour of your eyes exactly.'

'Really?' Janna felt herself blush scarlet – almost bridled like a filly herself under that warm approving gaze. But Mickeen hadn't finished yet.

'Silver they are amongst the grey, like snow in shadow – a rare sight indeed in this green, green place.'

Dion laughed at the expression in Janna's face.

'Don't mind him, January mine, he's lived alone too long and must pay the price for it. No woman will have him now that has not four hooves and a tail for a bridal train!'

'And am I not saving every penny I have in the world to be married, and have been these four years past?' Mickeen's voice rose in plaintive mock protest.

'Thank you, Mickeen. I'm honoured. I hope I bring her luck.' The words sounded stilted, but Mickeen looked pleased. Suddenly it seemed very important to Janna that Dion's friend should be pleased.

'And you the heart's own darling. Why did you not tell me, Dion Malloy?'

'Am I the fool that should tell you, Mickeen, and you looking for a wife these four years?'

Janna smiled, and blushed, and smiled again. She knew the two men were only teasing her, but she liked it, the banter, the exaggerated courtly grace of the words they used, the wry looks they gave each other. As they ushered her towards an ancient rattletrap of a horsebox, January Girl following docilely behind on her tiny hooves, Janna felt like a queen flanked by her knights at the head of a cavalcade. After coaxing the filly into the box with a handful of new grass Dion installed Janna in the magnificently dusty cab between Mickeen and himself. No need for conversation as they jounced down the farm track, and no possibility either.

'Where are we going now?' Janna mouthed to Dion over the earth-shattering din.

'To the races,' he mouthed back, grinning.

It was only when they reached the metalled road and Janna's eyes fell on her now hugely muddied rubber boots that she realised she'd left her own shoes behind, in the lee of Mickeen's crumbling drystone wall.

But by then that was the least of her worries. As the van thundered westwards, scaring up gulls from fields that glistened like velvet, she couldn't help raising a silent prayer of thanks for each minute that found her still alive. If only Mickeen hadn't been quite such a careful driver. The problem was January Girl. Her weight in the box behind made the old vehicle tricky to handle as a jumping bean, so Mickeen allowed the ass-carts and cyclists and horse-traps and fishermen bound for the Shannon such an enormously wide berth that half the time his outside wheel was up on the verge and Janna's heart in her mouth. She only hoped he never had to pass a pantechnicon, or they'd be in the next county. The sight of Mickeen, frowning face and hands gripped deathly white on the steering wheel, didn't help. It was indeed a long way to Tipperary, and not as the crow flew.

But at last, up a track white with limestone dust, somewhere between two seas on the Galway road, they found it. Not so much a race meeting as a party, a picnic, a fair – men in droopy tweeds and tobacco-stained moustaches, bright-eyed children, prime bloodstock tethered anyhow at the roadside, tinkers and their stone-faced women with plaits black with oil, dogs everywhere, stalls and hawkers and an open-air dance platform where three fiddlers played for themselves while boys ran in and out between the planks. The course itself was almost invisible, barely sketched out between the white-daubed rails.

'Just in time for breakfast!' announced Dion as he swung Janna down in the merciful silence after the engine coughed its last.

'But we've had breakfast already!' It must be past lunch-time by now.

'You can never have too many Irish breakfasts.'

After buttermilk bread and juniper smoked ham, wedged

237

into a towering edifice that Dion called a bookmaker's sandwich, Janna began to understand what he meant. It seemed as if she could go without sleep indefinitely as long as she kept on eating, and food tasted so good in this air. I'm going to regret this, thought Janna, as she bit deep into the bread, with its sea-sweet taste of soda. But she didn't stop. After her sleepless night she had to eat just to keep on her feet.

Mickeen ate nothing, but downed an Irish double whiskey – three times the quantity of an English single, naturally – to steady his nerves. Looking sober as a judge and reeling only slightly he headed off to confront officialdom and find his rider.

Janna, feeling fairly riderless herself, what with the two breakfasts and her backlog of fatigue, followed Dion into the crowd. It must have rained here only a little while ago, because there was a fine friendly smell of wet wool and crushed grass and damp leather. The winner of the last race, wild-eyed and steaming under his satin-edged blanket, was dancing under the eager pressure of half a dozen hands. There seemed to be no paddock, no centre to the gathering at all, just a free-for-all, with horses being saddled up wherever their jockeys fancied. They moved through the crowd like kings, shining and tall and masterful, bowing their heads in gracious appreciation of their subjects' loyalty. Every so often in the crowd there was a knot of more serious activity, fast talk and money changing hands, or a circle of faces round three grubby cards.

'What are they doing?' Janna stared, fascinated. Around her people milled, nudging, jostling her elbows, but for the first time in a crowd she felt no fear. It was as if the terrible sea voyage had dislocated her temporarily from her old self, set her adrift. Now, for an hour, for a day, she was a castaway. It was a strange feeling, reckless, almost free.

'I'll show you.' Dion shouldered his way through the crowd, brandishing a pound note. The cards flew, the crowd oohed and ahed, Dion pointed to a card, the man shook his head, turned it face upwards. The pound disappeared into his bulging pocket.

'You lost!' Despite herself, Janna was surprised.

'Of course.' Dion was smiling, quite unworried. 'That's what always happens with Find the Lady. If you could win, it wouldn't be worth playing in the first place.'

'Then why throw good money away?' Janna couldn't help feeling scandalised.

Dion shrugged. 'To see – an artist at his work, the magic of it. You should try it yourself, not Find the Lady maybe, but Crown and Anchor, Under and Over Seven . . .'

'I wouldn't dream of it.' Janna spoke with what she hoped was dignity. 'I don't approve of gambling.'

'Ah, you English . . .' Dion's eyes teased. 'I wonder, is it the love of winning or the fear of losing that offends you most? I take it you won't be backing January Girl, then?'

'I don't know.' Janna was sorely tempted. She almost felt as if the filly was her personal property now. 'Do you think she'll win?'

'There's no way of telling. It's her maiden race. You'd have to take a chance.'

Janna hesitated, then shook her head. 'In that case, no. It's not worth it.'

'Just as I thought.' Dion rolled up his eyes in mock despair. 'If Providence herself opened her arms to you you'd have to test her biceps first.' He sighed deeply. 'Well, if that's the way of it, you'll have to give me the money.'

'What?'

'We agreed, remember?' Dion's expression was innocence itself. 'Before we left No. 3.'

Janna set her teeth. 'I had no idea you intended to use it to back a horse.'

'Why else would I want it?' Dion seemed almost shocked. 'I have everything I need and more besides.'

Janna sighed in her turn. When in Rome . . . 'Very well, then.' Why did Dion always make her feel petty and small-minded, a timid little suburban housewife? 'I will lend you the money, but on one condition – that if you win, you use it for something worth while.'

'Worth while – well now.' His eyes twinkled at her. He

didn't seem to realise she only had his best interests at heart. 'How many new roofs can a body possibly need? Perhaps I should find myself a fine fat piggybank, start saving for my old age?'

'Be serious, Dion.' Someone had to be. Janna held out the wad of notes. It was an expensive point she was making, but maybe it would sink into that shaggy head. 'If you can't think of anything sensible, I will. Just leave it to me.'

'Very well so.' He took the money from her with an urchin's glee. 'I always wanted to be a scholarship boy.' He lifted her hand, dropped on it the lightest butterfly kiss. 'Let my life rest here.'

Janna winced as the entire wad disappeared into a bookie's leather satchel. She didn't want Dion's life – she just wanted to help him, straighten him out a little. This might be a roundabout way of doing it, but needs must when the devil drives . . .

And perhaps it was the devil himself who entered January Girl's flying hooves in the 2.30 – better known as the just about ten to three – and whisked her past the winning post a clear two lengths in the lead. Wonderful odds, too. If Janna hadn't been so dazed – it all happened so fast, and January Girl looked very different at full gallop, her ears laid flat and her jockey crouched into a tiny flailing ball over her shoulders – she could almost have felt disappointed. Glad for Dion, of course – but he hadn't been meant to win, not at all. It wasn't good for him. How on earth had he managed it? Him and his three-card tricks . . .

'I think we should celebrate, don't you? Wait here, I'll be back before you know it.' Janna could only nod as she watched Mickeen hoisted onto January Girl and carried off laughing. She hardly felt like a winner, somehow.

But when Dion came back she couldn't help but smile. Behind him, jingling and creaking, came a little piebald pony with crepe flowers on its bridle, drawing a painted yellow cart.

'You've bought it?'

'Without consulting you?' Dion looked properly shocked.

240

'How could I live with myself and do such a thing? No, but it's ours for the afternoon. Hop in.'

Janna had no idea it would be such fun riding in a horse-drawn cart. The road ahead was a different beast altogether, no longer a hazardous switchback but a peacefully unrolling ribbon. There was time to notice the shadows of clouds, count the greens, smell the air. She could hear bees. The swing and sway, the clop of hooves, the rhythmical nodding of the shaggy head in front, with its two velvety ears on their independent mountings, made an absorbing counterpoint. Under the rough brown-and-white coat the pony's haunches rolled like water. She could make out each hair in its straw-like tail. From time to time a shiver ran over its skin as if a mayfly had lighted on the surface of a pool.

All these things she seemed to see very clearly, with eyes outside her mind – and yet if she looked too closely the image blurred as if she'd misted up a glass. Perhaps it had something to do with the light, so pure but so variable that she could never quite pinpoint a colour before it brightened or faded beneath a cloud. They were heading due west, into the heart of the declining sun. Perhaps if they kept on going the day would never end.

After a while Dion gave her the reins to hold and she liked that too, the slightly damp, seaweedy feel of the leather, black with age and polish and pony sweat. Dion leaned back in the wooden seat with a great gust of a sigh.

'What a picture we must be making – John Wayne and Maureen O'Hara to the life . . .'

Janna burst out laughing. The empty air took up her laugh and returned it to her with a sigh.

'Where are your finer feelings, girl?' Dion gave her a look that was eloquently pained. 'This is not a comedy we're playing but a romance. The blue hills of Connemara, a beautiful girl and a pony with its back turned . . .'

'Don't try that on me, Dion.' Janna straightened her back. 'I'm holding the reins, remember.'

'That is so.' Dion frowned mightily. 'And I've no desire to end up in the ditch, me that bathed only yesterday – or was it

241

the day before? No matter.' He gestured grandly towards the horizon. 'A change of scene, then – let no-one say I am not versatile. Behold the endless plain – Hungary, I think – the gathering clouds. Revolution is in the air –'

'And the smell of manure, doubtless.' Janna spoke tartly, to cover a little thrill of unease. Dion's voice had dropped an octave, setting up sympathetic vibrations down her spine.

'Silence, woman. No manure in this drama.' He stared fiercely out to the blue distance. 'We are the embattled peasantry, you and I both, cast in the heroic mould. But lost, lost . . . At any moment they'll ride down upon us, the Cossacks with their cold steel, slice us from gullet to gizzard between one breath and the next –'

'Dion!' Her blood chilled. He was all too convincing. Seemingly at his bidding the sun slid behind a cloud. It was as if a door had closed. Suddenly the white road was stony grey, the clop of the pony's hooves a lonely sound, every bird's voice silenced. With the gilding gone the landscape was suddenly bleak and hard. Only now she realised it must have been changing for some time. No more lush grassy pillows, but black bogland scarred by the raised tissue of silicon-striped rock, pitted with whiskey-brown pools like hostile eyes.

'It's only a filum, girl.' Dion's eyes were wide and blue. 'Everyone comes here to make them, because there's no telephone wires to limit a man's imagination.'

'I see.' Janna was relieved. That was why the setting seemed so strangely timeless, as if they'd stepped back a hundred years. So simple a thing.

'And every Irishman, right down to the last Dublin Jackeen, cast in his own starring role.' Dion's voice mused. He sounded half asleep. 'It's what the world wants of us, after all.'

The sun came out again, making the rocks sparkle with mica, revealing the brown pools to be shallow after all, not bottomless pits leading down to the earth's core. But for Janna there was no going back to her light-hearted mood. Every boulder hid a Cossack.

'It's getting late. Shouldn't we be getting back?'

Now there was a little wind, cool, salty, the faint sad cry of some bird – a curlew, a plover? It might be her imagination, but to Janna the light seemed to be fading. She hoped Dion knew where he was going. A little coot scuttled nervously across the road ahead like an uninvited guest. Yes, this was a wild, bleak, abandoned place, even in summer. Grey and mauve and every shade of brown between, shading away to the far purple hills. A landscape like a bruise.

And then, seeping into her consciousness so slowly that for all she knew it might always have been there, came the sea. The road dipped a trifle and there it was, level, silvery, glass-still. On the horizon the faintest brush-marks of islands. Between, the etched black curve of a solitary boat, below, a half-moon of pale sand. A scattering of coloured pebbles, a scrawl of dark weed along the waterline, and nothing else. Not a soul, not a sound, not a single dividing line between sea and sky. Just emptiness and light.

The pony stopped, unbidden. The road had dwindled to almost nothing. Silently, Dion unhitched the animal, covered it with a blanket from the cart and tethered it at the verge, weighting the reins with a large stone. Ahead was a low whitish cottage, almost indistinguishable from the earth it rose from, the roof thatched with bleached grass, the tiny windows set deep. Behind it there was a cluster of smaller buildings, a few enclosures, haphazard as a child's toy outgrown.

Slowly Dion led her through the bones of what might have been a garden. Beside the door he hesitated.

'What is it?' Janna half expected a pit of snakes, a vandal's cave. Dion threw open the door. It leaned crazily on one hinge. Inside, instead of the expected darkness, was a limitless vista of milky sky. Half the roof was gone, the back wall crumbled, the frontage a mere façade.

'*Céad míle fáilte*. A hundred thousand welcomes, to the house where I was born.'

Water had gathered just inside the threshold. In one easy movement Dion lifted Janna up and over, setting her neatly on her feet inside. She stood there, for a moment lost for words. The cottage was so sad, with its spikes of rafters, its

243

little windows and walls protecting only emptiness – and yet there was something wholly, recklessly right about it, like a child's truth at a grown-up's party.

'The Emperor has No Clothes.'

Dion smiled, picked up a stone and sent it wheeling far up through the non-existent roof and into the endless sky.

'There is more enterprise in going naked, as the poet said.'

'But what happened? Where did they all go?'

Dion shrugged. 'Away. It is the tradition, in Connemara. My sister to Canada, my brothers to the States. The next parish to the west, that's how they think of it here.'

'Why not you?'

He smiled. 'I'm the baby of the family. Babies must always be contrary.'

'You should go, you know.' An idea had suddenly occurred to her. 'You're a painter – you should go to New York. New York is the place for artists, that's what everyone says.'

'So.' Dion stood very still, watching her. 'You would like me to go to New York.'

'I didn't say that.' Janna hesitated. 'But it would be good for you. You might be a big success. You should try anyway.'

'Would success make me a better painter, do you think?' She had the impression he was teasing her.

'It might.' Janna's voice strengthened. 'I think you should go. With the money you won today. Take a chance.' Janna paused. She still hadn't quite forgiven him for backing a winner and making it look so easy. 'Only this time, on something worth while.'

Silence. Clearly she'd taken him by surprise.

'But what about you, all alone in that old house?'

'Me?' Janna smiled. She could never be alone, in No. 3. And if Dion was gone . . . Suddenly she had a vision of herself in the parlour, receiving visitors, entertaining dinner guests. Coffee, candlelight, conversation – it would all be so much easier without Dion's footfall on the attic floor. 'Don't worry about me, I'd manage perfectly well.'

'The big man, the blond fellow – perhaps he'd look after you?' Janna felt herself blush. He'd read her mind too closely.

'His name is Gray.' She spoke with dignity.

'I had not forgotten.' Dion regarded her gravely. 'He means a lot to you.'

'Everything.' Janna sighed. 'You've seen him.'

'Hmm.'

'I think – I think if I could make him love me I'd be . . .' Janna's voice tailed away. There were no words for what she meant, it was beyond imagination.

'Home and dry?' Dion's tone was helpful. 'Past the winning-post?'

Janna gave him an old-fashioned look. How could he hope to understand, with his track record?

'He's the perfect man. My dream.'

'He has my sympathy.' Dion shook his head. Janna looked up sharply, wondering whether he was being deliberately insulting, but his face was bland. 'What does he do with his time, your Gray?'

'Well . . .' For a moment Janna didn't know what to say. She could only guess at the details of Gray's life. But she didn't want Dion to know that. 'He runs the estate, of course.'

'You'll marry him, then, and live in his big house?'

Janna hesitated. Somehow, the way Dion put it, it sounded so – ordinary.

'I haven't thought about it.' She felt her cheeks grow warm. She'd thought of nothing else for months.

'It's just that, being a practical man, I couldn't quite see him in No. 3.' Dion's tone was gently apologetic. Somehow that only served to make Janna more uneasy.

'No?' Minute by minute Janna was beginning to realise how much better it would be if Dion did actually go to New York. These discussions were – unsettling. How could she possibly lead a life of her own with him overlooking her affairs from the attic? 'Don't you like him, then?'

Dion shrugged. 'He's a man among men, there's no denying it. And doubtless the finest of fellows with two or three drinks inside him.'

Janna opened her mouth then shut it again. Dion was jealous, of course, of Gray's looks, his position, everything.

'I think you should go to New York.' Although she tried hard to control it, her voice came out a little high. 'You'd like it. There's a bar on every corner.'

'And me forgetting you were such a woman of the world.' Dion's face for once was expressionless. Janna shivered in a sudden cool breeze from the sea.

'Very well, then.' Dion turned away. 'Let us be getting back to – civilisation.'

'I can hardly wait.' Janna wrapped her arms round herself. She was angry, but not only with Dion. She'd come here on false pretences, after all. She'd assumed Dion would help her, just as he had with Liane. She'd thought it would be easy. But she'd forgotten how prickly he could be. As for kissing him – Janna shivered. Yesterday seemed like a century away.

Stumbling a little in her eagerness to get away, Janna followed Dion up the shadow of a path. Now she had no difficulty imagining why his family had left this place behind them. That was all she wanted now. If Mickeen couldn't drive her back to Dublin, she'd have to find someone at the race meet who could. There was sure to be an evening flight back to London, and she'd get on it somehow, even if it meant borrowing the money from Dion. With luck, she'd be back at No. 3 soon after nightfall. Tomorrow there'd be time to press her dress before Dene.

The cart, its sunny yellow faded to gamboge in the dying light, looked like an old friend. She'd be glad of the pony blanket round her shoulders on the way back.

She found Dion looking up the empty road with a faraway expression on his face. Something in his attitude stopped her in her tracks.

'What's the matter?'

He shrugged, raised one eyebrow in the direction of the cart.

'See for yourself.'

Janna looked. There, a little pathetic in the white dust, lay the blanket. But the pony was gone.

246

CHAPTER SEVENTEEN

Janna's first thought, as she searched the gathering dimness on the horizon was – Cossacks. Silent as wraiths, they'd swept down from the hills and captured the pony, leaving Dion and herself no means of escape. She shook free of the thought with an effort. It was just the Celtic twilight playing tricks with her nerves. Her second thought took her across the road to the spiky, shrubby grass behind which the lighter line of the sea shifted and whispered. The pony couldn't have gone far. It must be down there on the shoreline somewhere.

'I wouldn't waste any more energy, if I were you.' Dion's voice was dry. 'That beast will be halfway home by now.'

Janna looked up at him doubtfully.

'How can you be so sure?'

Dion shrugged. With one foot he rolled away the stone that had weighted the pony's reins. 'See that trace of iron on it, where he moved it with his hoof? He did it himself, on purpose. Doubtless he's been well trained. It's an old gypsy trick – they sell one horse in the morning, get another back, just like it, in the afternoon, and no-one's the wiser . . .'

'But if you knew that . . .' Janna controlled her voice with an effort. 'Why on earth did you hire a gypsy pony in the first place?'

'It slipped my mind, I'm afraid.' Dion smiled at her disarmingly. 'What with January Girl, and the winnings . . .'

Those winnings, thought Janna despairingly. I knew it was wrong from the first. Now look what's happened. I should have gone home then, while I had the chance.

'Not to worry.' Dion's teeth flashed white in the dimness. 'It's a fine night. It would be a shame to waste even a minute of it.'

'You don't understand.' Now the full extent of the disaster was beginning to sink in to Janna's mind. 'I've got to get back home today, I've simply got to. I'm due at Dene tomorrow, filming starts at 6 am on Monday morning!'

'Monday? But that's a whole day and more away.' Dion didn't seem remotely concerned. 'Don't worry, we'll get you to Dene in plenty of time, just you see.'

Janna gritted her teeth. Dion's casualness was infuriating. What did he know about deadliness, appointments? He either turned up late or not at all. All that side of life was left to her. She was the one who made lists, answered telephones, made sure bills were paid on time . . . She didn't expect him to understand about Gray, but what about No. 3? If she wasn't at Dene ready to shoot her scenes first thing on Monday morning, Fernand would be quite likely to withhold his second payment on the roof. And then where would they both be?

As for Dion's confidence that she'd get back on time, it was clear he hadn't realised tomorrow would be Sunday. She'd be lucky to get a flight at all – that is if she managed to reach the airport in the first place. On the way here she hadn't seen another human dwelling, not a single vehicle, let alone a bus-stop or a telephone. She might as well be on the other side of the world.

But there was no point in trying to explain that to Dion. He would simply shrug, smile, leave everything in the lap of the gods as usual. She watched, exasperated, as he picked up the pony blanket, shook it clean with what seemed to her exaggerated care, and arranged it round her shoulders.

'Hop in.' He gestured at the cart. Janna stared at him with what she hoped was withering scorn.

'Why? I can't exactly go anywhere!'

'I know that.' Dion's voice was soothing, as if to a maiden aunt. 'But you might as well be comfortable while you're waiting. I have things to do.'

But so have I, thought Janna in anguish. I wanted to get back home today, to be rested and ready for Dene. After two sleepless nights what kind of impression am I going to make

248

on Gray? I won't even have the chance to have a bath, press my dress, do any of the things Liane told me. This is terrible. I've planned so long, tried so hard. How can one day with Dion ruin everything?

And yet she was helpless. She sat, staring out to sea, where the incoming surf was edging up the sand, ice-white and just as cold. She pulled the blanket close, strained her ears in the hope of catching the throb of an internal combustion engine, but there was nothing but the rustle of grass and the hushing of the sea. She looked at her watch. Its small illuminated dial seemed like the last bastion of civilisation. Nine o'clock. Time to take her pill. She forced it down dry, almost choking on the irony of it, feeling as if the sky and sea were watching her and laughing at this poor human creature, as weighed down with senseless plans and precautions as a tinker with pots and pans. But she had no-one to blame but herself for what had happened. She should never have involved Dion in the first place – it was as good as asking for trouble . . .

Trouble himself, blue-eyed and black-haired, appeared suddenly at her elbow, hand upraised to lift her down. Stiffly, her rubber boots catching in the blanket folds, Janna clambered from her wooden throne. All the excitement of the day was gone. She felt cold and hungry and very, very tired. The thought of the long hours of darkness ahead was almost more than she could bear.

As she stumbled back down the shadow path and saw the cottage door open wide in a mockery of welcome Janna felt tears rise up in her eyes. She missed No. 3. She wanted to go home. No, she wanted to be home, magically, with a rafter fire in the grate and a cup of hot tea in her hand and water running in the bath . . .

'Welcome to the stable.' Dion smiled. 'After the horse has bolted, maybe, but we still have a door of sorts.'

And that wasn't all. As Janna entered she saw that in a corner of the cottage, between two sound walls, sheltered by a makeshift windbreak of old sacks weighted with stones, a small fire burned. More sacks over two mounds of what looked like heather lay on either side of the fire. Neatly ranged beside it were some potatoes with earth still clinging to their skins, two tin cans full of water and a third with small yellow flowers.

'Dion . . .' Surreptitiously Janna brushed her tears away with a corner of the blanket. She didn't know what to say. The cottage had become a different place, transformed. Firelight painted the walls, bringing them alive, fragrant blue smoke curled from the turfs. She was drawn in by the ancient magic of it, the warm, obedient light.

'Sit you down and warm yourself.'

Tentatively Janna subsided onto the mound Dion indicated. It was surprisingly comfortable. She held out her hands to the chirruping fire. With an expression of great concentration, Dion dug deep in the heart of it and revealed five small potatoes hidden in the embers. He handed three to her, punctiliously wrapped in his own handkerchief.

'I'll catch you a fish for your breakfast.' His smile flashed out, taking Janna by surprise. The potatoes were very hot but she couldn't wait for them to cool. They tasted good, charred and earthy. They warmed her from the inside. Small things . . . it was amazing what small things could do. Already she felt a little better, ashamed of her bad temper. Dion had risen to the occasion so much better than herself.

'Well . . .' She dusted off her hands, shook the earth and potato skin off Dion's handkerchief, handed it back to him. 'This is certainly an experience.' Remembering the experience she'd planned for, Janna blushed a little guiltily. At least that was out of the question now. She couldn't help feeling relieved.

'Cold feet?' Dion inquired solicitously. It was as if he'd read her mind. Janna was glad of the semi-darkness, glad too of the horse blanket and her rubber boots. Nothing could be less romantic.

'A little.' She looked down at her feet. 'It's these boots. I feel like the frog princess.'

Dion laughed, dug deep in his pocket. 'Here – I've been saving these for just such an emergency.' He unrolled the small ball with a flourish. It was a pair of fluffy woollen socks.

'Every Irishman carries a spare pair, just in case.'

Before Janna could deter him he reached forward, tugged off her boots.

'Warm your toes first,' he directed, with the authority of long experience. Janna held them out to the fire, wriggled them a little. She could barely move them. They seemed to have frozen into one block of ice. She noticed with sorrow a hole in the heel of her stocking, wished she'd had the foresight to bring a spare pair. But then she could never have imagined she'd be sitting here, a whole country away from home, miles from anywhere.

She looked down to see that Dion had impaled the socks on two sticks and was carefully toasting them over the fire. As she watched he reeled one in, pressed it against his cheek, nodded, then swiftly, dextrously, slid it over her foot.

'How's that?'

'Wonderful.' Janna half closed her eyes. Such a simple, sensual pleasure, cold skin in warm wool, like plunging her foot ankle-deep in tropical sand.

Dion was busy stacking the remaining potatoes in the embers.

'We'll have them cold, for breakfast. With the fish I'll be catching.' He saw her expression and laughed. 'No cheating now. You'll be hungry in the morning too.' He leaned back, dusted off his hands. 'Well, now.' He beamed at her. 'Fresh-dug potatoes, a good fire and better conversation. What else in this world could a man desire?'

Janna sighed. If only life were so simple.

'Problems, Miss Brown?'

'Please don't call me that.' It was all very well for Dion to make fun of her for being serious, but someone had to be. 'January's bad enough, but Brown is worse.'

'Oh, I don't know.' Dion's eyes teased. 'It could have been Gale, or Sale . . .'

'Don't be ridiculous.' Despite herself, Janna had to smile. 'Even my mother wouldn't have done that to me.' As soon as the words were out she wished she hadn't spoken. There was a short silence. She was uncomfortably aware of Dion's eyes on her, difficult to read in the flickering light.

'Did she hate you so much, then?'

'Of course not.' Janna spoke sharply. To her horror she felt tears again, pricking painfully at the back of her eyes. Now she knew why she'd almost cried coming up the path. It had reminded her of all the other times. The path, the open door – and nothing on the other side.

But she never cried about that any more. She was tired, that was all, and the smoke was getting in her eyes.

'It's just that –' Janna took a deep breath to calm herself. 'I don't think she wanted me, not really. I always felt – in the way somehow. She used to scrub me with a loofah.' She smothered a sound that was half laugh, half sob, not at all what she'd meant it to be. 'I think she was hoping she might wear me away altogether.'

'Oh, January.' Dion's voice was suddenly deep and soft as the sea. 'So much sadness in the world. Your poor mother! What she lost by not loving you.'

Janna blinked. She'd never thought of it like that. Had there been a path that led nowhere for her mother too? She looked at Dion, a little uncertain. He had a gift for turning everything upside-down, as if the world might make better sense that way.

'Your mother . . .' Suddenly she realised how little she knew about Dion's family, apart from what he'd told her today. 'What was she like?'

Dion shrugged. 'I hardly knew her. She was almost fifty when I was born. She had me in the change, died when I was only five. I was fed by my sister – she'd just had her first.'

'It sounds – incestuous.'

Dion smiled. 'I suppose it was, in a way. My sister was my mother, my niece my sister . . . I grew up thinking all women were related to me somehow! But it was a practical solution. It was best I should be taken for my sister's child, my father being ten years dead.'

Janna stared, wide-eyed. 'Then who . . .?'

'The lodger, who else? Only seventeen, poor lad, and chosen for the Church.'

'The Church?' Janna heard her voice go high.

Dion's smile widened. 'Are you shocked? No need to be. I like to think of it, him so young and lonely, missing his own mother doubtless. He'd be a better priest for it, I'm thinking.'

'So it seems quite natural to you?'

'As a horse is born to run.' Dion smiled at her in the half-dark. It didn't seem right that a man with such a sweet tooth should have not one filling in his head. And a priest's son to boot . . . Janna shook her head. Maybe she hadn't been wrong about the horns after all.

'But it doesn't seem right.' Janna tried hard to straighten out her thoughts. 'Fifty and seventeen – he should have been with someone his own age, surely?'

'Two virgins?' Dion laughed easily. 'A hopeless combination. You might as well try and start a fire with two damp twigs.' His eyes rested on Janna with a speculative gleam. She shifted uneasily on her sacking, wishing the plants underneath didn't crackle with every movement she made.

'I don't suppose you were ever a virgin yourself.'

'Not since I was fifteen.'

'Were you in love?' Janna tried to imagine Dion in love and failed. But it was easier to guess what he'd been like at fifteen. A few inches shorter possibly, chin a shade lighter, but otherwise much as he was now.

'Of course.' Dion nodded sagely. 'I was fifteen.'

'What about the girl?' Janna tried to sound stern. She must have been underage, after all.

'I wanted to marry her, but her parents disapproved, as well they might.' Dion sighed philosophically. 'Better marry the wind, her father said, and he was not wrong.'

'You're not the marrying kind?'

'I didn't say that.' Dion's eyes laughed. 'I'm open to offers. Now if a certain celebrated film star were to make me a proposal, in glorious technicolour, I would have to consider my reply very seriously indeed . . .'

'You mean me?' Janna relaxed a little. She was more at home with his bantering tone. 'I'm not famous, or likely to be.' Thinking of one of her coming scenes with Gray her face clouded. 'There's this bit in the film, with Eden . . .'

'A love scene, is it?'

Janna gave him a sharp look. How had he guessed? Was she that transparent? 'It's this – kissing business.' Janna shrugged, trying to sound casual. 'I think it's overrated.'

Dion laughed out loud. 'You just need practice, that's all.'

'Practice has nothing to do with it.' Janna spoke with as much dignity as she could muster in a pair of men's socks. 'In some cultures, you know, they don't do it all.' She wondered suddenly, uneasily, if she sounded too much like a library book.

'But nothing could be more natural, surely?' Dion's eyes twinkled. 'We all do it – dogs in the street, rats in their tunnels, babes in the womb even. Imagine that now. They say a little rat will know its siblings always, though it's not seen them since the day it was born. Once kissed, never forgotten. So many questions to be answered, when you taste a stranger. Who are you – where have you come from – where are you going – are you my friend? Yes.' Dion nodded gravely. 'It's an important business, kissing. Life or death.'

Janna eyed him doubtfully. She had the suspicion he was laughing at her. Rats, dogs indeed . . . 'I've seen what dogs do in the street, thank you.'

Dion shrugged. 'Very well, then.' He leaned forward, stirred the fire. 'What's your favourite food?'

The change of subject took Janna by surprise. She didn't like to talk about food, but perhaps she was safe enough here.

'Chips.' Instantly a vision of them, golden, sizzling, swam before her eyes.

'With vinegar or without?'

Janna sighed. 'With. And mayonnaise.'

Dion closed his eyes for a moment as if faint. 'Oh, sacrilege. The poor potatoes. But never mind.' He leaned back, apparently satisfied with the fire's progress. 'Well, then, there's your solution. All you have to do, before you kiss this Eden, is imagine that you are leaning over an exquisitely moist, savoury newspaper-bundle filled to the brim with piping-hot chips, malt vinegar and a great deal too much mayonnaise.'

254

He folded his arms, regarded Janna sternly. 'You would kiss a chip, would you not?'

'Not for long.' Despite herself, Janna smiled. 'I'd have to eat it, once I got that close.'

'My point exactly.' Dion nodded in perfect agreement. 'That's what a pair of lips is for, tasting and eating. Try mine.'

'What?' For a moment Janna couldn't be sure that she'd heard right.

'Try mine.' Dion spoke a little louder, clear enough for the smallest child to understand. 'Pretend I'm Eden, if you like.' He smiled obligingly. 'Or Gray. Or the doorstep of No. 3, or your most favourite aunt, I don't mind which. Go on. I promise I won't bite. I won't even move.'

Janna stared at him, utterly taken aback. She didn't know what to say, didn't even know how she felt. To be confronted so suddenly by the opportunity she'd planned for, only without any of the long elaborate build-up she'd prepared, left her numb with shock. Especially since she'd changed her mind.

'Remember –' Dion nodded encouragingly. 'The closer you get, the less there is to worry about. It's like boxing – once you're inside your opponent's defences, you're perfectly safe.'

Safe? Of course she was. Something in Janna stirred in response to the challenge. It was only surprise that had made her heart beat erratically, not fear. She had nothing to fear from Dion, she knew that. And he made it sound so easy, so simple, it seemed almost churlish to refuse. She hesitated, mentally assessing the distance between them. She could just about reach if she leaned forward. But even so . . .

'Don't forget to sniff first.' Dion reminded her. 'Then you can change your mind if you want to.'

Janna couldn't help but smile. Dion sounded exactly like a Boy Scout offering to escort an old lady across the road. Cautiously, like that rat in the tunnel, she moved towards him. Even as she did so she knew that if she hadn't been so tired, if it hadn't been for the smoke in her eyes and her hair and the safety of the heavy rubber boots, she couldn't have done it. But this was more like kissing a relation than a lover, just as he'd said. A matter of duty, not inclination. A sort of formality, one of those bridges that needed to be crossed then left behind without a backward glance.

She sensed the warmth of his skin long before she touched him. Tentatively, she breathed in. He kept very still. He smelled of green grass and newly-turned earth and apples. Almost edible, in fact. Their lips touched. As promised, Dion kept his still. They were warm and muscular and quivered a little with half-suppressed laughter.

'How was that?' Janna leaned back, looked up anxiously. Dion put his head on one side, debated a moment. 'A little – well, forensic. But not bad for a first try. Now I will kiss you.'

Before she could draw away he leaned forward, kissed her chastely beneath the ear.

'Oh.' Janna was both relieved and a little worried. She hadn't wanted to fire him with passion, but she would have liked some reaction to her own attempt. How else was she going to learn?

'Very well.' Dion nodded once, didactically. 'Now I am going to kiss you seriously, as a lover would kiss you. Are you ready?'

Janna nodded unhappily. She was afraid she wasn't going to be very good at this.

'I will keep up a running commentary as long as possible, like a driving instructor, to show you how it's done. First I pause, so, in the middle of a sentence –' Janna stared at him, mesmerised like a charmed bird. Suddenly he was close, so close she could count his lashes. His eyes were blue and fierce.

'Now, I can no longer control myself.' Janna shivered. Dion seemed to be able to control the pitch and timbre of his voice at will. Obediently, she closed her eyes. His mouth touched hers, suddenly supple, resourceful, so different from before that it took her breath away. It invaded her, melted her. All thought of what she should do next or how she should react fled from her mind. There were no rules left, no boundaries. When at last he withdrew his lips her mouth felt as if it belonged to someone else. They stared at each other. He was breathing hard. She felt as if she'd never breathe again.

'How was that?' At last Dion broke the silence.

'Very . . . er . . .' With an effort Janna gathered the shreds of herself together. 'Personal. I don't think I should kiss Eden like that.'

'Maybe not.' Dion looked at her a little quizzically. 'It depends on what happens next.'

'Next?' Janna felt her heart lurch.

'In the scene. The one you were worried about.' Dion's tone was patient. Janna felt herself blush.

'Of course.' Her heart was pounding. She tried hard to concentrate, remember the details of Fernand's script, but they escaped her. Fatigue. It was affecting her memory.

'Well? What happens next?'

'We – er –' Janna made a vague gesture. 'Make love.' That much she knew, because the plot hinged on Jeanne becoming pregnant and forcing Eden into marriage.

'Very well so.' Dion rose in one swift movement, kicked off his shoes without bothering to undo the laces and began to unbuckle his belt.

Janna stared, horrified. 'What are you doing?'

'Taking my clothes off.' Dion smiled. 'It is usual, I assure you. I'll help you in a minute.'

'Wait!' Dion was halfway through unbuttoning his shirt already. In the midst of her consternation Janna had to admit Liane would have given him full marks for attack. 'Please don't.' Her heart was thumping at her ribs, her face felt scarlet. 'There's no need. Really.'

'Of course there is.' Even in the half-light Janna could see the spark of amusement in Dion's eyes. 'You need the practice. And this is better than some draughty rehearsal room, don't you think?' Quicker than she would have believed possible, he was naked. She looked away. He was a primitive study in black and white, graphic as a cave painting.

'Dion.' Janna knew she must sound like a schoolteacher with a delinquent pupil but she couldn't help it. 'This is very embarrassing. Please put your clothes back on. Why, someone could come in at any minute!'

'And what if they did? You'll need to get used to that too, surely, on the set?'

'But this is different.'

'Why should it be?' Dion bent unconcernedly and added another turf to the fire, which gave an appreciative little sigh.

'Because . . .' Janna's voice faded. She felt disorientated, completely confused. *Because this is for real. Because this is us.* How could she begin to explain something so obvious? If only she could think straight . . .

'What's your first line?' Dion was standing now, perfectly relaxed, his black hair as usual standing on end, his eyes smiling at her. Now Janna felt as if she was the one who was naked.

'I don't have any.' With an effort Janna dragged her gaze away from his nipples, tiny and bewitchingly pink in the dark silky hairs. 'Mine isn't a speaking part.'

'The best kind.' Dion smiled. 'Then let's improvise.' He paused for a moment, deep in thought. 'How about – "You're the most beautiful woman I've ever seen." '

His voice seemed to have dropped a full octave. It reverberated inside Janna's bones. She gave a shaky laugh.

'You should be in movies.'

'Did I give it too much?' Dion looked concerned. 'Very well, then.' This time he spoke quietly, almost conversationally. ' "I love you".'

Foolishly, tears pricked at Janna's eyes.

'What's the matter?'

Janna sniffed. This sea air – it made your eyes water. 'No-one's ever said that to me before.'

' "I love you, I love you, I love you." That's three times, to make up for a world of fools.'

Janna felt the corners of her mouth turn down like a sad child's.

'What's the matter, January?' Dion's gaze was on her, steady, almost contemplative. 'They're just words. I love you, January.'

'Stop it.'

He shrugged. 'If you don't like my line, then give me another.'

Silence. Where was Fernand now? No instructions, no counting of paces, just silence and the rustle of the fire.

258

'Then you must touch me.' Dion's voice, calm, reasonable. 'I won't move, I promise.'

In a dream, because she was there, because she didn't know what else to do, because she could no longer stand there silent, looking, Janna reached out her hand, touched his cheek. It was warm, lightly stubbled, just as she'd expected, and yet different. More solid somehow. His lips twitched. Instinctively, afraid of what he might be about to say, she covered his mouth with her hand. And then, as her fingers touched his warm mouth, he closed his eyes, in a gesture of such perfect trust, such childlike pleasure, that Janna felt something hard and closed and dry in the centre of her body uncurl and melt away, leaving only emptiness. She took her hand away. Dion's eyes opened, the pupils swollen and dreamy.

'For the love of heaven, woman.' His voice was quiet, reasonable, patient. 'Will you now take off your clothes?'

Janna searched his face. What was there to be frightened of, after all? This was no ogre. This was Dion, her lodger, the man upstairs, familiar as her own carved newelpost, the man who could bend a $\frac{3}{4}$ inch copper pipe into a figure-of-eight without breaking it, who could pass through solid walls and make no sound.

'You think I should?'

'Yes.' His eyes were deeply, wholly serious. 'It's only fair.'

Janna had never realised her blue silk had so many buttons. Her fingers seemed suddenly clumsy. She stopped when she reached her slip.

'Off. All of it.' Dion needed no megaphone. Janna slipped the straps off her shoulders, felt the fabric slither the length of her body, felt air close on her naked skin.

'Now.' Dion's voice expressed nothing but heartfelt satisfaction. 'At last. After all this time. My very own January.'

Janna felt herself sway. She would have closed her eyes but she didn't dare. She braced herself to be touched, caught, held so tightly that it hurt, but nothing happened, nothing at all. She looked up to see that Dion was smiling, not triumphantly, or lustfully, or in ridicule, but with pure, bewitching friendliness. From somewhere, as if by magic, he'd summoned up two bottles of Guinness.

'I don't want to be drunk!' Janna's voice was higher than she'd meant it to be.

'You didn't want to be naked either.' Dion uncapped one bottle with a practised flick of the wrist against the door jamb, handed it to her. 'Better have some. It's full of iron. You may be losing some blood here.'

Janna thought she'd misheard for a minute, choked on the bottle rim. Was nothing secret from Dion? He met her accusing stare with an equable grin.

'There's an Irish laugh in everyone somewhere.'

Janna felt tears in her eyes, bubbles in her bloodstream. She licked the bitter froth off her upper lip and wondered if she could really be here, stark naked with Dion, toasting the loss of her virginity with bottled ale. It wasn't possible, surely. Her skin felt hot, her brain was whirling. She must be ill, out of her mind. Pneumonia perhaps, the first stages . . .

'My feet are cold again.'

'Ah, yes.' Dion's voice was mildly reproving. 'You should have left on my socks.' Janna choked again at the image of herself, naked but for two hugely woolly feet. What would Liane have said to that, she wondered.

'But I shall warm you.' Gently, Dion covered her foot with his own. Looking down she saw that his feet were even more beautiful than she'd remembered, high-arched, narrow-heeled, with toes as graceful as fingers. At that moment she realised she'd been cold all her life and never known it, a sleeper with her eyes tight shut against the morning sun, a hen imprisoned by a thin chalk line, a miser starving in a cellar full of gold.

'Thank you.' The words weren't adequate for what she felt, but they were all she could find to say.

'You English.' Dion laughed. 'At any moment you'll be asking me if you can leave the table.'

Janna shook her head. She'd come too far to run away this time, even though her heart was beating so fast and hard she could barely stand. And then, she found herself inside the circle of his arms. She held her breath for one shuddering moment then let it go. His warmth anchored her. So simple in the end, the touch of skin to skin, like entering a warm sea. Her head fitted into the hollow of his neck. He stood quite still, letting her hear his heartbeat like music in a nextdoor room. His hair smelled of salt and crushed grass. She closed her eyes. She could see so much better then, the gates of her mind thrown wide on another country, an infinite perfumed hinterland she'd never known existed till that moment. As he lifted her, laid her gently back against the sacking she felt suddenly weightless, free. His hands were very warm. Under his touch she felt as if she was shedding her familiar skin and growing another, as supple and smooth as a newborn baby's, elastic enough to contain a whole new world. Her other self, landlocked, so serious and dry, was left behind for ever.

She knew his mouth now, knew every curve. He covered her with his body, holding her close so that she would belong to him entirely. He moulded himself to her, strength meeting softness, until she didn't know where her limbs ended and his began. She breathed him in, felt his sigh, felt the weight of his longing like something always known, felt the centre of her body open to let that knowledge in.

And in return – nothing. No victory, no secret, no solution. Only this. The taste of salt. Honey at the flower's heart. A beat of time, indefinable as a colour, fragile as a single sound. Dividing, making whole. Letting the silence and the sea air and the sadness in, to be part of her for ever, like water through the reeds, finding at last its small way home to the sea.

'I'd like to meet your mother one day.'

'Why?' Laced in his arms Janna felt safe as a swaddled baby.

'Because of my interest in lineage, my little racehorse.' With one hand he traced the line of her thigh under the rough blanket. 'There's good limestone grass in these bones.'

'What on earth would you do with her?'

'Take her to the pub.'

'To the pub? My mother? She'd never go.'

'It's not naked that she'd be going. I shall ask her. Unless she'd signed the pledge?'

'Dion, you're drunk.'

'Now you do sound like your mother.'

'How would you know? You've never met her!'

'All mothers sound like that. You will one day.'

'Never.'

He laughed deep in his chest, folded her tighter in his arms.

'That's what they all say. Be grateful to your mother that you were born at all. She gave you the air, the sky, the sun – and me. Think of that, now. I am your mother's gift to you.'

'You're being Irish again.'

Janna felt his lips brush soft as doeskin against her ear. 'And why not? Someone has to be.' He curled himself round her like a cat, relaxed, and within instants she could tell from the sound of his breathing that he was asleep.

But Janna lay awake, wide-eyed, watching shadows cross the surface of the moon and stars career in the sackcloth sky. Darkness and light, strange as her own self, discovered. Young and old, empty and overflowing, a speck of dust, a diamond. Safe within his arms. Set free.

CHAPTER EIGHTEEN

Dawn turned the sky to mother-of-pearl. Janna opened her eyes on the beginning of the world. No sun, just light. Cool, unutterably clear. No wind, no birdsong. Silence like a bubble, poised, reflecting radiance.

Janna could feel Dion's naked body warm against her side. She didn't move for fear of waking him, hardly dared breathe in case she broke the spell. She felt so new. Raw, tender, fragile. Even her eyes seemed to have been washed clean in the night. Above the blanket all the colours looked so bright they might have been lit from inside. The grass, blue-green, she could see each blade of it, see each molecule of air in the blue sky. Has the world always looked like this, she wondered, have I been blind? It's all so different from what I thought.

Dion turned and she felt her heart turn too. Very slowly and carefully she eased herself up so she could see his face. He was still fast asleep. With his eyes closed he looked innocent, almost defenceless. She studied his face, amazed. There was so much about him she hadn't noticed before. How could she ever have thought him ugly? His skin was so white, his hair curled so beautifully against the nape of his neck, he breathed so neatly and silently, surrendered utterly to sleep, like a small boy, a tired, piratical little boy exhausted by pillage and plundering, one hand curled at his cheek, the other resting possessively against her side.

'I love you.' Janna whispered the words so quietly that his eyelids didn't even flutter. The words were lost in the dawn, became part of it. She wished she could stay there for ever, watching him sleep, learning his face, remembering, knowing there would never be a moment quite like this again. Perfect, endless, outside time.

Even as she lay there, motionless, hardly breathing, willing herself to remember this, everything, the feel of his legs against hers, the texture of the blanket, the silence, the light, there came a noise from the road outside. Dion stirred. Quickly, Janna slipped from the makeshift bed. Leaving Dion felt like severing a limb. She dressed as fast as she could, shivering from the cold, looked out of the window. There, by the cart, was a battered Volkswagen with variegated wings, one blue, one orange.

As Janna stared, the car horn sounded again, and a man got out, walked round to the front, looked around. He was wearing what looked like a long black skirt.

A priest! Of course! Janna's mind raced. Who else would be driving down a deserted country road at 6 am on a Sunday morning? Even as she watched the priest began to walk slowly down the path leading to the cottage, obviously concerned to find the owner of the abandoned cart. Janna's heart lifted. Dion had been right. She had a chance of getting to Dene in time after all, a god-given chance.

Then, looking back at the cottage interior, Janna's eyes fell on the two beds, only one of them rumpled, the fire ashes, the top of Dion's head poking out of the sackcloth, the empty Guinness bottles ... What would a priest make of such a scene, which told its own obvious, even faintly sordid story? What would a priest know of the way she felt, the smell of Dion's skin, the warmth that ran through her when he touched her, the miracle of waking up beside him in the dawn? Another thought, even worse to contemplate, sent her searching for her bag. She had to prevent the priest reaching the cottage door. This was a small parish, after all. It was just conceivable that the middle-aged man outside on the path might be Dion's father ...

Hurriedly, Janna smoothed her hands over her hair, went out, closing the door very carefully behind her. She was relieved to notice that the priest's eyes were brown. She didn't want to think of Dion every time she looked at him.

'I wonder ...' She saw the priest's eyes scan her blue silk and rubber boots with good-natured surprise, and blushed a little. 'Could you give me a lift to the nearest town?'

'Why, surely.' The priest smiled. 'I'm on my way there myself, to early-morning mass.'

As Janna climbed into the Volkswagen she looked once back at the cottage, wishing she could have stayed, to see Dion's face when he first opened his eyes and saw her there. But she was doing the right, the only sensible thing. Dion would understand, once he saw her clothes were gone. Dene was important for both of them, more than ever now. And it was foolish to worry about him, alone at the cottage. Dion was resourceful, no-one more so, and at least he had enough money now to get back to No. 3 under his own steam.

Janna smiled as she leaned back against the worn seat. No. 3. She'd see him there, very soon, just as soon as she could get away from Dene. That much was certain, Holy Writ. Sooner or later Dion would always come back to No. 3, because all his paints were there.

It was late on Sunday evening by the time Janna reached Dene. There was no-one to meet her at the station. She was glad of that, because her rubber boots would have been difficult to explain. Fortunately, as the ferry carried her back to Liverpool on a millpond sea, she had ample time to bathe and brush the grass seeds out of her hair. She hadn't enough money to fly, but she didn't care, now. She'd abandoned the idea of going home first. She didn't need to any more. As she walked in the summer darkness from Dene station to the big house, much as she had the first time, empty-handed, wearing the wrong clothes, she felt like a different person. She was filled with a sort of radiance, a combination of fatigue and excitement and pure happiness that made her feel she must glow in the dark like a firefly.

Even Dene looked different to her now. Smaller, somehow, with its classic lines interrupted by lighting towers and generators and fill-in screens, its razored lawns criss-crossed by cables. Maybe, once you'd slept all night beneath the stars, four walls could never seem quite so important again.

But even so, Janna's heart missed a beat at the thought of being here again, where it all began, seeing Gray once more.

265

'Till Dene.' His last words to her, promise and warning all in one. Would he see a change in her too, she wondered, would he see starlight and firelight written in her face, her eyes, the way she moved? That other Janna, dazzled and dazzling in her borrowed Fortuny, that one golden bubble of an afternoon in Monte Carlo, seemed like something from a past life. And yet – even now she couldn't be sure, not entirely, until she saw Gray again.

Luckily a night crew were still working in the Great Hall, setting up for one of tomorrow's scenes. They were too busy to notice anything odd about Janna's appearance as she stole in, relieved to see that Fernand's location manager had pinned a large plan of Dene complete with names and numbered rooms on a temporary notice-board rigged up by the double doors. She'd been put next to Julie, she was glad to see. She made her way up the stairs as quietly as she could. Her case was waiting on her bed.

Her last thought, as she curled up beneath the covers, the clean sheets feeling cold, almost unfamiliar against her skin, was of Dion. She felt joined to him somehow, as if there was space beside her in the bed where he should have been. But thinking of him made her feel warm. He was there in her mind, real, alive, every time she closed her eyes.

What seemed like only a minute or two later someone thundered on the door. Janna struggled from deep sleep to realise that it was 6 am. Bright sunlight was streaming through the window. Fernand will hate that, thought Janna sleepily. It will get in the way. And then, Dion will love it. I hope the sun is shining in Ireland too. Almost instantly she was wide-awake. There was so much to look forward to, so much to do. She leapt out of bed, showered, picked out a pair of black trousers, a plain white T-shirt, put them on, belted the trousers as an afterthought with her two-tone blue belt. Blue and black. She liked them very much. They were Dion's colours, the exact shade of his eyes and hair. She'd been drawn to them, despite herself, when she'd chosen her blue dress and black shoes. It was strange to think that she'd been wearing Dion, like a second skin, all along.

The mirror showed Janna that her clothes looked better than they'd ever done before. They hung well, making her look taller, more upright. Despite her lack of sleep, her cheeks were pink, her hair lifted with a life of its own, her eyes shone. And yet, somehow, her own reflection didn't matter so much to her any more. She felt good inside, where it counted.

A knock sounded at the door, a tousled head poked round.

'Julie!' Janna ran to the door, pulled Julie in, reached up to kiss her on both cheeks.

'Hey, Janna!' Julie smiled, looking a little uncertain for the first time since Janna had known her. 'What's happened?'

'I'm in love.' Even as she said the words Janna knew she'd needed to tell Julie from the first, to make it real. Julie was her friend, her reference point. Telling her made it – official.

'I know.' Julie looked not so much surprised as confused.

'You know?' Janna blinked, taken aback.

'Yes, you told me yourself. Don't you remember? In New York.'

'Oh, that.' Janna blushed. Gray had seemed so important to her then, but already she'd almost forgotten. Did that mean she was fickle? No, what she felt for Dion was solid, strong, she couldn't mistake it. 'That was someone else. It's over now.'

'I'm glad.' Julie smiled. 'I don't think he was good for you, the other one.'

'You're right.' Janna nodded. Gray hadn't been good for her, or her friendship with Julie. He'd cast a shadow which was only now beginning to lift.

'Who was he, anyway?' Julie's eyes were curious. Janna shook her head. She wasn't going to take any risks, not any more. Julie was too important to her, more important than Gray had ever been, she saw that now.

'I'll tell you someday.'

Julie sighed. 'I suppose you're not going to tell me about your new one, either?'

'That's right.' Janna smiled, linked her arm in Julie's as they went down to breakfast. 'But when I do tell someone, you'll be the first to know.'

Despite her new confidence, Janna was relieved that Gray

wasn't present at the breakfast table. After the meal was over cast and crew dispersed, Julie to the make-up room where she was to get ready for a scene in the pleasure garden, Janna to the rehearsal room she'd been allocated to block out her love scene with Gray.

Janna was the first to arrive. The room was small, clearly used mostly for storage. In one corner three wooden crates had been pulled together to represent, she supposed, a bed. Of course the scene itself would be shot in the ruined cottage in the grounds. Janna smiled. No wonder Fernand hadn't been able to resist that cottage. It was a nineteenth-century folly, more picturesquely ruined than any real ruin could ever be, the perfect setting for Jeanne and Eden's only major scene together, with its elements of betrayal and masquerade. It was clever, too, how Fernand had managed to work the cottage into the story. Out hunting with Eden and Julia, Jeanne falls from her horse. Eden goes back to rescue her, finds her injured, carries her to the nearest shelter, and there . . .

Janna's gaze fell uneasily on the three box crates. Fernand would instruct her, of course, and it wasn't as if she and Gray would be alone together, but even so she couldn't help feeling nervous. Before going to Ireland with Dion it had been her ignorance that worried her, but now it was her knowledge. Would she respond to Gray's touch as deeply and instantly as she had to Dion's? Perhaps, after her years of self-imposed loneliness, she was incapable of self-control? Perhaps Fernand, casting her as Jeanne, the loose woman, weak, sensual, greedy, had been wiser than she knew?

The door opened. Janna swung round, but it was only Fernand.

'Ah!' In his usual way, he seemed neither pleased nor displeased to find her there. When he was working, people were simply tools. If they were missing, they had to be found or replaced, that was all. He motioned her over, gave her one of those razor-sharp glances which seemed to read her mind. 'Janna. Please remember, everything depends on Jeanne in this scene. If she is not "sympathique", if she is wooden or professional, then no-one will care about her pregnancy,

Gray's proposal of marriage, her dilemma. We must see, not the whore in this scene, but the woman. Suddenly, out of the blue, she is confronted by something entirely strange to her – a man in love. Imagine what that must mean to a woman like Jeanne, whose body has belonged to so many uncaring men. She has no idea what to do, how to react, how to defend herself against something more than simple lust. She has no experience of love. Love is for ladies only. And yet if she succumbs she will place herself in terrible danger, betraying not only Julia, but herself.'

Janna swallowed. Fernand eyed her.

'Do you understand?'

'Yes.'

'And you will do it?'

'Yes.'

'Good.' Fernand looked at the crates through narrowed eyes. 'No nudity, of course, there is no need for anything so explicit. The audience will not know for sure whether Jeanne has succumbed to Eden until the final reel, so the revelation of her pregnancy will come as – just that, a revelation.' He swung round with that small, slanty smile. 'An immaculate conception, *n'est-ce pas*? You would have known all this, of course' – he paused reproachfully, 'if you had been at home, yesterday, when I called.'

'I'm sorry.' Janna gave him an apologetic smile. 'I've been – busy. Very, very busy.'

'Preparing your role, I hope.' Fernand's voice was stern.

'Yes.' Janna blushed. 'In a way.'

She was almost glad to hear the door open behind her. She turned to see Gray. Once more, she was taken aback by his beauty. He seemed to carry his own lighting around with him, always Rembrandt, always high-key. His skin was lightly tanned from the weeks in Nice, a smooth even shade of chamois brown which accentuated his blondness. His hair was a little longer than when she'd last seen him. He'd brushed it back from his forehead. His pale blue cashmere sweater exactly matched the colour of his eyes. And she'd forgotten how tall he was. For a moment she wondered how Fernand was going to arrange for them to kiss each other at all.

'Hello, Janna.' At the sound of Gray's voice, against her will, Janna's heart beat faster. Could he possibly remain so cool after he'd kissed her, even in rehearsal? Fernand would make them do it again and again until he was satisfied, she knew that. She risked just one look into Gray's eyes. What she saw there sent a not unpleasant shiver chasing down her spine.

'Hello, Gray.' Janna turned away with an attempt at casualness, though every inch of her body prickled in awareness of his eyes. She felt something strange coursing through her body, a sort of strength she hadn't known she possessed. She felt almost – powerful, as if Gray could be hers any time she chose, just as Liane had said. She looked up to see Fernand watching her too, speculation in his gaze.

'Very well, *mes enfants*.' Fernand spoke quietly. No need for a megaphone this time, with only the three of them in the small dusty room. 'You know the script. Gray, you enter here.' With the chalk he always carried in his trouser pocket Fernand marked two crosses on the floor. 'You carry Janna to the bed, lay her down, keeping hold of both her hands. Then, the speech – then –' He made an expressive gesture with his hands. 'Janna?' Janna nodded. Her heart was beating too loud for her to speak. 'Remember, you are wearing an ankle-length riding costume. Your hat has fallen off, your hair come loose. So. Now you know all you need to know. *Allez-y.*'

Fernand took up his position by the single window, frowning. Gray and Janna looked at each other for a moment. Then, gracefully, Gray removed the script from Janna's hands, laid it face down over his own copy. Janna's face flamed. Suddenly that seemed like the most intimate gesture she'd ever seen. He stepped forward, put one arm behind her shoulders, bent slightly and with what seemed no effort at all lifted her. His cashmere sweater was very smooth against her cheek. Remembering she was injured, Janna let her head fall against his chest. Being in Gray's arms was completely different from being in Dion's. He was stronger, taller, and yet, strangely, she felt less safe. She was almost relieved when he laid her gently on the three box crates.

He knelt beside her, his hands imprisoning her own, forcing

her to look at him. Fernand's words spilled from his mouth, but Janna hardly heard them. She was lost in the detail of Gray's face, never seen so close before. Not a trace of stubble on his chin, not a single smudge of paint. Every feature handsome, classic, from aristocratic nose to close-set ear, and yet there was nowhere for her eyes to rest, no focus anywhere. The speech ended. Janna half closed her eyes, feeling almost faint. She opened them to hear Gray speaking her name, Jeanne's name, hoarse with the undertone of pure desire. He leaned over her, blocking out the light from the single window. Their lips met.

Relief washed over Janna, making her realise how much she'd feared this moment. She liked Gray's mouth, smooth, expert. She liked the taste of his lips, they were pleasantly warm against her own, but that was all. Whatever magic Dion and Ireland had created wasn't here. Her body responded with pleasure and gratitude and relief. She almost smiled behind her kiss. It was simple, after all. It was going to be all right.

'Good.' Fernand nodded as they drew apart. 'Now, again.'

They took up their marks again. This time, Janna smiled into Gray's eyes. As she did so she realised it was the first genuine smile she'd ever given him. I was so frightened, before, she thought. But not any more. Because of Dion, no more fear. This time, too, Gray held her closer when he picked her up in his arms. Perhaps he was nervous too, thought Janna. She let herself relax against his chest. When the scene was over he smiled at her, a different smile, the kind she'd seen him give Julie.

'Why, Janna.' Gray's mouth quirked up at one corner. 'I had no idea you were such a woman of the world.'

He's flirting with me, thought Janna, pleased and amazed and subtly gratified. She recognised the game from her days with Julie.

'I thought you'd never notice.'

'Enough, *mes enfants*.' Fernand called them both to order. 'Time for the real thing.'

After all the preparation, filming the short scene didn't take

271

long. For once, the light was kind, remaining consistent from beginning to end of each take. For once Fernand didn't shout and curse behind the lens. For once, as Janna got up from her cottage bed after Fernand called 'Cut!' she knew before he spoke that everything had gone well. She even felt that Gray had become a friend. She still didn't understand him, he was still her mystery man, but they'd created something together, and that made a sort of bond.

The rest of the day was her own. Filming had gone so smoothly that she had time to take her blue dress to the cleaner's, mend the hole in her stocking, study the floor plan for tomorrow's wedding scene on the green baize notice-board, and catch the end of Julie's garden scene. She was going to be good, that was clear. Amongst the roses she looked like a rose herself. I wish I had a long neck like Julie's, Janna thought. But then maybe Dion likes short ones.

She made herself wait till after 7 pm before telephoning No. 3. As she'd expected, there was no answer. Even if Dion was back so soon, he rarely heard the telephone from his attic room. She spent two very pleasant hours composing him a postcard. When Fernand's usual messenger came to collect the cans of newly-exposed film for urgent processing in London, she managed to persuade him to take her card as well. The post was too slow. She wanted Dion to hear from her as soon as he got in. She only wished she could be there herself, to welcome him home.

But if all went well, tomorrow would be her last day at Dene. She was only needed for the wedding scene, which involved so many of the cast that Fernand insisted it must be shot in one day, because convening so many people and cos-tumes again would be a continuity nightmare. There weren't even to be the usual run-throughs, to save time.

That night, still tired from Ireland, Janna went to bed early but could hardly sleep from excitement. She woke in time to pack her case before breakfast, even though she wasn't due on set until the afternoon. Fernand wanted westerly light for the chapel scene, something to do with the stained glass. After breakfast, there was a hiatus. Julie and Gray were busy rehearsing a scene together, in fact everyone but herself seemed to have somewhere to go and something to do. But Janna didn't mind. Already her mind had raced ahead, to No. 3 and Dion. As she wandered from room to room, trying hard not to get in anyone's way, she realised she felt just as nervous and excited as a real bride, as if from today, her life too would be completely changed.

She was so absorbed in her thoughts that she missed lunch, only recovered herself in time to remember her dresser was waiting to fit her costume. Not Lisa this time, but a girl she'd never seen before. Everything changes, Janna thought. A week ago, that would have upset me, but not now. She stood patiently while she was arrayed in a cloud of antique Honiton lace, complete with flowered veil and white silk slippers. Looking in the mirror she saw a bride above all brides, white and perfect, fragile as spun glass, a chrysalis inside its exquisite cocoon. Not Janna Brown any more, but a symbol, a figurehead. Serious-faced, the dresser adjusted her veil very carefully, and warned her that the old lace was brittle, she must make no sudden movements, just in case.

Once dressed, Janna wondered what best to do. There was very little she could think of that didn't involve sitting or smudging her shoes or risking the intricate seaming of her tight-fitting bodice. At all costs she wanted to avoid lengthy repairs, or even worse, a re-shoot. And it would be some time, she knew from past experience, before light and sound and the arrangement of extras were choreographed to Fernand's satisfaction in the Chapel. If only Julie were here . . .

Carefully, lifting her heavy skirt so that it didn't touch the ground, Janna went in search of her friend. She wasn't in the Chapel, or in her trailer, or in the grounds, as far as she could see. She must be inside the House somewhere. Janna entered the covered passageway leading from the Chapel to the House. As she emerged into the Great Hall her heart beat a little faster, as it always did. In her lovely bridal white she could almost imagine she belonged there by right, the betrothed of the Lord of the Manor, being escorted to her bridal chamber by a retinue of attendants, the way before her strewn with rose petals, a footman with a burning taper striding ahead. She'd have bathed in milk and powdered with orris root, fasted till she was light as a flower petal, a butterfly.

Slowly, Janna ascended the marble stair. There was no-one in sight, she was Mistress of the House. Just a harmless fantasy, a sort of preparation for her role. Drawing out the moments, she paraded down the dim corridor leading to the State Apartments, nodding at the dark portraits as she passed. They didn't frighten her now. They were simply people, long gone, with their own hopes and fears. Goodbye, goodbye. After today, they wouldn't matter any more. Through the gilded and marbled doorways, beneath the coiled and clustered cherubs, until at last, with her shadow company milling about her, Janna was there, face to face with the Great Bed.

It lay, a huge, fallen blossom, rosy, scented. Faded petals open wide, but empty. No Julie. Janna turned away, lingered one last time. From the window, high above the park, she looked down on the green landscape, rolling away endlessly like the sea. Not an Irish green at all – richer, mellower, with an undertone of ancient gold, but somehow less sure, less sweet. Silently, Janna said goodbye to the sculpted hills, and the two-hundred-year-old oaks by the lake, and the gate-keeper's lodge, and the dragon-faced gargoyles on the roof, and the pale sweep of immaculate drive. They belonged to a dream and would remain there, a seamless fabric, a timeless, ancient tapestry. But there would be no Janna Brown at its intricately patterned heart. She'd be somewhere else, where grass grew long, under the stars.

'Janna!' She started, torn from her reverie so abruptly that she could feel the coloured threads unravelling still. 'I didn't expect to find you here.'

It was Gray. Caught off-balance, Janna didn't know what to do or say. She felt somehow guilty, a trespasser, an intruder, a poacher caught by the gamekeeper in the grounds. It was partly what he was wearing, the severe, almost sombre tones of full morning dress.

'You look – beautiful.' Gray's voice was very soft, his gaze just a little unfocussed. Janna was suddenly very glad of her

274

veil. 'Like a little china doll.' His voice seemed to turn Janna to china, fragile, breakable, ready to shatter at the touch of a hand into a million tiny pieces. She held herself together with an effort.

'So – we are to be married this afternoon.' The words so light, so without inflection that Janna had to rerun them in her mind before she could understand what he was saying.

'Yes.' She tried hard to mimic his lightness, recover the camaraderie of yesterday. 'I'm looking forward to it.' But her words, too, seemed meaningless, mere gracenotes over the real conversation that was going on between them, dark and ponderous as a drum-beat.

Silently, in unbearable slow motion, Gray took a step towards her. Janna's heart leapt into her mouth. It was as if he were walking over her skin. She felt the imprint on her flesh. Shivers prickled over her back and neck. And yet, she couldn't move. She could feel the warm blood draining from her face and pooling somewhere deep in the recesses of her body. Time stretched out, to snapping point.

Gray was close now, close enough to touch. Panic released Janna's muscles. She backed away, felt the lintel of the high window press against the base of her spine, swayed.

'Careful!' Gray reached out authoritatively to pull her back. His hand on the bare skin of her wrist was dry and strong. Janna closed her eyes. She'd nearly fallen. Her heart was racing so fast she felt faint. She tried to draw her arm away but Gray didn't let go. He was looking at her, searching her face under the veil. Janna felt her cheeks burn, turned her head away. She didn't want him to see Dion there. Suddenly she felt guilty, unclean. What would Gray think of her if he knew? He would never understand.

'You know . . .' Gray's voice was different now, a little hoarse. 'You know I have been thinking of this for a long time, Janna.' Denials, hot, passionate, rose to Janna's lips, but meeting Gray's eyes she couldn't lie. She knew. Of course she knew. She'd dreamed of this, just exactly this, so often and so long. The guilt of those dreams weighed on her. He knew, she knew. How could she explain that everything had changed?

'Please let me go.' Janna tugged again but his grip didn't loosen. A faint smile curved his lips, as if he was looking at a fractious, disobedient child.

'Never.' Trapped, Janna looked up at him. He was strong. She remembered how easily he'd lifted her into his arms once before and shivered. She could feel that same strength running down his arm and into hers like an electric current, cold, numbing. Silence. She fought to stay calm. He pulled her towards him.

'Please. Gray. My dress . . .' Terror for the fragile lace gave Janna a moment's strength. She strained away, felt his grip loosen, half closed her eyes in relief. It was just a game after all. He was going to let her go.

But no. Instead of releasing her, his fingers moved on the fastenings down her spine, expert, swift. 'No!' Too late. The lace fell back on her shoulders, she felt the starched veil prickle on bare skin. Under it she was half naked. Desperately Janna struggled to recapture the lace, hide herself again, gave a small moan of fear as she heard the fragile fabric tear. Between the lace and Gray she was trapped, helpless, unable to move.

Now he was smiling, a blind, bright smile. This was no dream. Pinning her arms to her sides he was urging her towards the Great Bed.

'No!' Breathless, forgetting the lace at last, Janna struggled against him. 'I don't want this!' Gray didn't hear her. It was like fighting the wind. The dress fell, a shell of lace. Beneath the veil Janna felt more naked than if she'd been wearing nothing. Gray imprisoned her with his body. She could feel the fastenings of his black frock coat pressing through the gauze against her skin.

'You're so different, Janna.' Gray's voice was a whisper. Janna froze, indicted. He knows, she thought wildly. He knows. It's my fault, it's all my fault.

Gray reared up, touched her body through the veil. His hands were hard, his face unreadable, preoccupied. This isn't real, Janna told herself. This can't be happening to me. If I close my eyes it will go away.

But it didn't. She could smell him now, clove-scented soap,

the tang of lime cologne. He pressed against her, heavy, insistent, but he was no nearer. She was lost, cold, far away. No feeling in her, no wordless tide unfolding to bring her home. She opened her eyes and he was still there, pinioning her. Her whole body ached under that gaze, which looked so closely but didn't see. Her throat filled, choking her. She turned her head away, helpless. It didn't matter what she did. Gray didn't see her. For him, she didn't exist.

It was that that hurt most, a hard dull ache, not just in her body but in her heart. Tears crept slowly from the corners of her eyes to gather in the hollows of her ears.

No kisses. Only tears, and pain, and sadness spreading deep inside her like a bruise. It was as if the Gray she'd known, the courtier, the cavalier, had died and she was mourning him, alone. She'd never felt so alone. To be so close to another human being and yet so far away . . . She lifted her eyes to the rose-pink canopy above her, trying to escape, looking down on herself and wondering how many other women had lain like this over the centuries beneath some urgent, oblivious man. Her tears were for them, and for herself, and for the golden braiding that was coming away and could never be bound again. The end of girlhood, the end of dreams.

At last, when Janna felt she couldn't bear a moment more, Gray eased himself away, breathing hard, and slid one arm beneath her shoulders. She lay completely still, empty of tears and pain and breath, a motionless rabbit in its snare. Her body felt chilled and stiff, as if it didn't belong to her any more.

'Janna, you're wonderful.' Gray's voice, a contented murmur in her ear. Janna flinched. Could it be, could it really be that even now he had no idea how she felt, hadn't understood her at all? Suddenly she felt stifled, suffocated, as if the ancient rosy folds of the Great Bed had fallen round her, filling her lungs with dust.

I've got to get away, she thought. I want to see the sky. I want Fernand to call out 'Cut' and tell me this was only a run-through, not real at all. She took a deep shuddering breath, flexed her sore, bruised body in preparation. One more minute to recover and then she would escape, forget everything that had happened, blot out each and every memory with a pure effort of will. It could be done. It would be done. It was the only way.

But a minute was a hundred years too long. Footsteps, eager, hurried, sounded down the corridor. Janna swung her bare feet to the floor but it was too late. Standing in the doorway, her face a powdered mask under a ravishing peony-pink hat, was Julie.

CHAPTER NINETEEN

No-one spoke, no-one moved. They seemed trapped for ever, Gray, Julie and herself, like flotsam in a frozen sea. Underneath, slow and terrible, black water moved. In the silence Janna was aware of something breaking. Nothing would ever be the same. No forgetting, now.

Julie's lips moved, the words coming out oddly, like a badly-matched sound track.

'See you in Church.' She shrugged, attempted lightness painful as a blow.

And then there was no more time. The sound of Julie's footsteps running back down the corridor. A breathless reassembling of clothes. Janna couldn't reach the fastenings at the back of her dress. She had to stand, silent and still, while Gray's fingers moved with aching slowness over each button-hole. Once he brushed against her skin and her whole body seemed to shrink away in revulsion. When it was done, it was as if an iron cage had closed around her ribs, she could hardly breathe. No air left in the room, no way of meeting Gray's eyes. No time, no time to think or feel or forget. All she longed for was to be alone.

But there was no escape, not yet. The Chapel was hot and bright under the lights, the air thick with the smell of lilies. Great sheaves of them were arranged in black lacquer vases, stripped of every leaf and wired so they held their graceful pose. A fashionable mutilation of the day. Janna looked away. She could almost hear the flowers screaming. Her eyes fell on the tomb of the third earl's wife who died in childbirth. In the crook of her marble arm was a small bundle, lovingly wrapped.

Janna tore her eyes away yet again. Her heart felt as if it was about to burst open. Oh, Dion. I was yours, and now what am I? She felt lost, disorientated, memories of Ireland overlaid by the image of herself and Gray in the Great Bed. How could she ever forget? Her own body felt like a stranger's, aching under the lace. But it was her own fault. She'd been trapped by her dreams, like those flowers wired on their perfect stems. She'd paid the price for that now, a thousand times over. Oh, Dion . . .

Thinking of Dion made her eyes fill with tears. Desperately Janna lifted her eyes to the rose window above the altar, but that was no better. It reminded her of Julie's peony hat. I've betrayed them all, she thought, Dion and Julie and the marble lady who died for love. Even Gray. He's not to blame, not really. He didn't see me, but that's because I hid myself away. I wanted to be different, for him. And I didn't see him, either. I invented him, made him into what I thought I needed, closed my eyes to everything about him that was real.

Knowing that, knowing that in the end it took two to make love without loving, Janna needed all her courage to turn as Fernand directed and place her kid-gloved hand on Julie's arm. It was Julie's role as Jeanne's protector to give the bride away. Together, to a scratchy recording of 'Adeste Fideles', they paced the endless mosaic aisle leading to the altar where Gray waited. Julie's face was averted, her profile pure and remote under the brim of her hat. Janna focussed on the strands of her embroidered veil. This was worse than any real wedding could ever be. She felt like a sleepwalker, condemned to pace this aisle for the rest of her life. When the moment came for Gray to lift her veil and kiss her on the lips her whole body cried out in protest, and memory, and pain. Not now, the kiss. She couldn't bear it.

But she did, because she had no choice, not only once but over and over again, until Fernand was satisfied. And then, at last, she was allowed to go.

'Don't forget, Janna.' Fernand's voice followed her. 'The second week of September, for the studio scenes with Julie. Allow a week, with over-dubs.'

Janna nodded. She couldn't speak. In the safety of the

trailer she stripped herself of the Honiton lace as if it burned.

It was late by the time she got back to No. 3. As she opened the door there was nothing in her mind, no plan. She wanted to see Dion, that was all. If he wasn't there, she'd wait for him. She needed him. He would explain. He would understand. He would make things right again. Because whoever and whatever she betrayed, Dion would remain the same. Dion made sense. He was another world, a sure star. Someone to come home to.

As she entered the familiar hall, her eyes fell on her own post-card lying on the floor. She tore it up hastily, glad that Dion hadn't seen it. So much had happened since those careful, inno-cent lines.

But Dion was back. Janna realised that, with a joyful lifting of her heart, as she passed the parlour door on her way up to the attic. She'd left it closed, but now it was wide open. Dion didn't like shutting doors. Janna ran up the rest of the stairs, knocked just once on the trapdoor. This was an emergency, Dion would understand.

There was no reply. Perhaps he was asleep already. I'll kiss him awake, Janna thought. Each kiss will take me a step nearer home. The trapdoor wasn't locked. She swung it open care-fully, saw that the interior was dark. Dion must be asleep, after all. Quietly, aware of the beating of her heart, she eased herself up the ladder and through the trap. It was the first time she'd ever come this far. It took a few moments for her eyes to adjust to the dimness. And then, for a blank, confused moment, she wondered whether she'd come to the wrong house by mistake. Because there was nothing there. No Dion, but that wasn't all. No clothes, no paints or canvases, not even a speck of dust any-where. Everything was unnaturally tidy and clean, as if no-one had ever lived there, the mattress stripped, the box shelves empty, the skylight closed tight, the door locked.

Stunned, unable to think, barely able to take it in, Janna stood in the middle of what had been Dion's room. There was nothing left, not a message, not a clue as to where he'd gone. Not even a drawing pinned to the rafters. It was as if the room had simply turned its back on her.

A creak of floorboards sounded behind her. 'Dion!' She spun

round, breathless with relief. But it was just the trapdoor settling on its hinges. She was alone, perfectly, completely alone. Suddenly she was aware as never before of all the noises in the old house, the creak of timbers, the rattle of pigeon feet on the slates, the sigh of empty air.

Dion is gone. She said the words to herself, slowly and carefully, but they made no sense. He couldn't be gone. It wasn't possible, not while she had his face so clear in her mind's eye, while her body ached with the need to touch him, when there was so much she needed to tell him, so many things that only he could understand.

But the room didn't lie. Slowly, stumbling a little on the rungs, Janna went down the ladder, closed the trapdoor carefully, uselessly, behind her. It seemed to make a different sound from before. Empty, hollow. It felt as if Dion had taken the heart of the house with him. Now, like her, it was simply a shell.

Slowly, heavily, she went downstairs to the parlour and sat down. Her body couldn't seem to register the fact that Dion had gone. Need for him gnawed deep inside her, a dull ache, an emptiness. What will I do without him, she thought. What will happen to me? How will I live, from day to day?

I don't understand. She rubbed her knuckles hard against her eyes. He loved me, in Ireland. I couldn't be wrong about that. It was too strong, too real.

'Janna, you're wonderful.' She shivered suddenly, remembering. It wasn't Dion who'd said that to her, but Gray. She buried her face in her hands. Love was never the same for two people, the Great Bed had shown her that. Perhaps, for Dion, she'd been just another girl. He'd known so many, why should she be any different?

Because I love him, she thought, every cell in her body rising up in protest. I love him so much I can't believe he doesn't feel something for me in return. She pressed her hands against her aching eyes. Something, maybe. But not enough. If he loved me, he wouldn't have gone away. If he loved me, he would have left a message, somewhere, to tell me where he'd gone.

She took her hands from her eyes. She felt cold, a deep internal chill even though the night was warm. She knew she should light a fire, but she couldn't, even though the grate was ready laid with coal. It would make her think too much of Ireland. She couldn't watch the flames alone.

Her eyes rested on the grate. Suddenly, hope flickered like a flame. She hadn't laid a fire before she left, and yet the grate was full of coal. Had Dion laid it? Was he meaning to come back after all?

She leaned forward eagerly, slid to her knees before the fire. Now she realised it wasn't coal she'd seen in the grate at all but something else, the last thing she would have expected. Shining, coal-black – a pair of shoes. It took her a full minute to recognise them as her own, the ones she'd left behind at Mickeen's farm, a hundred years and many more miles ago.

Janna's hands shook as she lifted the shoes out of the grate. She didn't know what to think. They'd been cleaned and polished, not a speck of Irish bog clung to the soles. Who had done that, Mickeen? Or Dion? Suddenly it mattered very much. She found herself holding the shoes very close to her. Suddenly it mattered more than anything, that Dion should have remembered to return her shoes, her little racing shoes.

Then, with a blinding flash that rocked her back on her heels, it came to her. Where Dion had gone, and why, and who had sent him, with his heart in his pocket and money to burn.

New York. Her own challenge, issued with such careless bravado, irresistible to a racing man. New York. An ocean away, the other side of the world.

It was then she realised for the first time that he was gone, the finality of it. He was far away, beyond her reach. She wouldn't wake one sunny morning to hear his footsteps on her ceiling, his voice on the stair. Knowing that, at last, she dropped her head and let them fall, all the tears she'd been holding inside her because there was nowhere else for them to go, scalding her eyes, wrenching at her throat, running down her cheeks and dripping onto the tips of her beautifully polished, almost new, patent-leather shoes.

*   *   *

The door. A different sound from the telephone, louder, less regular, more difficult to ignore. Janna stirred in her well of sleep. The doorbell troubled her. Like the sunshine behind her shutters, it told her time was passing, she was still alive.

But all she wanted to do was sleep. In sleep everything stayed the same. Her eyes opened and closed on the same room, only the light flexing its muscles outside the window made any change.

The doorbell sounded again, peremptory. Slowly, Janna levered herself to a sitting position, hoping to catch the nausea unawares. but it rose with her, despite the fact that she hadn't eaten for days. She'd tried feeding the sickness or starving it in turn, but whatever she did it wouldn't go away. It followed her everywhere, her constant companion as she tossed and turned on a voyage with no hope of arrival, an endless Irish Sea.

The floor was dusty under her bare feet, reminding her of how much she'd meant to do in the house before the last studio shoot. She had the money now, refunded by the council, but she'd done nothing. The cheque stood propped on her mantelpiece, still in its envelope. She couldn't seem to remember why she'd cared about hand-planed skirtings, eighteenth-century leaded lights. Everything had changed, since Dion had gone. All she wanted now was sleep, to sew herself up behind the curtain of her eyes for ever and a day. As if, somehow, that might bring him back.

Memories. They flooded in with the sunshine as Janna drew back the bedroom shutters. Pain and brightness together, the window filled with yellow and gold, a last fruit of summer light, ripe, ready to fall. It had been so long . . .'

'Good afternoon.' The voice of the light, blinding, familiar. Automatically, Janna looked down to the alley below. What she saw there robbed her instantly of thought and speech. Gray! She would have stepped back from the window but she couldn't move. His face, upturned, transfixed her. The full shock of his presence crashed in on her two heartbeats later, thunder after lightning. Blood rushed to her face, making her feel faint. Her stomach churned.

'Excuse me for disturbing you unannounced.' Gray leaned back that smooth pale head, narrowing his eyes. There was some expression in his voice that seemed out of place. 'I'm looking for Miss Brown.'

It was then, with a shock that rocked her a full pace back into the shadows of her room, that Janna realised what it was that seemed so strange about him. A simple thing, yet terrible in its way. He hadn't recognised her. Looking for the Janna Brown he'd last seen he hadn't expected a pale face at a window, a crumpled kimono, unbrushed hair. A sudden image of herself and Gray laced together in the Great Bed flashed across Janna's mind and she burned with shame. He'd seen her naked, but now he didn't know her. Somehow that made it worse, what they'd done, almost obscene.

'She . . .' Janna's throat constricted. She didn't know what to say. All she wanted was to disappear back into the shadows and the safety of her room. 'She's not at home.' She bit her lip. She'd almost told him that Miss Brown was dead. That was how she felt. Somehow, with Dion gone, Miss Brown had ceased to exist.

'Oh.' Gray looked a little puzzled. 'Will she be gone long?'

'She's in New York.' The words spilled out before Janna could stop them, part Julie's old excuse for unforeseen emergencies, part wishful thinking. Dion would have known me, Janna thought, pain stirring underneath her heart. Dying, blinded, in the dark – Dion would know me anyhow, anywhere. Looking down at Gray her vision was suddenly blurred with tears. Go now, she pleaded inwardly. Please, please go.

'Would you tell her –' Gray paused a moment, then changed his mind. 'No, perhaps not. Thank you.' A nod, a brisk dismissive smile and he was gone.

Janna let down the window sash very slowly. She felt faint and breathless, her heart thundering in her ears. It was as much as she could do to reach the door. She took one stair at a time, holding tight to the banister rail. Her head swam. She felt weak, weak and heavy, every movement an effort, as if she was very old.

As she passed the hall mirror Janna stopped dead. Looking back from the glass was a drowned girl, eyes wide and staring in her swollen face. Her hair was dull and lifeless, her skin very pale. I look ill, Janna thought. What is the matter with me? No wonder Gray didn't recognise me.

'I'm not myself.' Janna heard a stranger's voice ring out in the emptiness, high and thin, and knew that it was true. Something was happening to her, something beyond her control. She was either ill, or dying, or losing her sanity. Which of the three she had to know.

'Nothing to worry about, nothing at all.' The doctor bent over his pad. 'But I'll prescribe a course of vitamins, just to be safe. I'm a little concerned about your weight. Have you been eating properly?'

Janna shook her head. The thought of food made her feel faint.

'That will right itself in due course. Give it time.'

'I'm afraid I haven't got much time to spare.' It was the last week of August already. A shiver went down Janna's spine as she realised that if Gray hadn't rung so insistently at her door she might have lost track of time completely, forgotten all about Fernand's last studio scene. She'd so nearly let him down. She looked pleadingly at the doctor, hoping against hope that he could help her salvage in two short weeks what remained of Janna Brown.

The doctor's gaze rested fleetingly on her left hand. When he next spoke some of the clinical briskness had left his voice.

'I see you are not married. Perhaps that is worrying you a little? Have you –' he paused delicately. 'Have you enough to live on?'

'Yes.' That was so far from being a worry now that Janna was momentarily confused. She looked back at him questioningly.

'What about after the baby comes?'

'I beg your pardon?'

'The baby.' The doctor leaned forward, speaking very carefully and clearly, as if to a foreigner. 'Have you enough to live on after the baby comes?'

286

'What baby?' Janna felt faint once more. She must have misheard, surely?

The doctor said nothing, looking at her over his glasses with a strange expression, half doubt, half sympathy. Then he came round to her side of the desk, drew out a chair.

'Your baby, Miss Brown. You're pregnant.'

'No, I'm not.' Janna shook her head. It wasn't possible. 'I'm on the pill, you prescribed it for me yourself, don't you remember?'

'I know. But you must have missed a day, somewhere. There's no doubt about it, I'm afraid. You're pregnant. Between three and four months, I should say.'

Janna stared at him. Suddenly her heart began to race, with a wild and disbelieving joy. Dion's child! She was carrying inside her Dion's child! Something, something remained, something she could keep for ever, something to remind her of Ireland, and the races, and the little house with no roof, and Dion's smile. Everything wasn't lost. No – it was just beginning . . .

And then a small cold chill ran over her. She'd been so careful to take her pill, every day in Ireland. And after, faithfully, until that evening when she'd come home and found Dion gone. She'd stopped then. With Dion gone, there was no point. She hadn't even been surprised when her periods hadn't returned. That always happened when she didn't eat.

She listened, dazed, hardly comprehending, as the doctor explained, once, then again. It was always advisable to finish a course of tablets before ending treatment, he said. She'd been unlucky, but it happened.

'I did warn you.' The doctor's expression softened when he saw her face. 'But there you are. It doesn't make a great deal of difference how it happened, after all.'

'It does to me.'

Suddenly the full weight of what had happened hit her, the bitter irony. A mistake, the most awful, terrible mistake. Gray's child. Not Dion's, but Gray's. The child of the man who this very afternoon had seen her face to face and failed to recognise her.

'It's been a shock, I can see that.' Now the doctor's face was scrupulously impersonal. 'You must think everything over very carefully. You have a choice whether or not to keep this baby, but not for long. Come back and see me in two weeks at the very latest.'

Already, as she stumbled out of the doctor's surgery and into the summer streets, Janna felt like a murderess. She wasn't dying, but this was worse, far worse than anything she could have imagined. Gray's child was inside her. No matter what she did, she'd never be free again. She'd been invaded, colonised, her old self lost for ever. Whatever she did, whether she destroyed the child or kept it, she would be irrevocably changed. She looked around her wildly. It was the school holidays. There seemed to be children everywhere. One ran by, laughing, swinging on its protesting mother's arm. A tide of revulsion rose in Janna's throat. How could she destroy this child, her child? It hadn't asked to be born. And yet how could she keep it? How could anything living have been conceived by that loveless, arbitrary coupling in the Great Bed?

I won't love it, she thought, with a sort of pain. How could I ever learn to love such a child, looking at me with its father's eyes? But how can I condemn any child to live as I did, unwanted, always in the way? Nausea rose, threatening to overcome her. She clung to the iron railings, impaled by the irony. I don't love this child, she thought, with sudden clarity, and I never will. Just as my mother never loved me.

CHAPTER TWENTY

'It's not the script that is dead, it is you!' Janna shrank away before the expression in Fernand's eyes. 'You, Janna, are about as convincing as a wooden clothes peg on a washing line!'

'Well, this is Pinewood, isn't it?' Julie's voice, interceding. Janna felt a pang of gratitude. She and Julie might not be on speaking terms but they could still speak up for each other.

But Fernand was in no mood for lightness this morning.

'You too, *ma belle Julie*.' Now he included Julie in his scorn. 'What's the matter with you both? You're supposed to be two fully-grown women passionately in love with the same man, yet you show as little emotion as if you were competing for a dinner menu!'

Janna looked down.

'And what have you been doing these past months, Miss Brown?' Fernand's eyes rested accusingly on her face. 'Late nights, I suppose. *Les – les discos!*' He spat out the word. 'Women! Not one of you is to be trusted for a single moment! How could you do this to me, Janna? This may be a night scene, but I can hardly place all of you in darkness!' He paused. 'You at least, *ma belle Julie*, you have lost weight. I approve.'

Awkwardly, Janna tugged at the folds of her semi-transparent nightdress in an attempt to hide her rounded waistline.

'I give up.' Abruptly, Fernand turned away. 'In any case, it is time for lunch. Take yourselves off or you'll spoil my appetite altogether.'

In silence Janna and Julie made their way off the sound stage. Janna saw that Julie's face mirrored her own tension.

We look older, she thought, both of us. As if we've been living double time. She put a jacket over her nightdress. Gray's shadow hung between herself and Julie like a third presence.

'Oh, sod it.' Julie had dropped a contact lens. The tension lessened for a moment as they both dropped to their knees with the ease of long habit. They both spotted the tiny plastic disc at the same time, lunged with a crow of triumph, collided. Their eyes met. Tentatively, Janna smiled.

'Lunch?' Julie's voice was hesitant.

Janna nodded. She didn't trust herself to speak. If she did, everything might spill out at once. Questions hammered in her mind. Am I going to tell her? Can I tell her? What can I tell her?

The big dining area, lined with panelling salvaged from the wreck of the Mauretania, matched Janna's mood. She felt as if she was sinking too, slowly and surely, with no flags flying.

'You've changed.' Again that hesitancy, so unlike Julie.

'So have you.' It wasn't only Julie's manner that seemed different. As Fernand had said, she'd lost weight, while Janna had gained it. They'd probably take the same dress size now, despite their difference in height. Janna felt small and dull and frumpish, just as she had in the beginning.

'This scene . . .' Julie's forehead creased. 'It's not working, even I can see that.'

Janna shook her head in agreement. Once the scene would have mattered to her as much as it clearly did to Julie, but not now. There were too many other things on her mind.

'Do you mind if I ask you something? Something personal?'

Janna's heart plummeted. Here it comes, she thought dully. 'Go ahead.'

'Am I –' Julie hesitated. 'Am I any good? As a film actress, I mean?'

Janna blinked in surprise. It wasn't like Julie to show this sudden lack of confidence, let alone ask anyone else's opinion. And yet – she herself had seen what happened to Julie on film, how her glow became tinselly, her voice flat, her movements theatrical. What could she say? It would be easy to lie, but somehow she couldn't bring herself to do that. Julie deserved better.

'I think you're wasted on film. It's just – not your style.'

Julie laughed. 'I knew you'd tell me the truth, Janna.' She sounded oddly relieved. 'For my own good. You know something? I think you must be the only person in the whole world who's ever seen me without my mascara and lived to tell the tale.'

Janna smiled. What friends they'd been, she saw that now. The image of their friendship shimmered before her, beautiful, far away, like a mirage. And then, at that very moment, for the first time, the baby kicked, a restless little squirm of movement that made Janna gasp out loud.

'What is it?' Julie leaned forward anxiously, almost knocking over her Coke.

'I'm pregnant.' It was out at last. Silence. Janna half closed her eyes. The baby, its work done, subsided inside her, quiet as if it was listening.

'Gray?'

Janna nodded. She couldn't bring herself to look up and meet Julie's eyes.

'But didn't you . . .'

Janna read her mind. 'Yes. I was on the pill.' She sighed. 'But after I came back from Dene I stopped. Too soon, I'm afraid.'

'That wedding!' Julie cast up her eyes. 'It doesn't surprise me, not one bit. I knew it was all wrong.'

'A Freudian slip, you mean?'

'The only kind worth wearing, that's what I say.'

Janna looked up in astonishment. Yes, there was a twinkle in Julie's eyes. She couldn't believe it. Any minute now she'd be laughing. Seeing Janna's face, Julie was instantly penitent. 'I did mind, honestly I did.' She stared pensively off into the middle distance. 'When I caught you and Gray in the Great Bed I minded a lot.'

'I'm sorry.' Janna looked down.

'No, you don't understand.' Julie smiled something like her old smile. 'Not about Gray so much, but about the Bed. It was my place, my special place. He shouldn't have taken you there. He should have known.'

'I see.' A huge weight seemed to lift from Janna's shoulders, she was suddenly dizzy with relief.

'I knew you would. You understand about these things, because of No. 3.' Julie paused, her tone suddenly solicitous, as if she was enquiring after a mutual friend. 'How is No. 3, by the way?'

'Bearing up. Just.' Janna felt a pang of guilt. She'd neglected No. 3. She'd let it down, badly.

'You know, Janna . . .' Julie's voice was suddenly wistful. 'I envy you.'

'What?' Janna searched Julie's face for signs of amusement but there were none.

'You've got everything. A home of your own, talent, a baby. I wish I were you, Janna.'

'You're crazy. Here I am, unmarried, pregnant, and you wish you were me?'

Julie nodded, blue eyes serious.

'Babies love you, don't they? You don't have to work at it, they just do. You're so lucky. It'll be like – starting all over again. Only this time you'll have someone of your very own.' She gave a little laugh. 'That's what I always wanted, even when I was tiny. A sister. Someone who'd love me just because I was there. I always had to try so hard to make Father love me. There was always something missing. I was never enough for him. It was a strange feeling.' Julie frowned. 'As if I'd lost someone, somewhere. Like on a station platform, you know? All the noise and all the people, and you run about all over the place, and then you think you've found the person you're looking for, only it turns out to be someone else, a complete stranger.' She gave a little shrug. 'I was lonely, I guess. But it wasn't just company I was looking for, it was someone special. Two hearts beating as one. It sounds corny, I suppose. But I used to get it sometimes with men, just for a bit. That was all I ever really liked, lying together afterwards.'

Janna stared at her with suddenly new eyes. Julie the

seductress, Julie the glamorous and golden – had she never looked beyond that lovely façade, had no-one?

'Julie . . .' Janna spoke in a sudden rush. Lucky Julie, in the end. She'd be able to do things in the right order. 'I think you should get married, settle down, have babies. Lots of them.'

'Mmm.' Julie nodded. 'It was always at the back of my mind that I'd do just that. One day. If the worst came to the worst, you know? Marry Gray, surround myself with children and dogs, become a real country lady. Sort of an insurance policy. But now . . .'

'Now I've ruined everything.' Janna bit her lip. 'Oh, Julie. I'm so sorry.'

'No, no!' Julie seemed genuinely distressed. 'It's got nothing to do with Gray and you, I promise. It's just that – well, I can't. Have babies, I mean. I had some pain in New York, went for a check-up. Pelvic inflammation, that's what he said. Too many men, I expect.' She sighed. 'I wish I'd known. I always wanted a little girl. I'd have been a good mother, I know I would, once I'd settled to it. And now –'

'You'll make a wonderful godmother.' The words were out before Janna even realised what she was saying. But in that instant she knew she'd taken an irrevocable step. For the first time, because of Julie, she'd dared to think of the baby inside her as a real person. Now, she knew, she was going to keep this child. Whatever happened, it was hers.

'I'd like that.' Impulsively Julie reached out a hand across the table. 'I'd be family then, wouldn't I?'

'Oh, yes.' Feeling suddenly weak with the knowledge of what she'd just done Janna rested one hand on her stomach. 'This little bump's going to need all the relatives it can get.'

'Talking of relatives . . .' Julie spoke slowly, thoughtfully. 'What about Gray? Are you going to tell him?'

Janna shook her head. The fact that she'd decided to keep the baby made no difference on that score. There was no question of marriage between herself and Gray, she knew that now. They were worlds apart. He would never ask her and she didn't expect it of him. Of course, being a gentleman, he might insist on supporting her and the child, but that would mean including him in her own life once more, and she couldn't do that, even to provide her child with the father she herself had never known. Gray was a shadowy figure banished to the edges of her consciousness and he must stay that way. She'd manage, somehow.

'And Dion?'

'Dion?' Janna felt heat rise to her face. 'Have you seen him then?'

Julie nodded. 'In New York. At a party.'

Janna looked down. She could barely speak. 'How was he?'

'Fine . . . he seemed to know everyone.'

Janna swallowed. Jealousy seared through her body like a flash fire, leaving her empty and strangely calm. Why should Dion remember her? His life was full, the world his friend.

'It was just after I'd found out about my tubes.' Dear, prosaic Julie. 'I was rather upset.'

'So you told him all about it?' Dear, dangerous Julie.

'I did, actually. He's very easy to talk to, isn't he?'

'Yes.' Janna closed her eyes for a second, remembering. She could feel in herself like an actual physical hunger the need to hear Dion's voice again. 'What else did you talk about?'

'You.' Julie looked thoughtful. 'He said you were a very unusual woman. Rare as a live fish in the Liffey, those were his very words.'

'Oh.' That scalding heat again, as if she had one layer of skin too few. Had Dion been making fun of her, had they laughed together over her, the two of them? She could hardly bear it.

'And something else to do with fishing.' Julie frowned. 'What was it? Oh, yes. He said falling in love with you was like angling for trout with a live mayfly. The worst sort of madness. Only an Irishman would ever attempt it.' Julie beamed, evidently pleased with her effort of memory. Janna tried to return her smile but couldn't. Her face felt numb. And yet what had she expected Dion to say about her, after all?

'And then . . .' Julie paused, fractionally, then went on. 'Then we went to bed.'

So simple, almost matter-of-fact, and yet Janna's heart turned right over inside her body, like that sole live fish in the Liffey, the foolish optimist, gasping and choking in the poisoned water. Alive, but not for long. No sight, no breath, just pain and air that burned. She should have known. She should have guessed. Dion had good taste. And it was no more or less than she had done herself, after all. So why did her heart convulse and jerk against itself, all its valves gaping wide in a long soundless scream of mourning for the lost sea currents, the green freedom that would never be hers again? It was gone, that future, if it had ever existed. Goodbye, goodbye . . .

'He said to be sure to tell you that.' Julie looked half guilty, half determined. 'He said it would be good for you. He said it would set you free.'

Silence. No more to say. It's strange, thought Janna. I always wanted to be free.

She looked up to see Julie watching her, a little anxiously. 'Still friends?'

Janna nodded. That at least was simple, incontrovertible fact. Julie hadn't blamed her for Gray – how could she blame Julie for Dion? And they'd been through so much together, she and Julie, there was no need for words.

The bell sounded, summoning them back to the small dark womb of Sound Stage Two. They stood, in unison, pushed back their chairs. Janna knew without needing to ask that Julie's mind was on the scene ahead of them. It was hard for her, to carry alone the whole weight of the dialogue, slung round her neck like an albatross. And Janna hadn't helped, with her woodenness, compounded of guilt over Gray and indecision about the baby. Perhaps, now, it would be different. They'd reached a plateau of understanding, a sort of resting place. Not the old unthinking friendship, but maybe stronger in its way.

It takes two to be friends, thought Janna. It's harder than it looks. Sometimes you have to say the difficult things as well as the easy ones. And sometimes, which is harder, nothing at all.

*　　*　　*

A dim room, silvered over by moonlight. Nothing stirs. In the oaken bed, coverlet thrown back, imperceptibly breathing, lies a sleeping girl. Behind her, silently, the door opens.

A sudden noise, a floorboard creaking like a pistol shot. Julia sits up, gasps, her hands to her face. Silence again. A shadow on the wall. Across Julia's white face comes fear, recognition, surprise. She slips from her bed, reaches out a hand, withdraws it suddenly. Two girls now, strangely alike in their white muslin nightdresses, face each other in the darkened room.

No words still. Julia leans forward, her lips framing questions, but Jeanne looks from left to right, then shakes her head, a short, fierce movement. Her face is expressionless, yet beneath it something stirs. From round her neck, attached to a slender chain, she takes a simple gold ring. Julia gasps, her eyes light up with a sort of shocked pleasure. Jeanne hands her the ring, watches gravely as she slips it onto her left hand, spins to the mirror, stands for a second quite still, then whirls full circle, holding out the skirts of her nightdress as if she is dancing. Catching sight of Jeanne she stops dead.

Julia reaches behind her to the dresser drawer, takes out a sheaf of money, big paper notes, holds it out to Jeanne. Jeanne shakes her head vehemently. Julia looks puzzled, asks a question with her eyes. Jeanne stares at her. Slowly, two tears fall down her expressionless face. She lays one hand, simply, over her heart.

Julia's face twists. She turns away, lays aside the money on the dresser. Jeanne, tentatively, touches her on the arm. Julia shrugs away her arm, but Jeanne will not be rebuffed. She waits, patiently, holding out her hand, palm upwards, like a gypsy. Understanding breaks on Julia's face. A little contemptuously she slides off the ring, drops it into Jeanne's palm. Jeanne bows her head a fraction. Her eyes close for a second. Then swift as a shadow she glides to the door.

Julia hesitates. Her eyes rest on the pile of notes on the dresser. Curiosity, puzzlement, resentment chase across her face. At the last moment she recalls Jeanne at the door, an imperious beckoning. Her lips frame the beginning of a word – 'Why?' Before she can utter it Jeanne lays one finger over her mouth. Their eyes meet. Slowly Jeanne takes Julia's hand and lays it, firmly but with a sort of resigned tenderness, over her abdomen.

Julia recoils, her white face shocked. Then, very slowly, like a flower bending under rain, she leans forward, disbelief fading into something else, a concern that is almost maternal. Gently she lowers Jeanne to her own bed, lifts the lace coverlet up around her shoulders. Jeanne is crying now but does not seem to know it. Mistress and whore sit side by side on the rumpled bed, huddled together like exhausted children, while caught by a breath of air from the half-open window the paper money lifts and floats and scatters at their feet like autumn leaves.

'Cut!' Silence, unbroken by a single movement, sweeter even than the rattle of applause. Janna and Julie looked at each other and smiled.

'So.' Fernand watched them still, stroking his chin. 'You decided to dispense with my dialogue altogether.'

Wordlessly, in unison, they nodded.

'Do I mind?' Fernand asked himself, rhetorically. 'What can I say?' He smiled. 'Nothing. I have no dialogue.' He spread his hands wide. 'Very well, *mes enfants*, my little Siamese twins. *C'est fini*. You may go home.'

Home. Janna looked at Julie. Something had happened on the sound stage, in the silence. They were family now, closer than they'd ever been. She knew without needing to be told that when they both went home it would be together, to No. 3.

297

CHAPTER TWENTY-ONE

'Sandwiches?'

Janna held out the packet for inspection.

'Purse?' Obediently, she tapped her bag.

'Ticket?' She opened her coat, displayed the small card rectangle tucked neatly into her top pocket.

'Address book?'

'Address book?' Janna blinked, astonished.

'You never know.' Julie looked a little guilty. 'You might need to ring the hospital or something.'

'Really, Julie . . .' Janna shook her head. 'The baby's not due for three months yet.'

'Even so.' Julie refused to back down. 'You should have brought it, just in case. Vitamins?'

'Julie!' Janna looked at her friend with mingled affection and exasperation. She felt nervous enough without Julie making things worse. 'I'm not going to stay overnight. Wild horses couldn't make me.'

'But you might have to.' Julie's face was dark. 'There might be a train strike, or a derailment, or a snowstorm –'

'Snow? In November? I don't think so.' Janna tried to smile. She understood why Julie was making difficulties where none existed. She'd been against the idea of this journey from the beginning. She didn't realise that if Janna was going to go it had to be now or never. In a month or so winter weather and her advancing pregnancy would make it only too easy to postpone the journey – and after the baby was born it would be too late.

But even now, Janna wouldn't have found the courage, if it hadn't been for Dion. His attic was bare, but he'd left something behind after all – a different way of looking at the world and the people in it. He'd shown her that sometimes you couldn't plan for every eventuality. Sometimes, you had to step straight forward into the dark.

So it was because of Dion, finally, that Janna was here once more, at Liverpool Street Station, on the site, she now knew, of the old Bedlam, where wild-eyed madwomen had wept and torn their hair, chained against the wall. Not so far from where she'd started, a mere eighteen months ago.

Janna had only to glance down at her own body to see how much had changed since then. Her outline was barely recognisable – and yet, curiously, she'd lost the last of her old longing to be thin. Nowadays even Julie's perfectly proportioned body looked somehow incomplete to her eyes. She wanted every woman to be pregnant, every space filled. Wherever she went she seemed to see other pregnant women, other invisible babies suspended in their watery cradles, other dreamy, preoccupied eyes. The thought of her own baby inside her was a sort of warmth, a protection, as if she was carrying a magic talisman.

But would the baby protect her today?

'You'd better get on the train. I've reserved you a corner seat.'

Julie, her mission accomplished, hurried away. She'd seen something for the baby in a shop window on the way to the station, she said, one of those Moses baskets frilled with real Nottingham lace. Janna knew it was no use dissuading her. She'd bought so many things already for the baby, board-books and pastel-coloured jumpsuits, a specially soft bath towel with a tiny hood in one corner, a mobile featuring Donald Duck and Mickey Mouse, three pairs of small white pram shoes, bonnets and shawls and bootees and hand-embroidered quilts . . . 'You can never have too much for a winter baby,' Julie said.

Janna shivered. She missed Julie already. But this was something she could only do alone.

The journey was over all too soon. Before Janna was really ready she found herself standing on the familiar station platform, her breath a thin spiral in the chilly air. The platform was deserted. No-one used this line outside the commuter rushhour. It took her ten minutes in a pay-phone booth to find a taxi.

Then, foolishly, when the moment came to tell the driver where she was going, Janna couldn't remember the address. She should have brought her book with her after all. It was just that she'd never arrived before quite like this, on her own.

But not alone, not really. The baby kicked once, then settled. 'This is for us both,' Janna whispered. 'I'll be good if you will.' A little comforted, she turned to the driver. 'Never mind.' She mustn't panic now. She was so near. 'I know the way.'

How could she ever mistake that road, straight and narrow between stunted trees? They all grew sideways, because of the biting easterlies that whipped across this flat land even in summer, forcing everything to bend before them or die. Spring came late and winter early. In memories it was always November, the days drawing in. The ground hard, each grass-blade sugared with frost. Black twigs admonishing the windowpane.

Janna closed her eyes. Some memories never died. They stayed frozen in time. She could feel herself shrinking, forgetting everything she'd learned so painfully, all the milestones and manoeuvres falling away. She was going back, trapped like a reed by the encroaching ice.

The familiar gate, the familiar path. A little grass. Mostly paving, pre-cast concrete slabs, geometrical. The door still black, the knocker stainless steel. So practical. No time to waste on polishing . . .

It took all Janna's courage to open the gate. The old feeling seemed to rise up from the ground under her feet like marsh gas, drugging her, making her eyes blur. Had she ever really been away? If she had, then it didn't count. Like a miner, for her there was only one kind of work worthy of the name, and that lay here. Down the pit.

But I will finish it this time, she thought. I must be whole when I walk down this path again. For the baby. For myself.

The door opened, as she'd always known it would. The

porch, dark, smelling of wax and linoleum. An impatient face, strange and unchanged, under well-ordered steel grey curls.

All the words Janna had been preparing fell away. Without meaning to, with that long-ago child's doomed eagerness to please, she smiled.

'Hello, Mother.' What could she possibly say, after so long? She felt her smile flicker out like a candle-flame in a vacuum. No air, no light in the mineshaft now, but no room to turn round either. The only way was on.

'Oh.' Her mother stood there for a long moment, wrinkling her eyes up against the light. She'll soon be needing bifocals, thought Janna, suddenly. 'It's you.' The corners of her mouth turned down, in that way she had. But it didn't hurt so much as before. It was as if Janna was looking out of someone else's eyes, Julie's maybe, or Dion's. She saw an elderly woman, very upright, a little stiff, the skin on her hands wrinkled and reddened. Mother never wore rubber gloves, they weren't hygienic. Her poor hands . . . 'Are you coming in?'

Janna hesitated, just for a moment. But it was all right. She didn't have to go in any more. And so, at last, she could.

'Yes, please.' She stepped into the porch. Everyone had porches here, because of the wind. It made the entrance hall dark. As a child she'd feared the darkness of that hall, so full of breakables, but now – it was strange, she felt more at home here as a visitor than she'd ever done when it was her home.

'Well, now.' Her mother was bustling, her cheeks a little pink. She looked almost – pleased. Janna couldn't remember ever seeing that expression on her face before. Or perhaps I never learned to read her, she thought suddenly. Maybe there's more than one kind of short sight. 'What are your plans?'

An involuntary smile twitched the corners of Janna's mouth. It was so familiar, and yet so strange. How she'd always hated that emphasis on plans and projects and achievements – and yet she shared it with her mother, she saw that now. They were great planners, the both of them. 'I'd like to talk. If you've got time. And later, perhaps –' For a moment Janna's courage faded, then she remembered the wide still sea and the smell of grass and Dion's head sticking up out of the blanket and she realised suddenly that it didn't matter any more. If her mother said no, it wasn't the end of the world. No-one was that powerful. 'Perhaps we could go to the pub?'

'Why not?' Brisk, matter-of-fact, but to Janna as astonishing as a thunderclap. 'That is –' her mother's face clouded momentarily, 'if you know where it is?'

And at that, seeing her mother's expression, half guilty, half hopeful, Janna had to smile, because she didn't know either. They'd lived here like strangers, exiles, afraid to venture beyond the city gates. 'We could always ask,' she ventured, a little shyly, because all this was new, all the old landmarks changed. 'Later on. There's plenty of time.'

'The *pub*?' Julie leaned forward, her eyes enormous. She looked as shocked as if Janna had said a brothel. 'But I thought your mother was –'

'So did I.' Janna paused for a moment, cupped her hands round her mug of cocoa. The warmth was comforting. They were in the front parlour, fire lit against the night, Janna in her dressing gown. Just like old times. But she still felt unreal, almost stunned. So much had happened, it would take her a while to make sense of it all.

'Whatever made you think of asking her in the first place?'

'Oh, I don't know. Something someone said to me once.' A long time ago. Oh, how I wish Dion could have seen me. I think he would have approved.

'What about the baby, did she notice?'

'Not then. I was wearing my coat. I still hadn't made up my mind how to approach it.'

'OK, so you're in the pub. What next?'

Janna smiled. 'I got her a Guinness.'

'I hope you didn't have one!'

'No, orange juice.' From now on, Janna knew, its sour, slightly metallic taste would be associated in her mind with that halting, shadowed conversation, its many silences, pale November sunlight falling long across the bar. 'In the end, I don't know, it just came out. I said, "I'm drinking this because I'm pregnant".'

'And what did she say?'

'She said, "That's right, you can't be too careful if you're pregnant". It was as if I was one of her patients on the ward.'

'How terrible!'

Janna shook her head. 'No, I liked it. She sounded – interested, even approving. I always wanted her to approve of me and I think that was the first time.'

'She didn't ask you about the father, or if you were married or anything?'

'Not a word.' Janna smiled. 'And you know what? I suddenly realised something – a sort of revelation. She's a career woman. It's as simple as that. She's just not interested in anything outside her work. The only surprising thing was why she ever had me in the first place.'

'You should have asked her.'

'I did. Not in so many words. I asked her about my father first, what sort of man he was, his medical history, that kind of thing. I said I needed to know because of the baby. She understood that.' Janna paused. She still couldn't quite believe it, couldn't be sure she'd got it right. 'Then she said the most extraordinary thing. She said she was very sorry she couldn't help me more because she'd never met him.'

'Never met him?' Julie blinked. 'I don't understand.'

'Neither did I. I told her so. And then, it was strange. She just – looked at me, as if she'd come to the bottom of a long column of figures and didn't want to add them one more time. "You weren't mine," she said. "I had to take you".'

'And then she told me the rest, the whole story. She'd been working in the private wing, on the obstetrics ward. One of the patients had her baby delivered under anaesthetic, was left to recover in a side ward. Later that night she went into a coma and no-one knew why. She was bleeding badly. Too late, they found out there'd been a terrible mistake, instead of one baby she'd been carrying twins.'

'How awful!'

'I know. Of course, they had to get the second baby out, to try and save the mother, but it was no use. By that time she'd lost too much blood. An hour later, she died.

'It was no-one's fault, not really. That kind of mistake happens even now. The trouble was, the woman was the wife of someone important, and the consultant in charge was right at the beginning of what promised to be a brilliant career, and so –'

'They hushed it up!'

'I'm afraid so. No-one expected the second baby to live long. After a birth like that, everyone agreed it would be best if it did die. What use would another baby, probably damaged, be to a grieving husband?

'By the time they realised the baby was going to live after all, the secret had been kept too long. They couldn't just produce another child like a rabbit out of a hat. So my mother said she'd take it.'

'But why?' Julie looked puzzled. 'If she was so keen on her career, why on earth did she lumber herself with a baby?'

Janna smiled a little. 'Because she was in love. With the consultant. They'd been having an affair. She admired him tremendously, knew he was destined for great things. She couldn't bear the thought of his future being ruined by a mistake anyone could have made. So she said she'd take the baby away, right away, where no-one would ever find out what had happened.

'He was very grateful. He advised her not to come back for at least six months, for her own sake, to allay any possible suspicions. And then they could go on just as before . . .

'It was only afterwards, when she went to check on the baby in its incubator, that my mother realised exactly what he'd meant. He wanted her to get rid of the baby, safely, out of sight. It was a terrible shock to her, she said. Not so much what he had in mind, because she knew that sort of thing goes on more often than people think, but because it showed her that despite everything they'd been to each other, he hadn't understood her at all.'

Janna paused. 'You see, my mother may be ambitious, but she's straight as a die. She wouldn't compromise medical ethics for all the career opportunities in the world. So that same day she left for East Anglia, taking me with her. And she never saw her lover again.'

'But surely –' Julie leaned forward eagerly. 'If you know where he worked, this consultant, you could trace him, maybe find out who your real parents were?'

'I'm afraid not. He died last year, or my mother wouldn't have told me, even now. She's very – scrupulous.'

And I'm grateful to her, Janna thought. For me, she gave up almost everything – her job, her lover, her freedom. No wonder she resented me. And yet she stuck by the decision she'd made.

Janna put down her mug of cocoa, now cold, and stretched, feeling every ligament in her body loosen. She was thinking of something her mother had said before she left. 'You know, I like you better now you're grown-up. I wasn't a very good mother to you, I know that. I always felt bad that I couldn't love you as a child should be loved. But now I don't have to worry any more. Because – well, you're all right, aren't you? You're all right.'

It wasn't a question – it was a simple statement of fact. And for the first time in her life Janna realised it was true. She hadn't got everything right, she never would, but she knew now that like her mother, she'd – muddled through.

Janna closed her eyes for a second. She felt very light and free, as if she'd tied up her whole past into a bundle and thrown it overboard. Now she could see it bobbing in her wake, mercifully small and insignificant compared with the expanse of sea and sky.

'It explains so much.' She spoke half to herself, stretching out her hands to the fire. 'I used to have this dream. It kept coming back, always the same. I'd be somewhere warm and safe, better than anything I'd known, and then, without warning, the walls would close in. I'd begin to choke. I'd feel this terrible pain up my spine, as if I was being snapped in two. I'd try to scream but couldn't make a sound. The pain would go on, for ever and ever, until I could feel my heart stop beating, until I knew I was going to die.

'Then, just before the end, I'd wake up. And that was

worse. Because I felt so alone. As if I'd forgotten something terribly important, and for that, I'd have to suffer in exile for the rest of my life. As if it was a crime that I'd been born at all.' She frowned. 'And I suppose it was, in a way. Maybe I knew, even then, that it was because of me that my real mother died. Maybe I thought I'd killed my twin too.' She remembered Dion's baby rats, once kissed and never forgotten. Perhaps it had been like that for her. She'd always felt – divided, incomplete. Maybe, all her life, she'd been haunted by that lost presence in the close warm darkness of the womb. They said that twins could hear each other's heartbeats, sense every movement. She'd read that one pair, identical, had been born holding hands.

'And now?'

'Now . . .' Janna paused. The loneliness was still there. It was a part of her and always would be, but now it had a human face. There'd be no more nightmares. 'Now I'm a new person. Even my birthday's changed. I was so undersized when my mother took me away from the hospital that she was able to pass me off as six months younger than I really was. It all helped to cover the tracks.' She turned to Julie and smiled. 'So I'm six months older, all of a sudden. Believe me, after today, I feel it.'

Julie counted silently on her fingers. 'Six months – that means you were born in – June, maybe July. Any idea which?'

Janna shook her head. 'She wouldn't tell me, just in case. The consultant is dead, but his wife is still living, and somewhere I might have a twin. Too many people might get hurt.'

'You know which hospital, though?'

'Oh, yes. My mother worked there after all. She could hardly keep that a secret. It's strange – it's where I went when I was ill, before I met you. It was brave of her to send me there.'

'Wait a minute.' Julie had gone a little pale. When she spoke next her voice sounded breathless. 'This may sound like a funny question, Janna, but what's your blood group? Do you know?'

'I certainly do.' Janna spoke with feeling. 'I've given

enough blood samples at the ante-natal clinic. It's AB. Only 2 per cent of the population have it, apparently. But don't worry, it's a universal recipient. If I need a transfusion when the baby's born any blood will do.'

'I know.'

'Really?' Janna was a little surprised. Julie wasn't usually interested in technicalities.

'Because I'm AB too. I found out when I went for my check-up in New York. And there's something else. Do you know where I was born?'

'In New York, wasn't it? While your father was at the Embassy?' Julie shook her head. 'He sent my mother to London two weeks before the birth. He wanted his "son" born British. And my mother died, in hospital, the day after I was born.'

They stared at each other for a long moment. The fire had gone out but Janna didn't feel cold. She felt very strange, but not cold.

'You mean . . .'

Julie nodded. Her eyes seemed very large and bright.

'I'm afraid so. In the private wing of a large teaching hospital not so very far from where we're sitting right now.'

In silence, like two children meeting for the first time over a picket fence, they looked at each other. Eyes. Hair. Skin. Expressions and habits and mannerisms, blending, dissolving, superimposed and overlaid like a lantern-slide show.

'Not identical.' Janna's voice was light, tentative.

'But alike.' Julie's voice returning out of the half light. Why had Janna never noticed before that their voices were so similar in pitch and timbre, an eerie playback? 'Especially now.'

'I think so.'

'We always felt –'

'In tune. I know.'

'We always liked –'

'The same things. The same people.'

Unspoken names hung in the air. Dene. Dion. Gray . . .

'Oh, dear.' Julie's face was a baffling mixture of amazement and dismay. 'This changes everything.'

'Only for the better.' It had been a day of so many surprises that Janna felt she could cope with anything. My sister, she thought, with a glow of pride. My beautiful, beautiful sister. 'Just think, you've been promoted. From godmother to aunt!'

'That's not the point. I couldn't love you or the baby more anyway.' Oh, lovely, practical Julie!

'What are you worrying about, then?'

'Don't you see?' Julie's face was twisted into a mask of concern. 'If what we think is true, then you're not Janna Brown any more, you're Janna Le Franceys of Dene.'

'So I am.' Strange – it was what she'd wanted. Six months ago she'd have given everything to be just that, to belong – but now it didn't matter any more. 'What difference does it make?' Nothing had changed, not really.

And yet, looking at Julie's face, Janna felt the lightest, faintest chill, as if November had entered their cosy parlour, hoarfrost in his hair.

'Gray.' Julie felt it too. Her voice was low. She seemed suddenly older, her face tired, her eyes remote. 'You'll have to tell him about the baby now.'

'No!' It was torn from Janna in a sort of gasp, but even as she spoke she knew that Julie was right. Now, truly, everything was changed. Whether she liked it or not, she'd been born again. The baby inside her was a Le Franceys twice over. The choice was no longer hers to make.

'Oh, Julie.' Tears rose suddenly to Janna's eyes. 'I wanted it to be just us. You and me and No. 3.'

'I know.' Julie reached out her hand. 'I almost wish you hadn't told me. I wish . . .' Her voice trailed away. She stirred the fire with the poker, but there was no life left in it, only a coil of smoke heavy with ash. They watched it disappear up the chimney, taking their future with it.

'I can't tell him.' Janna's voice was a whisper. 'Will you?' Julie didn't hesitate for a moment. No matter how much it cost her, family came first.

'I'll tell him.' She took a deep breath. 'And then I'll take the next plane back to New York.' Janna flinched but Julie went on, inexorably. 'It's the only way. You and Gray – you'll want to talk things over. It may take a while. There's no point in me being here. And in any case . . .' Her voice went a little ragged. 'I don't think I could stand it, you know?'

Janna nodded, suddenly numb. For everything to disappear, so suddenly, all their plans . . . 'Will you come back for the birth?'

'Yes, please. Just ring me – I'll jump on the first plane out.' Julie smiled. 'I might even bring you a bagel.'

'Promise?'

'Sure.'

A long pause in which they avoided each other's eyes. Then Julie spoke, abruptly. 'He'll want to marry you, you know.'

'How can you be so sure?'

'Easy.' Julie shrugged. 'He's like me. He believes in family.'

'I see.' Marriage . . . Suddenly, to Janna, it sounded like a word in a foreign language. Cold, incomprehensible. She couldn't imagine what it might be like to be married to Gray. The idea seemed unreal, almost irrelevant. But if he asked her, what right did she have to refuse?

And then it came to her, in long sickening rush, exactly what it was that she'd lost along with the ragbag bundle of her past. It was only now that she could admit to herself that it had ever existed, squirrelled away in the deepest, most private compartment of her mind, the small, faint hope that one day, when spring was setting the air alight and sparrows fighting over the chimney-pots and grass racing up between the cobbles, she'd open the door of No. 3 and find him there, blue and black and welcome as a swallow – Dion, smiling at her as if it was the first time.

But now? If and when she ever saw Dion again it would be as another's man's wife, the mother of his child. And even he, escape-artist that he was, master of trapdoors and chalk-marked stairs, couldn't spirit that fact away.

'What about Dion?' It was as if Julie had read her mind. 'When I last saw him he said he was going to come back soon.'

'Come back?' Suddenly Janna was terrified. 'He can't!'

'He may have to. He said his money had almost run out.'

'You'll have to stop him.' The idea that Dion might see her carrying Gray's child made Janna feel almost physically ill. He mustn't come back. She couldn't bear it. She'd be all right. She'd recover herself in time, just so long as Dion stayed away.

'How can I?' Julie smiled an unsteady smile. 'He's a free agent.'

'Wait a minute.' Fear lent wings to Janna's brain. 'Tell me, Julie, what exactly were you planning to do in New York when you got back?'

'I hadn't really thought.' Julie seemed suddenly at a loss. 'The usual, I suppose. A bit of modelling, another film maybe. That's if I can get one. I'm not good enough, really.'

'Maybe not.' Janna leaned forward, hands clenched to stop them shaking. 'But there's something else you're good at. People. That's a gift too.'

'So?'

'So —' Janna took a deep breath. If Julie suspected why she was doing this, she'd never agree. 'So there's something you can do to — help me out. Find Dion, take him in charge, and make him a success.' She swallowed. 'A big success. So big that coming back to No. 3 is the last thing on his mind. You can do it, no-one better. You know all the right people. All you need is a bit of capital to start you off, and I've got that. Believe me, it would be worth every penny to me.'

'But —' Despite her doubtful expression it was clear that Julie was intrigued. 'Isn't Dion going to think that a bit odd, in the circumstances?'

Janna avoided her eyes. 'Why should he ever find out? If he asks, you can tell him he's got some kind of rich admirer, an anonymous patron. An elderly widow with artistic leanings and money to burn.'

'But I thought . . .' Julie's face was still puzzled. 'I thought you'd never even seen his paintings?'

'I haven't.' Janna felt a pang of sadness. One more regret out of so many. All the missed opportunities — but it was no use grieving for them. She'd never see Dion's paintings now. Unless, in ten years' time, she went to a retrospective exhibition, for old time's sake. Just so long as the artist wasn't standing by. 'But you have. Is he any good?'

'I've no idea.' Julie smiled, apologetically. 'I wasn't wearing my lenses. Not that it matters, really.'

'Exactly. Will you do it, Julie? For me?'

'I'll give it a try.' Julie shook her head. 'But I still don't understand. Why?'

Janna shrugged, pretending lightness. 'I just don't want him here, that's all. There'll be Gray, and the baby – Dion would only be in the way.'

It was the final release. It hurt. She'd handed Dion over to Julie. From now on Julie would be his angel, his inspiration, his guide, in the ways that only Julie knew. And yet, deep down, Janna felt sure Dion would approve. This was a gamble, the best possible use of the money that she didn't want and wouldn't need, probably the last such gamble she'd ever have the chance to make. Life with Gray would be safe, secure, in Dene's gilded cage. From now on there would be no more impromptu excursions to the races, no more long-odds outsiders chasing in to scoop the pool. So just this once she would back the horse she fancied, win or lose.

'There's only one condition.' Her decision taken, Janna felt suddenly exhausted. Her eyes felt sore, her back ached. She knew what she'd done, none better. She'd sent them away, Julie and Dion. She'd said goodbye. Now, she was conscious of nothing beyond pain and the need, whatever happened, to survive. For the baby. If she could hold onto that thought she'd be all right, in the end. For the baby.

'Yes?' Julie's eyes were bright again. She looked almost excited. By comparison, Janna felt a hundred years old.

'Tell him I'm to be married. Tell him I'm happy, very, very happy. But please – don't tell him I'm pregnant.'

CHAPTER TWENTY-TWO

A week later, the doorbell rang. Janna hurried down the stairs, somehow sure that when she opened the door it would be Dion standing there.

But it was Gray. He stood there, unsmiling, for a long, awkward moment, while Janna felt her foolish hopes fall away to nothing. Of course Dion wouldn't come, once he knew about Gray. He'd respect her decision. He'd want her to be free to choose, to govern her own life, a grown-up woman now.

'Well, Janna.' Gray's voice sounded different, a stranger's voice. Janna swallowed. Her throat felt swollen, as if she'd been crying, the words she'd meant for Dion lodged there still.

'Come in.' She tried to smile. She saw his arms were full of roses, winter blooms flown in from some distant sunny land, perfect in their plastic shroud. As she took them she felt the thorns hard and sharp in her hands. Gray's eyes rested curiously on her overalls. 'Sorry about these.' Janna gestured as best she could, burdened with the flowers. 'I'm in the middle of plumbing in a washing-machine.'

Gray's eyebrows went up. 'Surely it would be better to employ a professional?'

Janna looked down at her hands, whitened with sealing compound, and wondered for a moment what Gray would say if he knew that the mother of his child and potential bride could no longer afford a plumber because she'd invested almost all her capital in a crazy Irish artist somewhere on the other side of the Atlantic. There was enough left for her to live on till the baby came, but that was all.

'It's all right.' She felt her face colour. 'I know what I'm doing. I had a good teacher.' Unbidden, Dion's voice came into her mind. 'Copper is so beautiful, you must be kind to it always. Stroke it, and like a ginger cat it will follow you home.'

It was a relief to be able to turn away and lead Gray up to the parlour. She'd tidied it only that morning. She spent a lot of time keeping house now. It helped to occupy her mind, even though she had to fight back the feeling, every time she blackleaded the grate or polished her barleycorn balustrade, that she was wasting her time. How much longer would she be here, after all?

That, really, was up to Gray. This was hardly a straight-forward courtship, more like a proposed merger, with one very important sleeping partner holding the deciding vote.

'We have things we must discuss, Janna.'

'Yes.' Janna eased herself into one of the two Windsor chairs she and Julie had bought together. Then, she'd found its straight back a little uncomfortable, but now it was a friend, a second spine. She folded her hands protectively over the baby, looked up to find Gray's eyes on her with a faintly troubled expression, as if she herself was an object in a saleroom and he wasn't quite sure of her authenticity. She steeled herself. 'Julie told you?'

'Not exactly.' At last, a small smile. 'She sent me a telegram.'

'It must have been a long one.' A flicker of fellow feeling passed between herself and Gray. The atmosphere lightened a little. Perhaps, thought Janna, perhaps it's not going to be so bad after all. At least we've got Julie in common.

'You're sure it's my child?' Janna flinched. Hope faded as swiftly as if it had never been. And yet, he was not wrong to ask. This could so easily have been Dion's child. A few days – but what a difference they would have made, all the difference in the world. Dion, she knew without a moment's doubt, would have been here with her, painting walls, sharing plans, revelling in every moment of her pregnancy. He'd have made a good father too, she could see him now, crawling on all fours, making drawings jump off the page . . .

'Yes, I'm sure.' She drew herself up with as much dignity as she could. It was up to her to make the best of things, for the baby's sake. Now, it sensed her anxiety and stirred. She smoothed one hand over its outline. Oh, baby, she thought. I had no idea being a mother was so hard.

'I suggest a January wedding. There are a lot of formalities to complete, arrangements to make. The ceremony will be at Dene, of course. I don't think St Paul's would be suitable, under the circumstances.'

Hearing the note of regret in Gray's voice Janna was suddenly abashed. She wasn't the only one who was going to lose out because of this baby. Behind his detached façade Gray was clearly mourning vanished opportunities of his own.

'I'm sorry, Gray.' She spoke with a rush. 'I wish it didn't have to happen like this. Couldn't we – couldn't we delay the wedding till February, after the baby's born?' Just in case, was her unspoken thought. It might not be born alive – a terrible thing, but it would at least mean she and Gray would be free.

'I'm afraid not.' Gray smiled, a small, tired smile. 'There's the question of inheritance, you see. I've taken legal advice. Even now a legitimised son hasn't quite the same rights as a legitimate one. We must marry before the child is born.'

'Oh.' So complicated, so technical, the traps of property, and so difficult to escape. 'What if it's a girl?'

Gray rubbed his hand across his forehead, gave a sigh. 'It makes very little difference. There'll be others.'

Janna's heart sank. Other children – she hadn't thought of that. It sounded so – dry, so formal, utterly loveless, the arranging of genes like cut flowers in a vase. But she had no choice any more.

'Very well, then. Just let me know when the date is fixed and I'll be there.' Janna stood up. Gray followed suit, gracefully, seeming very tall in the little room. This house doesn't suit him, Janna thought suddenly. Whatever made me think it would?

'I'll take care of all the other arrangements, just leave it to me. I've booked a maternity nurse for two weeks before the child is born. You'll need help in the house. There's a room for her to stay, I take it?'

Janna nodded dumbly, a lump in her throat. So she wasn't even to have No. 3 to herself for much longer. But he was right, of course he was. He couldn't be there himself.

'After the child is born the nurse will accompany you to Dene. The nursery suite is being renovated for her arrival. Then there's the question of a nanny. Do you wish to be present at the interviews?'

Again, Janna shook her head. She couldn't speak. A maternity nurse, a nanny, a separate suite – was she going to lose the baby too?

'Very well, I will see to it.' Gray paused, bent to kiss her lightly on the cheek. 'Please don't bother to see me out.' Janna felt tears prick at the corners of her eyes. It was as if she'd become invisible, a child again, for whom decisions had to be made, an encumbrance. But what could she expect? Dion would have picked her up, baby and all, and whirled her round the room with whoops of delight, but Dion was different. Gray had done all he could. He would treat her well – she could feel confident of that – and hopefully he would love his son. She, for her part, must try very hard to be a good wife, to keep her side of the bargain.

From the parlour window Janna watched Gray's pale head until he disappeared into his car. It had begun to rain. Slowly, wondering how she could feel so empty and heavy at the same time, she went downstairs to finish plumbing in her washing machine. As she smoothed polyfilla into holes in the plaster she wondered if one day her child would turn on her, bitter and accusing. 'Why did you marry my father? You never loved him. Why was I ever born?'

And how could she ever explain? No child would understand. Children thought only of love, she knew that. She'd been a child herself, only six months ago.

More Polyfilla. Janna dug deep, forced a great trowelful into the gaping hole round the outflow pipe. It was astonishing how much this dry old plasterwork could absorb with no visible signs of improvement. This was a thin house and always would be, no matter how hard she tried to feed it up. But she wouldn't stop just because of that. She was going to enjoy them if she could, these last few weeks of being January Brown.

But as the days went by January Brown, who could skip downstairs without having to pause for breath halfway, and turn over in bed without thinking twice, receded further and further into what seemed like another life. It was as if Janna had herself become a baby, or an invalid. Parts of her body simply stopped working. The most ordinary actions became difficult, even impossible. She couldn't bend to pick up anything if she dropped it – and she was always dropping things now, her fingers seemed to be stuffed with cotton wool – without a strange, dowager-like sideways curtsey. She couldn't sit comfortably without a cushion propped in the small of her back, or get up without bracing herself with her arms. She couldn't even see to put on her own shoes. At night, sometimes, as she felt her bones creaking in their sockets and every ligament stretching till she was one large ache, she wondered if her body would ever be hers again.

Instead of counting sheep she forced herself to count blessings. She was lucky, really. She had a roof over her head, a father for her child. She was young and strong and healthy. Strong houses are built of little bricks, Dion said.

It helped to think of that at the hospital clinic when they talked darkly of her small bones, told her that a woman of her height should have had her pelvis X-rayed before conceiving. On hearing that the baby's father was over six feet tall they shook their heads gloomily as if that was no more nor less than could be expected from an unplanned pregnancy.

Julie didn't help, either. She refused outright to use the telephone in case Janna tripped on the stairs on her way to answer it, so telegrams fell through No. 3's letterbox like snow. Questions and more questions, almost as if Julie was the one who was six months pregnant and counting the hours. She'd chosen not to come to the wedding, something which Janna understood perfectly, but she was still determined to drive Janna to hospital when she went into labour. She'd worked out all the details in advance, right down to having a hire car with extra room in the back seat waiting at the airport.

'I promise to be extra careful – I'll drive all the way in first gear if you like! If any harm came to the baby because of me I'd never forgive myself . . .'

But it was good to know that Julie was making progress with her new career. She'd added other artists to her stable already. Janna felt maternal towards her – in fact by this time she felt maternal to almost everything and everyone, lampposts, sparrows, sunsets, herself, even her own mother. But Julie was special. Julie was family, the other half of herself. Somehow, Janna felt that Julie's success would make up for her own lost opportunities. Julie's telegrams were full of excitement, a heady mixture of hope and ambition and certainty that whatever happened, she'd found her niche at last.

'I'll never be an actress – but who cares? You were right. I can feel it – I'm good at this agent business. And I like it. I like private views, and hangings, and dressing-up, and giving advice, and lunch . . .'

But on the subject of Dion and his work Julie said very little. Janna had to read between the lines to guess how his career was going.

'I sold "Roofs 1" today, to a lovely man, a White Russian. He was thrilled, said it made him feel young again – or maybe that was me! Anyway, I told him it would be a very good investment. "That too," he said, and giggled.'

'Roofs 1' . . . Janna wondered, a little wistfully, what that might be. Perhaps it had even been painted at No. 3. You could see a lot of roof, from the attic.

It was frustrating not to know more, but Janna knew she mustn't ask – that wouldn't be fair. Dion's career was Julie's baby, in all ways. If Janna stuck to the rules she might earn the rank of fairy godmother, if she was lucky. So she kept her replies encouraging but non-committal, and felt in that fact a sort of pride.

Slowly, on their hands and knees, the weeks inched by. November closed in a flurry of wind and rain, and one December morning Janna opened her front door to collect the milk and found it half frozen on the stone step. Winter was going to come early this year. But she didn't mind. She had her pride in Julie to keep her warm, and the baby. It was like a sort of central-heating boiler inside her. No matter how frosty the air she didn't feel a moment's cold. Her cheeks were pinker than she'd ever seen them. No two pairs of gloves for her this winter, no woollen tights. She didn't need them. When she went out to the shops she noticed how people in the street seemed to lean in towards her, as if she was radiating warmth like a chestnut-seller's brazier full of hot coals.

Then it was Christmas. Janna could have gone to her mother's, but the memory of past childhood Christmases, her mother's awkward attempts to generate jollity and festive feeling for an audience of one, deterred her. Her mother would be happier at the hospital, where she could be useful and have things to do. As for Dene – well, she could have gone there, she supposed – Gray was hardly likely to show her the door if she turned up, but he didn't invite her and there was no reason why he should. Until they were married she would be simply an embarrassment to him.

No, she would spend Christmas alone. Alone, but not lonely. The baby accompanied her upstairs, downstairs, listening agreeably when she discussed the weather, kicking approvingly when she sat down to rest her legs, utterly still when she sang. She lit two candles on Christmas Eve, one for Julie and one for Dion, and gave herself permission to open her presents on the stroke of ten instead of midnight, because she needed her early nights.

First Gray's, because its wrapping paper was in such good taste that it made her a little nervous. Inside, in a dark blue velvet-covered box, was a ring, a lovely sapphire set in white gold, for their engagement. According to his accompanying card, it had belonged to Julie's mother, and Julie's father's mother, and five other mistresses of Dene before that, reaching back almost three centuries. Janna slipped it on, but it stuck at her knuckle. Pregnancy had made her fingers swell. With a little shiver she pulled it off and put it aside. It was probably enormously valuable. She'd better take it to the bank. It was a relief to put it away. The sapphire would have suited Julie so much better anyway, because of her eyes. She wondered for a moment what Gray would make of her present to him, a set of white linen handkerchieves she'd embroidered with his initials in dark blue silk. Maybe a little dull, handkerchieves usually were, but what could you give a man who had everything, especially when you didn't have much money to spend?

Her mother's parcel was big and bulky and very thoroughly strapped with tape. Inside was a bottle-sterilising unit, complete with six bottles, sterilising fluid, bottle brush and three tins of milk powder. Janna couldn't help smiling. She was going to breastfeed her baby – she was looking forward to it – but all the same she could appreciate her mother's gesture. It seemed that babies brought out the best in everyone. She hoped her mother would make good use of her set of stainless-steel kitchen knives.

Last of all, Julie's present. Janna had sent her two pairs of the most amazing tights, spidery red lace, for the famous Julie legs. She knew Julie would love them, just as Julie had known she would love her Christmas stocking of goodies for the baby. A minute pair of doeskin moccasins embroidered with little blue and red beads, a baby-sized ankle chain adorned with the smallest diamond in the world ('Start her off on the right foot, that's what I say'), a pair of crocheted mittens no bigger than egg-cosies, a share in a Californian gold mine, a shocking-pink elephant with an aggrieved squeak, a plastic-backed bib with a picture of Wonderwoman and finally a pocket-sized edition of the *Kama Sutra*, complete in every detail, right down to the scarlet morocco binding and gold-blocked title. On the flyleaf Julie had written a dedication: 'For my beautiful niece – do what I did but do it better.'

Right at the bottom of the stocking was a square of white card covered in Julie's schoolgirl printing. Janna smiled. Julie had made a special effort, because it was Christmas. Ten lines at least – it must have taken her hours.

'Happy Christmas, darlings! And good news. Fernand has set a date to show the rough-cut to distributors here in New York. All very secret and hush-hush, you know what he's like. He hasn't let another copy of the print out of his sight, even the invitations are going out under a provisional title. Incidentally, he's thrilled by the idea of us being twins, he says he feels personally responsible. Everything on film happens in real life sooner or later, he says. Kisses – and keep taking the vitamins!'

That was all, except for Julie's glorious sprawl of a signature. Making a mental note to tell her most people didn't use a capital L in the middle of a word, Janna turned over the card to discover that it was actually a printed invitation made out in her name.

'A Special Preview Showing of Fernand Kim's Latest Film,' it read. And then underneath, in a slim elegant typeface taking up half the space – 'SISTERS'.

In smaller letters, like the subtitle of a learned monograph, a byline: 'A study in the pornography of love'.

Janna was intrigued, she had to admit it. It was very French, that subtitle, as tantalising as a flutter of Liane's oiled eye-lashes.

Not, of course, that it made any difference to her. As far as she was concerned, New York might as well be on the moon. She put the card on her mantelpiece, invitation side to the wall.

Two days later, in the first post after the Christmas holiday, Janna received another invitation, even grander, with engraved lettering and gold-embossed crest, to her own wedding at Dene. The date had been set for a week's time, just four days after the New York preview of *Sisters*. January 3rd. Her old birthday, as it happened. She wondered if Gray would have chosen it if he'd known.

Birthdays and deathdays . . . The nearness of the two dates made Janna feel restless. She could, in theory, attend both events – but of course that was out of the question. It would be folly even to think of flying at eight months pregnant, for a start.

She mentioned that fact, a mere twenty-four hours before the preview, at her weekly check-up.

'Oh, no – you mustn't think of yourself as an invalid.' The doctor's tone was encouraging. 'You should go. Staying at home worrying isn't going to do you any good. You'll be all right as long as you have plenty of rest. I'll give you a letter, in case there's any difficulty at the airport.'

Janna stared at him, utterly shocked. She hadn't been worried, not at all. Right till this moment her mind had been perfectly clear.

But now? The doctor had let her down when she most needed him. If only he knew. Now it was in her like a hunger, a desperate, passionate need to know, not just what Fernand had made of his film, but what Dion had made of his life.

CHAPTER TWENTY-THREE

The sight of Julie, waving furiously from behind the barrier in the arrivals hall, almost made Janna feel she'd been right to come. Paying for her ticket had used up her last month's house-keeping money – she didn't know what she was going to live on when she got back, but it was worth it to see her sister again. She hugged Julie, as well as she could over the bulge, and the bunch of hothouse lilies her sister was carrying tickled her nose.

'You look wonderful.' Julie had been beautiful before, but now she was impressive, someone to be reckoned with. No more fuchsia eyeshadow and triple coats of lipgloss, just a hint of mascara and powder completing her career woman's outfit of pale grey cashmere sweater and slacks under a swirl of cape in a brilliant blue that matched her eyes. Only a trace of the old flamboyant Julie showed in the tasselled boots and the gold hoops that swung in her ears.

'You like it?' Julie flung back her cape, extended one arm in a regal gesture. 'I call it my Statue of Liberty look – bring me your poor, unprotected artists, and I will make them a million dollars!' She tucked her arm in Janna's. Walking beside her, Janna felt like a schoolgirl in her flowered smock and flat heels. She wondered if she'd ever wear her blue silk dress again. Somehow, it didn't seem suitable for a lady of the manor. Gray wouldn't want the mother of his child to play the siren, any more than he'd like her to have a career of her own.

By some miracle of organisation, again so unlike the Julie she'd been used to that Janna could only wonder, a yellow cab was waiting to take them straight to the preview theatre. Once inside the cab Janna could afford to relax a little. It was safe and dark and private, the right sort of place to voice the question that had been burning in her mind all the way across the Atlantic.

'How's Dion?'

'He seems fine.' Julie's face was a dim blur against the neon backdrop. 'But I worry about him sometimes.' Suddenly she laughed. 'I sound like a mother hen, don't I? But that's how I feel about my artists. Most of them are more incompetent than I ever was. They need me, they really do. Selling their paintings for them is like finding good homes for orphans. If I get a really good price for one I feel as thrilled as if one of my orphans had won a scholarship to Yale!'

Janna smiled. Julie's enthusiasm was infectious. But there was only one of Julie's artists that mattered to her.

'Why are you worried about Dion? Isn't he selling well?'

'That depends on what you mean by well.' Julie frowned a little. 'He's beginning to sell, but not as much as I would like. The trouble with Dion is he's not really interested in making money. There's one of his paintings I could have sold five times over, but he won't let it go at any price. I keep trying to tempt him by telling him how many yards of canvas he could buy for what I'd get for that one piece, but it makes no difference. He's a stubborn devil. He says he wouldn't be less of an artist if he never painted another stroke. I don't understand that, do you?'

'I'm not sure.' Against her will Janna remembered soft, invasive air, the smell of summer grass, blue hills, sky close enough to touch. She couldn't go back there now, but she wouldn't forget, not ever. So maybe you could be an artist without once setting brush to canvas.

'Hey . . .' Julie swung round in her seat, eyes bright. 'Maybe you should have a talk with Dion, sort him out for me. It's in all our interests, after all. It'd be fun, too – just think, we could see the New Year in together, all three of us, maybe book a table at Sardi's –'

'No!' A knife-twist of panic, sharp and deep. For a moment Janna forgot everything, Gray, and the baby, and the wedding, all thoughts of the future swept away in her sudden, overpowering thirst for one face, one voice. But she couldn't see Dion again, not now, not ever. It would hurt too much to say goodbye.

Even in the dimness of the cab Janna could see that Julie looked surprised and a little offended. Shakily, she hurried to explain.

'It's just that – well, the wedding's only a few days away and I haven't even found a dress that fits yet. So there won't be any time for – sight-seeing this time around, much as I'd love to.'

'No bagels?' Julie's tone was wistful.

'Well, maybe one.' Janna smiled. 'At the airport before I go.'

And then, before Janna had a chance to ask any more questions, the cab drew up outside the viewing theatre. The pavement was icy under Janna's feet. She drew her loose knitted poncho around her and was glad of Julie's arm as they hurried in. The interior was quiet and dim, curiously spartan, blank walls sculpted into eggshell curves. No press or photographers or first night glamour, no smoked salmon canapés and chilled champagne, just a small white-clothed table equipped with red and white wine, ice and chunky glasses. And in the middle of the theatre a solid line of five backs facing the blank white screen.

'The money,' Julie whispered, mentioning the names of three big distributors and one chain of art houses. To the right of them, another group of blue-suited backs, a little more excitable, shifting restlessly as they waited for the screening to begin.

'More money – but on our side,' whispered Julie. Of course, the backers. Janna studied the anonymous backs. They might not look it, in their city uniform, but they were gamblers too. And without them, she'd have had no roof over her head. I wish them luck, thought Janna, remembering Dion. I hope they win.

Fernand entered to a scattering of applause. He made no speech, simply nodded courteously in acknowledgement as he took his seat in the centre row. He signalled, without turning round, and the lights dimmed.

Janna was glad of the friendly dark. This was another good-bye. There'd be no more film-making for her, she knew that. Already she missed it, the rising at dawn, the interminable waiting, the false starts, the re-takes, the failures – all of them transcended by the faint, fragile hope of getting it right next time, of doing better, reaching one more hand's span towards that star.

As the credits opened she almost closed her eyes. It would be herself on that screen, in front of this, her first audience. She could hardly bear to watch. And yet, by the time that moment came she was so caught up in the story and its players that she didn't even recognise the sad-faced girl in her shabby Edwardian lace as herself. There was so much more to the film than she'd ever suspected from her own part. How could she waste any time judging her own performance when there was Gray to consider, such an apt piece of casting, all grace and courtesy, that she could almost have fallen in love with him all over again? Almost. And then there was Julia, highly-strung, over-bred, her flounderings painful to watch. A netted butterfly, too beautiful, too bright. And Dene . . . It was the perfect setting, lush, ornate, a velvety scented trap for poor human hearts, bleeding to death over the hand-embroidered damask but trying desperately to leave no stain.

All except for Jeanne. From the beginning her eyes showed she came from another world, looking out with a sort of wry fatalism, an almost modern awareness, from behind the mask of time. Jeanne was real, the explosion of passion between herself and Eden as shocking as a terrorist's bomb. Janna half expected to see mortar detonating, flying debris, flesh ripped beyond repair.

Yes, Fernand had been clever, very very clever. He'd used every inch of his material, cut like a master couturier. There was as much resemblance between the rushes Janna had seen and this edited version as there was between a caterpillar and a newly-hatched butterfly. And this was only the rough-cut. Music, post-synch work and some of the dubbing had still to be added.

But even without music, as Eden and Jeanne, newly-married, drove away from Dene in his white Hispano-Suiza, and Julia, her face set with the burden of Jeanne's corrupted past, flung herself onto her grey hunter and raced after them, Janna's heart was in her mouth. Julia spurred her horse like a madwoman, a Fury. Her hat came loose and rolled away unheeded, her hair tumbled from its pins and flew free. Would she catch the lovers before they reached the gates? Would this be the end of three lives, with truth the executioner?

She did catch them, wheeling her horse to block the drive with a desperate force that made it rear, wild-eyed. A close-up of scything hooves, dangerously close to the windscreen. Eden's eyes horrified but Jeanne's expressionless, pinned to her clasped hands as if one look up at Julia's face would turn her into a pillar of salt.

The long, terrible silence as Julia stared down, panting, her mouth twisted, wind-whipped water in her eyes. It was over, it must be. Her lips parted to speak. Her face filled the screen, narrowing in on her accusing eyes. Only now something was happening. Her eyes were changing, blurring. Swimming up from beneath was another girl's face, looking out from behind Julia's eyes. The image strengthened, steadied. Mistress and servant, maiden and whore. The eyes. One darker than the other, a sky that promises rain. Bruised eyes, naked eyes. Jeanne's black and white beneath Julia's gold, the shadow of war over a last Edwardian summer, in an angel's face the eyes of a chained soul in Purgatory, waiting, waiting for the world to turn, waiting to be set free.

Suddenly, the screen was empty. Blackness, night without end. The only sound a heartbeat, fading. But then, slowly, resolving itself out of the shadow like an old print, came a familiar image, the essence of summer and seaside, salty, innocent. A sea of silk, lace-trimmed. An empty sky, shining sand. And two girls in their white dresses, running hand in hand.

The end. Challenge, and question, and unspoken command. Choose. Choose now. It's up to you.

'It was us, wasn't it.' They were almost the first words Janna had spoken since she and Julie left the theatre, slipping out before the lights went up because neither of them could bear to wait for conversation and congratulations. Julie left her flowers behind in her seat. There seemed no point in giving them to Fernand now. He knew what he'd done, he knew he was going to win the Palme d'Or, and make people cry all over the world, and, what was probably more important to him than any amount of applause or awards, make himself enough money and credit to finance his next film.

Julie sighed. 'Us and everyone else.'

Janna knew what she meant. She was thinking of Gray, and Dion, and the mess people made of their lives. Maybe we're all refugees from love, thought Janna. All of us, even Fernand. Running away from love, and death, and time – all the big words that are so strangely hard to say. Looking ahead she seemed to see her future very sharp and small and pinpoint clear, as if through the wrong end of a telescope.

'I wish . . .'

'What?'

Janna shrugged. 'I wish real life had a better director.'

Julie said nothing. She stared out at the winter darkness for a moment, then leaned forward and rapped on the cabby's protective glass. 'Turn around! We've changed our minds.'

'What are you doing?' Janna was shocked. 'I'll miss my plane!'

'Don't worry, I'll get you there in time, I promise. But there's something you've got to see first.'

CHAPTER TWENTY-FOUR

'What is this place?' Janna looked up into the gloom, awed. It reminded her of nothing so much as the engine-room of a great cruise liner, docked and silent, waiting for its crew of maintenance engineers. A cavernous space slung with huge pipes and cables thick as her arm, criss-crossed with a scaffolding of platforms and metal stairs.

Without answering, Julie flicked a switch and a battery of lights blazed down from what looked like a circus performer's net stretched midway between the floor and the faraway ceiling. Bare brick walls, every crack and cranny mercilessly etched, doors with their concrete lintels showing – nothing hidden, nothing disguised. It was the first time Janna had seen a building entirely without its clothes. The effect was raw, startling.

'Follow me.' Julie seemed to know her way around, unlocking doors and turning off alarms in a very expert fashion. She led the way up a clattering metal stair to a mezzanine storey. Janna emerged into a wide, low-ceilinged area, rubber-floored, eerily silent. Big white screens had been set up at an oblique angle to the walls. Julie snapped on more switches, flooding the area with light.

Of course, Janna thought. This is where the building keeps its clothes. The screens were hung with paintings, each rectangle of colour like a window opening in a blank wall. It was strange how the paintings' presence brought the building to life, giving it a proper human scale, like footprints leading across a deserted beach. But why had Julie brought her here?

'You're privileged.' Julie was smiling. 'The exhibition doesn't actually open till Friday.' She handed Janna a catalogue. It was entitled 'Irish Eyes: An Exhibition of Paintings by Dion Malloy'.

'Dion?' Janna knew there couldn't be two Dion Malloys in the world, but all the same she found it as difficult to believe as the sight of her own face on the cinema screen an hour before. 'Our Dion?'

'The one and only.' Julie's face looked a little bleached by the hard light. It was strange to come straight from the darkened theatre into this brilliance. 'Listen, I'm going to leave you to look around. I'd like to know what you think.'

Still stunned, Janna could only nod. When Julie had disappeared back down the stairs she closed her eyes for a moment. She didn't want to look at Dion's paintings, she didn't dare. Supposing they weren't any good? Or worse – supposing they were – passable, even pleasant. It wouldn't be enough for her . . .

But she must look, of course she must. This meant a lot to Julie, she wouldn't be fobbed off with a few vague generalities. Janna opened her eyes, took a firm grip on the catalogue. At least she was alone, just herself and Dion's paintings. The chance she'd wanted, to say goodbye.

She moved closer, gearing herself up, trying to empty her mind. First impressions counted for so much, she didn't want to let Dion down. She wanted to like his paintings, but more than that, she wanted them to mean something, to express the Dion she knew, to ring out clear and true as a bell.

Her eyes rested on – colour, layers of it, unmuddied, somehow transparent. Janna felt a little of her anxiety leave her body like a sigh. How had Dion managed to get so much depth and light into a flat surface? Stillness and silence – but the colour seemed to quiver, like the flick of a trout over tortoiseshell stones, dream clear for a moment and then gone.

She blinked, feeling her vision blur with the effort of looking and not looking. They troubled her, these paintings, like a conversation with someone she loved on a bad telephone line. She thought she knew what he was saying but she could never be quite sure. The trouble was at her end, of that she could be certain. Her brain might be filled with static but there was no mistaking the authority of the voice that travelled down the line. A phrase here, a sentence there, came through majestically clear.

She moved slowly down the line, looking, wondering. A sky, boundless, a milky pool. A tree like the first tree, about to pick up its roots and walk. A horse.

Oh yes, a horse. Of course. Janna couldn't help but smile, remembering. Painted almost roughly, simple as a child's drawing, but a thoroughbred nonetheless, its coat smooth as silk, its eye liquid gold. It looked as if it had been painted only yesterday, the oil still buttery, irresistible. A cream-cake of a painting, she could have eaten it on the spot, horse and all.

He'd called it, simply, 'Good News'. The name of some champion hurdler, doubtless – or maybe, knowing Dion, a rank outsider come in to win with a twinkle of tiny hooves and a roguish roll of the eye. And yet – looking at that horse Janna suddenly felt she didn't know Dion at all, had never known him. Those dextrous hands, those faraway eyes . . . What she'd give to look through those eyes for a day, an hour, to see what he saw, to feel it, skin to skin. Good news, good news . . .

It felt like a mortal sin to leave the golden filly without stroking her neck, pulling her velvet ears, but there was more to see and very little time. Janna rounded a corner into relative darkness. Julie hadn't come this far into the gallery to turn on the lights, but even in the dimness it was clear that the whole width of the opposite wall was taken up by one large painting, a sort of altarpiece. Framed by its own twin spotlights, it was obviously the pride and prize of the whole exhibition.

She located the switch, flicked it and then – shock hit her so hard that she took an involuntary step backwards.

Damn.

How could he?

The pain, the essential pain of recognition. It's me. He knows me. He remembers. He's seen me, right through to the bones.

Janna felt raw, burning all over as if she'd been flayed alive. She was there, in the painting, not just her face and body but the whole of her, her past, her future, her heart itself, mothy wings pinned wide in the light. Even her house. Those were her very own bricks, her wall flowers, every shade of clay from rose to rust.

She looked away, looked back. She was still there, that other girl, but now Janna saw that the basement room where she sat so still and quiet in the darkness was full of white silk. Reams of it, bolts and bales and rippling streams of it, lining the walls, spilling across the barely suggested table and over the flags to pile against the walls like drifting snow.

So cold, so blank, so virginal, a cocoon for a fragile creature that only flew at night. And yet, under the girl's fingers, stitch by laborious stitch, flowered a magic garden, a jungle of private thoughts, green and gold and scarlet tendrils coiling and swirling over the sill and out into the light, to clothe the green growing world.

Janna didn't know how long she stood there in front of the painting. She forgot where she was, who she was, all the schedules and appointments and departures. She knew that it didn't matter, just as Dion had said, whether or not he sold his paintings. Wherever they were, they existed. He knew his own talent as well as she'd once known, right down to the last millimetre, the measurement of her hips.

She knew too, without a moment's hesitation, that no matter how much it cost, she must have this painting. She was going to need it, more than anyone else could possibly need it, to remind her she was alive, to give her space to breathe. It was only when she looked in the catalogue that she realised, with a sickening sense of loss, the one invisible but irreconcilable difference between herself and the girl Dion had painted. The girl in the painting, for all her poverty and solitude, belonged to herself, utterly. She was not for sale. A hundred years from now she'd still be there, somewhere, eyes bent over her silk, sewing her dreams.

A footfall, a faint intake of breath.

'Julie?' No reply. Janna swung round, caught in the full glare of the twin spotlights she couldn't make out for a moment who it was. Inside her the baby suddenly kicked, butted its head against her ribs, bone on bone.

331

And then, he was there. No bravado, no insolence, simply there. Dion. In a long, heart-stopping moment, with the clarity of someone drowning in still water, Janna saw three things. He had had his hair cut. It made him look older, smarter, more defined. He was wearing loose blue overalls, the soft midnight shade of a French porter's uniform. Many pockets. Not one of them buttoned. And – he had flowers in his eyes.

'January.' She'd forgotten his voice, the way it warmed the air, melted every bone in her body. It made her think of rumpled, sweet-smelling things, sunshine on cotton, hot bread, babies at bathtime . . .

His eyes travelled down, then up again. Seeing first amazement, then delight, Janna knew, with a sort of agonised, slow motion detachment, that this was the worst moment of her whole life. No, not quite the worst. That was still to come. She could hear it buzz and hum in the rails as she lay there helpless, bound to the line. Near and getting nearer, hurtling down the track at a hundred miles an hour. The express. No stopping it now. Savage, inevitable, and dead on time.

'I'm sorry, Dion.' Whose voice was that, chill and distant as a station announcement? 'It's not your baby.'

The engine's roar, the stench of burning oil. Steel slicing through flesh to grate on bone, over and over, until there was nothing left of her, nothing at all.

'Goodbye.'

Dion didn't move or speak. He seemed turned to stone. She hoped she'd never see that look on anybody's face again. It was more than one heart could bear. Head down, she blundered past him, past the golden filly with her quizzical eye, the walking tree, the boundless sky, and away, down the hard stair and out in the wide wintry world.

Only then, in the safety and darkness of a cab heading for the airport, her teeth chattering and her breath coming in great shuddering gasps, could she allow herself to realise how fatally, cruelly near she'd come to having everything she wanted. That look in Dion's eyes – why hadn't she seen it before, why hadn't she understood? Now it was too late.

Not for Dion – he made his own sunshine and always would – but for her.

Hell has a glass roof, she thought, dully. So the lost souls can look up and see just how near they came to Paradise. It's the thought that love might be only a touch away that makes them want to die.

CHAPTER TWENTY-FIVE

Eleven hours later Janna closed the door of No. 3 against a flurry of sleet from an aluminium sky. The air in the hall tasted damp and metallic. Even No. 3 didn't feel like home any more.

Cold, dry-eyed, Janna crept upstairs and into her bed, fully-clothed. She lay there, immobile, while her mind went spinning away in great loops and cartwheels, as if she was still somewhere up there over the Atlantic, helpless, suspended. Leaving. Always leaving . . .

Hours passed, in and out of a twilit sleep. She kept waking to find her cheeks wet, the taste of salt in her mouth. Dion's face. Her heart couldn't believe she would never see him again. It kept crying out, pulling at her like a small child at its mother's skirts. When is he coming? Is it time yet? He should be here. I want him. You fetch him for me, now, right now . . .

At some point, between darkness and darkness, recognising a faint pang of hunger, she got up and went to the kitchen, washed down some dry biscuits with a glass of water. The water was ice-cold. Drinking it felt like swallowing a sword. She crept back into sleep, to dream she was drifting high above the lightless world under a great white flower of a parachute. The harness cut under her arms, across her ribs, but it was worth every pain to fly, free and weightless, a moth on secret wings. But then, suddenly, she was falling. Down, down, the black earth open to devour her. Silk descended, choking, muffling . . .

Blind, breathless, Janna woke to find the sheet over her face. Looking out she saw the room filled with a strange, dead light, white but opaque, as if her vision was still cobwebbed over with silk. Stiffly, she got up, pulled the bedspread round her shoulders. The floorboards were marble cold under her bare feet as she went to the window.

What she saw reflected her own state of mind so exactly that it came as a shock. The end of the world. The sky had fallen, everything was upside down. Unearthly white where the cobbles should be, a dark grey cobbled sky. No life or colour anywhere, no sound. A strange, bleached, widow world, laid in a dark drawer between layers of cottonwool.

Perhaps she was dead then, and this was heaven? It was white enough. All that white. Her mind moved painfully, remembering. Dion's painting . . .

Snow! A thrill of alarm coursed through her. Snow was everywhere, piled in huge drifts against the alley, silted right up against the basement windows of the house opposite. It must have fallen steadily while she slept.

The muscles of her stomach tightened in fear, went on tightening. The spasm lasted for longer than she'd expected, making it difficult for her to breathe. Hunger, perhaps – and yet she didn't feel hungry, not at all.

Then it came to her. Placing one hand on her abdomen she could feel it stir and flex, like the first tremor of an approaching earthquake.

Janna waited, appalled, her breathing ragged, her heart racing, as her mind filled with unknown terrors. But there was nothing more. No more spasms, just that uneasy tightness. All the same, she thought, I'd better ring the hospital. Just to be sure.

Slowly, carrying her weight like a trayful of priceless lead crystal, she made her way to the stairs. She felt fine now, as if that vice-like cramp had nothing to do with her at all.

But halfway down the stairs, with terrifying suddenness, she was caught by another spasm, a spiral of pain so ferocious that she had to cling to the balustrade just to stay on her feet. Its razor-sharp point probed deep in her body, pulling, wrenching, tugging. At last it retreated, but this time not completely. It hadn't given up. It would be back. Janna could feel its corkscrew tip still deep in her, waiting.

She drew herself upright with an effort. Thank God for the

phone. A hundred years ago they'd have had to harness horses, salt the road, battle through drifts to reach her. All she had to do was get to the bottom of the stairs and through the parlour door.

Just as she stepped off the last tread she felt a sudden release of pressure in her lower abdomen. Warmth, wonderful welcome warmth flooded her. It was like wading into a tropical sea, so pleasant and soothing that she knew the worst must be over. The pain could only have been stomach cramps, after all.

But then she felt wetness, growing cold on her clothes and skin. Panic struck her, all the more savage after her relief. What was it, blood? Perhaps she was bleeding to death?

Before she could find out she was doubled up by a cramp so violent that it drove every other thought out of her head. She sank on her knees, there on the hall floor, with an agonised moan. Pain . . . She'd never known what pain was till now. And she was alone, alone!

At last, with appalling, cat-like abruptness, the pain released her. She crouched, shivering, on the hard boards, wondering how long she had before it pounced again. Quickly, with trembling hands, she checked under her skirt. No blood. How could there be so much pain without blood? Just wetness, with a sweet, almost spicy smell.

A glimmering of memory surfaced in her mind. The waters. The waters had broken, a warm, salt, internal sea. Clinging to her scrap of knowledge like a ship-wrecked sailor to a piece of driftwood Janna negotiated the last few steps to the parlour door. Her soaked clothes were cold and uncomfortable but that didn't matter once her hand was on the telephone. She'd be all right now. She'd be safe. If an ambulance couldn't get through yet at least they'd send someone, a professional. They'd get help to her somehow, they always did.

She lifted the receiver with a half-sob of relief, craving the automatic, responsive purr of the dialling tone.

But nothing came. Just silence, the same dead, empty, cottonwool silence there was everywhere, as if snow had silted right into the room.

No-one can hear me, Janna thought, with a sort of blankness. No-one in the whole world. Dimly, like the high-pitched whistle of a bomb falling from a great height, she sensed the approach of her next pain, the one with her name etched on it with letters of fire. Too soon, too soon – the pains shouldn't be coming so close together, they didn't give her time to recover her strength. Her hand shook as she forced the receiver back on its rest, tried again.

Nothing.

The pain hit her like a tidal wave, building, cresting, then peaking again, higher and higher, until there was no room in her for anything but that, the endless, all-consuming pain.

How many more? Surely no more as bad as that, it wasn't possible. Laboriously, her legs shaking, every muscle quivering with the effort, Janna dragged herself to the parlour window. The front door was locked but they could always go for help to break it down.

It took almost all she had to lift the sash. Icy air rushed in, searing her lungs and making her eyes water. White everywhere, beautiful, hospital white. No-one in sight. She called, weakly. The snow absorbed her voice, deadened it. No reply. In the windows opposite, not one light. On the white carpet beneath, not a single track.

And now, fatally, remorselessly, whispering down like flowers on a bier, more snow began to fall. It fluttered in through the open window onto Julie's Shiraz, but didn't melt. The room must be cold now, almost freezing. Janna reached for the sash to lower the window again but it had jammed and she no longer had the strength to free it. She must leave it open wide, for her important visitor, the pain. Now she was beginning to know its habits and mannerisms, learning to dread its step on her stair . . .

But its face was never the same. No matter how hard she struggled to rip each mask away there was always another beneath, grinning, leering. A cavalcade, a menagerie. Monsters, wild beasts, machines. Dragons and pantechnicons and dentists' drills, sharks and wild bears and bacon slicers, pains with daggers and pains with saws, pains that crushed and pains that stretched and pains that held her close as a mother only to rend her soft flesh with a mad dog's jaws.

Down on all fours like an animal Janna battled to survive. Her back arched in a crossbow-bend of agony she heaved and groaned and knew that this was the end. She couldn't live through this, no-one could.

Abruptly, with a convulsion that seared the skin off the back of her throat and turned her stomach inside out she vomited, a pool of mucus and liquid and greyish lumps of half-digested bread in the middle of Julie's Shiraz.

'Oh, no.' Janna spoke aloud, half gasp, half retch. Dying was one thing, but to be found frozen and foul in a pool of her own vomit, on the boards she'd sanded with her own hands, was too much to bear. Her parlour, her lovely parlour . . . 'Please, no more.'

But her body took no notice. It was intent on its own spring cleaning, beating, pounding, churning, scouring every nook and cranny with scalding liquid.

Another huge wave of nausea, all the more appalling because there was nothing left to come up. But her body wouldn't accept that she was empty. It forced a few drops from her mouth, punched her stomach for more. She retched, limp, barely able to breathe. Her throat was raw, her eyes streamed. I can think of better ways of dying, she told herself bleakly. What is the baby trying to do, climb out of my throat? I must give it a few sex education lessons. Feebly, because there was nothing else she could do, she laughed.

It was then that she saw him, the angel. Merciful Providence, knowing she hadn't the strength to make it on her own, had sent him to fetch her home. A black angel, even a little ugly, but an angel nevertheless. Slowly, Janna let herself go. The cold was its own anaesthetic. Pretty soon the angel would unfold his wings and lift her with him. There'd be no more pain, ever, only the swift uprush of air . . .

But what was the angel doing with her second-best Windsor chair? Janna blinked. Dying or not she felt a spurt of outrage as with an air of angelic concentration he broke the chair across his knee and threw it in the grate. Now he was closing the window. How could they fly away together if the window was closed? Not only a vandal but incompetent, her angel . . .

He was building a fire now, with coals. Perhaps he was a devil after all – his hair was black enough. A devil sent to torture her . . .

A colossal pain, like a skyscraper building falling straight onto her unprotected body, stopped all thought. When the dust settled, Janna's vision was suddenly crystal clear. She saw the fire in the grate, sparks dancing upwards, she saw the dark stain on the Shiraz where the pool of vomit had been and was no more, and she saw Dion.

'You're in New York!'

'Don't talk.' His face, strange and wonderful as a map of the world. 'How could I be? You needed me.' He lifted a glass to her lips. The rim was blessedly cold against her cracked lips, the water liquid gold.

'How did you get in?'

'How do you think?' He brushed the hair gently back from her face. 'Through the trapdoor.'

Of course. She leaned against him. Dion, always the stage devil.

'Here.' He took her hands, folded them round something hard and cool. 'I brought you a present.'

She looked down. It was a bucket, the orange one from the scullery, glowing like the sun. She hugged it to her. She'd never properly appreciated its beauty until now. Oh, bucket. Oh, Dion.

'I love you.' She was going to die but she wanted it said now, before she was sick again.

'Bucket love, I know.' He was smiling at her, his wide-open window of a smile. His hand on the back of her neck, warm, strong. 'I love you too.'

'But I smell!' It was wrenched from her, a sob of humiliation.

'Like a navvy after a night on the tiles.' His smile didn't waver for so much as a second. 'Who cares? I love you.'

'Really?'

An anaconda pain, coiling up from the pit of her stomach. She retched drily, half-choked. 'Oh, dear.' She pushed the words out between grunts and gasps. 'This isn't very romantic.'

'Business before pleasure always.' His voice was a dark smile, a rich murmur. 'I'll bring you flowers later.' She could smell him too, his skin, his hair. He was the outside, the world, the air. Green moss, honey. Every sense in her body was suddenly alive and super-acute. The pain was no longer her enemy. She rode it like a lion, rejoicing in the huge muscles under her, hot, powerful.

But somewhere, down an echoing gorge, she fell off the lion and couldn't get back on again. No heat now, only bitter cold despite the fire, an icy hostile sea. No hope of landfall, no light anywhere. Black sky, salt water, utter weakness. Drowning, adrift. A fog of nausea.

'I feel so sick. I can't go on.'

'Yes, you can.' His arms around her, his mouth warm against her neck. 'You've done it before. Remember the Irish Sea?'

'How could I forget?' Pain, and laughter, and retching. She buried her face in the bucket, breathed deep. Her own bucket, newly rinsed, smelling not of her, simply of itself, a wonderful, modern, plastic smell. Oh, the uses of a bucket! From now on she'd keep one by her always, just in case.

Just in case. The Irish Sea. Something flashed in her brain, a tiny bright explosion like a Very light. No time to consider where it came from or why, but it brought with it new strength and hope. The Irish Sea. She mustn't forget. The sea, the sea.

She rode with it now, plunging deep with a reckless ardour, no longer a water-logged boat but a dolphin, buoyed by the waves.

'Aah . . .' There was a strange sort of exhilaration in it after all. The sea would carry her to land in its own time – all she had to do was let herself go. And remember, remember. The way she'd felt in Dion's arms, connected, part of everything, her body made new and her mind set free. What was pain after all but her body telling her it was alive and busy with life . . .

Strong arms round her, lifting her like the sea. It was hot

now in the room. He'd piled as much as he could onto the fire. Stripped to the waist, he shone, the skin on his chest and shoulders warm and golden.

'Dance, January.' His voice in her ear. 'Dance with me.' Half-standing, half-kneeling, she swayed. There was nowhere to go but his eyes. All that was left of January Brown slipped out of her eyes and into his, taking refuge there, a fish returning to the highwater pool where it was born, a bird flying straight up into midsummer sky. Keep me for me, she thought, keep me safe. There was no more to say. She needed him and he was there.

Their bodies melted. She felt every defence in her dissolve. Something was taking her over, something grand and terrifying and humiliating all at once, a terrific urge to become two. She was unfurling like a peony, not splitting but expanding, huge pink waves of muscles opening wide.

For the first time in her life, with a concentrated, steadfast passion, she knew exactly what to do. She buried her head in his neck, her fingers tangling in his hair. From her lips came a long-drawn-out moan, a warrior's shout of triumph, a lament, a rejoicing. Warm weight between her legs, the weight of the world. She leaned against him, his strong solid body.

'Slow now, slow . . .'

Suddenly there was time, time enough to build a house, throw wide its door and let the sunlight in. Opening, opening . . . They leaned together to frame an arch, a cathedral of flesh and blood and bone, and between, golden and glistening, came the miracle, sliding soft and slow into four hands' cradle, with a rush of rosy water and a faint, whispering cry.

Janna, kneeling, looked down. Her morsel of flesh, her basket of plums. Hot and hard, ripe and raw. First fruit, sweeter than anything, right down to the stone.

The first look. So simple, so strange. A child with the world in its eyes.

Peace, silence, looking. Never enough looking, a lifetime

wouldn't be time enough to answer that enormous question, cloudy blue shading to violet, summer night with stars.

Dion lifted the baby to her. Little arms crabbed sideways, a mew of protest clawed her heart. So small, so fragile, but so strong, so perfect, right down to the matched pink pearls of toes and tiny sea-shell ears.

A flood of warmth and disbelief and joy swept Janna back against the cushions. She opened her arms wide to the baby, skin to buttery skin, heart to heart. With one hand she nested that hot, wobbly head, smelling so delectably of peach pie and cinnamon, under her chin, with the other, very gently, she traced one flower-petal ear. Yes. Julie's eyes she had, her little baby girl, but her ears . . . Tiny, velvety, close-set – and pointed. The ears of a diminutive elf or a leprechaun. Dion's ears.

'We did it!' Laughing and crying, Janna reached out to draw Dion into the magic circle, now and for ever. A birth, a death, a new world, and they the only man and woman in it. 'You and me and the Irish Sea!'

They lay together, the three of them, and watched the last of the Windsor chair gild the walls with flame.

'Shall we put the other one on?'

'Let's not.' Dion eyed it consideringly. 'It will be good for breast-feeding.'

Little Julie opened one eye, folded her lips back round Janna's nipple, looked from one to the other in what seemed like perfect agreement. Dion reached out, captured one waving starfish hand in his own.

'Not many babies have the Irish Sea for godfather.'

'I know.' Janna felt as if she'd died and gone to heaven. 'It was being sick that did it. I lost my pill somewhere between Liverpool and Dublin.'

'The best thing you ever did.'

'You too.' They smiled at each other, broad, foolish, glorious smiles.

'The wedding tomorrow, I think.' Dion's tone was magisterial. Janna had never seen him look so serious. What a father he would make.

'Oh?' She couldn't resist the chance to play hard to get, one last time. 'I rather fancied a long engagement . . .'

'You've had that, with interest.' Dion gave her a stern look. 'Which reminds me – why aren't you wearing my ring?'

'Ring?' She blinked. 'What ring?'

'I thought as much.' He dug in his pocket. 'I found it where I left it for you, inside your little black shoes. I was sure you'd find it, the next time you wore them.'

'But I never did! I couldn't bear to, at first, and then – well, my feet swelled and they didn't fit . . .' Janna's voice died away. She stared at the ring on Dion's palm. It was lovely, a simple silver circlet bearing a tiny heart clasped by two hands.

Dion slid the ring onto her finger. It fitted perfectly. She knew that every time she saw it she would think of the baby, their baby, pulsing out into their joined hands.

'It's a Claddagh ring. A gypsy blessed it for me.'

'The same one who hired you that pony?'

'The very same.' He grinned. 'In his eyes, of course, we're as good as married already. All the best tinker weddings begin with an elopement.'

'Even so . . .' Now it was Janna's turn to be serious. She cradled the baby's head in one hand, smoothed back the slick of dark hair. 'We should do it properly, for little Julie.'

Dion nodded sagely. 'What better reason. A special licence should do the trick. I'll get onto it right away, straight after I've rung the hospital.' Janna was glad to see he didn't even try to move.

'And then –?'

'We'll live happily ever after.' Not a question, a declaration of intent.

'Till the Irish Sea runs dry.'

'In No. 3?'

'Of course. The attic for you –'

'And the parlour for you.'

'The bedroom –'

'For both of us. And the rest –'

'For the children.'

They smiled at each other in perfect agreement. Looking

343

ahead, in the golden darkness, Janna saw how it would be. Growing old with Dion would be like living for ever. He'd be so beautiful when he was old, her ugly man. His hair would go white but his brows and lashes would always be dark, his eyes blue as the back of beyond. He'd cheat time to the end, her magic man.

And she'd be there, with him, to the end. They belonged together, they fitted, two odd-shaped pieces of wood mitred into each other with a craftsman's cunning, leaving just enough space between for the wood to move, to weather every wind that blew. Room to expand and shrink, room to grow.

The baby stirred, hiccupped, gave a diminutive creaky sigh.

'Isn't she beautiful?' Two voices as one.

'Just like her mother.' Dion's eyes were Fortuny velvet, enfolding her like a cloak. 'The beautiful girl in the basement.'

'You mean that was me, all along?'

'Who else? Look at you now. You're the most beautiful woman in the world.'

And Janna, meeting his eyes, knew that it was true. She looked down at the sleeping fragrant bundle in the crook of her arm, and felt pride well up in her, pride and love and triumph and pure joy. One silken thread, fragile but strong enough to bind the world. For all her pain, something perfect. From the dusty cocoon, at last, silken wings.

He brought toast, and warm milk with nutmeg in it, and an old flannel sheet to wrap the baby in.

'Happy New Year.'

They kissed, and heard bells chime over snow.

Danielle Steel

A captivating bestseller . . .

WANDERLUST

At 21 Annabelle Driscoll was the acknowledged beauty, but it was her sister Audrey – four years older – who had the spine and spirit. She had talent as a photographer; she had the restless urge of a born wanderer.

Inevitably it was Annabelle who was the first to marry, leaving Audrey to wonder if life were passing her by. The men she met in California were dull, worldly. Even in New York, they failed to spark her. Only when she boarded the *Orient Express* did she realise she was beginning a journey that would take her farther than she had ever dreamed possible . . .

0 7221 8307 0   GENERAL FICTION   £3.50

AN ENTHRALLING SAGA OF LOVE, COURAGE
AND DEFIANCE . . .

THE PRINCESS OF
POOR STREET

EMMA
BLAIR

They called it Black Friday in Parr Street when the factory
closed. Whole families in the slums of Glasgow felt the cruel
sting of hardship and despair. Vicky Devine's father,
George, was devastated. But young Ken Blacklaws wasn't
going to be defeated. Come what may, he would make a
success of his life.

Maybe that's why Vicky loved him so much.

As Ken ruthlessly fought his way out of poverty, his
ambition knowing no bounds, Vicky's love grew in strength
and defiance. During his lifetime, Ken would break the law
and Vicky's heart, but never could he break her spirit . . .

Also by Emma Blair in Sphere Books:
STREET SONG

0 7221 1943 7   GENERAL FICTION   £2.99

A remarkable novel from an extraordinary writer . . .

Barbara Erskine
LADY OF HAY

*FASCINATING, ABSORBING
AND ORIGINAL*

'You must forget, Joanna. Matilda is dead. Let her rest.' Jo
smiled sadly. 'She can't rest, I can't rest . . . The story has
to be told . . .' Her gaze slipped past him. 'I have to live
again . . .'

WALES: 1175. Matilda, Lady of Hay, trapped in a loveless
marriage, barred from her lover and threatened by brutal
death at the hand of King John.

LONDON: 1986. Jo Clifford, hard-hitting journalist
planning to debunk reincarnation; hypnotised across the
ages into the harsh reality of Matilda's life . . . and
impending death.

0 7221 3359 6   GENERAL FICTION   £3.95

A selection of bestsellers from Sphere

FICTION

WHITE SUN, RED STAR	Robert Elegant	£3.50 ☐
A TASTE FOR DEATH	P. D. James	£3.50 ☐
THE PRINCESS OF POOR STREET	Emma Blair	£2.99 ☐
WANDERLUST	Danielle Steel	£3.50 ☐
LADY OF HAY	Barbara Erskine	£3.95 ☐

FILM AND TV TIE-IN

BLACK FOREST CLINIC	Peter Heim	£2.99 ☐
INTIMATE CONTACT	Jacqueline Osborne	£2.50 ☐
BEST OF BRITISH	Maurice Sellar	£8.95 ☐
SEX WITH PAULA YATES	Paula Yates	£2.95 ☐
RAW DEAL	Walter Wager	£2.50 ☐

NON-FICTION

INVISIBLE ARMIES	Stephen Segaller	£4.99 ☐
ALEX THROUGH THE LOOKING GLASS	Alex Higgins with Tony Francis	£2.99 ☐
NEXT TO A LETTER FROM HOME: THE GLENN MILLER STORY	Geoffrey Butcher	£4.99 ☐
AS TIME GOES BY: THE LIFE OF INGRID BERGMAN	Laurence Leamer	£3.95 ☐
BOTHAM	Don Mosey	£3.50 ☐

All Sphere books are available at your local bookshop or newsagent, or can be ordered direct from the publisher. Just tick the titles you want and fill in the form below.

Name_____

Address_____

_____

Write to Sphere Books, Cash Sales Department, P.O. Box 11, Falmouth, Cornwall TR10 9EN

Please enclose a cheque or postal order to the value of the cover price plus:

UK: 60p for the first book, 25p for the second book and 15p for each additional book ordered to a maximum charge of £1.90.

OVERSEAS & EIRE: £1.25 for the first book, 75p for the second book and 28p for each subsequent title ordered.

BFPO: 60p for the first book, 25p for the second book plus 15p per copy for the next 7 books, thereafter 9p per book.

Sphere Books reserve the right to show new retail prices on covers which may differ from those previously advertised in the text elsewhere, and to increase postal rates in accordance with the P.O.